SECONDHAND HEROES

IN THE TRENCHES

JUSTIN LAROCCA HANSEN

DIAL BOOKS FOR YOUNG READERS

FOR BARBARA, CRUCY, WAYNE AND FRANK
FOR PUTTING THE TEAM TOGETHER.

DIAL BOOKS FOR YOUNG READERS
PENGUIN YOUNG READERS GROUP
AN IMPRINT OF PENGUIN RANDOM HOUSE LLC
375 HUDSON STREET, NEW YORK, NY 10014

LYRIC ON PAGE 45 FROM "BLINDED BY THE LIGHT,"
MUSIC AND LYRICS BY BRUCE SPRINGSTEEN.

MANUFACTURED IN CHINA
ISBN 9780803740952 PAPERBACK
ISBN 9780735228108 LIBRARY BINDING

1 3 5 7 9 10 8 6 4 2

TEXT SET IN CCWILDWORDS

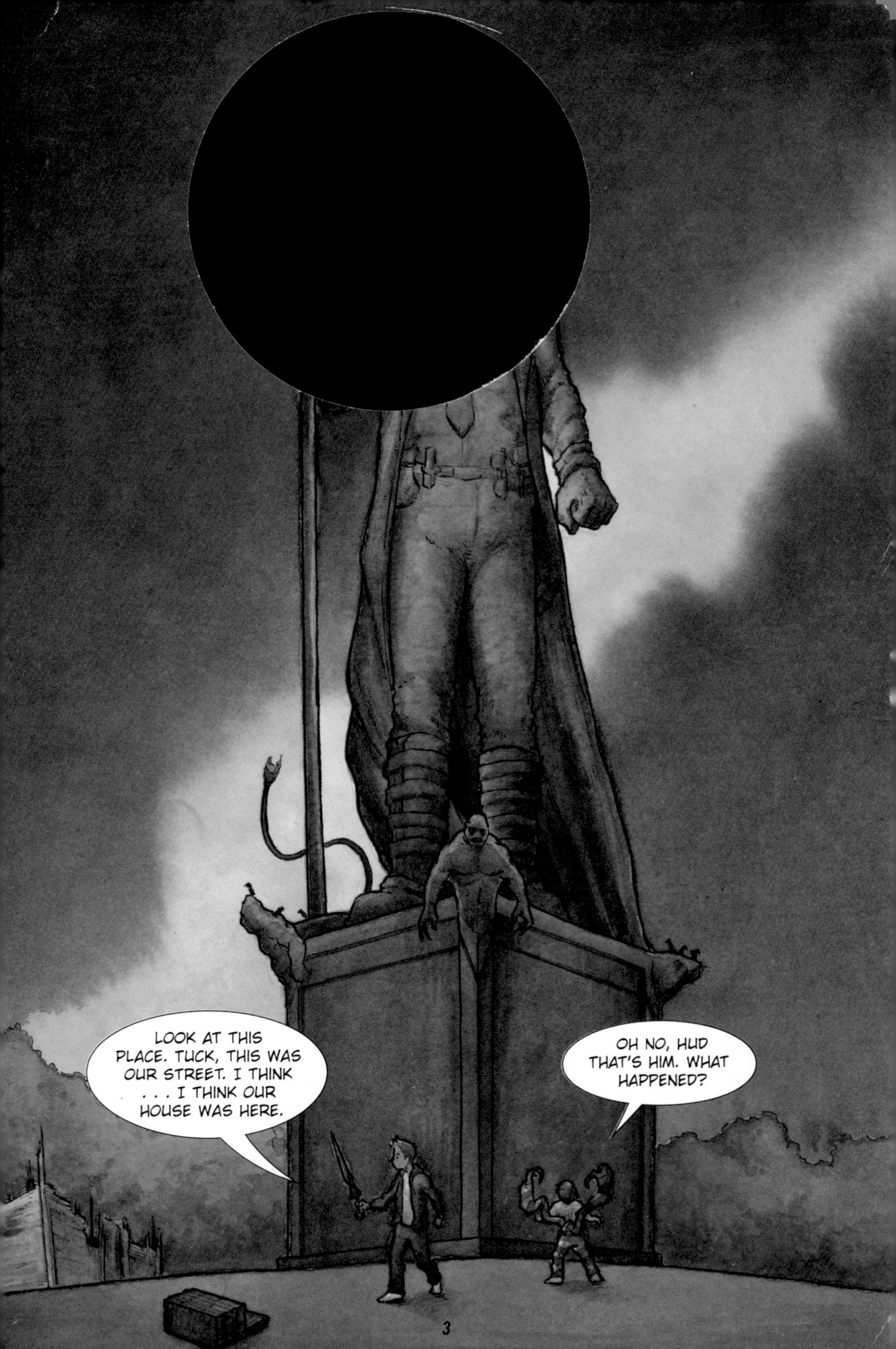
LOOK AT THIS PLACE. TUCK, THIS WAS OUR STREET. I THINK . . . I THINK OUR HOUSE WAS HERE.
OH NO, HUD THAT'S HIM. WHAT HAPPENED?

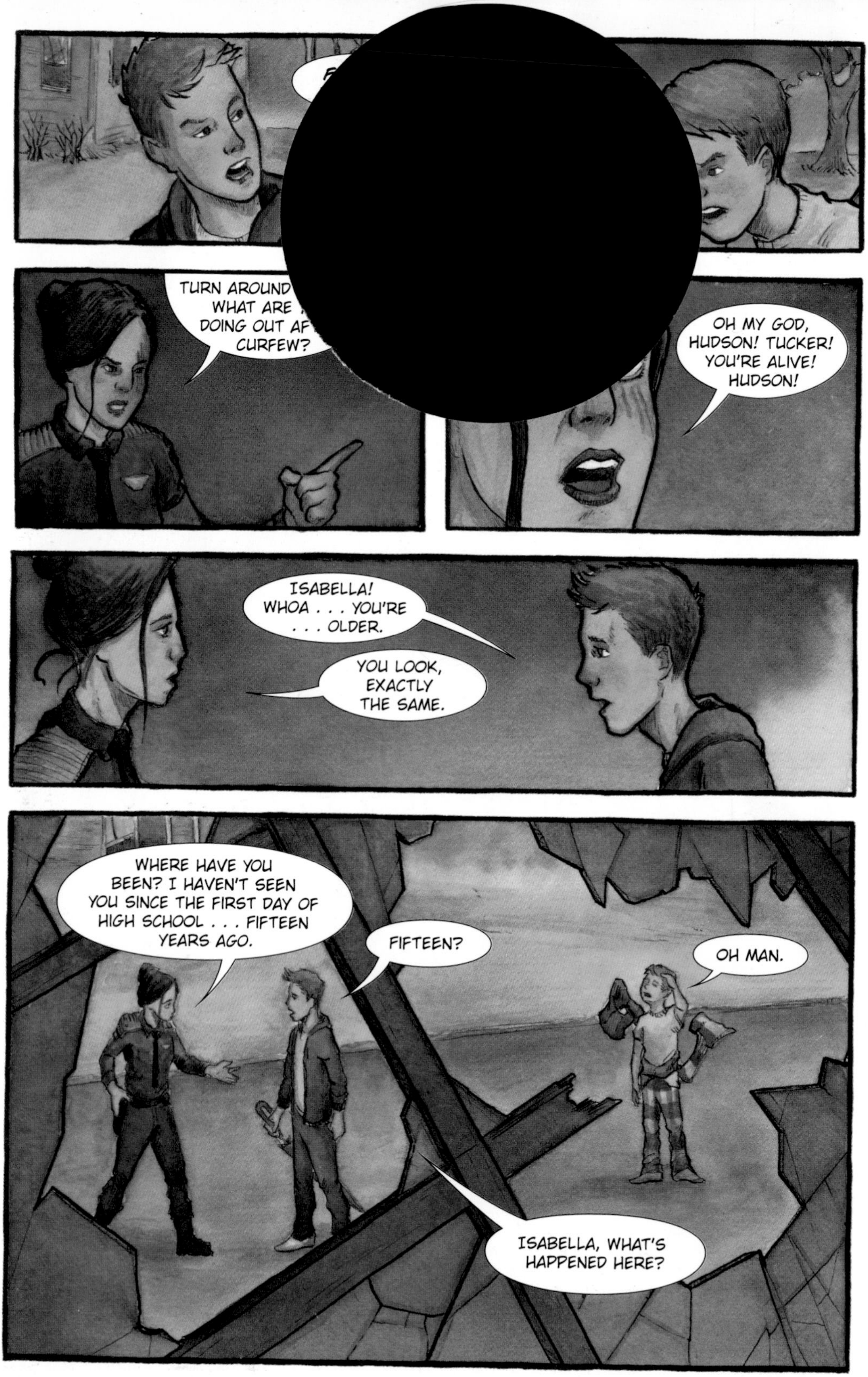

[redacted]
TURN AROUND [redacted] WHAT ARE [redacted] DOING OUT AF[redacted] CURFEW?
OH MY GOD, HUDSON! TUCKER! YOU'RE ALIVE! HUDSON!
ISABELLA! WHOA . . . YOU'RE . . . OLDER.
YOU LOOK, EXACTLY THE SAME.
WHERE HAVE YOU BEEN? I HAVEN'T SEEN YOU SINCE THE FIRST DAY OF HIGH SCHOOL . . . FIFTEEN YEARS AGO.
FIFTEEN?
OH MAN.
ISABELLA, WHAT'S HAPPENED HERE?

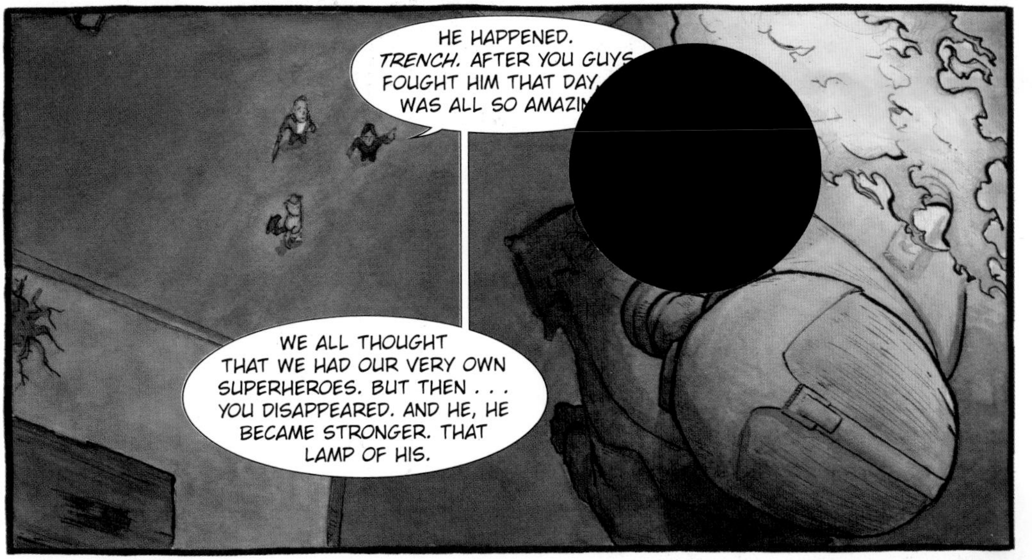
HE HAPPENED. *TRENCH.* AFTER YOU GUYS FOUGHT HIM THAT DAY, WAS ALL SO AMAZIN [redacted]
WE ALL THOUGHT THAT WE HAD OUR VERY OWN SUPERHEROES. BUT THEN . . . YOU DISAPPEARED. AND HE, HE BECAME STRONGER. THAT LAMP OF HIS.

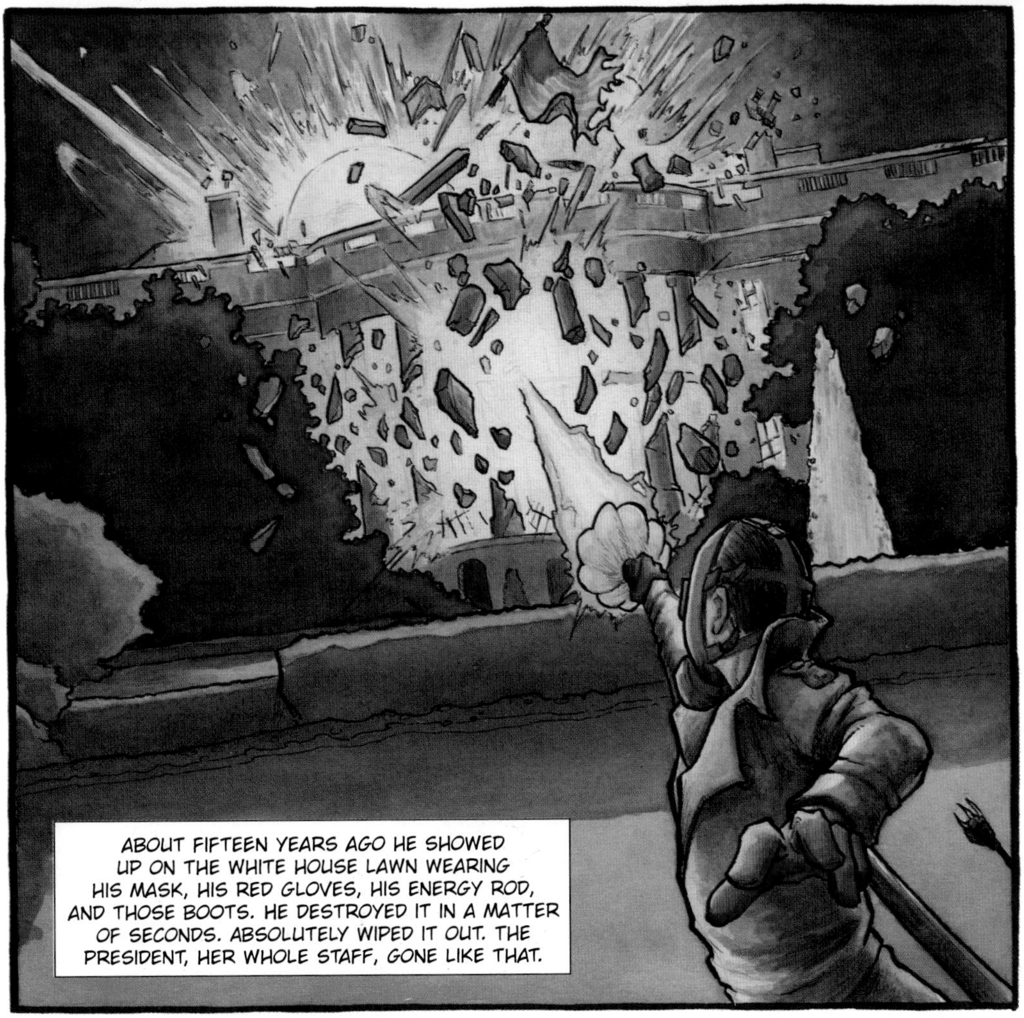
ABOUT FIFTEEN YEARS AGO HE SHOWED UP ON THE WHITE HOUSE LAWN WEARING HIS MASK, HIS RED GLOVES, HIS ENERGY ROD, AND THOSE BOOTS. HE DESTROYED IT IN A MATTER OF SECONDS. ABSOLUTELY WIPED IT OUT. THE PRESIDENT, HER WHOLE STAFF, GONE LIKE THAT.

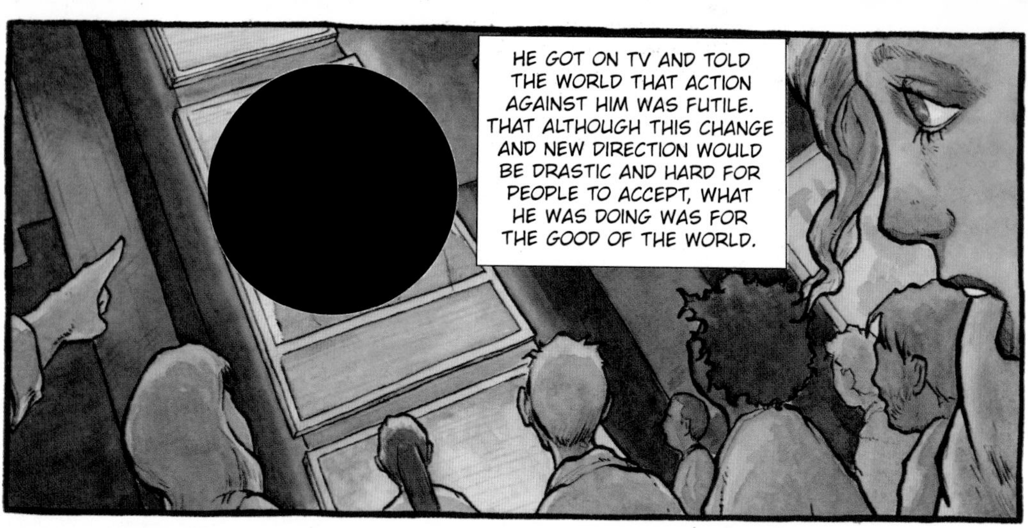
HE GOT ON TV AND TOLD THE WORLD THAT ACTION AGAINST HIM WAS FUTILE. THAT ALTHOUGH THIS CHANGE AND NEW DIRECTION WOULD BE DRASTIC AND HARD FOR PEOPLE TO ACCEPT, WHAT HE WAS DOING WAS FOR THE GOOD OF THE WORLD.

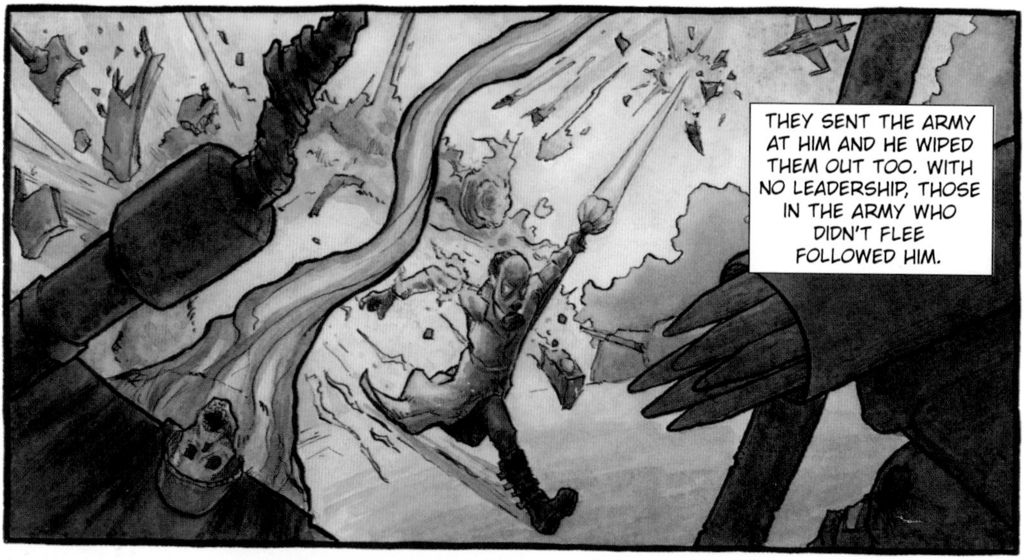
THEY SENT THE ARMY AT HIM AND HE WIPED THEM OUT TOO. WITH NO LEADERSHIP, THOSE IN THE ARMY WHO DIDN'T FLEE FOLLOWED HIM.

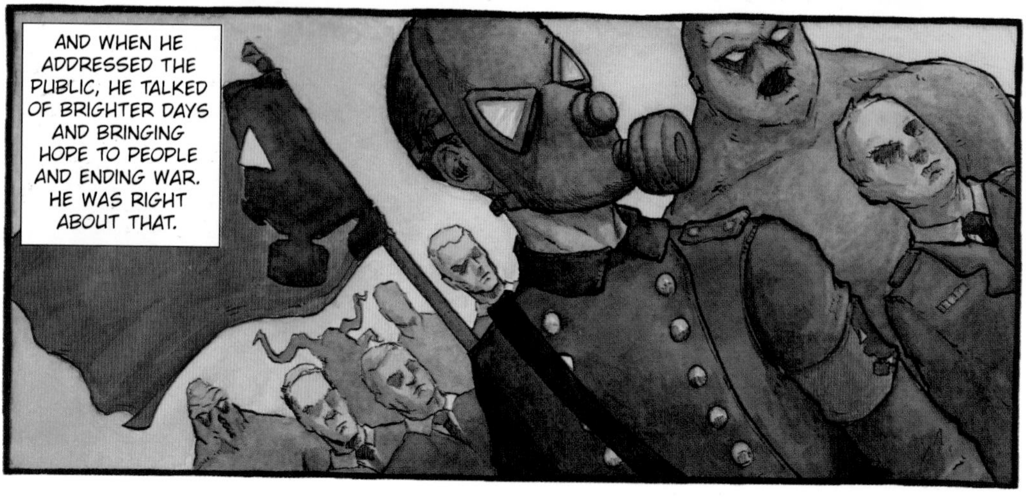
AND WHEN HE ADDRESSED THE PUBLIC, HE TALKED OF BRIGHTER DAYS AND BRINGING HOPE TO PEOPLE AND ENDING WAR. HE WAS RIGHT ABOUT THAT.

THERE'S ONLY BEEN ONE WAR IN THE LAST FIFTEEN YEARS.

A REBELLION.

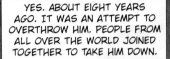

YES. ABOUT EIGHT YEARS AGO. IT WAS AN ATTEMPT TO OVERTHROW HIM. PEOPLE FROM ALL OVER THE WORLD JOINED TOGETHER TO TAKE HIM DOWN.

MY BROTHER WAS ONE OF THE LEADERS. SO WAS YOUR SQUIRREL FRIEND, STEEN. HE TOLD US ALL ABOUT YOU AFTER IT LOOKED LIKE YOU WEREN'T COMING BACK. I FOUGHT TOO. BUT HE ANNIHILATED US.

BY THEN HE HAD MOST OF THE WORLD ON HIS SIDE, AND HE HAS POWER AND ABILITIES THAT NO ONE ELSE HAS. THERE WERE A FEW WITH ABILITIES LIKE HIM, BUT HE DESTROYED THEM TOO. AND THEN HE HAD THEIR POWER. ONLY I AND A FEW OTHERS SURVIVED AND ARE FORCED TO SERVE HIM.

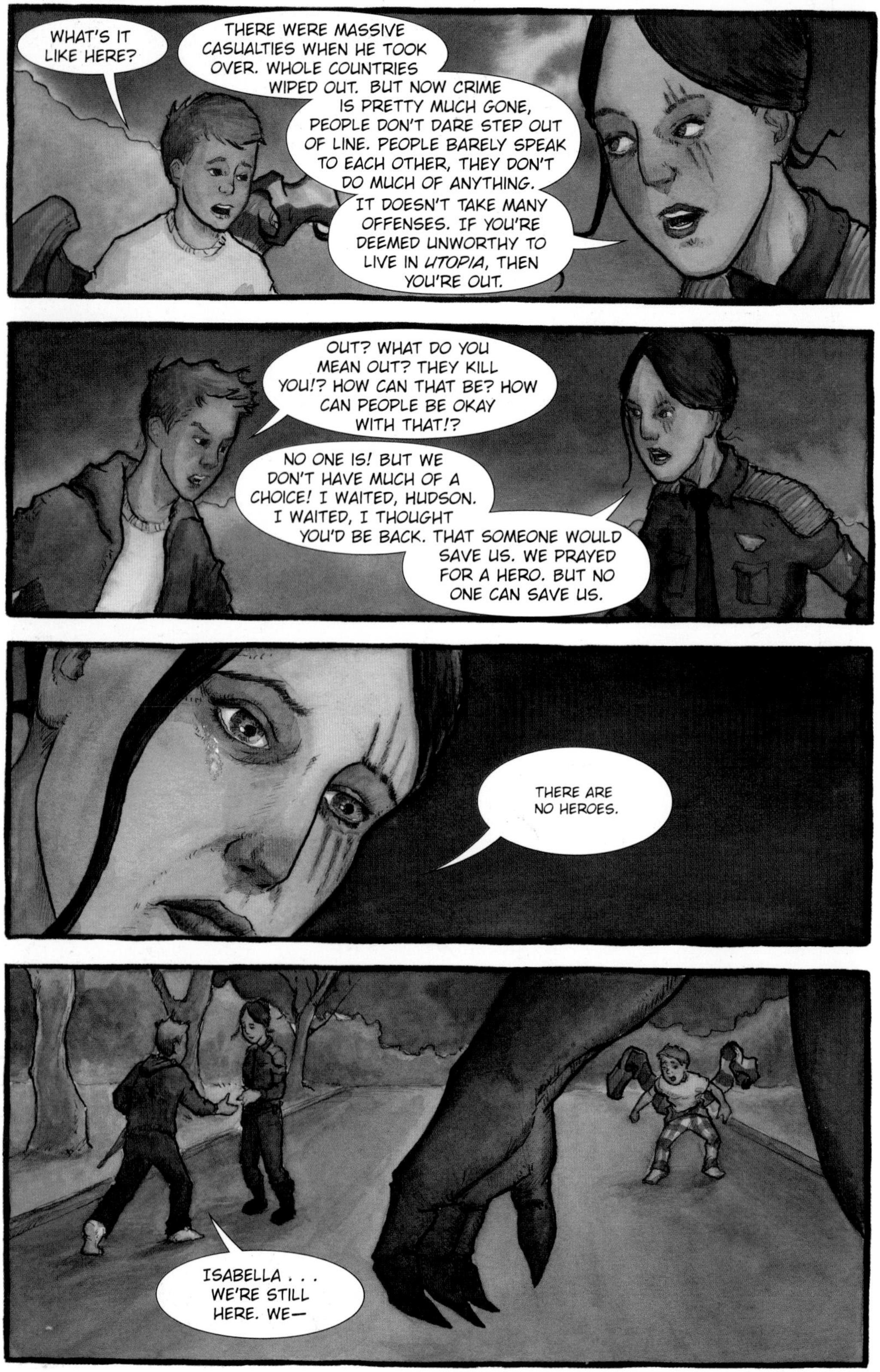
WHAT'S IT LIKE HERE?
THERE WERE MASSIVE CASUALTIES WHEN HE TOOK OVER. WHOLE COUNTRIES WIPED OUT. BUT NOW CRIME IS PRETTY MUCH GONE, PEOPLE DON'T DARE STEP OUT OF LINE. PEOPLE BARELY SPEAK TO EACH OTHER, THEY DON'T DO MUCH OF ANYTHING.
IT DOESN'T TAKE MANY OFFENSES. IF YOU'RE DEEMED UNWORTHY TO LIVE IN *UTOPIA*, THEN YOU'RE OUT.
OUT? WHAT DO YOU MEAN OUT? THEY KILL YOU!? HOW CAN THAT BE? HOW CAN PEOPLE BE OKAY WITH THAT!?
NO ONE IS! BUT WE DON'T HAVE MUCH OF A CHOICE! I WAITED, HUDSON. I WAITED, I THOUGHT YOU'D BE BACK. THAT SOMEONE WOULD SAVE US. WE PRAYED FOR A HERO. BUT NO ONE CAN SAVE US.
THERE ARE NO HEROES.
ISABELLA . . . WE'RE STILL HERE. WE—

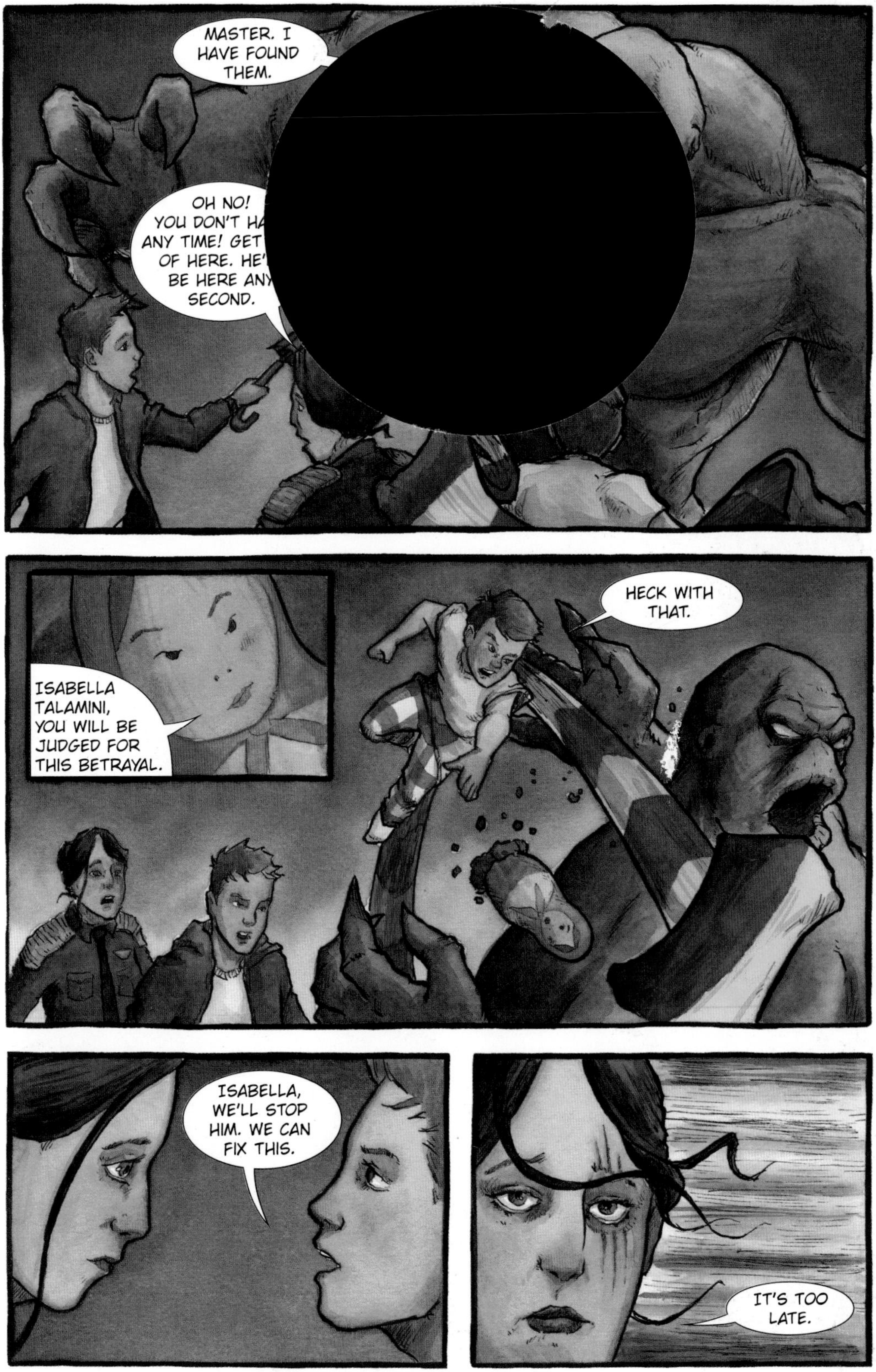
MASTER. I HAVE FOUND THEM.
OH NO! YOU DON'T HA[redacted] ANY TIME! GET [redacted] OF HERE. HE'[redacted] BE HERE ANY [redacted] SECOND.
ISABELLA TALAMINI, YOU WILL BE JUDGED FOR THIS BETRAYAL.
HECK WITH THAT.
ISABELLA, WE'LL STOP HIM. WE CAN FIX THIS.
IT'S TOO LATE.

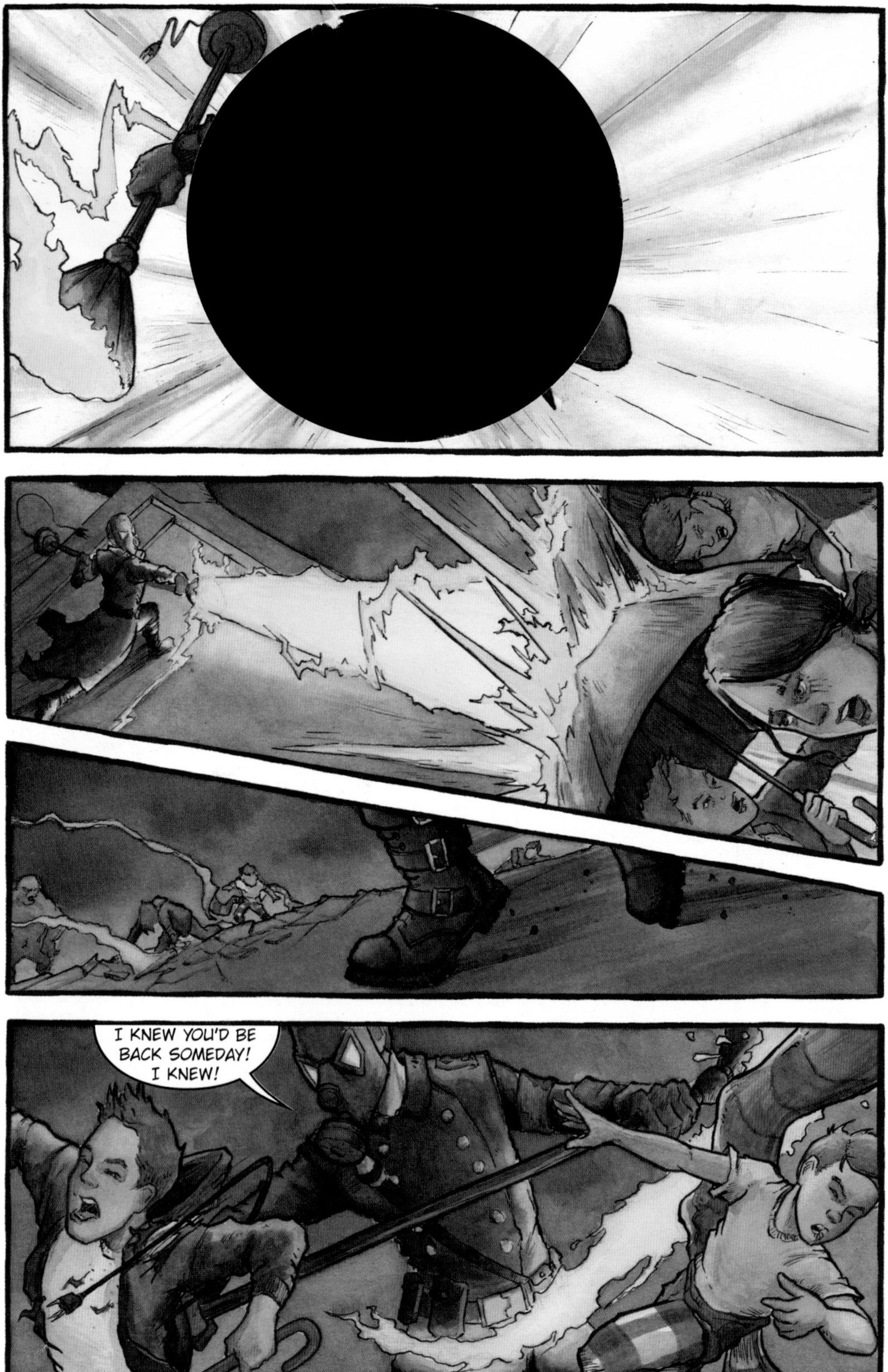
I KNEW YOU'D BE BACK SOMEDAY! I KNEW!

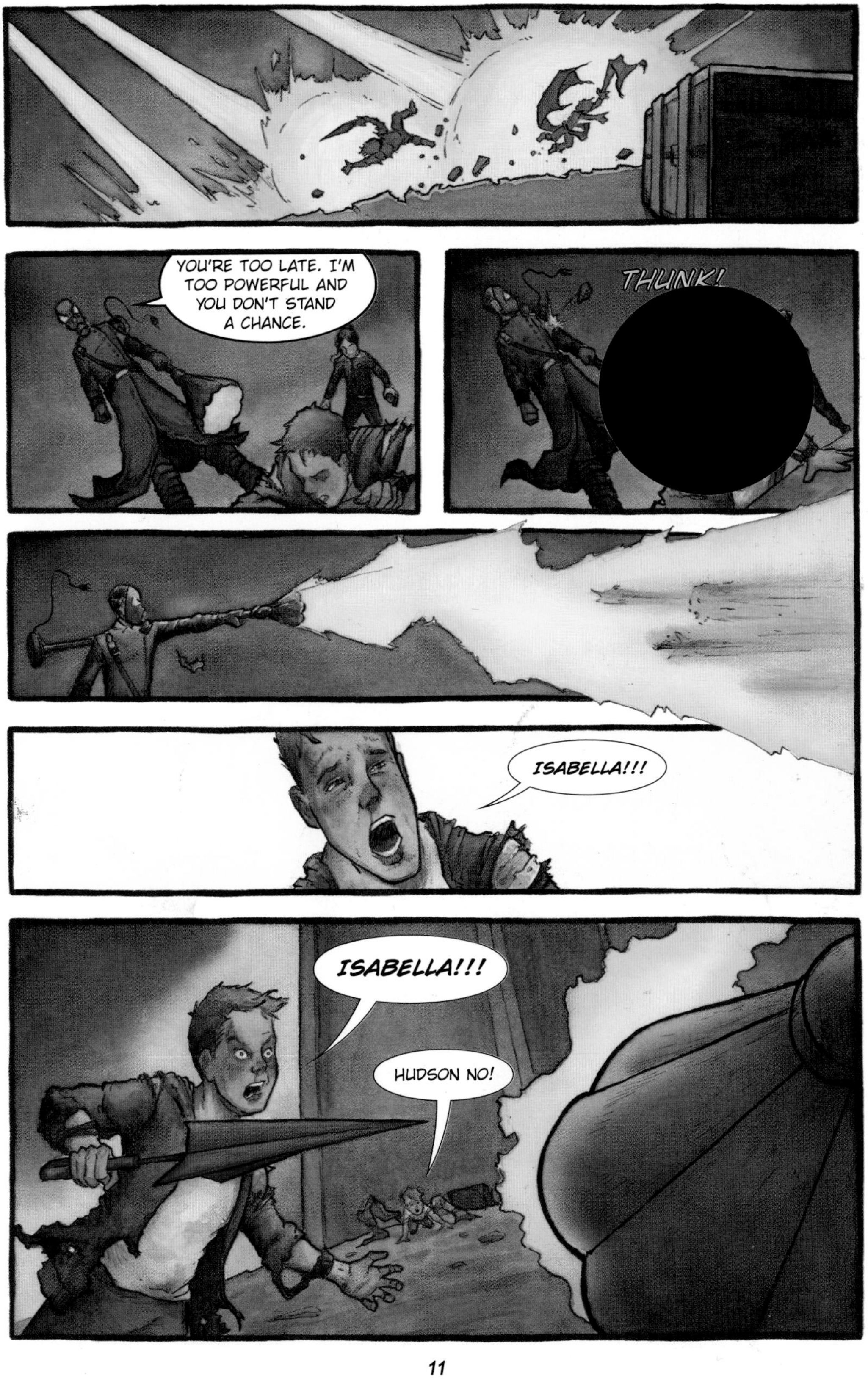
YOU'RE TOO LATE. I'M TOO POWERFUL AND YOU DON'T STAND A CHANCE.
THUNK!
ISABELLA!!!
ISABELLA!!!
HUDSON NO!

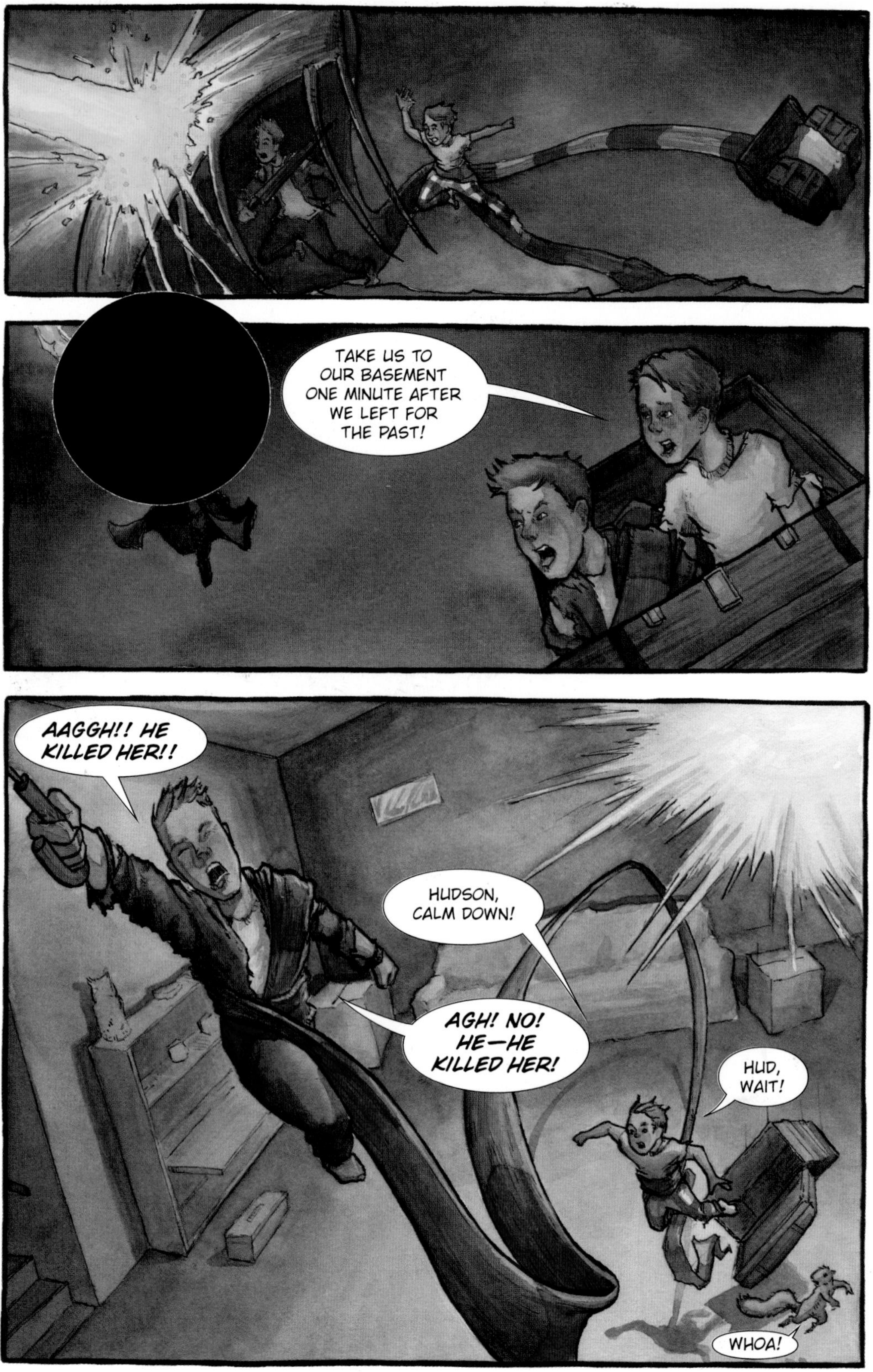
TAKE US TO OUR BASEMENT ONE MINUTE AFTER WE LEFT FOR THE PAST!
AAGGH!! HE KILLED HER!!
HUDSON, CALM DOWN!
AGH! NO! HE—HE KILLED HER!
HUD, WAIT!
WHOA!

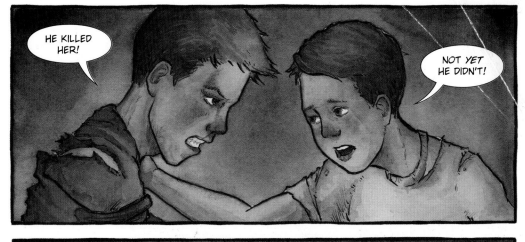

HE KILLED HER!

NOT *YET* HE DIDN'T!

RIGHT...THAT WAS THE FUTURE.

BUT I DON'T UNDERSTAND. HOW COULD THAT HAPPEN? WERE WE DEAD?

WAIT, WAIT, LET ME THINK. NO. WE WERE NEVER THERE. HE DIDN'T HAVE MY UMBRELLA OR YOUR SCARVES. WE WENT STRAIGHT FROM THE PAST TO THE FUTURE, THAT'S A FUTURE WITHOUT US IN IT. WE *HAVE* TO STOP HIM. WE CAN'T LET THAT HAPPEN.

WE CAN'T LET HIM GET HIS HANDS ON ALL THOSE OBJECTS. ESPECIALLY THAT LAMP. STEEN, DID YOU SEE ANYONE BUY A TALL LAMP AT THE YARD SALE?

DUDES, *WHAT* IS GOING ON? DOES THE TRUNK, LIKE, BEAT THE CRAP OUT OF YOU OR SOMETHING?

IN A MINUTE! DID SOMEONE BUY A LAMP?

HMM. YEAH, DUDE. CHUBBY OLD BALD GUY.

MR. HARRIS.

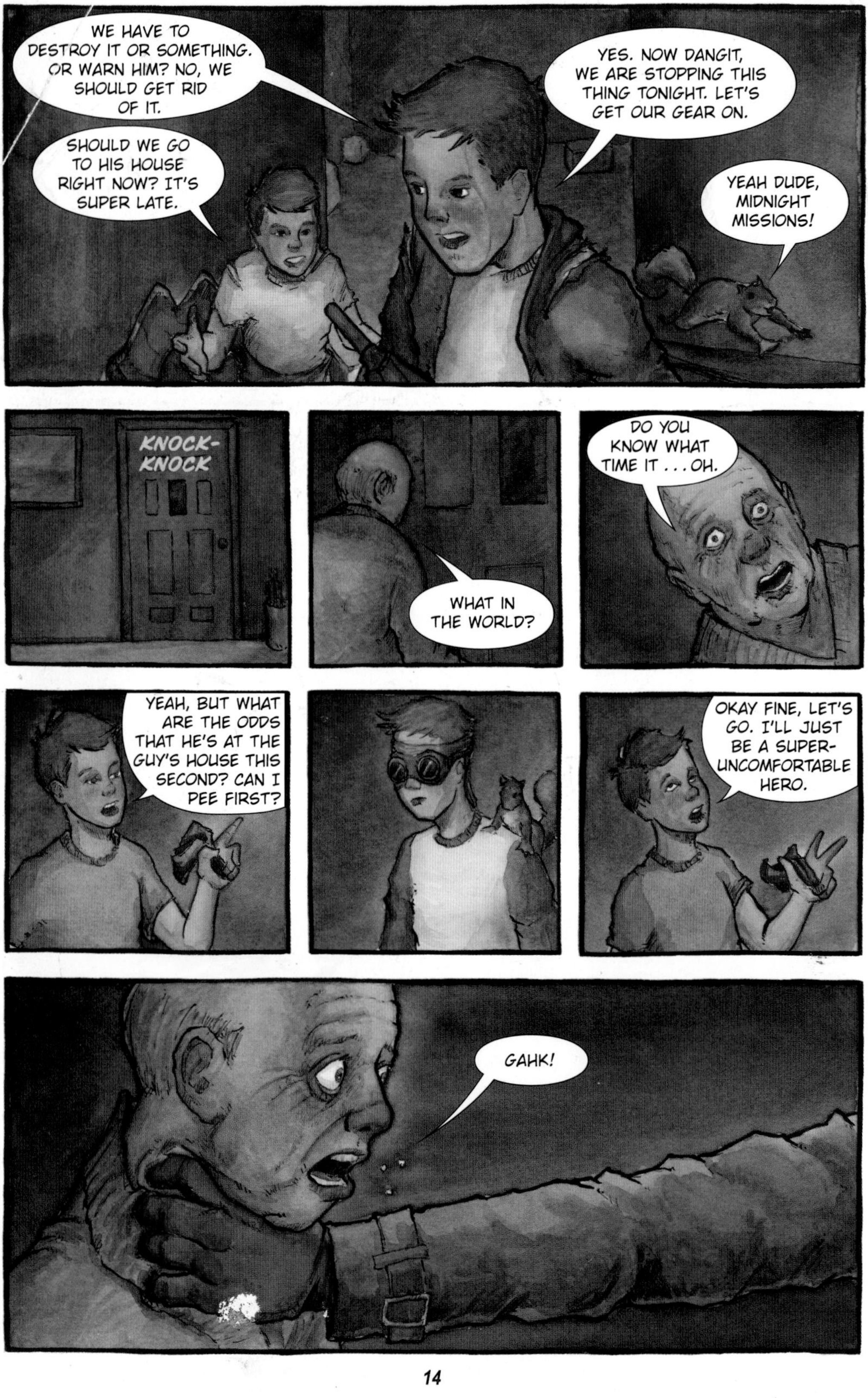
WE HAVE TO DESTROY IT OR SOMETHING. OR WARN HIM? NO, WE SHOULD GET RID OF IT.
SHOULD WE GO TO HIS HOUSE RIGHT NOW? IT'S SUPER LATE.
YES. NOW DANGIT, WE ARE STOPPING THIS THING TONIGHT. LET'S GET OUR GEAR ON.
YEAH DUDE, MIDNIGHT MISSIONS!
KNOCK-KNOCK
WHAT IN THE WORLD?
DO YOU KNOW WHAT TIME IT . . . OH.
YEAH, BUT WHAT ARE THE ODDS THAT HE'S AT THE GUY'S HOUSE THIS SECOND? CAN I PEE FIRST?
OKAY FINE, LET'S GO. I'LL JUST BE A SUPER-UNCOMFORTABLE HERO.
GAHK!

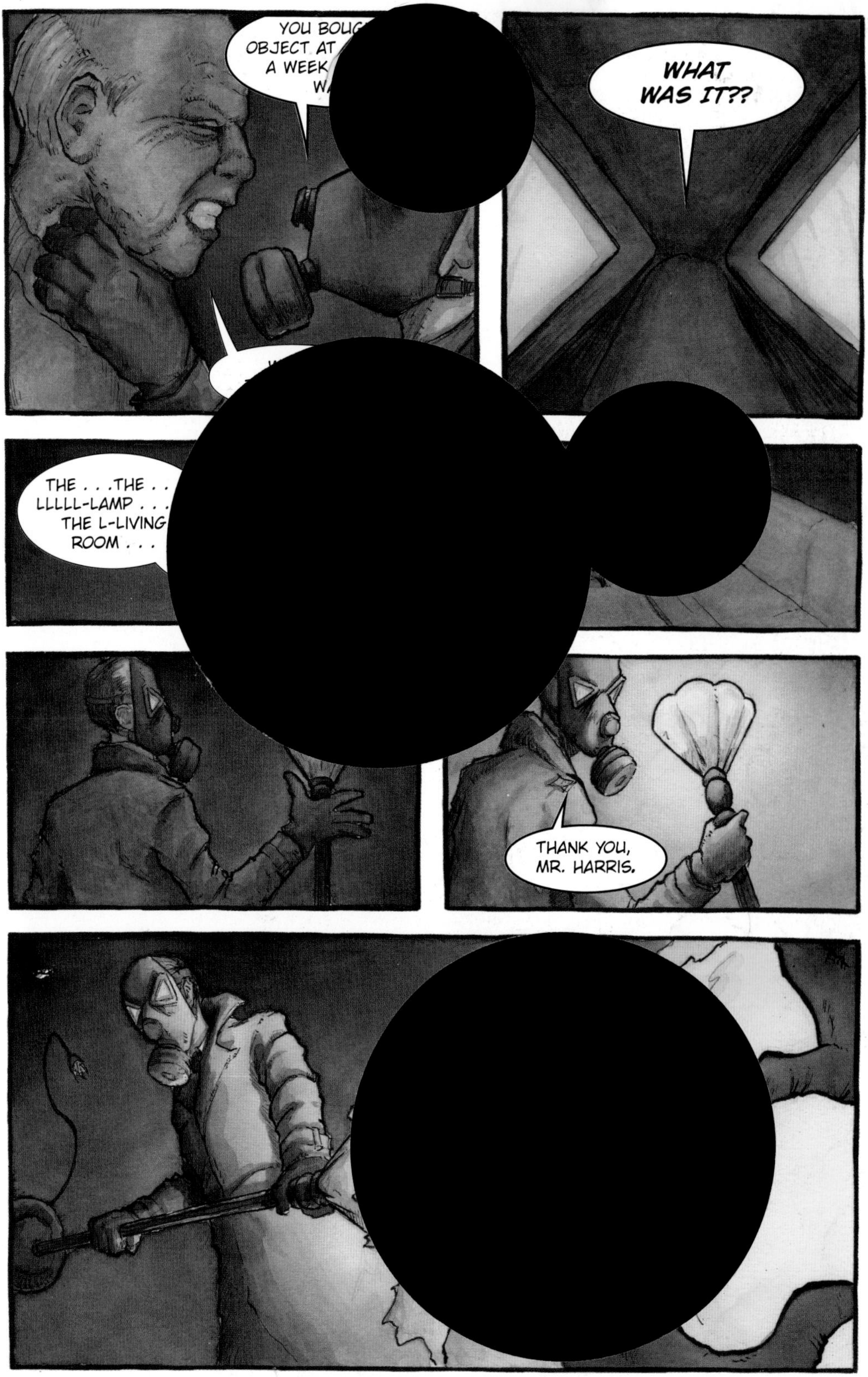
YOU BOUG[redacted] OBJECT AT [redacted] A WEEK [redacted] WA[redacted]
WHAT WAS IT??
[redacted]
THE . . .THE . . [redacted] LLLLL-LAMP . . . [redacted] THE L-LIVING [redacted] ROOM . . . [redacted]
[redacted]
THANK YOU, MR. HARRIS.
[redacted]

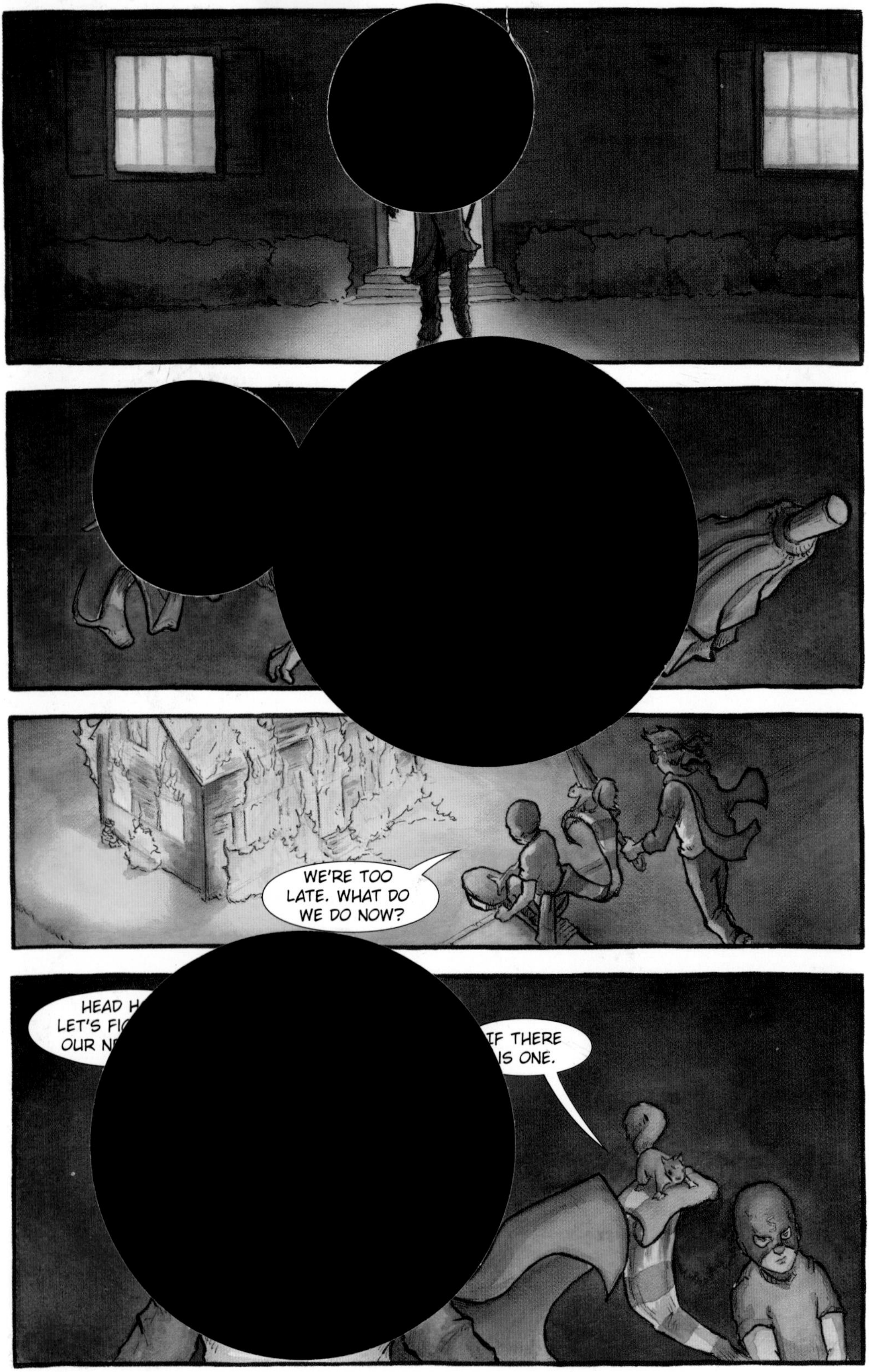
WE'RE TOO LATE. WHAT DO WE DO NOW?
HEAD H[redacted] LET'S FI[redacted] OUR N[redacted]
[redacted] IF THERE [redacted] IS ONE.

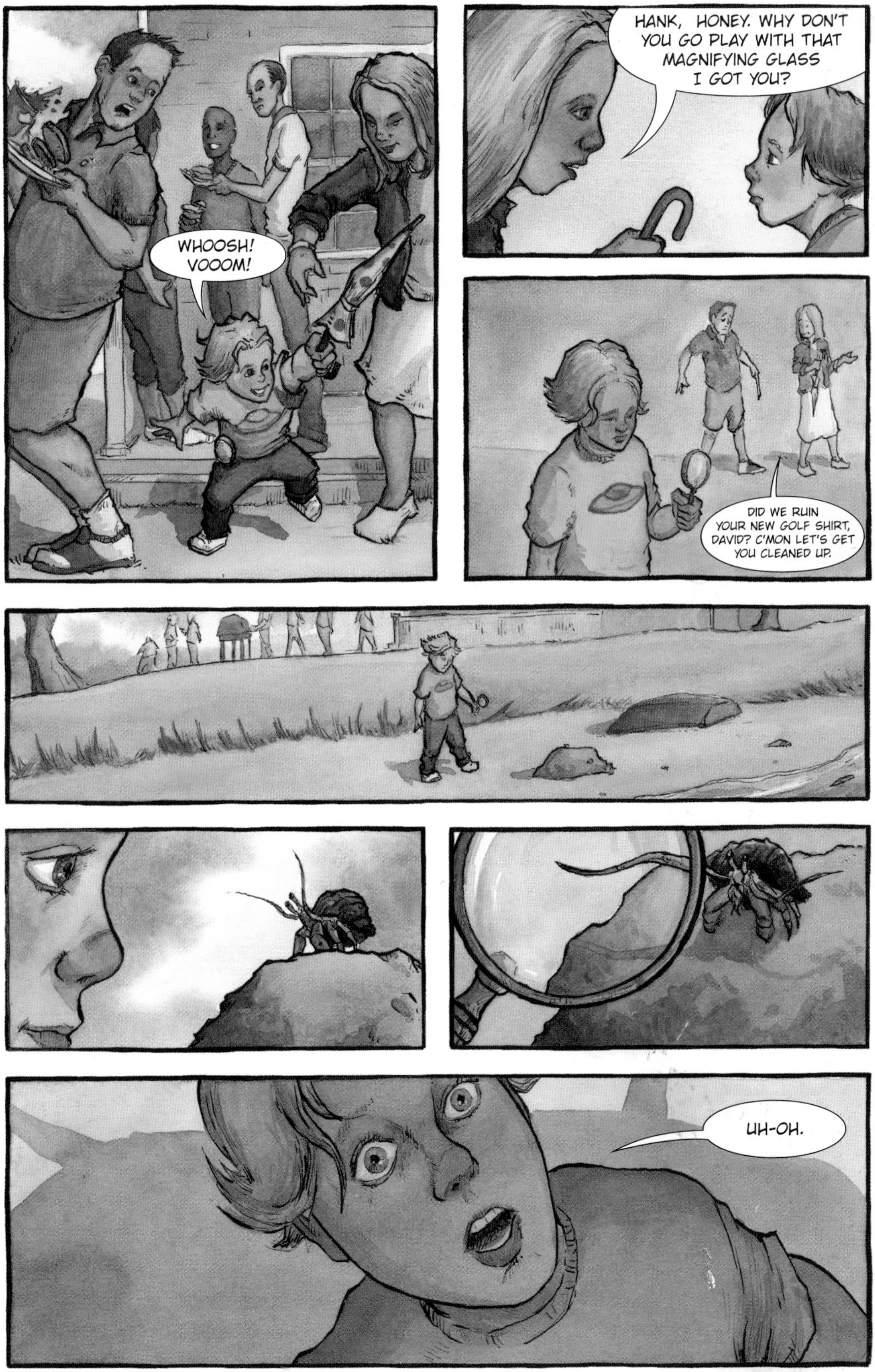
WHOOSH! VOOOM!
HANK, HONEY. WHY DON'T YOU GO PLAY WITH THAT MAGNIFYING GLASS I GOT YOU?
DID WE RUIN YOUR NEW GOLF SHIRT, DAVID? C'MON LET'S GET YOU CLEANED UP.
UH-OH.

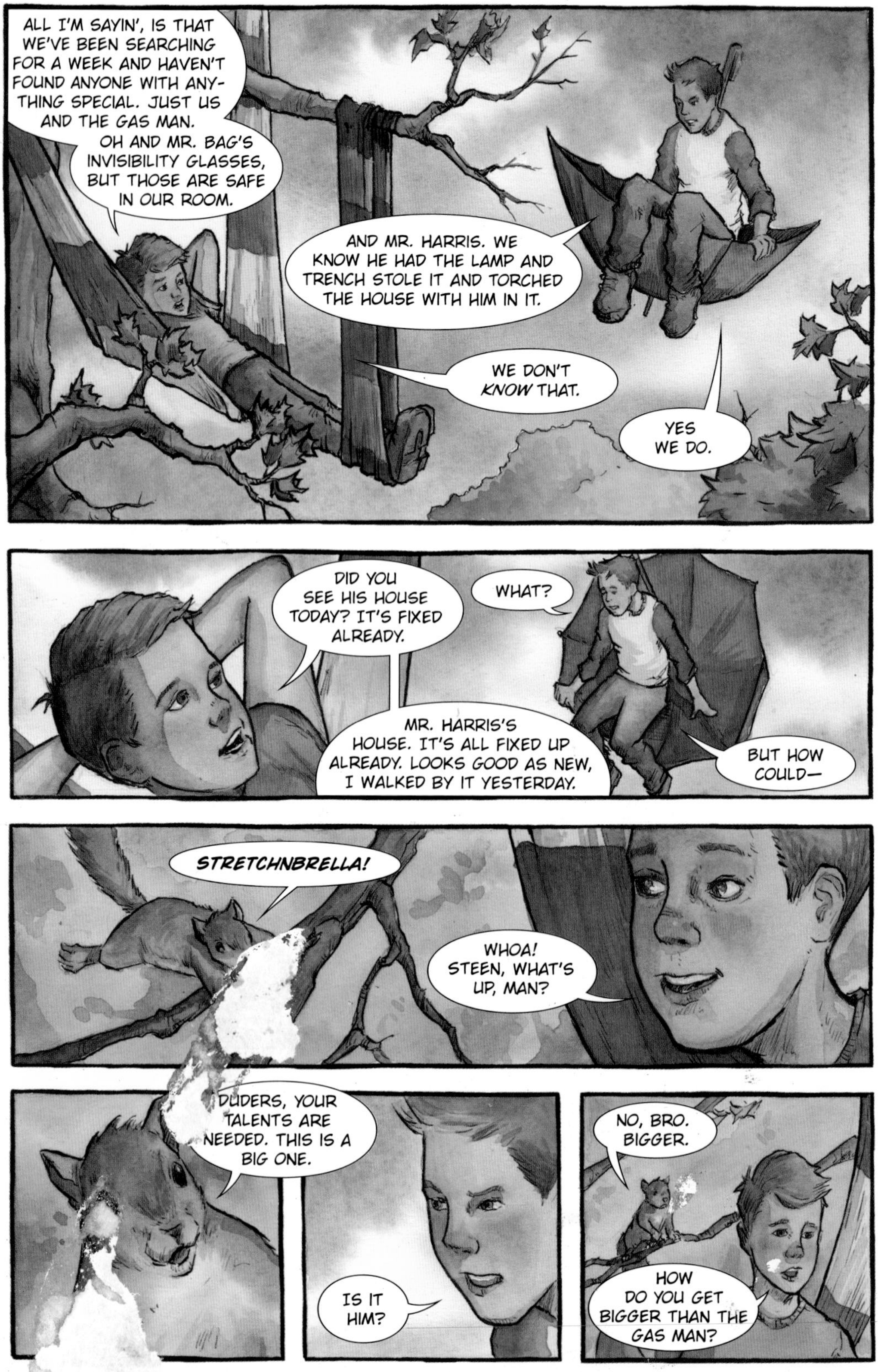

ALL I'M SAYIN', IS THAT WE'VE BEEN SEARCHING FOR A WEEK AND HAVEN'T FOUND ANYONE WITH ANY-THING SPECIAL. JUST US AND THE GAS MAN.
OH AND MR. BAG'S INVISIBILITY GLASSES, BUT THOSE ARE SAFE IN OUR ROOM.
AND MR. HARRIS. WE KNOW HE HAD THE LAMP AND TRENCH STOLE IT AND TORCHED THE HOUSE WITH HIM IN IT.
WE DON'T *KNOW* THAT.
YES WE DO.
DID YOU SEE HIS HOUSE TODAY? IT'S FIXED ALREADY.
WHAT?
MR. HARRIS'S HOUSE. IT'S ALL FIXED UP ALREADY. LOOKS GOOD AS NEW, I WALKED BY IT YESTERDAY.
BUT HOW COULD—
STRETCHNBRELLA!
WHOA! STEEN, WHAT'S UP, MAN?
DUDERS, YOUR TALENTS ARE NEEDED. THIS IS A BIG ONE.
IS IT HIM?
NO, BRO. BIGGER.
HOW DO YOU GET BIGGER THAN THE GAS MAN?

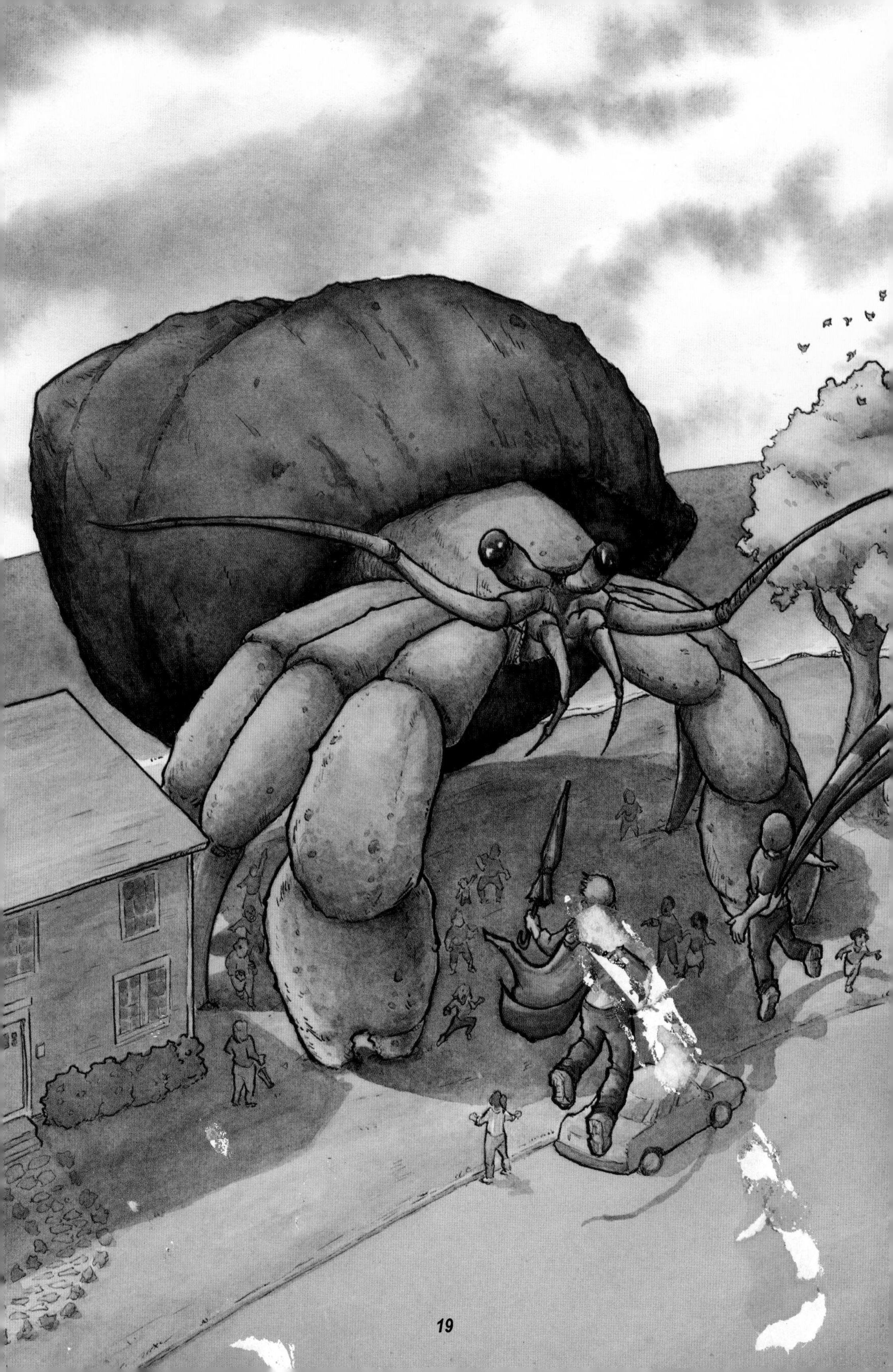

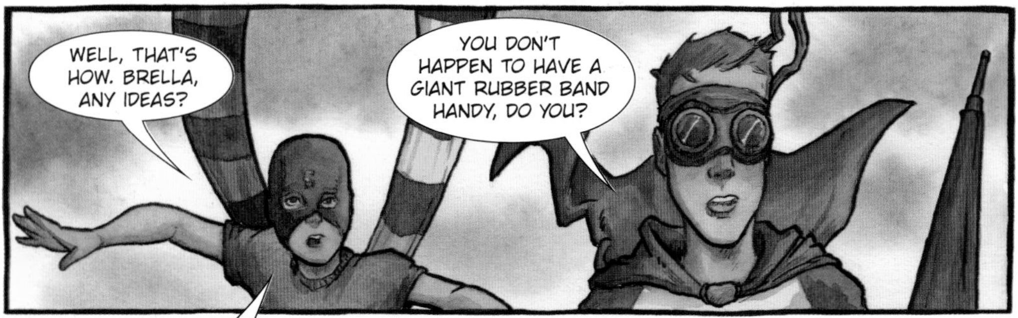
WELL, THAT'S HOW. BRELLA, ANY IDEAS?
YOU DON'T HAPPEN TO HAVE A GIANT RUBBER BAND HANDY, DO YOU?

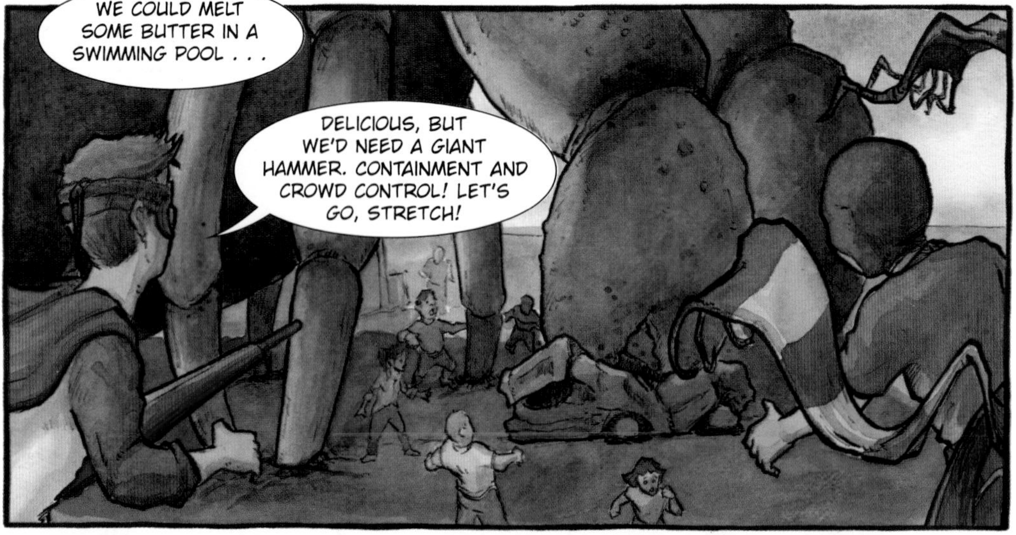
WE COULD MELT SOME BUTTER IN A SWIMMING POOL . . .
DELICIOUS, BUT WE'D NEED A GIANT HAMMER. CONTAINMENT AND CROWD CONTROL! LET'S GO, STRETCH!

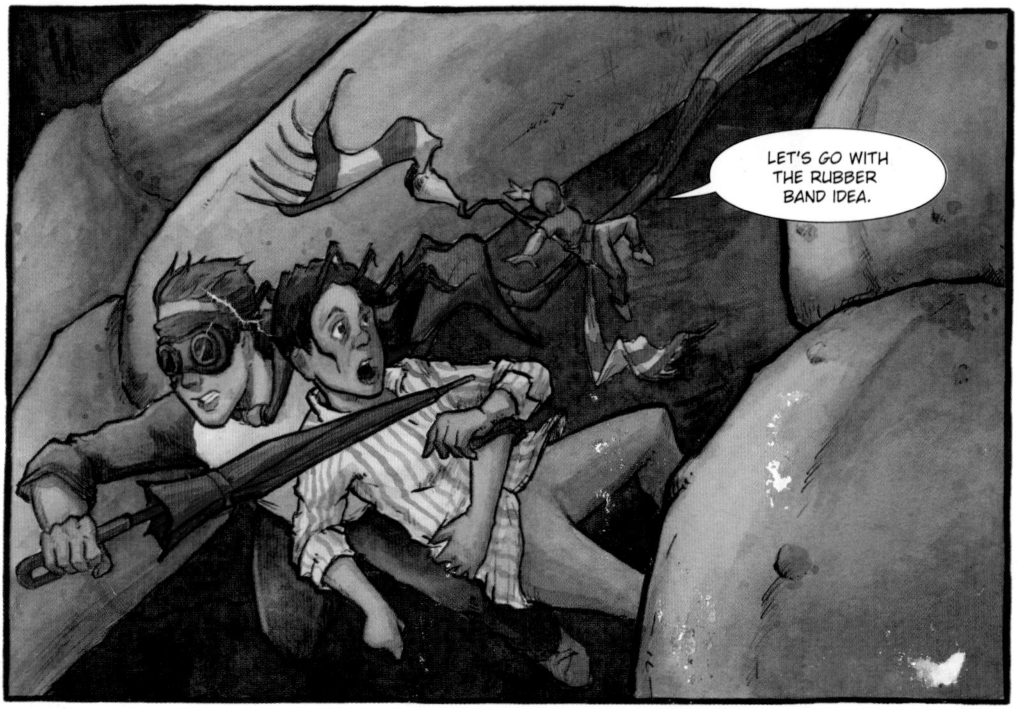
LET'S GO WITH THE RUBBER BAND IDEA.

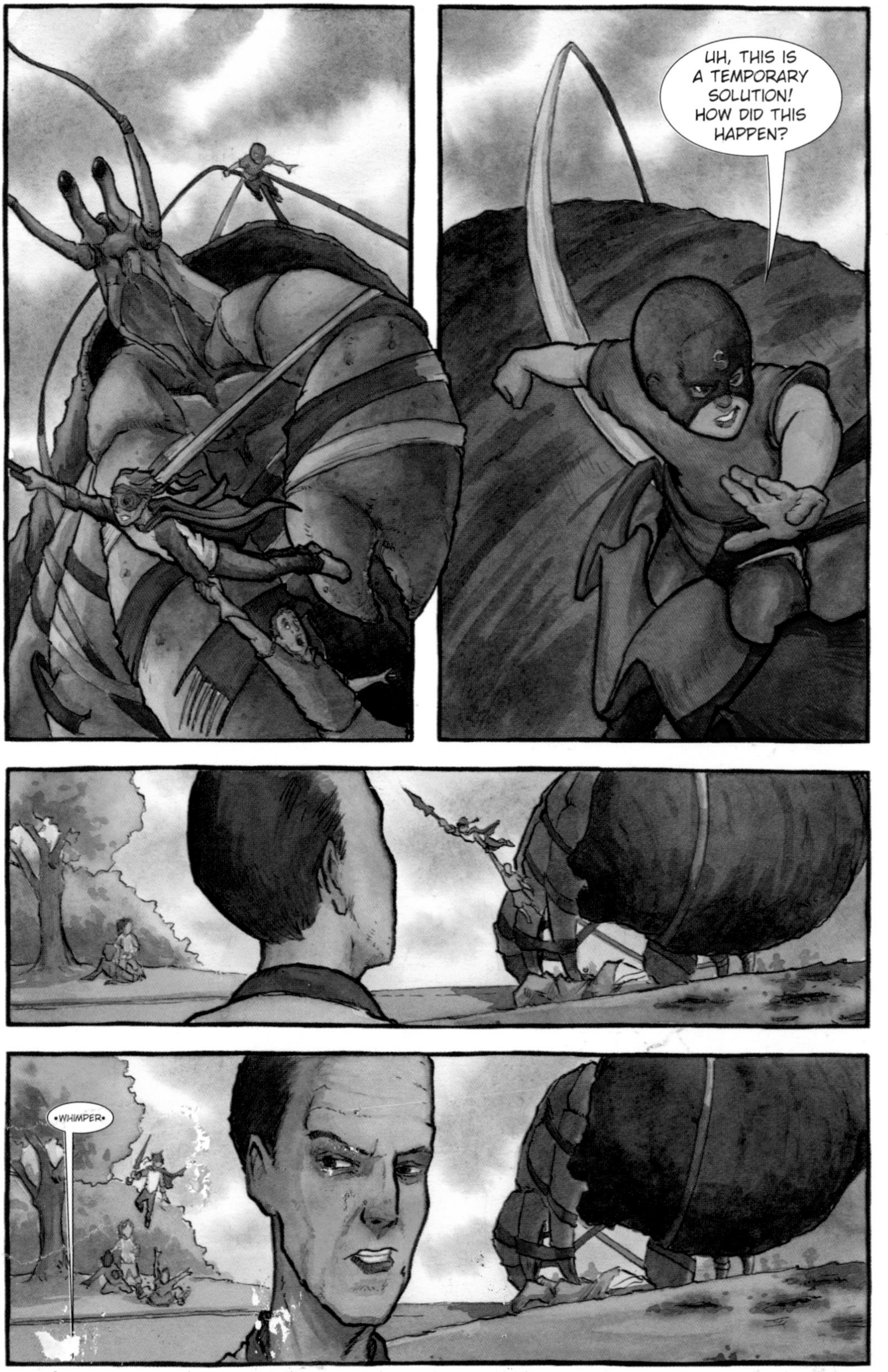
UH, THIS IS A TEMPORARY SOLUTION! HOW DID THIS HAPPEN?
•WHIMPER•

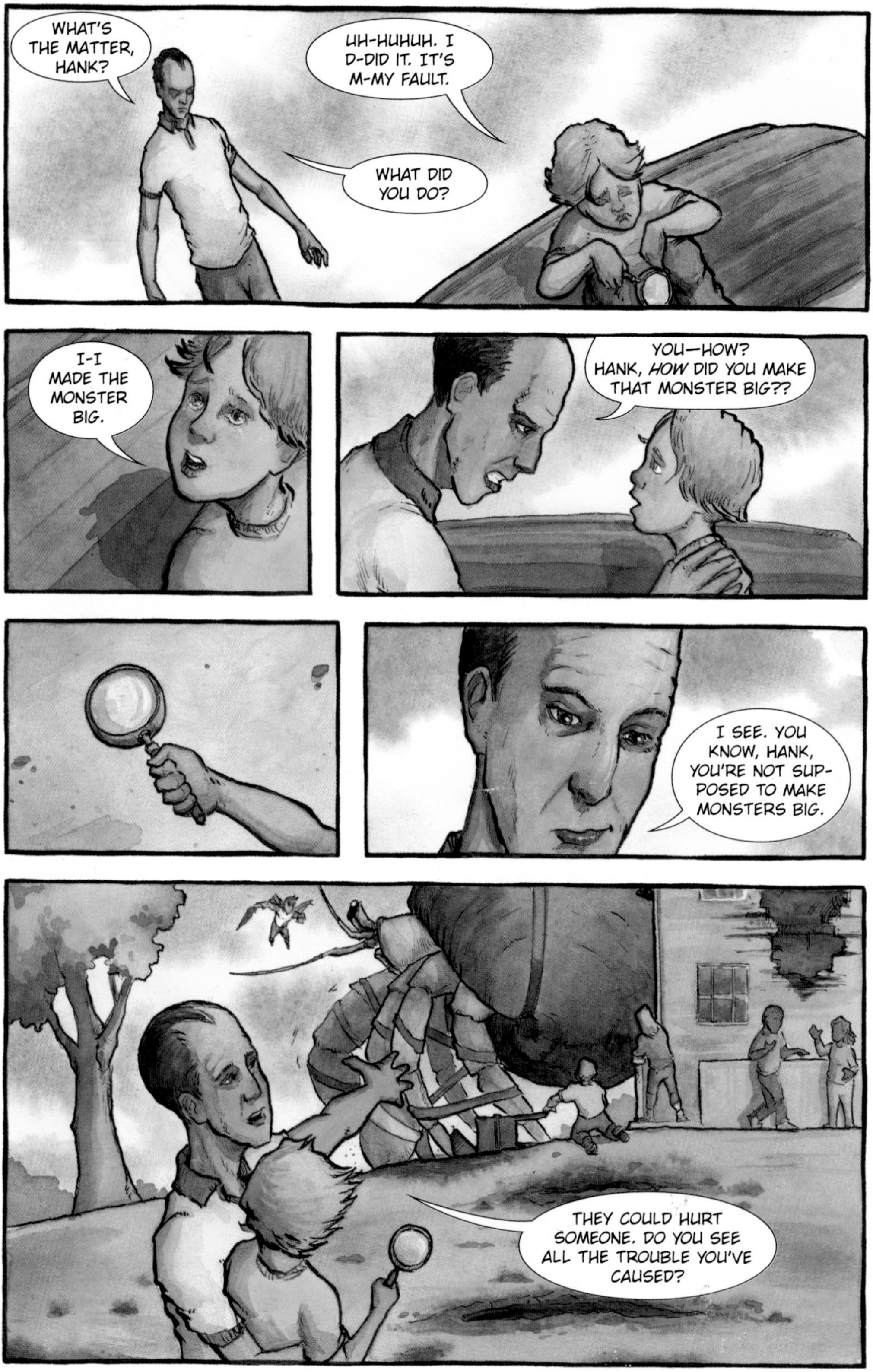
WHAT'S THE MATTER, HANK?
UH-HUHUH. I D-DID IT. IT'S M-MY FAULT.
WHAT DID YOU DO?
I-I MADE THE MONSTER BIG.
YOU—HOW? HANK, *HOW* DID YOU MAKE THAT MONSTER BIG??
I SEE. YOU KNOW, HANK, YOU'RE NOT SUP-POSED TO MAKE MONSTERS BIG.
THEY COULD HURT SOMEONE. DO YOU SEE ALL THE TROUBLE YOU'VE CAUSED?

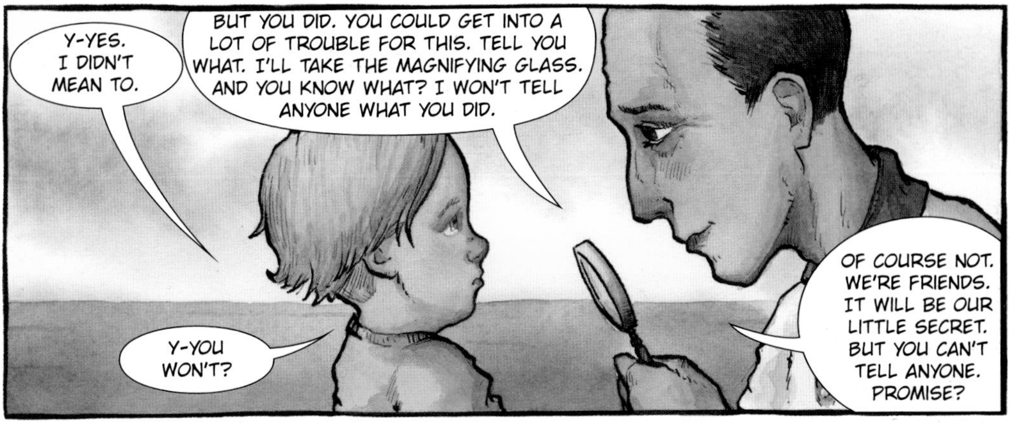
Y-YES. I DIDN'T MEAN TO.
BUT YOU DID. YOU COULD GET INTO A LOT OF TROUBLE FOR THIS. TELL YOU WHAT. I'LL TAKE THE MAGNIFYING GLASS. AND YOU KNOW WHAT? I WON'T TELL ANYONE WHAT YOU DID.
Y-YOU WON'T?
OF COURSE NOT. WE'RE FRIENDS. IT WILL BE OUR LITTLE SECRET. BUT YOU CAN'T TELL ANYONE. PROMISE?

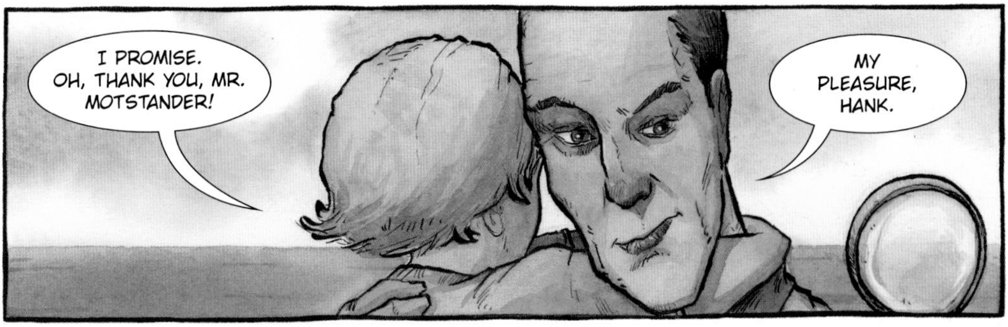
I PROMISE. OH, THANK YOU, MR. MOTSTANDER!
MY PLEASURE, HANK.

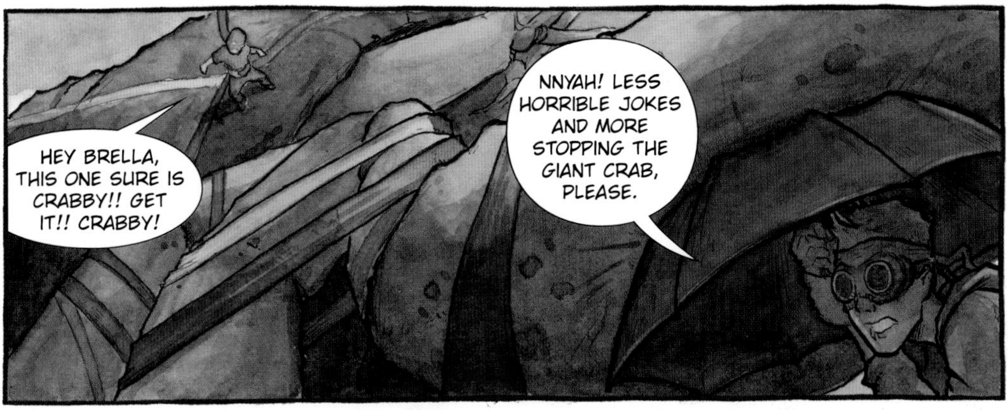
HEY BRELLA, THIS ONE SURE IS CRABBY!! GET IT!! CRABBY!
NNYAH! LESS HORRIBLE JOKES AND MORE STOPPING THE GIANT CRAB, PLEASE.

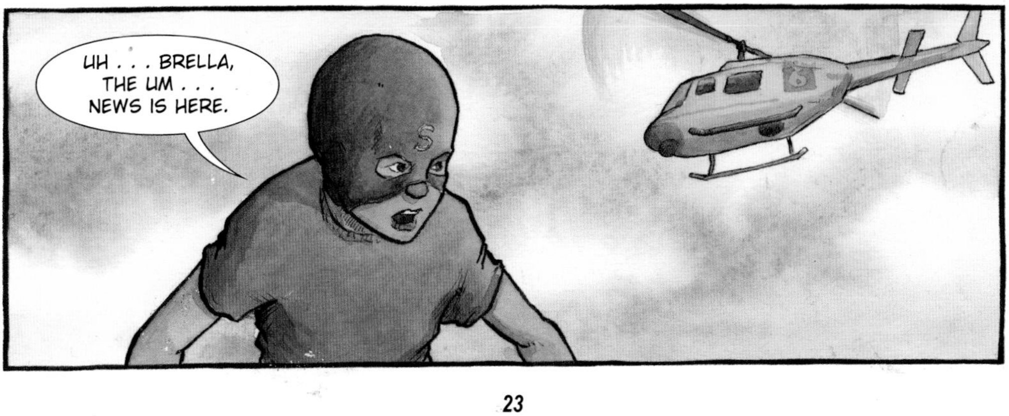
UH . . . BRELLA, THE UM . . . NEWS IS HERE.

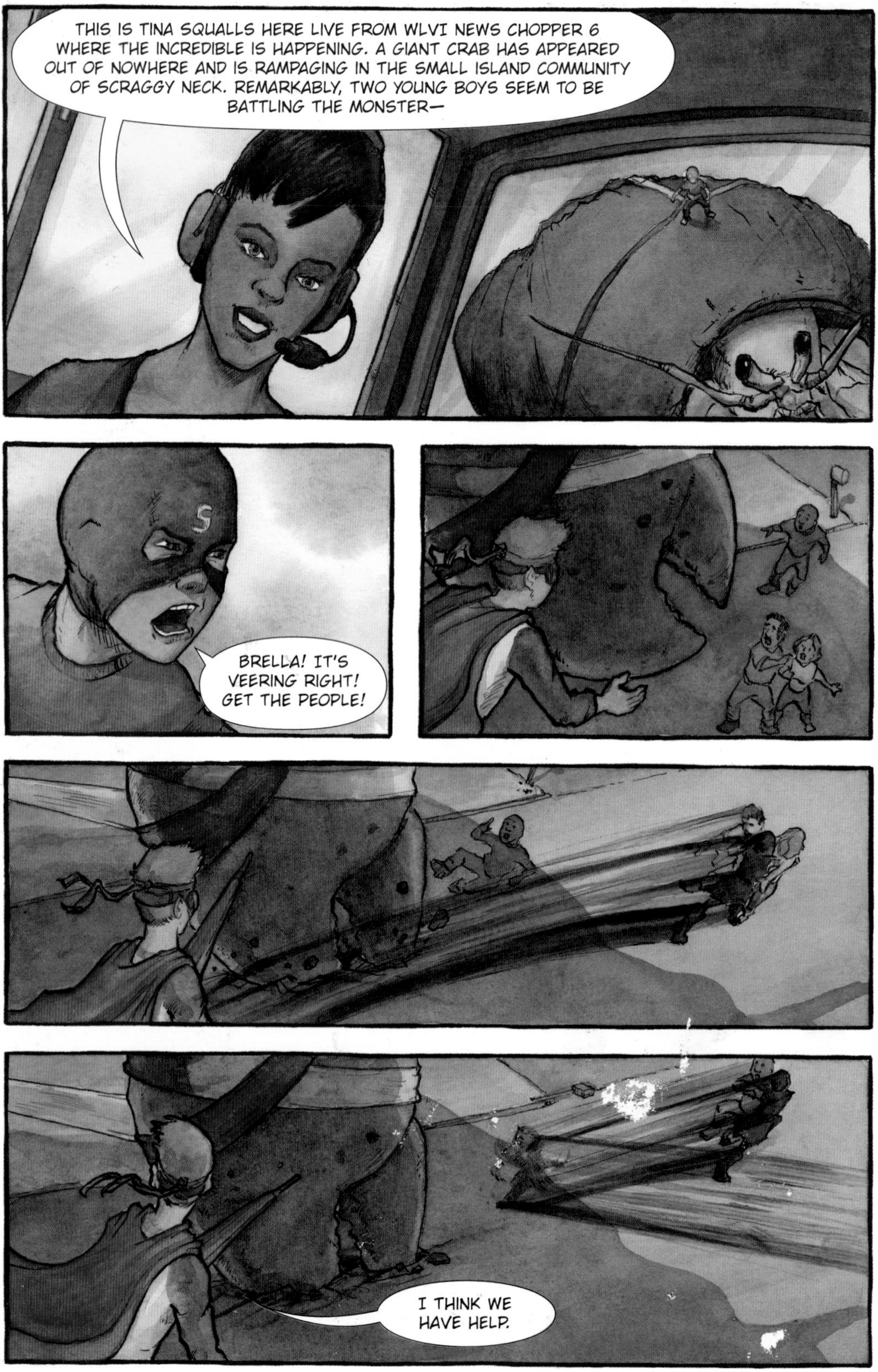
THIS IS TINA SQUALLS HERE LIVE FROM WLVI NEWS CHOPPER 6 WHERE THE INCREDIBLE IS HAPPENING. A GIANT CRAB HAS APPEARED OUT OF NOWHERE AND IS RAMPAGING IN THE SMALL ISLAND COMMUNITY OF SCRAGGY NECK. REMARKABLY, TWO YOUNG BOYS SEEM TO BE BATTLING THE MONSTER—
BRELLA! IT'S VEERING RIGHT! GET THE PEOPLE!
I THINK WE HAVE HELP.

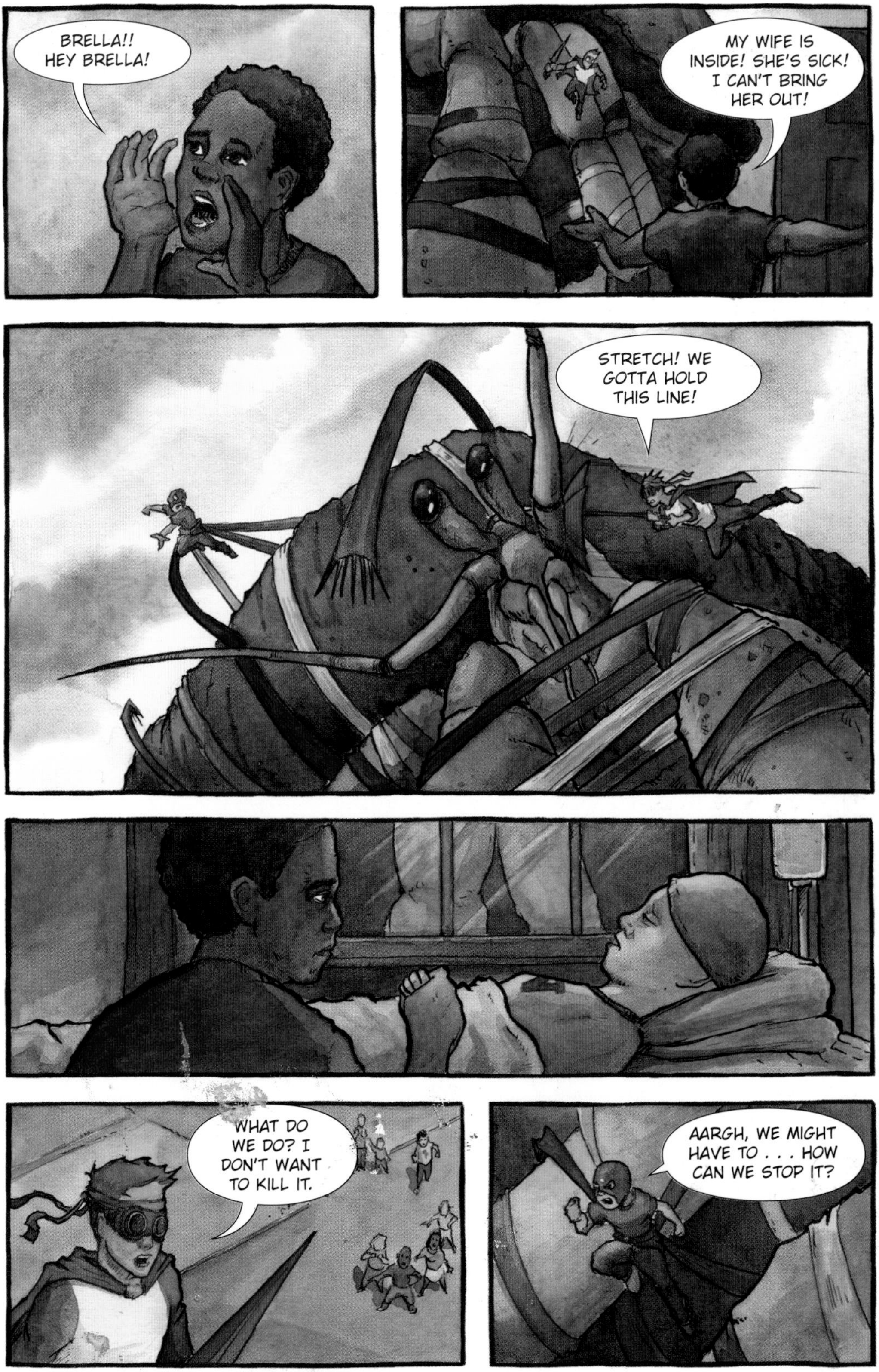
BRELLA!! HEY BRELLA!
MY WIFE IS INSIDE! SHE'S SICK! I CAN'T BRING HER OUT!
STRETCH! WE GOTTA HOLD THIS LINE!
WHAT DO WE DO? I DON'T WANT TO KILL IT.
AARGH, WE MIGHT HAVE TO . . . HOW CAN WE STOP IT?

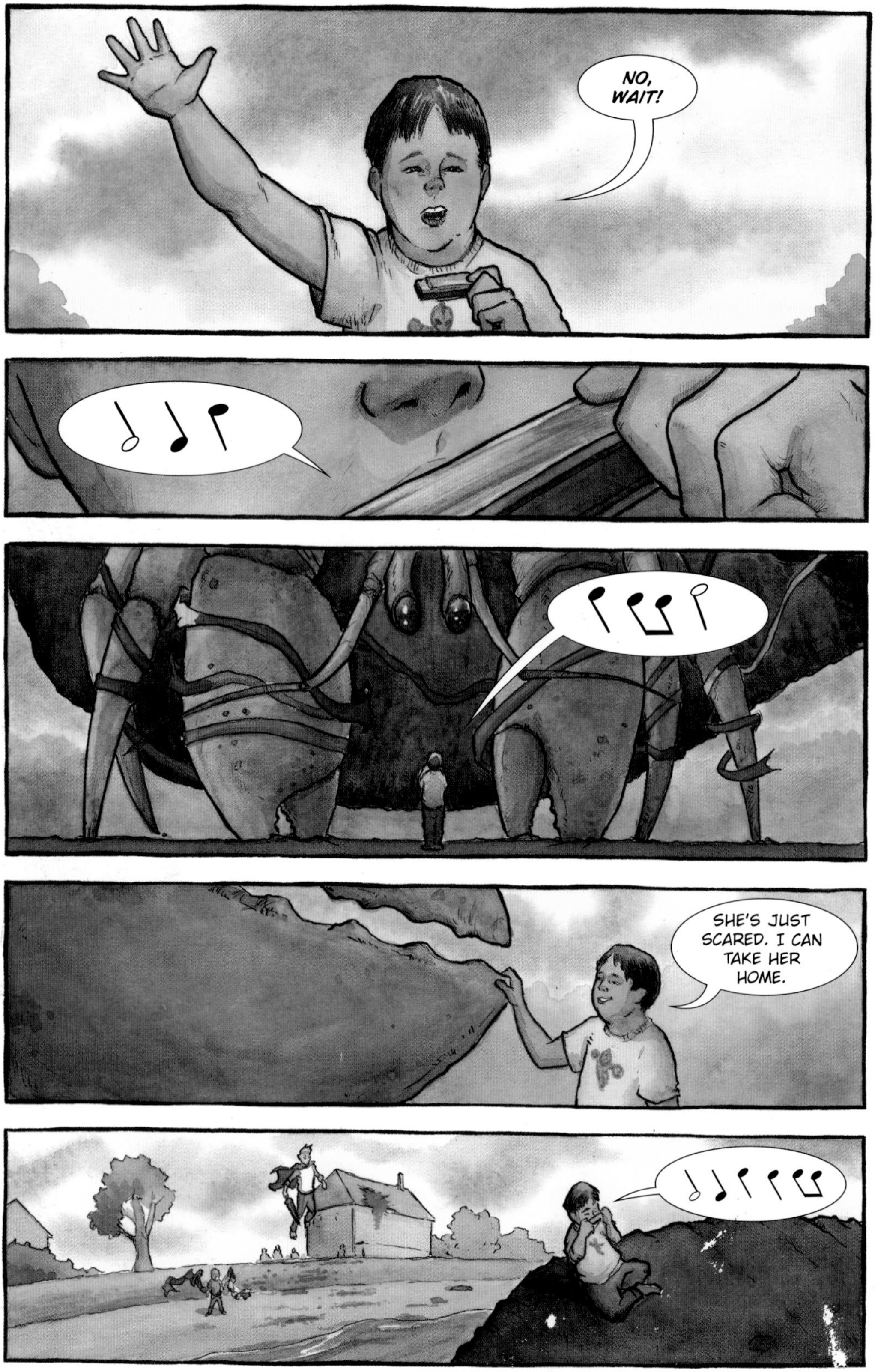
NO, WAIT!
SHE'S JUST SCARED. I CAN TAKE HER HOME.

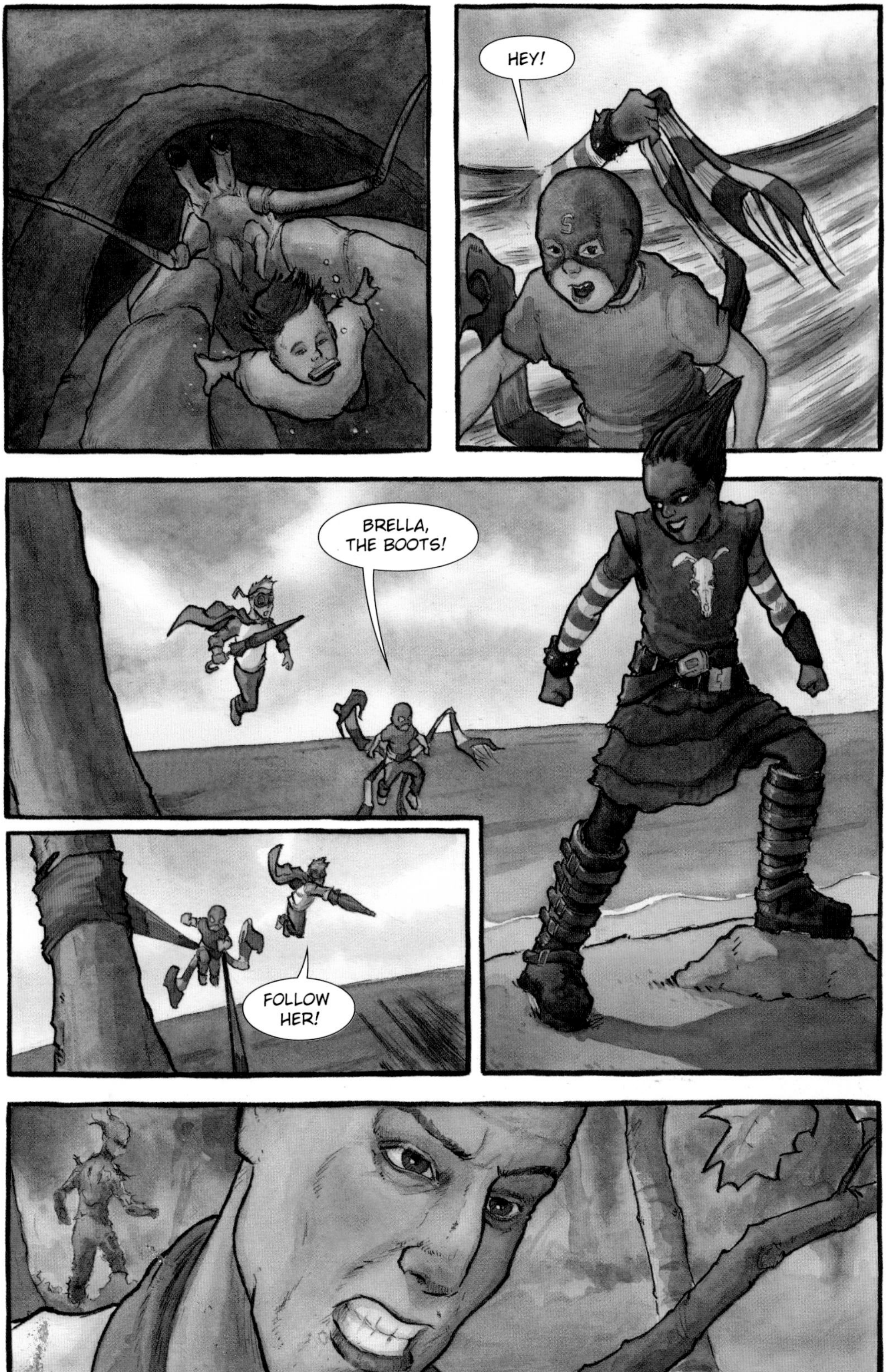
HEY!
BRELLA, THE BOOTS!
FOLLOW HER!

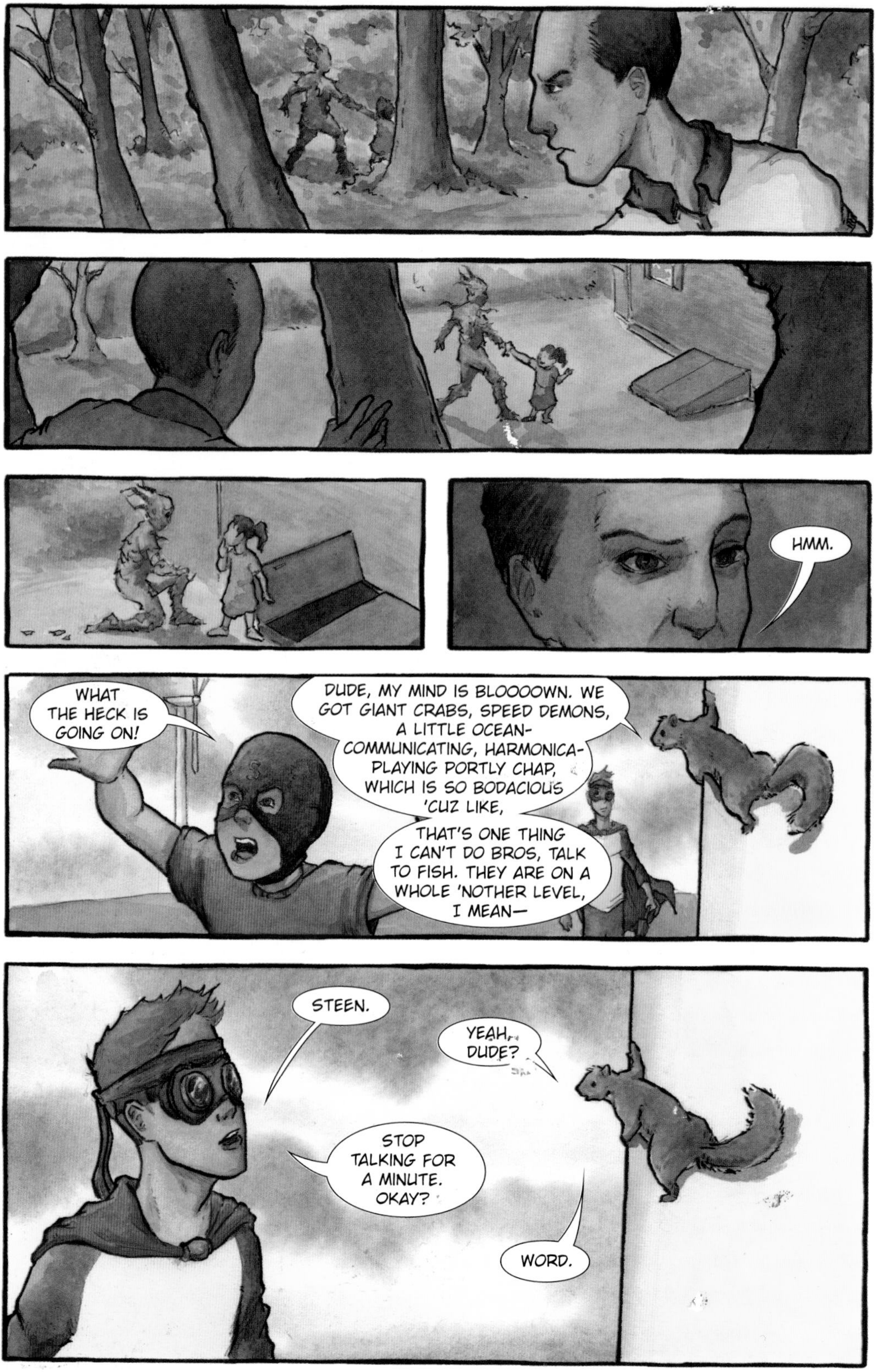
HMM.
WHAT THE HECK IS GOING ON!
DUDE, MY MIND IS BLOOOOWN. WE GOT GIANT CRABS, SPEED DEMONS, A LITTLE OCEAN-COMMUNICATING, HARMONICA-PLAYING PORTLY CHAP, WHICH IS SO BODACIOUS 'CUZ LIKE,
THAT'S ONE THING I CAN'T DO BROS, TALK TO FISH. THEY ARE ON A WHOLE 'NOTHER LEVEL, I MEAN—
STEEN.
YEAH, DUDE?
STOP TALKING FOR A MINUTE. OKAY?
WORD.

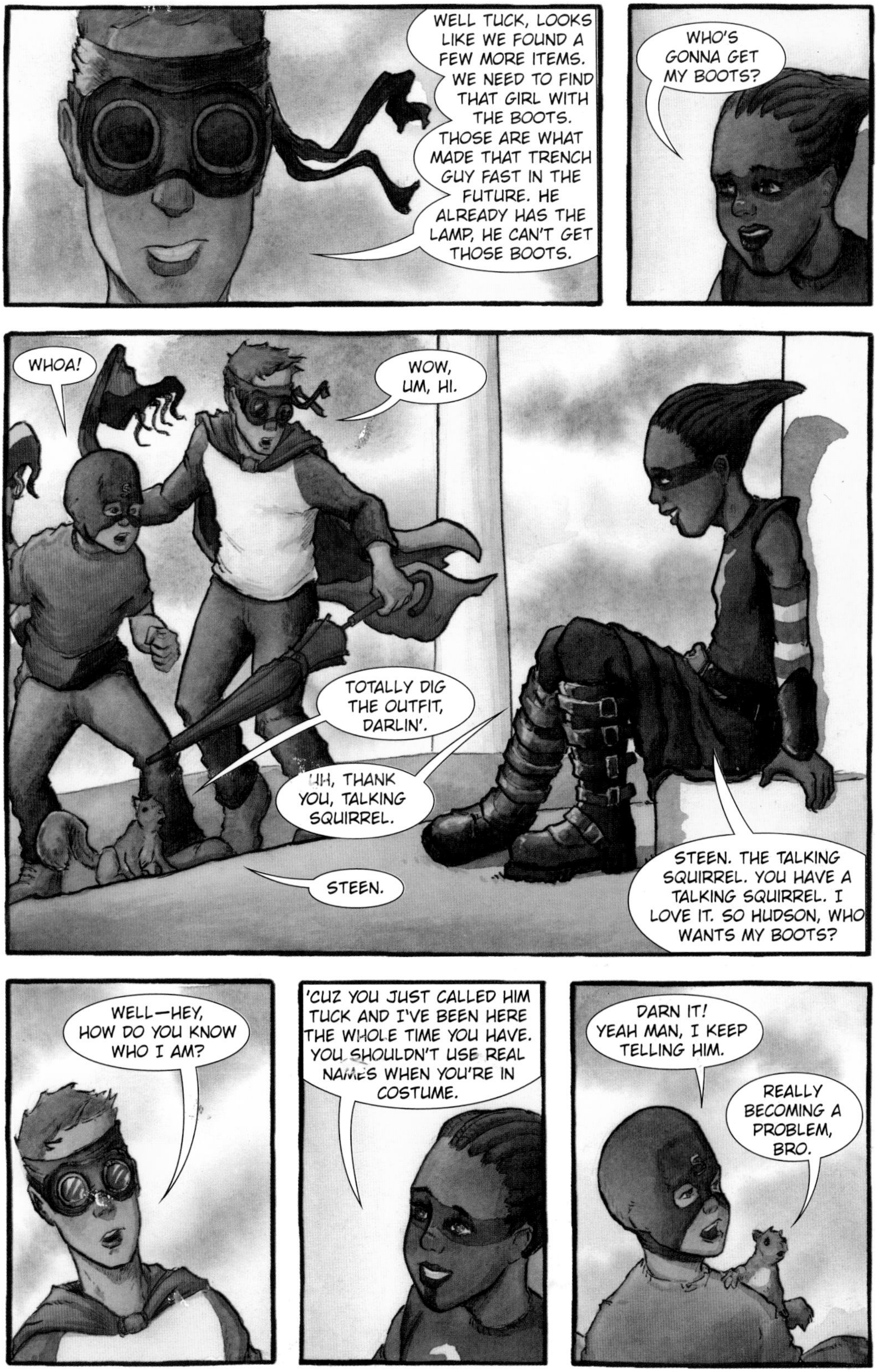
WELL TUCK, LOOKS LIKE WE FOUND A FEW MORE ITEMS. WE NEED TO FIND THAT GIRL WITH THE BOOTS. THOSE ARE WHAT MADE THAT TRENCH GUY FAST IN THE FUTURE. HE ALREADY HAS THE LAMP, HE CAN'T GET THOSE BOOTS.
WHO'S GONNA GET MY BOOTS?
WHOA!
WOW, UM, HI.
TOTALLY DIG THE OUTFIT, DARLIN'.
UH, THANK YOU, TALKING SQUIRREL.
STEEN.
STEEN. THE TALKING SQUIRREL. YOU HAVE A TALKING SQUIRREL. I LOVE IT. SO HUDSON, WHO WANTS MY BOOTS?
WELL—HEY, HOW DO YOU KNOW WHO I AM?
'CUZ YOU JUST CALLED HIM TUCK AND I'VE BEEN HERE THE WHOLE TIME YOU HAVE. YOU SHOULDN'T USE REAL NAMES WHEN YOU'RE IN COSTUME.
DARN IT! YEAH MAN, I KEEP TELLING HIM.
REALLY BECOMING A PROBLEM, BRO.

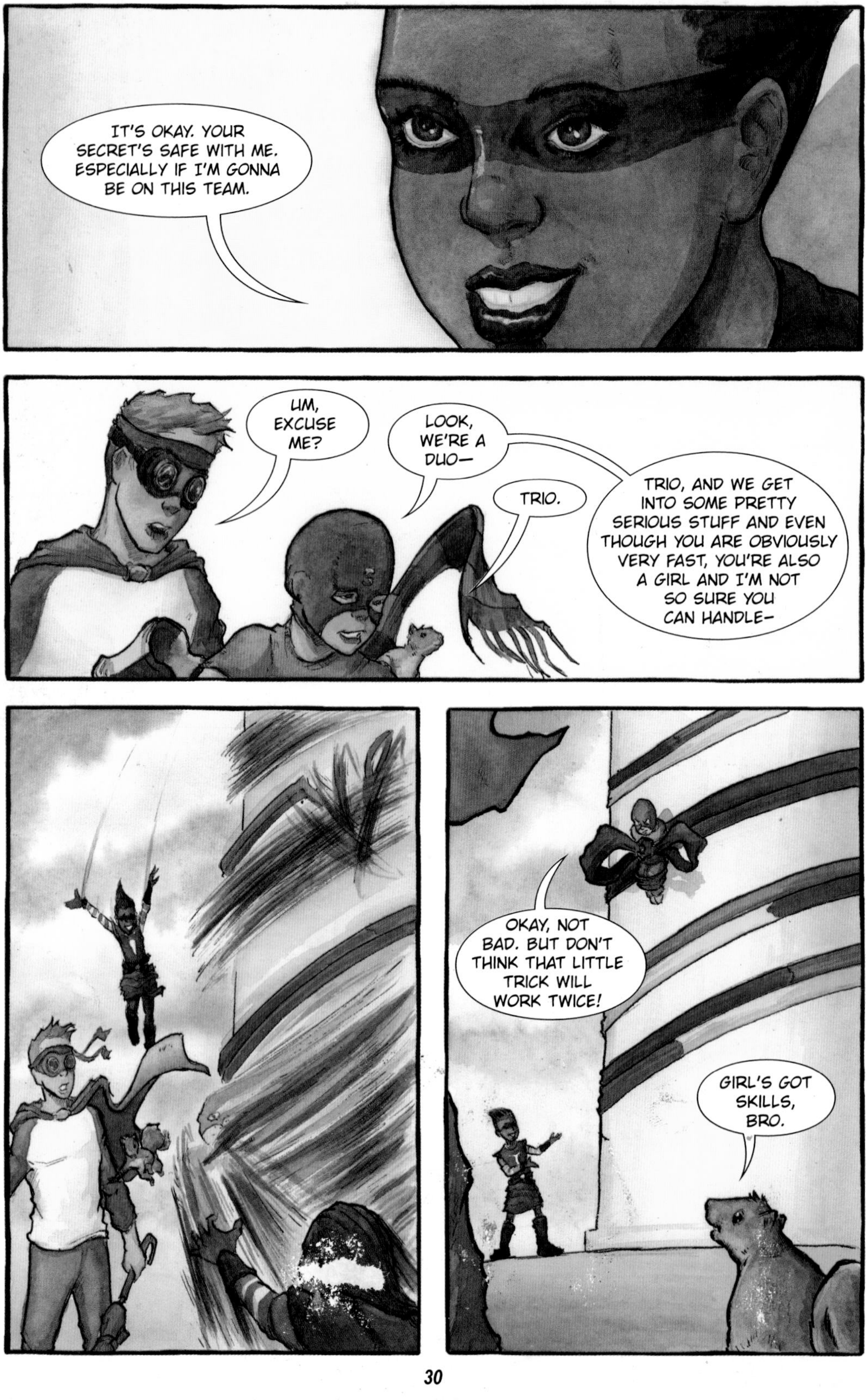
IT'S OKAY. YOUR SECRET'S SAFE WITH ME. ESPECIALLY IF I'M GONNA BE ON THIS TEAM.
UM, EXCUSE ME?
LOOK, WE'RE A DUO—
TRIO.
TRIO, AND WE GET INTO SOME PRETTY SERIOUS STUFF AND EVEN THOUGH YOU ARE OBVIOUSLY VERY FAST, YOU'RE ALSO A GIRL AND I'M NOT SO SURE YOU CAN HANDLE—
OKAY, NOT BAD. BUT DON'T THINK THAT LITTLE TRICK WILL WORK TWICE!
GIRL'S GOT SKILLS, BRO.

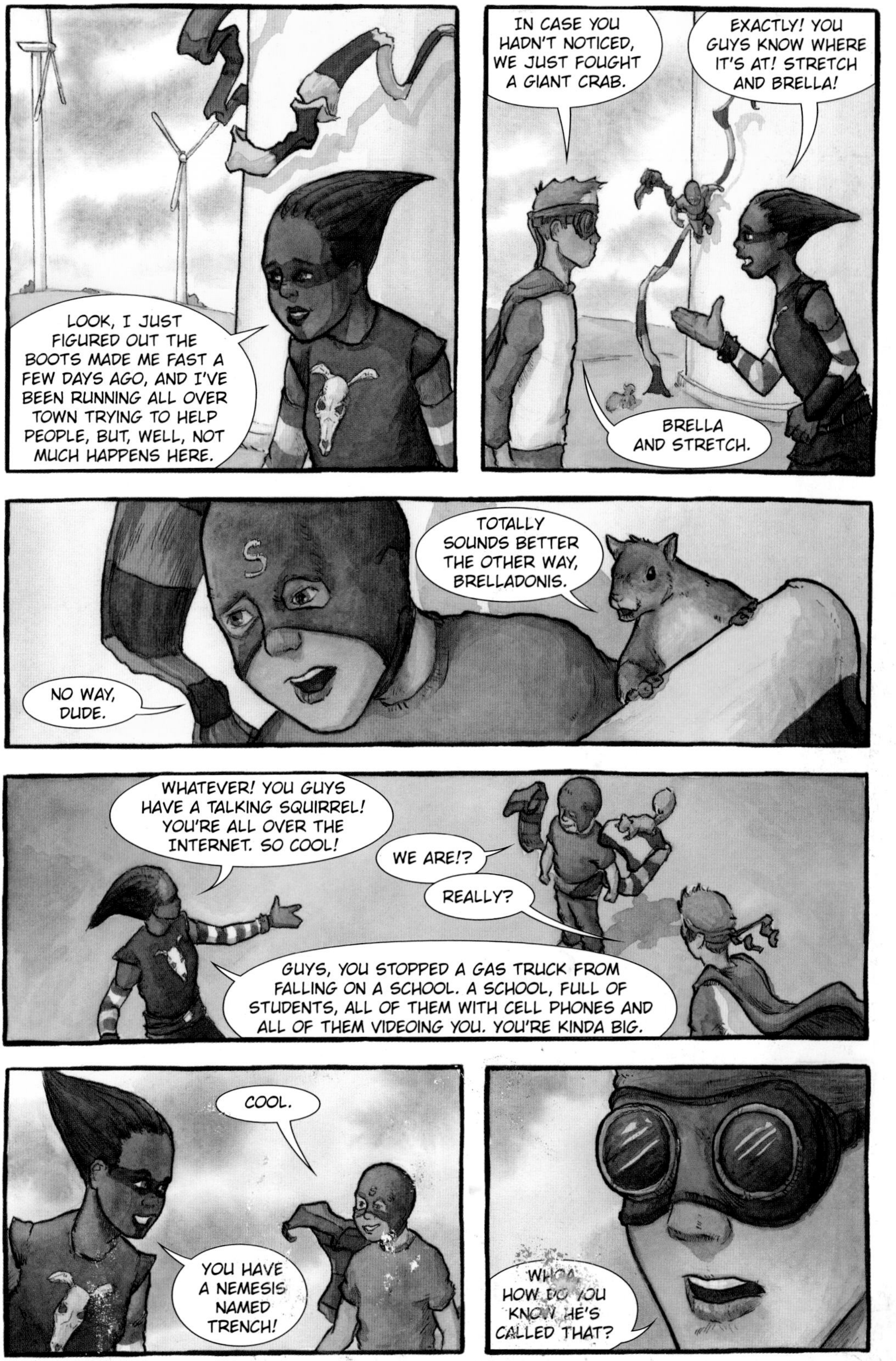
LOOK, I JUST FIGURED OUT THE BOOTS MADE ME FAST A FEW DAYS AGO, AND I'VE BEEN RUNNING ALL OVER TOWN TRYING TO HELP PEOPLE, BUT, WELL, NOT MUCH HAPPENS HERE.
IN CASE YOU HADN'T NOTICED, WE JUST FOUGHT A GIANT CRAB.
EXACTLY! YOU GUYS KNOW WHERE IT'S AT! STRETCH AND BRELLA!
BRELLA AND STRETCH.
NO WAY, DUDE.
TOTALLY SOUNDS BETTER THE OTHER WAY, BRELLADONIS.
WHATEVER! YOU GUYS HAVE A TALKING SQUIRREL! YOU'RE ALL OVER THE INTERNET. SO COOL!
WE ARE!?
REALLY?
GUYS, YOU STOPPED A GAS TRUCK FROM FALLING ON A SCHOOL. A SCHOOL, FULL OF STUDENTS, ALL OF THEM WITH CELL PHONES AND ALL OF THEM VIDEOING YOU. YOU'RE KINDA BIG.
YOU HAVE A NEMESIS NAMED TRENCH!
COOL.
WHOA. HOW DO YOU KNOW HE'S CALLED THAT?

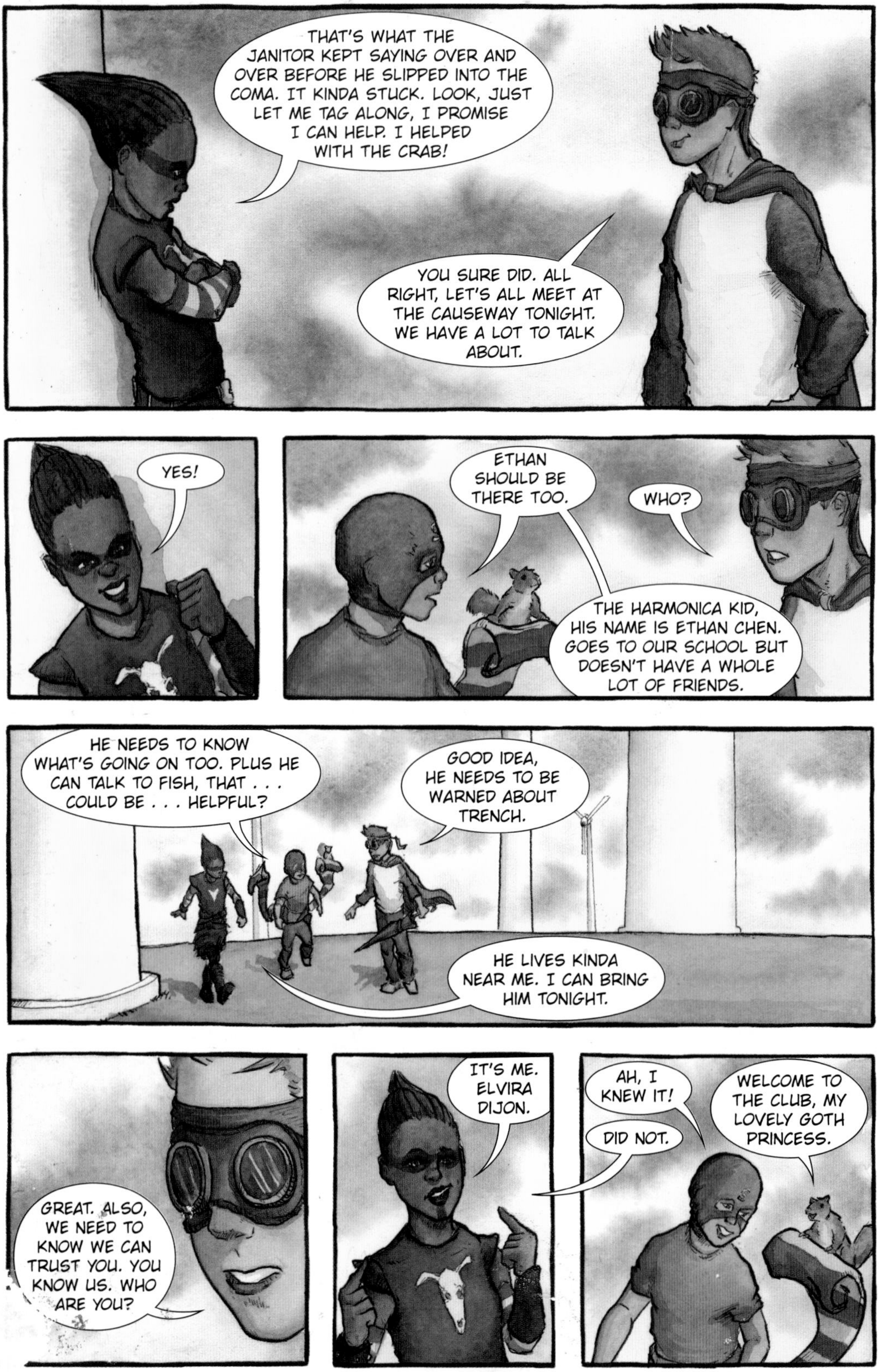
THAT'S WHAT THE JANITOR KEPT SAYING OVER AND OVER BEFORE HE SLIPPED INTO THE COMA. IT KINDA STUCK. LOOK, JUST LET ME TAG ALONG, I PROMISE I CAN HELP. I HELPED WITH THE CRAB!
YOU SURE DID. ALL RIGHT, LET'S ALL MEET AT THE CAUSEWAY TONIGHT. WE HAVE A LOT TO TALK ABOUT.
YES!
ETHAN SHOULD BE THERE TOO.
WHO?
THE HARMONICA KID, HIS NAME IS ETHAN CHEN. GOES TO OUR SCHOOL BUT DOESN'T HAVE A WHOLE LOT OF FRIENDS.
HE NEEDS TO KNOW WHAT'S GOING ON TOO. PLUS HE CAN TALK TO FISH, THAT . . . COULD BE . . . HELPFUL?
GOOD IDEA, HE NEEDS TO BE WARNED ABOUT TRENCH.
HE LIVES KINDA NEAR ME. I CAN BRING HIM TONIGHT.
GREAT. ALSO, WE NEED TO KNOW WE CAN TRUST YOU. YOU KNOW US. WHO ARE YOU?
IT'S ME. ELVIRA DIJON.
AH, I KNEW IT!
DID NOT.
WELCOME TO THE CLUB, MY LOVELY GOTH PRINCESS.

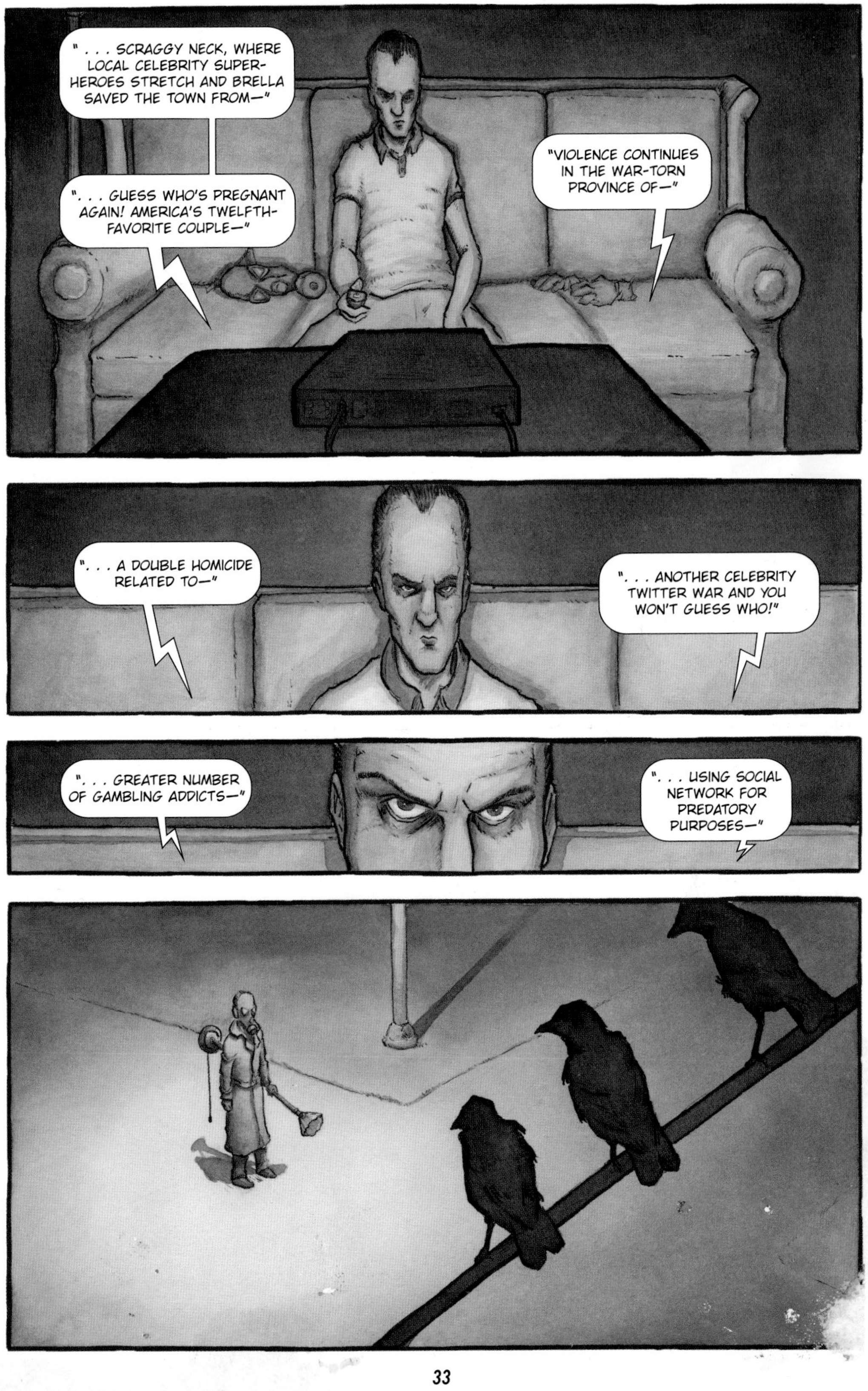
" . . . SCRAGGY NECK, WHERE LOCAL CELEBRITY SUPER-HEROES STRETCH AND BRELLA SAVED THE TOWN FROM—"
". . . GUESS WHO'S PREGNANT AGAIN! AMERICA'S TWELFTH-FAVORITE COUPLE—"
"VIOLENCE CONTINUES IN THE WAR-TORN PROVINCE OF—"
". . . A DOUBLE HOMICIDE RELATED TO—"
". . . ANOTHER CELEBRITY TWITTER WAR AND YOU WON'T GUESS WHO!"
". . . GREATER NUMBER OF GAMBLING ADDICTS—"
". . . USING SOCIAL NETWORK FOR PREDATORY PURPOSES—"

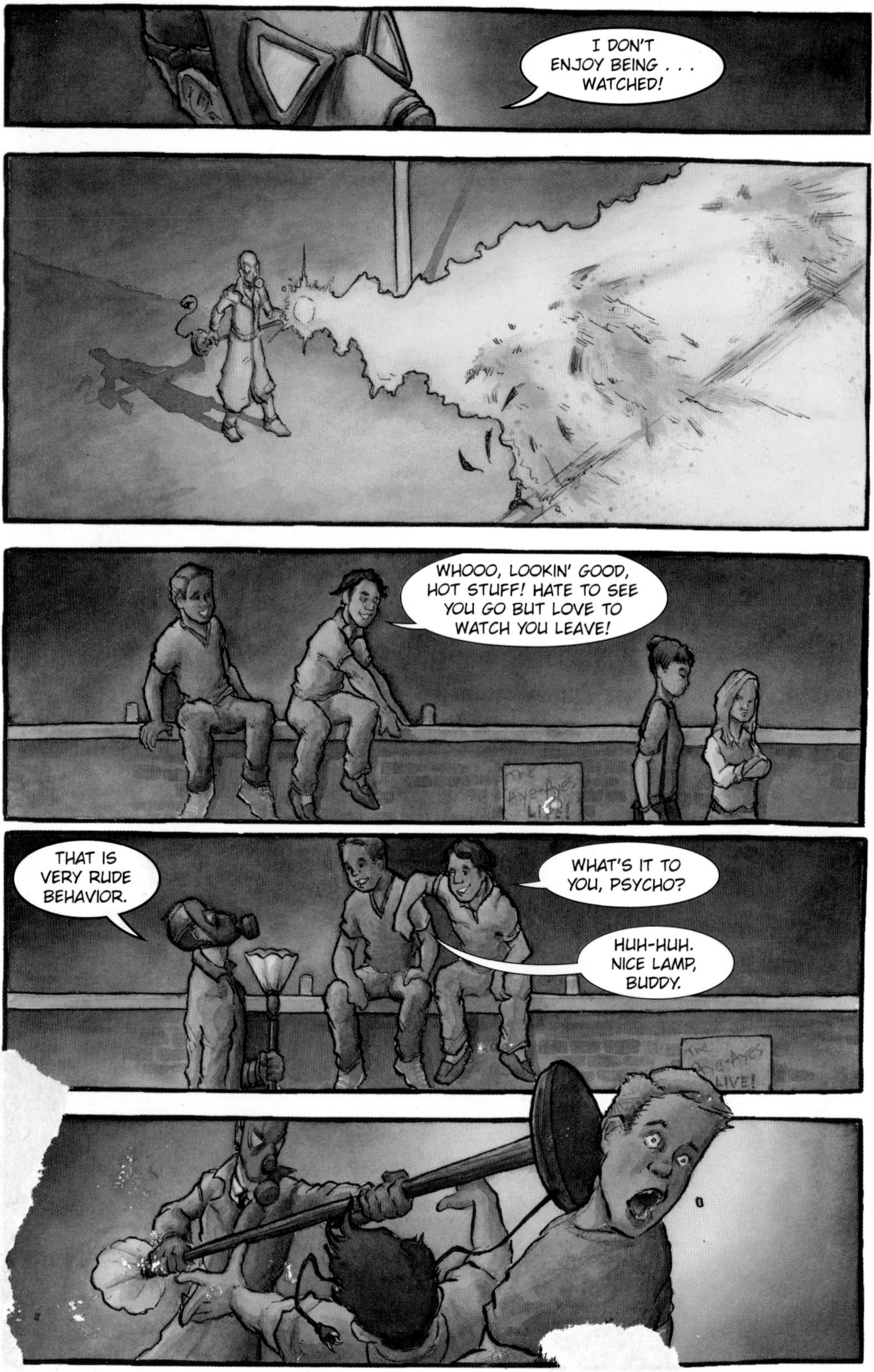
I DON'T ENJOY BEING . . . WATCHED!
WHOOO, LOOKIN' GOOD, HOT STUFF! HATE TO SEE YOU GO BUT LOVE TO WATCH YOU LEAVE!
THAT IS VERY RUDE BEHAVIOR.
WHAT'S IT TO YOU, PSYCHO?
HUH-HUH. NICE LAMP, BUDDY.

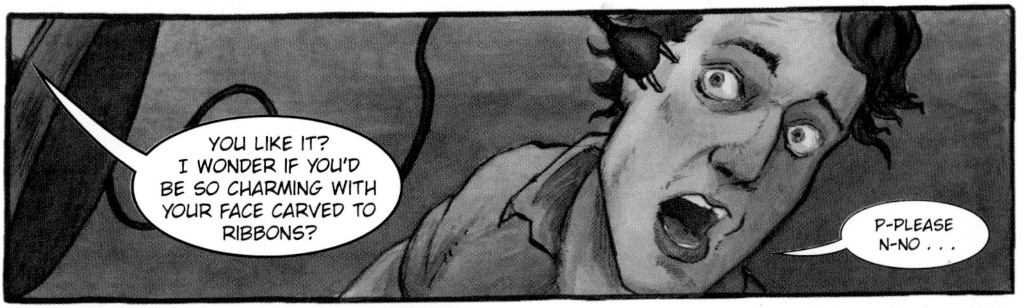
YOU LIKE IT? I WONDER IF YOU'D BE SO CHARMING WITH YOUR FACE CARVED TO RIBBONS?
P-PLEASE N-NO . . .

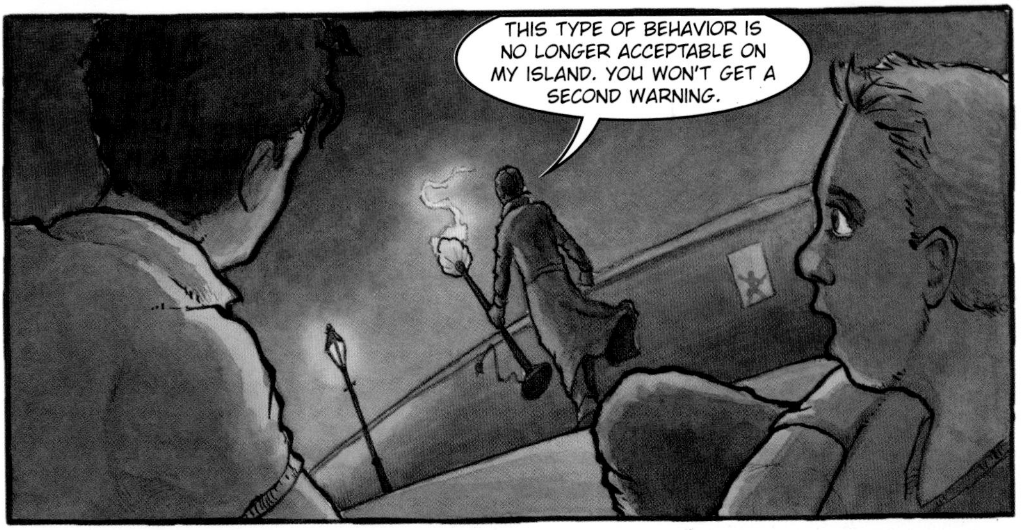
THIS TYPE OF BEHAVIOR IS NO LONGER ACCEPTABLE ON MY ISLAND. YOU WON'T GET A SECOND WARNING.

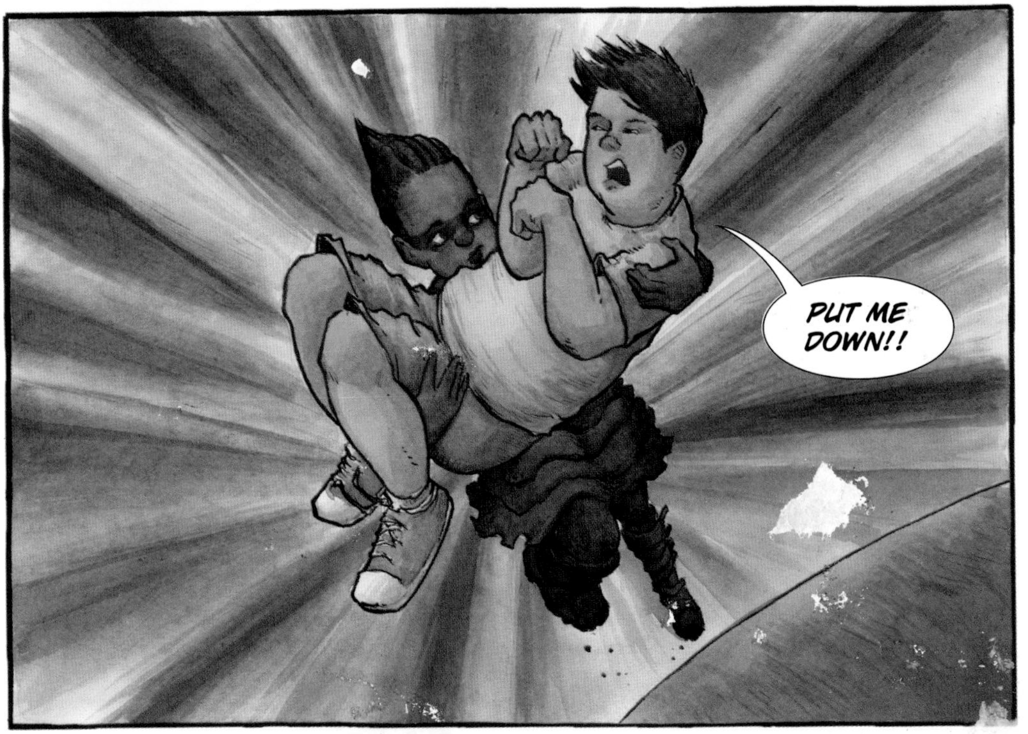
PUT ME DOWN!!

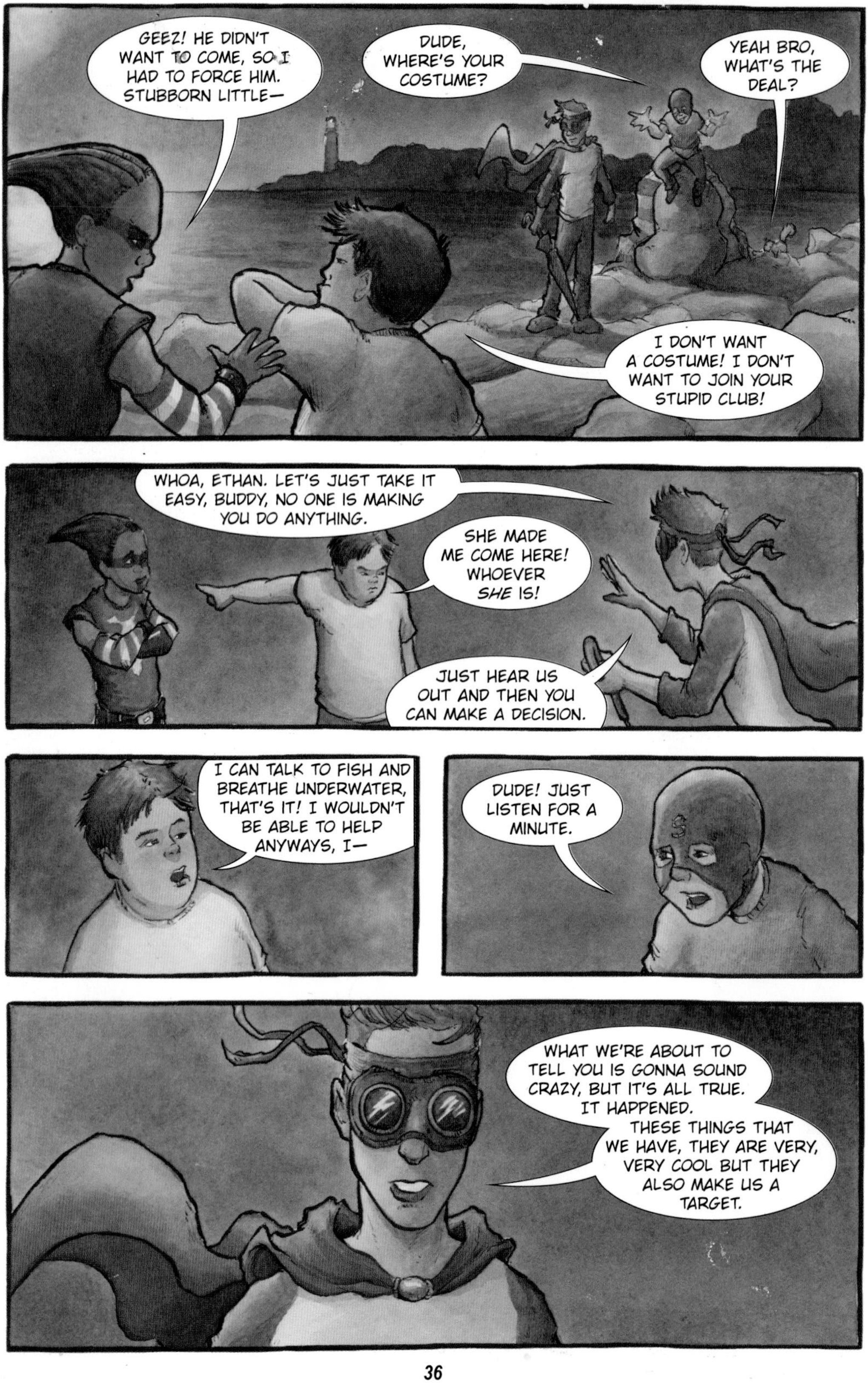
GEEZ! HE DIDN'T WANT TO COME, SO I HAD TO FORCE HIM. STUBBORN LITTLE—
DUDE, WHERE'S YOUR COSTUME?
YEAH BRO, WHAT'S THE DEAL?
I DON'T WANT A COSTUME! I DON'T WANT TO JOIN YOUR STUPID CLUB!
WHOA, ETHAN. LET'S JUST TAKE IT EASY, BUDDY, NO ONE IS MAKING YOU DO ANYTHING.
SHE MADE ME COME HERE! WHOEVER *SHE* IS!
JUST HEAR US OUT AND THEN YOU CAN MAKE A DECISION.
I CAN TALK TO FISH AND BREATHE UNDERWATER, THAT'S IT! I WOULDN'T BE ABLE TO HELP ANYWAYS, I—
DUDE! JUST LISTEN FOR A MINUTE.
WHAT WE'RE ABOUT TO TELL YOU IS GONNA SOUND CRAZY, BUT IT'S ALL TRUE. IT HAPPENED.
THESE THINGS THAT WE HAVE, THEY ARE VERY, VERY COOL BUT THEY ALSO MAKE US A TARGET.

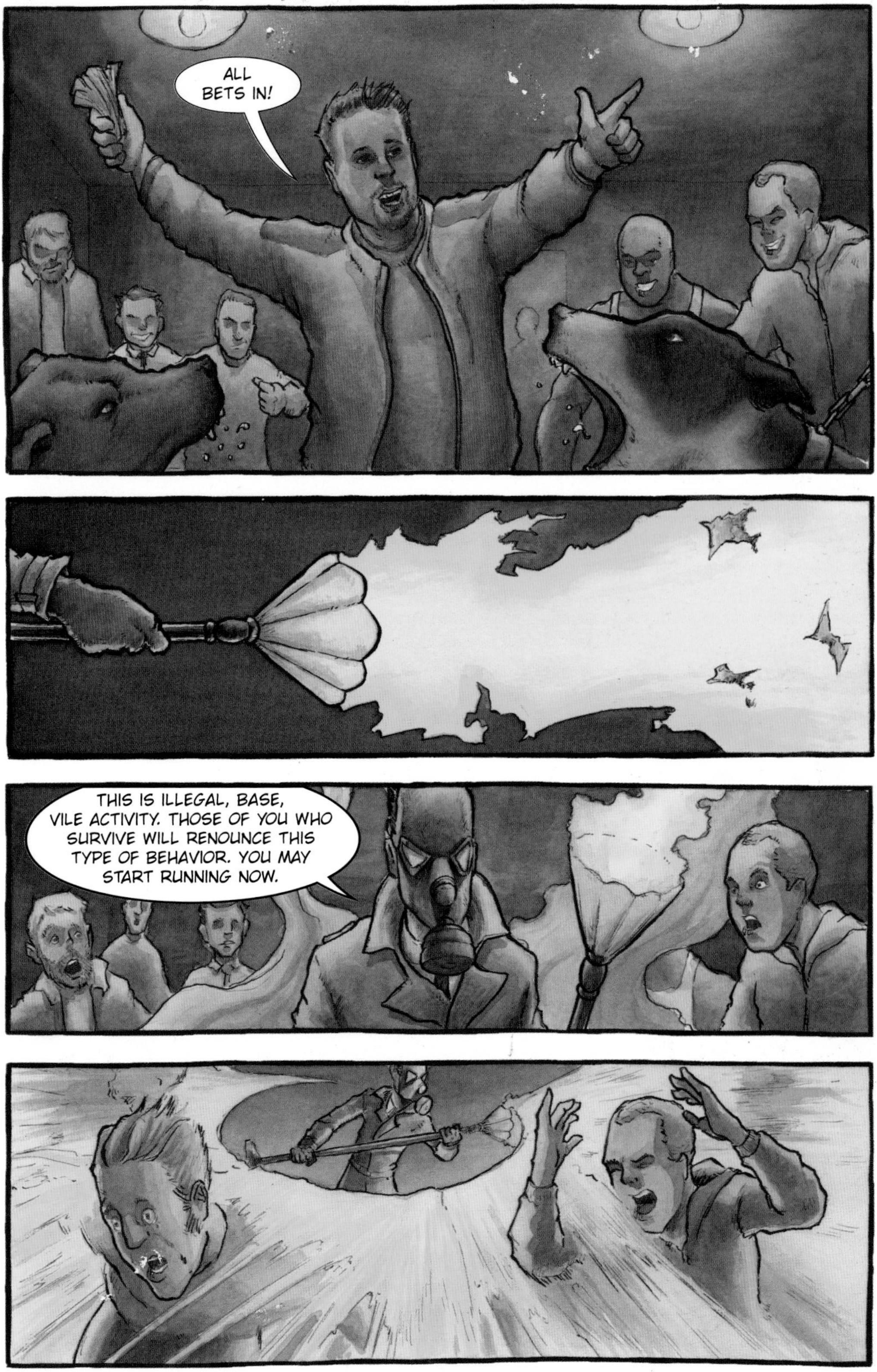
ALL BETS IN!
THIS IS ILLEGAL, BASE, VILE ACTIVITY. THOSE OF YOU WHO SURVIVE WILL RENOUNCE THIS TYPE OF BEHAVIOR. YOU MAY START RUNNING NOW.

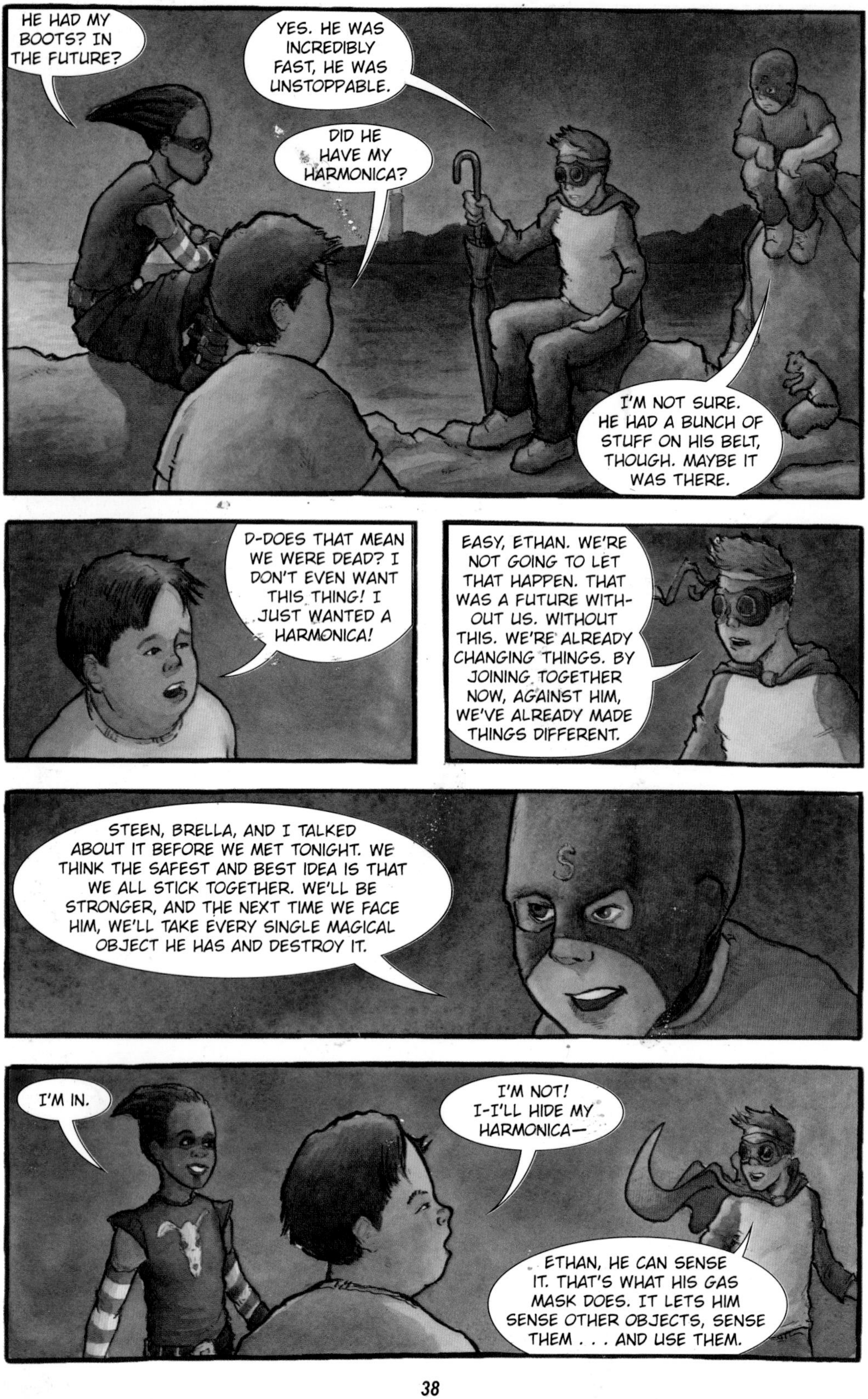
HE HAD MY BOOTS? IN THE FUTURE?
YES. HE WAS INCREDIBLY FAST, HE WAS UNSTOPPABLE.
DID HE HAVE MY HARMONICA?
I'M NOT SURE. HE HAD A BUNCH OF STUFF ON HIS BELT, THOUGH. MAYBE IT WAS THERE.
D-DOES THAT MEAN WE WERE DEAD? I DON'T EVEN WANT THIS THING! I JUST WANTED A HARMONICA!
EASY, ETHAN. WE'RE NOT GOING TO LET THAT HAPPEN. THAT WAS A FUTURE WITH-OUT US. WITHOUT THIS. WE'RE ALREADY CHANGING THINGS. BY JOINING TOGETHER NOW, AGAINST HIM, WE'VE ALREADY MADE THINGS DIFFERENT.
STEEN, BRELLA, AND I TALKED ABOUT IT BEFORE WE MET TONIGHT. WE THINK THE SAFEST AND BEST IDEA IS THAT WE ALL STICK TOGETHER. WE'LL BE STRONGER, AND THE NEXT TIME WE FACE HIM, WE'LL TAKE EVERY SINGLE MAGICAL OBJECT HE HAS AND DESTROY IT.
I'M IN.
I'M NOT! I-I'LL HIDE MY HARMONICA—
ETHAN, HE CAN SENSE IT. THAT'S WHAT HIS GAS MASK DOES. IT LETS HIM SENSE OTHER OBJECTS, SENSE THEM . . . AND USE THEM.

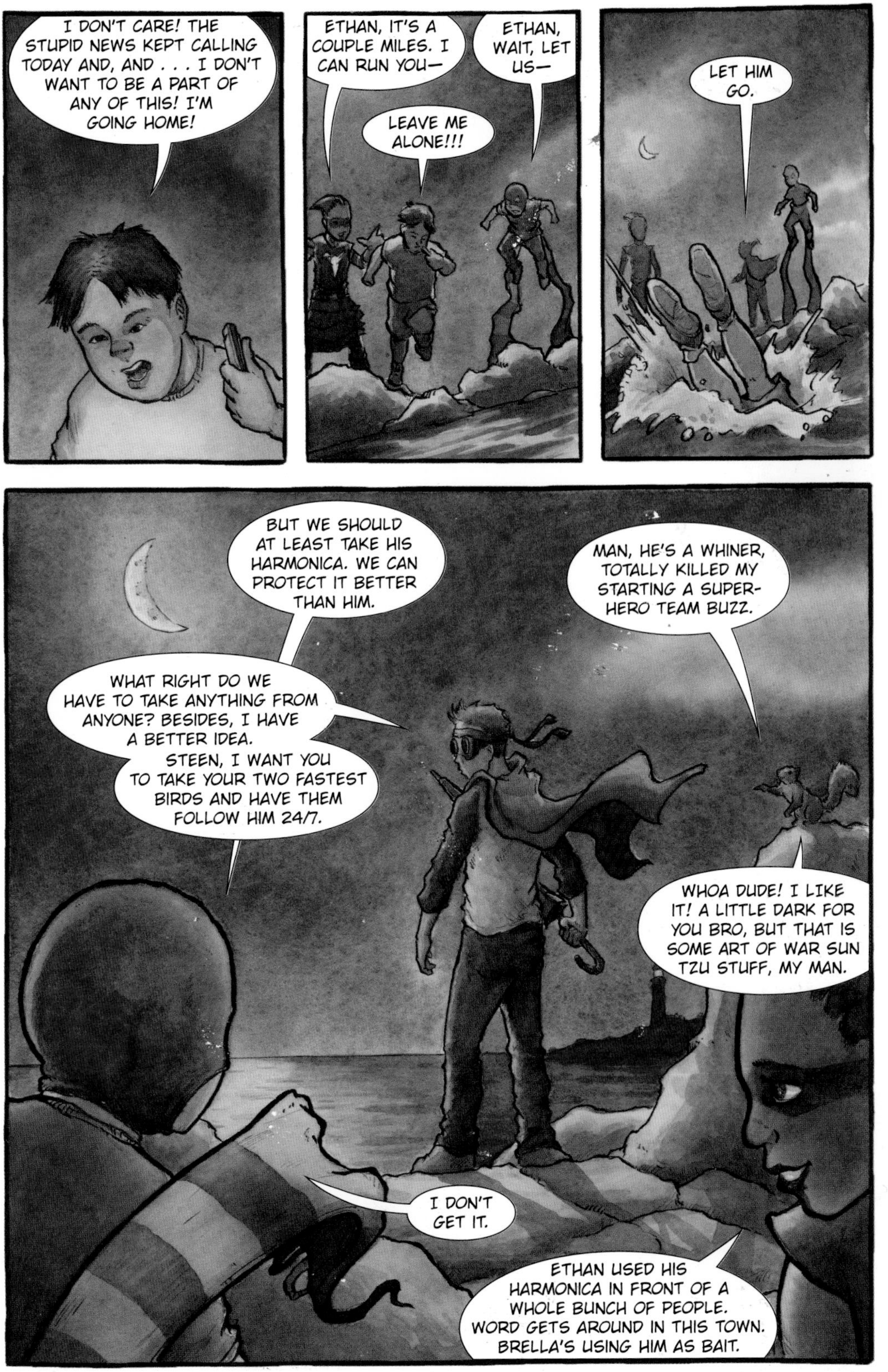
I DON'T CARE! THE STUPID NEWS KEPT CALLING TODAY AND, AND . . . I DON'T WANT TO BE A PART OF ANY OF THIS! I'M GOING HOME!
ETHAN, IT'S A COUPLE MILES. I CAN RUN YOU—
LEAVE ME ALONE!!!
ETHAN, WAIT, LET US—
LET HIM GO.
BUT WE SHOULD AT LEAST TAKE HIS HARMONICA. WE CAN PROTECT IT BETTER THAN HIM.
WHAT RIGHT DO WE HAVE TO TAKE ANYTHING FROM ANYONE? BESIDES, I HAVE A BETTER IDEA.
STEEN, I WANT YOU TO TAKE YOUR TWO FASTEST BIRDS AND HAVE THEM FOLLOW HIM 24/7.
MAN, HE'S A WHINER, TOTALLY KILLED MY STARTING A SUPER-HERO TEAM BUZZ.
WHOA DUDE! I LIKE IT! A LITTLE DARK FOR YOU BRO, BUT THAT IS SOME ART OF WAR SUN TZU STUFF, MY MAN.
I DON'T GET IT.
ETHAN USED HIS HARMONICA IN FRONT OF A WHOLE BUNCH OF PEOPLE. WORD GETS AROUND IN THIS TOWN. BRELLA'S USING HIM AS BAIT.

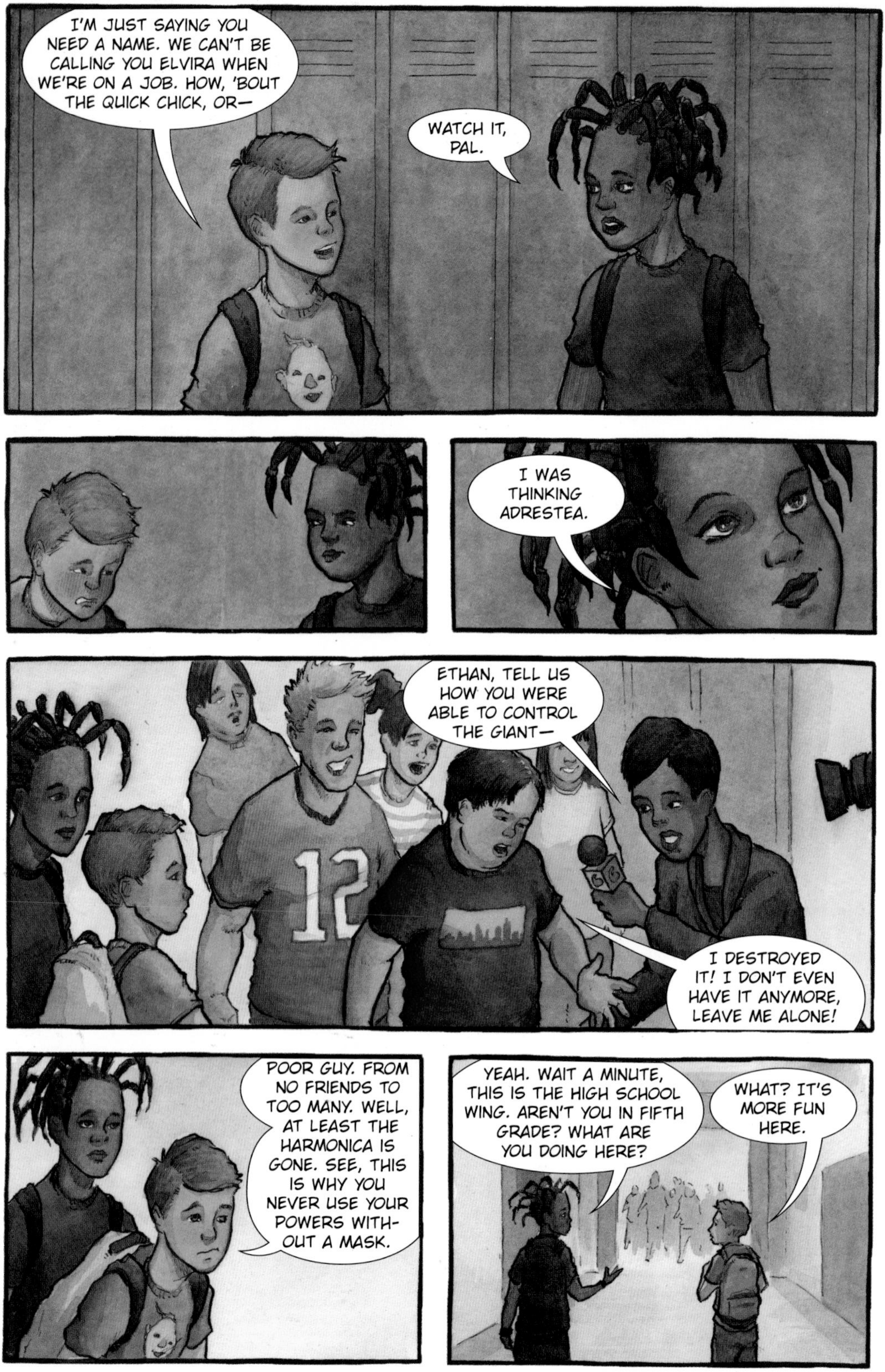
I'M JUST SAYING YOU NEED A NAME. WE CAN'T BE CALLING YOU ELVIRA WHEN WE'RE ON A JOB. HOW, 'BOUT THE QUICK CHICK, OR—
WATCH IT, PAL.
I WAS THINKING ADRESTEA.
ETHAN, TELL US HOW YOU WERE ABLE TO CONTROL THE GIANT—
I DESTROYED IT! I DON'T EVEN HAVE IT ANYMORE, LEAVE ME ALONE!
POOR GUY. FROM NO FRIENDS TO TOO MANY. WELL, AT LEAST THE HARMONICA IS GONE. SEE, THIS IS WHY YOU NEVER USE YOUR POWERS WITH-OUT A MASK.
YEAH. WAIT A MINUTE, THIS IS THE HIGH SCHOOL WING. AREN'T YOU IN FIFTH GRADE? WHAT ARE YOU DOING HERE?
WHAT? IT'S MORE FUN HERE.

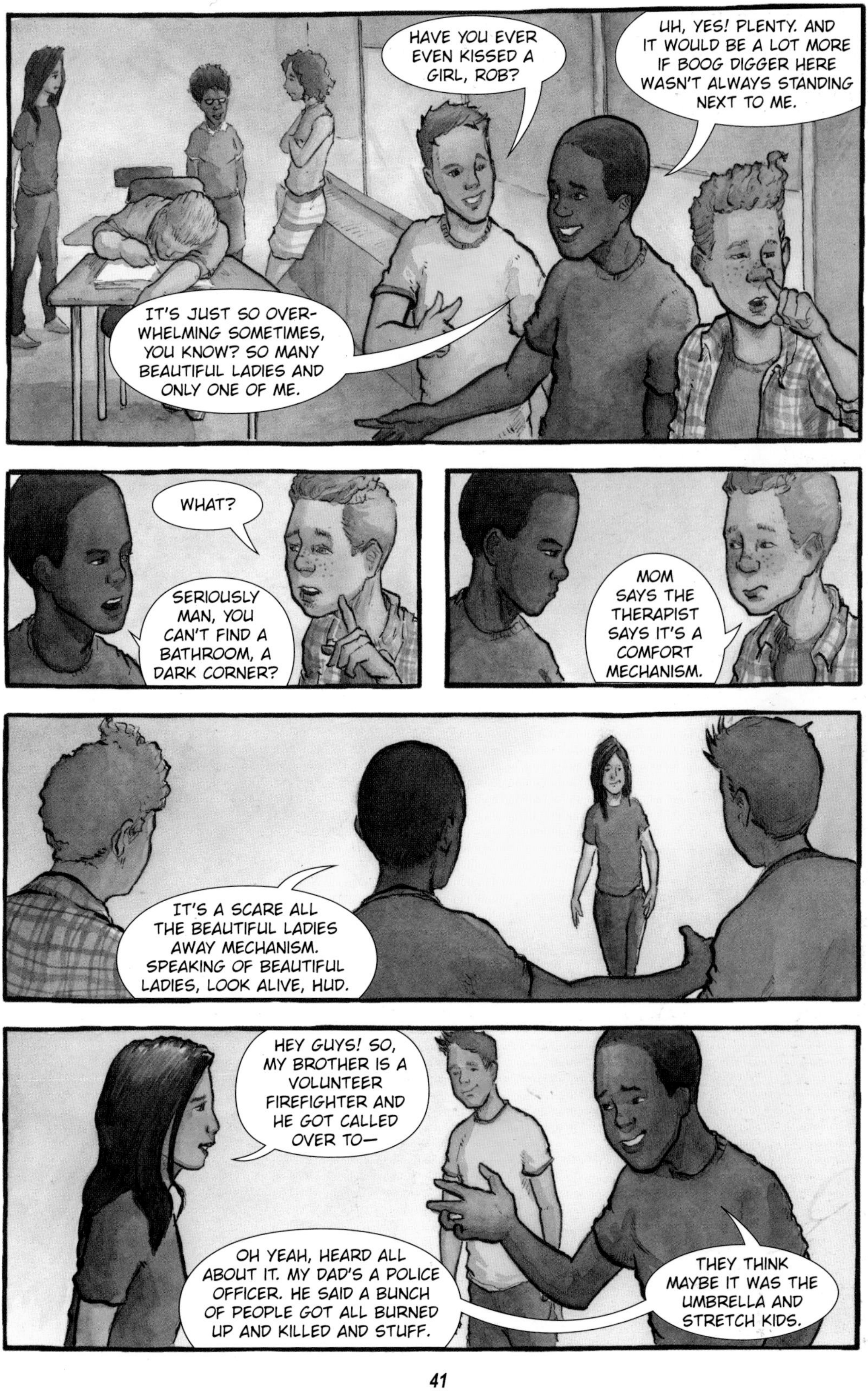
HAVE YOU EVER EVEN KISSED A GIRL, ROB?
UH, YES! PLENTY. AND IT WOULD BE A LOT MORE IF BOOG DIGGER HERE WASN'T ALWAYS STANDING NEXT TO ME.
IT'S JUST SO OVER-WHELMING SOMETIMES, YOU KNOW? SO MANY BEAUTIFUL LADIES AND ONLY ONE OF ME.
WHAT?
SERIOUSLY MAN, YOU CAN'T FIND A BATHROOM, A DARK CORNER?
MOM SAYS THE THERAPIST SAYS IT'S A COMFORT MECHANISM.
IT'S A SCARE ALL THE BEAUTIFUL LADIES AWAY MECHANISM. SPEAKING OF BEAUTIFUL LADIES, LOOK ALIVE, HUD.
HEY GUYS! SO, MY BROTHER IS A VOLUNTEER FIREFIGHTER AND HE GOT CALLED OVER TO—
OH YEAH, HEARD ALL ABOUT IT. MY DAD'S A POLICE OFFICER. HE SAID A BUNCH OF PEOPLE GOT ALL BURNED UP AND KILLED AND STUFF.
THEY THINK MAYBE IT WAS THE UMBRELLA AND STRETCH KIDS.

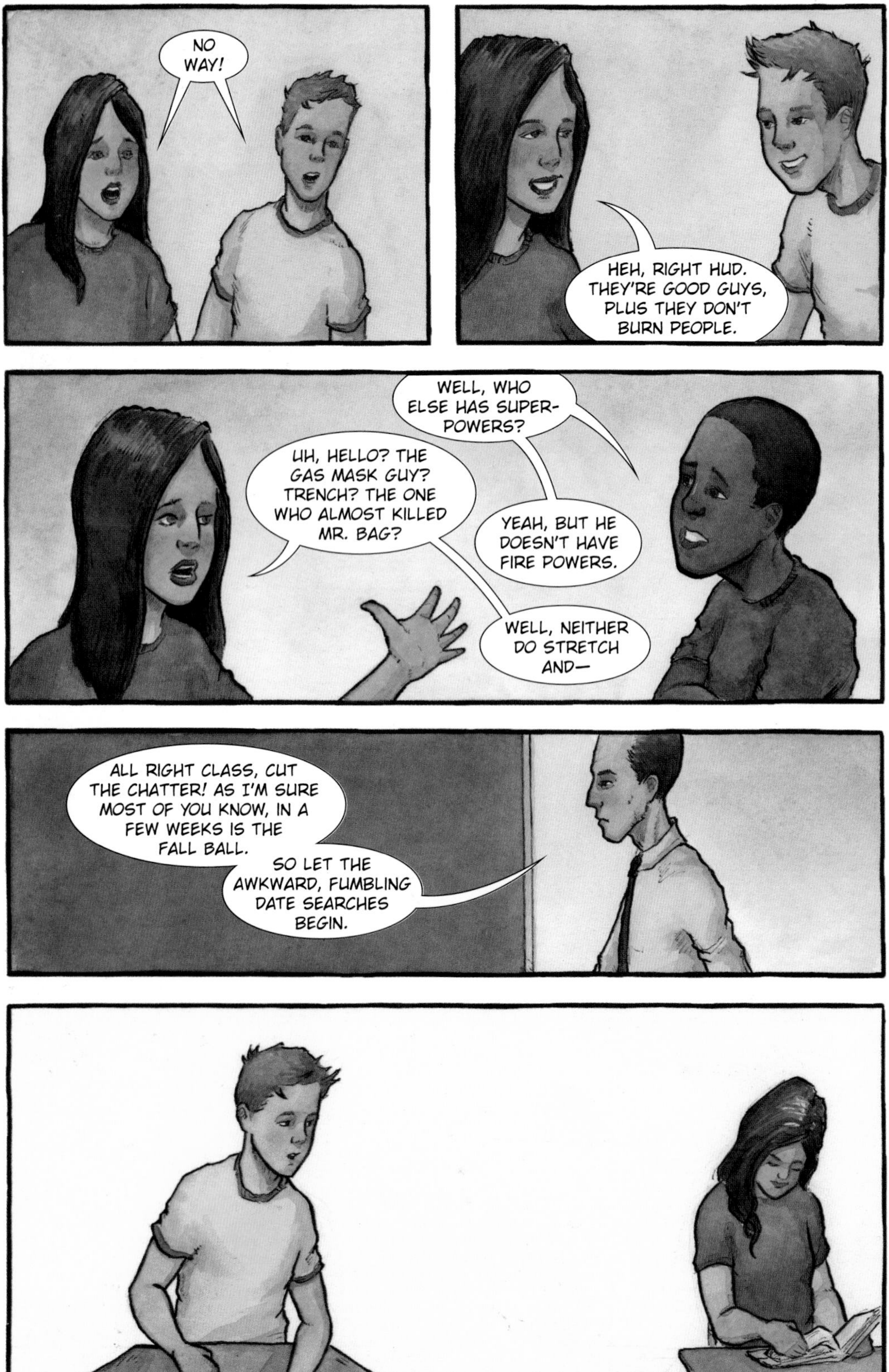
NO WAY!
HEH, RIGHT HUD. THEY'RE GOOD GUYS, PLUS THEY DON'T BURN PEOPLE.
WELL, WHO ELSE HAS SUPER-POWERS?
UH, HELLO? THE GAS MASK GUY? TRENCH? THE ONE WHO ALMOST KILLED MR. BAG?
YEAH, BUT HE DOESN'T HAVE FIRE POWERS.
WELL, NEITHER DO STRETCH AND—
ALL RIGHT CLASS, CUT THE CHATTER! AS I'M SURE MOST OF YOU KNOW, IN A FEW WEEKS IS THE FALL BALL.
SO LET THE AWKWARD, FUMBLING DATE SEARCHES BEGIN.

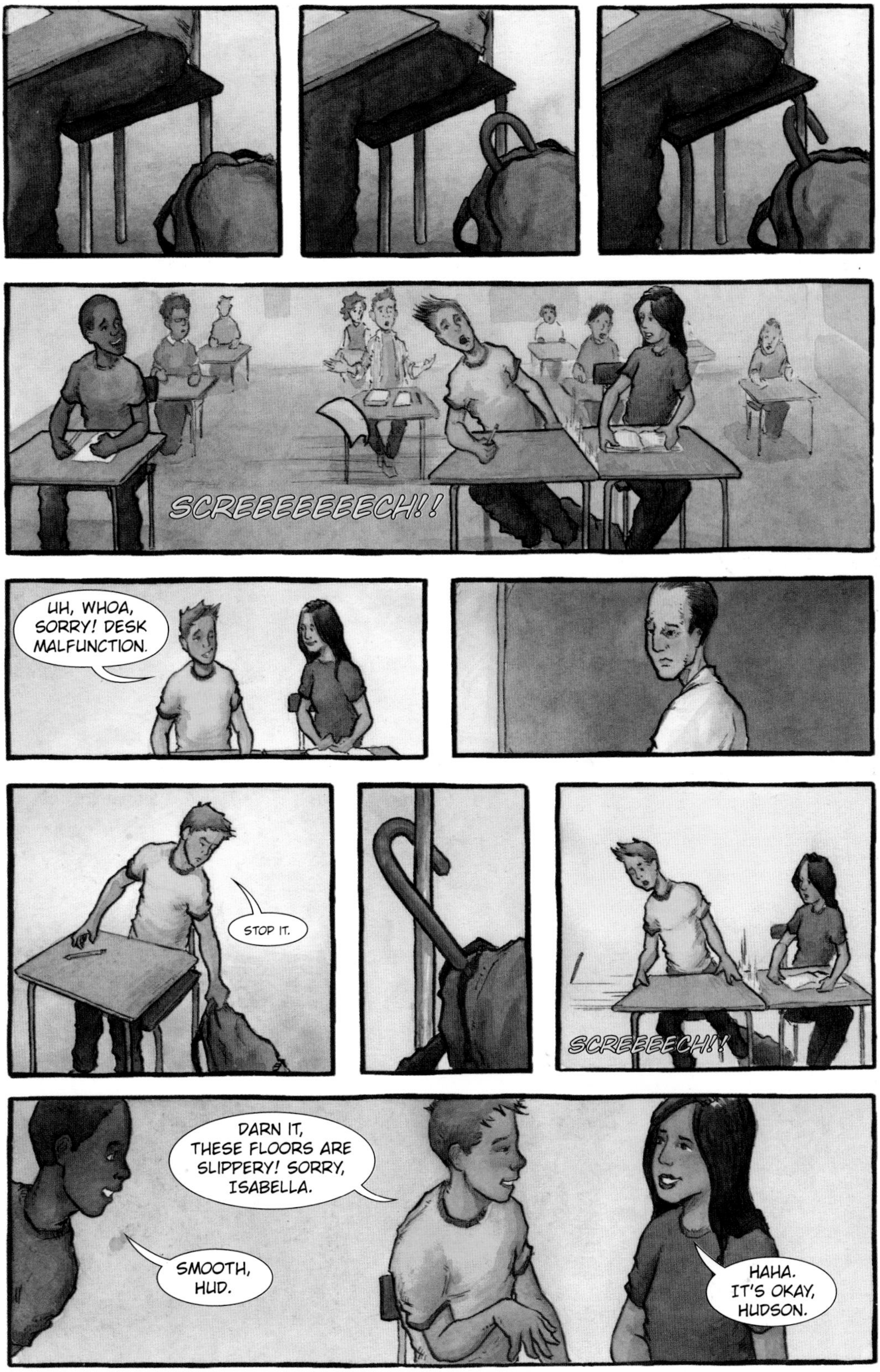
SCREEEEEEEECH!!
UH, WHOA, SORRY! DESK MALFUNCTION.
STOP IT.
SCREEEECH!!
DARN IT, THESE FLOORS ARE SLIPPERY! SORRY, ISABELLA.
SMOOTH, HUD.
HAHA. IT'S OKAY, HUDSON.

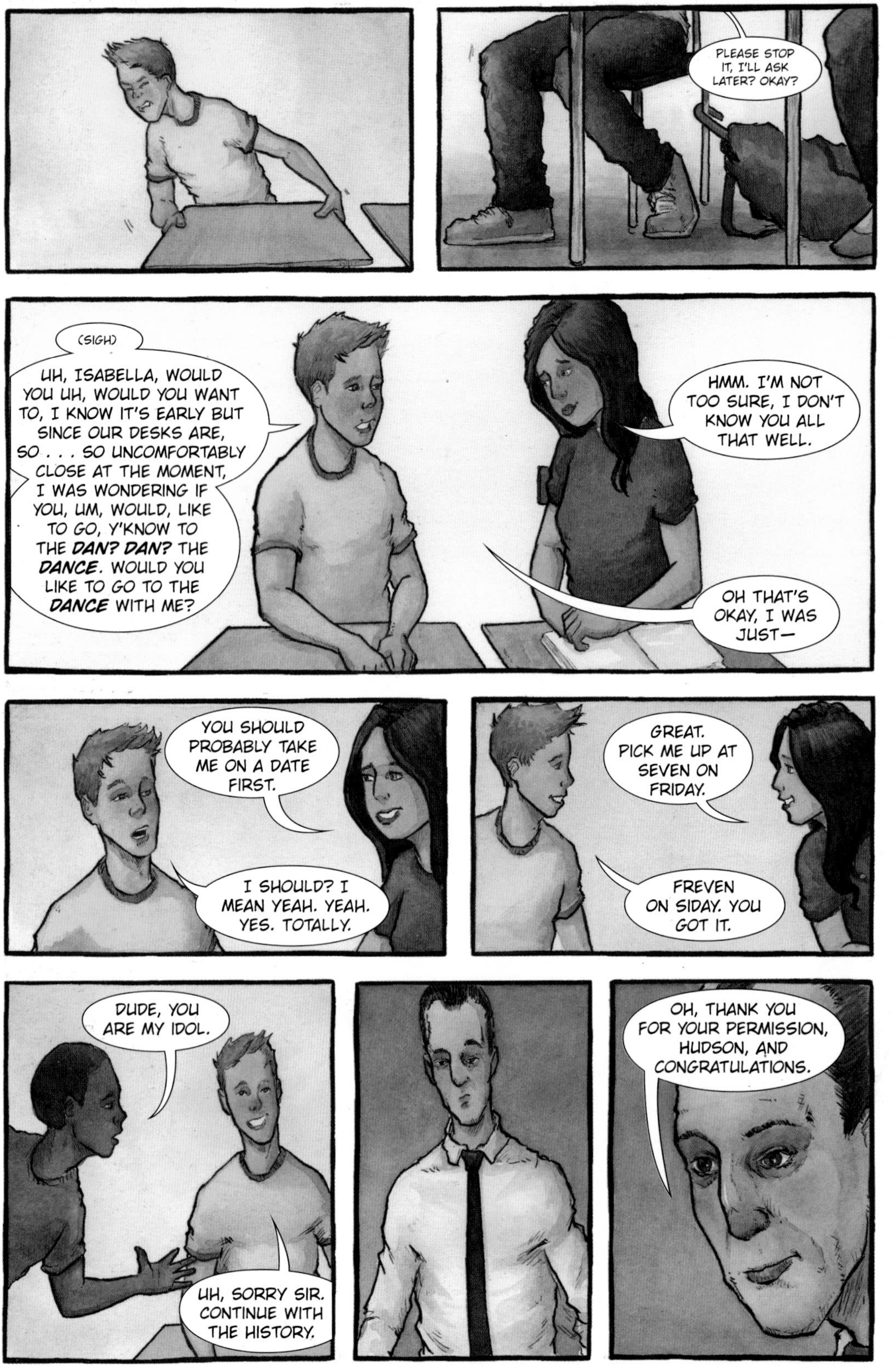
PLEASE STOP IT, I'LL ASK LATER? OKAY?
(SIGH)
UH, ISABELLA, WOULD YOU UH, WOULD YOU WANT TO, I KNOW IT'S EARLY BUT SINCE OUR DESKS ARE, SO . . . SO UNCOMFORTABLY CLOSE AT THE MOMENT, I WAS WONDERING IF YOU, UM, WOULD, LIKE TO GO, Y'KNOW TO THE ***DAN? DAN?*** THE ***DANCE***. WOULD YOU LIKE TO GO TO THE ***DANCE*** WITH ME?
HMM. I'M NOT TOO SURE, I DON'T KNOW YOU ALL THAT WELL.
OH THAT'S OKAY, I WAS JUST—
YOU SHOULD PROBABLY TAKE ME ON A DATE FIRST.
I SHOULD? I MEAN YEAH. YEAH. YES. TOTALLY.
GREAT. PICK ME UP AT SEVEN ON FRIDAY.
FREVEN ON SIDAY. YOU GOT IT.
DUDE, YOU ARE MY IDOL.
UH, SORRY SIR. CONTINUE WITH THE HISTORY.
OH, THANK YOU FOR YOUR PERMISSION, HUDSON, AND CONGRATULATIONS.

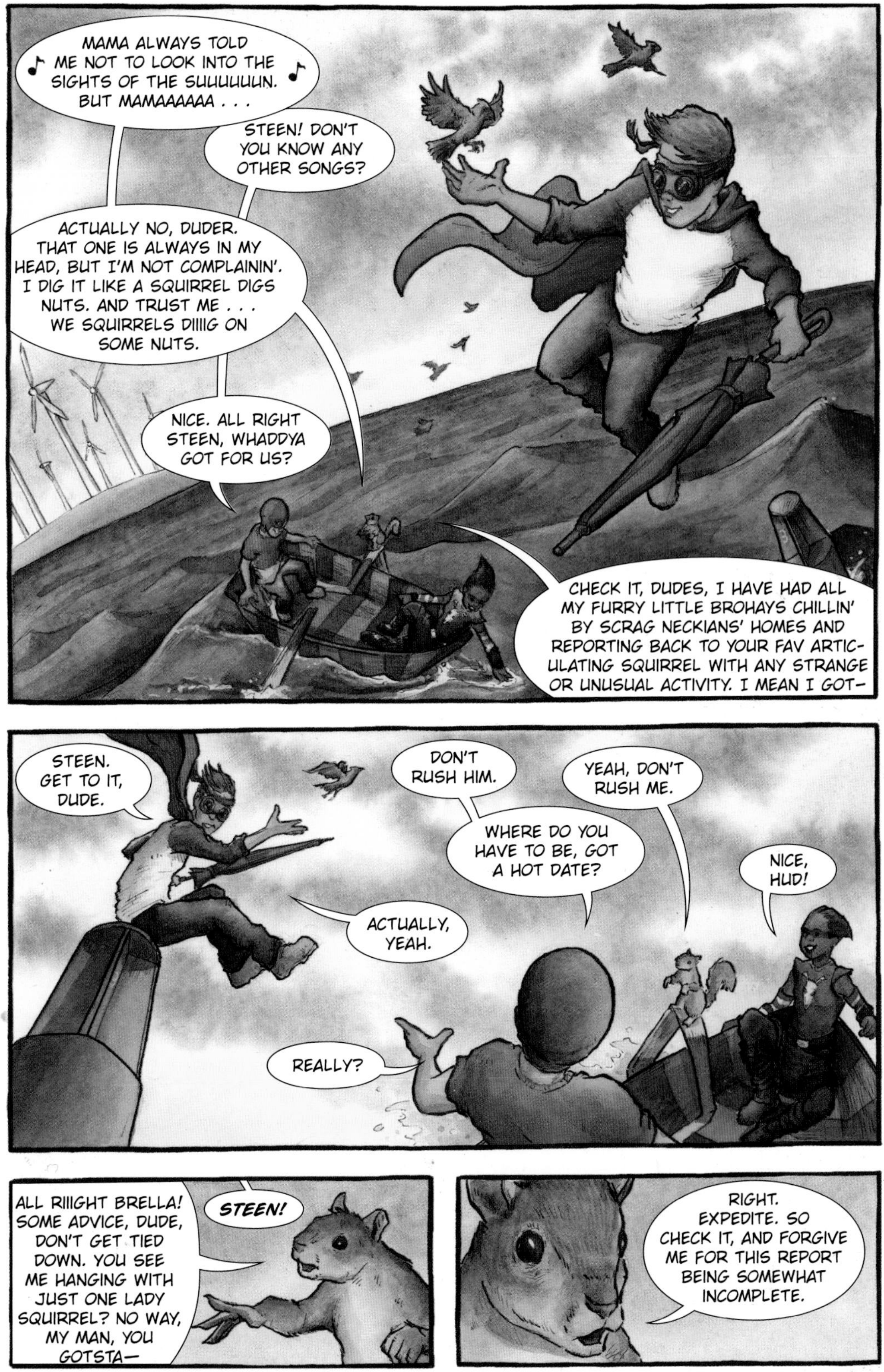
MAMA ALWAYS TOLD ME NOT TO LOOK INTO THE SIGHTS OF THE SUUUUUUN. BUT MAMAAAAAA . . .
STEEN! DON'T YOU KNOW ANY OTHER SONGS?
ACTUALLY NO, DUDER. THAT ONE IS ALWAYS IN MY HEAD, BUT I'M NOT COMPLAININ'. I DIG IT LIKE A SQUIRREL DIGS NUTS. AND TRUST ME . . . WE SQUIRRELS DIIIIG ON SOME NUTS.
NICE. ALL RIGHT STEEN, WHADDYA GOT FOR US?
CHECK IT, DUDES, I HAVE HAD ALL MY FURRY LITTLE BROHAYS CHILLIN' BY SCRAG NECKIANS' HOMES AND REPORTING BACK TO YOUR FAV ARTICULATING SQUIRREL WITH ANY STRANGE OR UNUSUAL ACTIVITY. I MEAN I GOT—
STEEN. GET TO IT, DUDE.
DON'T RUSH HIM.
YEAH, DON'T RUSH ME.
WHERE DO YOU HAVE TO BE, GOT A HOT DATE?
NICE, HUD!
ACTUALLY, YEAH.
REALLY?
ALL RIIIGHT BRELLA! SOME ADVICE, DUDE, DON'T GET TIED DOWN. YOU SEE ME HANGING WITH JUST ONE LADY SQUIRREL? NO WAY, MY MAN, YOU GOTSTA—
STEEN!
RIGHT. EXPEDITE. SO CHECK IT, AND FORGIVE ME FOR THIS REPORT BEING SOMEWHAT INCOMPLETE.

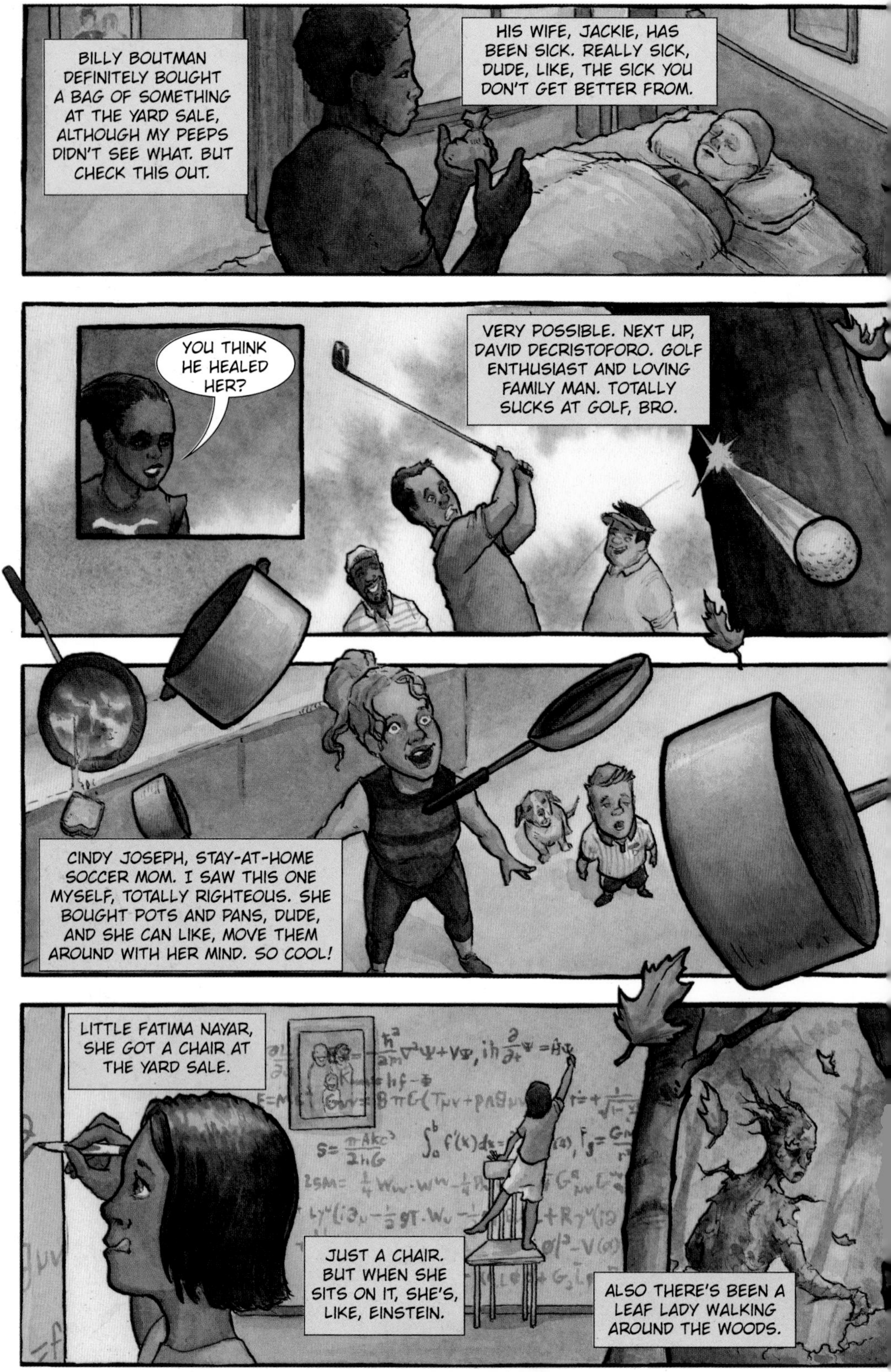
BILLY BOUTMAN DEFINITELY BOUGHT A BAG OF SOMETHING AT THE YARD SALE, ALTHOUGH MY PEEPS DIDN'T SEE WHAT. BUT CHECK THIS OUT.
HIS WIFE, JACKIE, HAS BEEN SICK. REALLY SICK, DUDE, LIKE, THE SICK YOU DON'T GET BETTER FROM.
YOU THINK HE HEALED HER?
VERY POSSIBLE. NEXT UP, DAVID DECRISTOFORO. GOLF ENTHUSIAST AND LOVING FAMILY MAN. TOTALLY SUCKS AT GOLF, BRO.
CINDY JOSEPH, STAY-AT-HOME SOCCER MOM. I SAW THIS ONE MYSELF, TOTALLY RIGHTEOUS. SHE BOUGHT POTS AND PANS, DUDE, AND SHE CAN LIKE, MOVE THEM AROUND WITH HER MIND. SO COOL!
LITTLE FATIMA NAYAR, SHE GOT A CHAIR AT THE YARD SALE.
JUST A CHAIR. BUT WHEN SHE SITS ON IT, SHE'S, LIKE, EINSTEIN.
ALSO THERE'S BEEN A LEAF LADY WALKING AROUND THE WOODS.

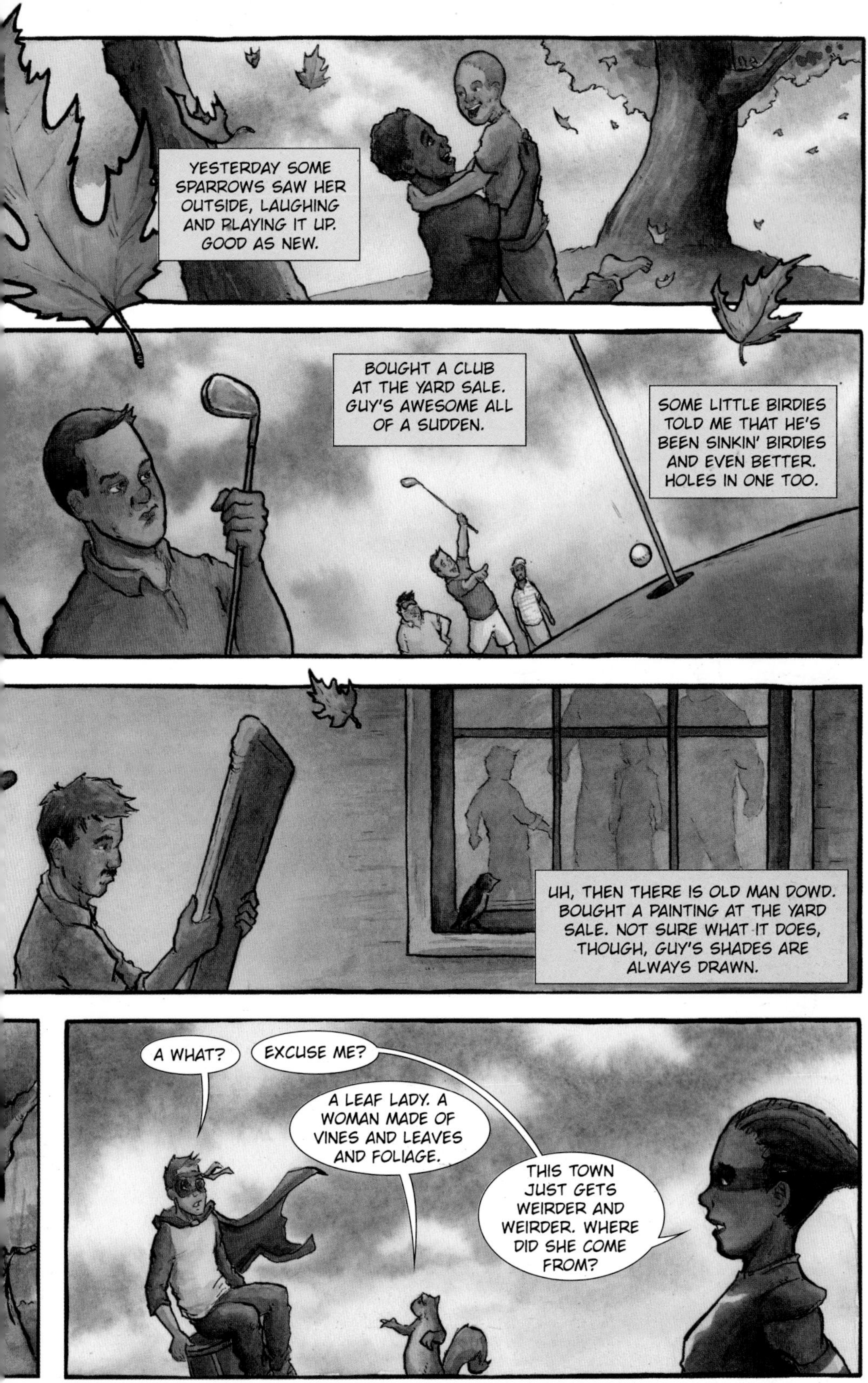
YESTERDAY SOME SPARROWS SAW HER OUTSIDE, LAUGHING AND PLAYING IT UP. GOOD AS NEW.
BOUGHT A CLUB AT THE YARD SALE. GUY'S AWESOME ALL OF A SUDDEN.
SOME LITTLE BIRDIES TOLD ME THAT HE'S BEEN SINKIN' BIRDIES AND EVEN BETTER. HOLES IN ONE TOO.
UH, THEN THERE IS OLD MAN DOWD. BOUGHT A PAINTING AT THE YARD SALE. NOT SURE WHAT IT DOES, THOUGH, GUY'S SHADES ARE ALWAYS DRAWN.
A WHAT?
EXCUSE ME?
A LEAF LADY. A WOMAN MADE OF VINES AND LEAVES AND FOLIAGE.
THIS TOWN JUST GETS WEIRDER AND WEIRDER. WHERE DID SHE COME FROM?

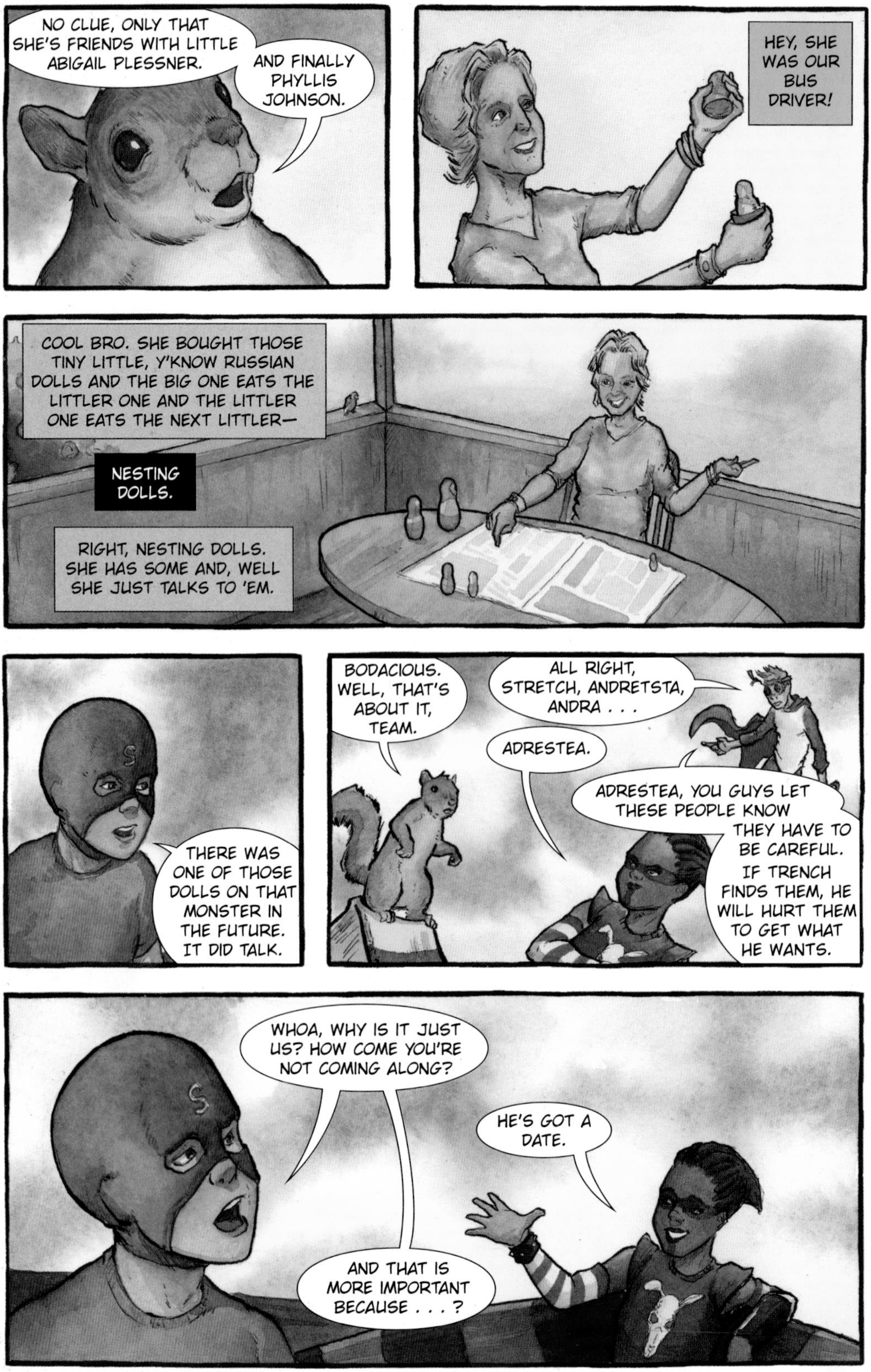
NO CLUE, ONLY THAT SHE'S FRIENDS WITH LITTLE ABIGAIL PLESSNER.
AND FINALLY PHYLLIS JOHNSON.
HEY, SHE WAS OUR BUS DRIVER!
COOL BRO. SHE BOUGHT THOSE TINY LITTLE, Y'KNOW RUSSIAN DOLLS AND THE BIG ONE EATS THE LITTLER ONE AND THE LITTLER ONE EATS THE NEXT LITTLER—
NESTING DOLLS.
RIGHT, NESTING DOLLS. SHE HAS SOME AND, WELL SHE JUST TALKS TO 'EM.
THERE WAS ONE OF THOSE DOLLS ON THAT MONSTER IN THE FUTURE. IT DID TALK.
BODACIOUS. WELL, THAT'S ABOUT IT, TEAM.
ALL RIGHT, STRETCH, ANDRETSTA, ANDRA . . .
ADRESTEA.
ADRESTEA, YOU GUYS LET THESE PEOPLE KNOW THEY HAVE TO BE CAREFUL.
IF TRENCH FINDS THEM, HE WILL HURT THEM TO GET WHAT HE WANTS.
WHOA, WHY IS IT JUST US? HOW COME YOU'RE NOT COMING ALONG?
HE'S GOT A DATE.
AND THAT IS MORE IMPORTANT BECAUSE . . . ?

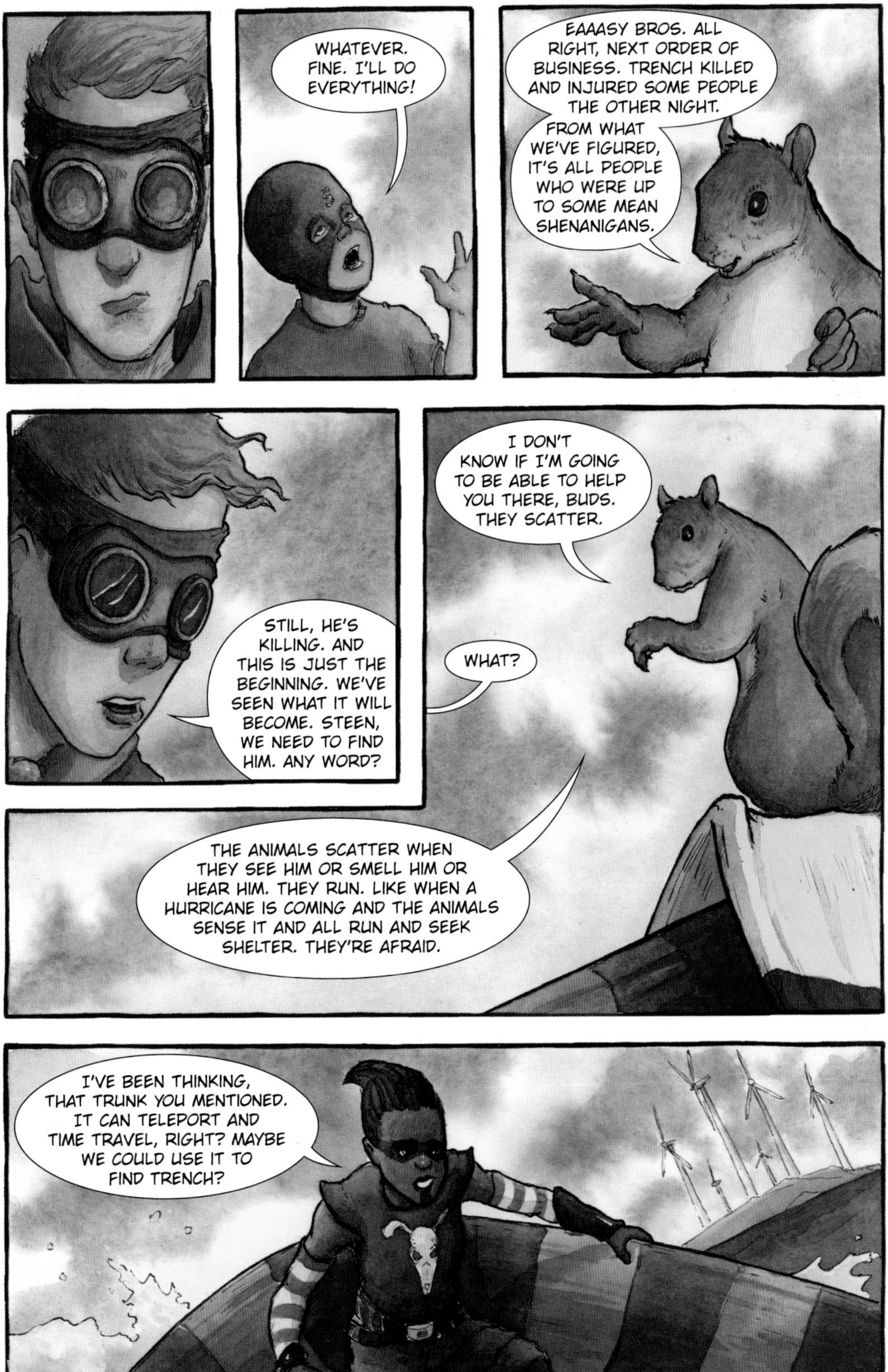
WHATEVER. FINE. I'LL DO EVERYTHING!
EAAASY BROS. ALL RIGHT, NEXT ORDER OF BUSINESS. TRENCH KILLED AND INJURED SOME PEOPLE THE OTHER NIGHT.
FROM WHAT WE'VE FIGURED, IT'S ALL PEOPLE WHO WERE UP TO SOME MEAN SHENANIGANS.
STILL, HE'S KILLING. AND THIS IS JUST THE BEGINNING. WE'VE SEEN WHAT IT WILL BECOME. STEEN, WE NEED TO FIND HIM. ANY WORD?
I DON'T KNOW IF I'M GOING TO BE ABLE TO HELP YOU THERE, BUDS. THEY SCATTER.
WHAT?
THE ANIMALS SCATTER WHEN THEY SEE HIM OR SMELL HIM OR HEAR HIM. THEY RUN. LIKE WHEN A HURRICANE IS COMING AND THE ANIMALS SENSE IT AND ALL RUN AND SEEK SHELTER. THEY'RE AFRAID.
I'VE BEEN THINKING, THAT TRUNK YOU MENTIONED. IT CAN TELEPORT AND TIME TRAVEL, RIGHT? MAYBE WE COULD USE IT TO FIND TRENCH?

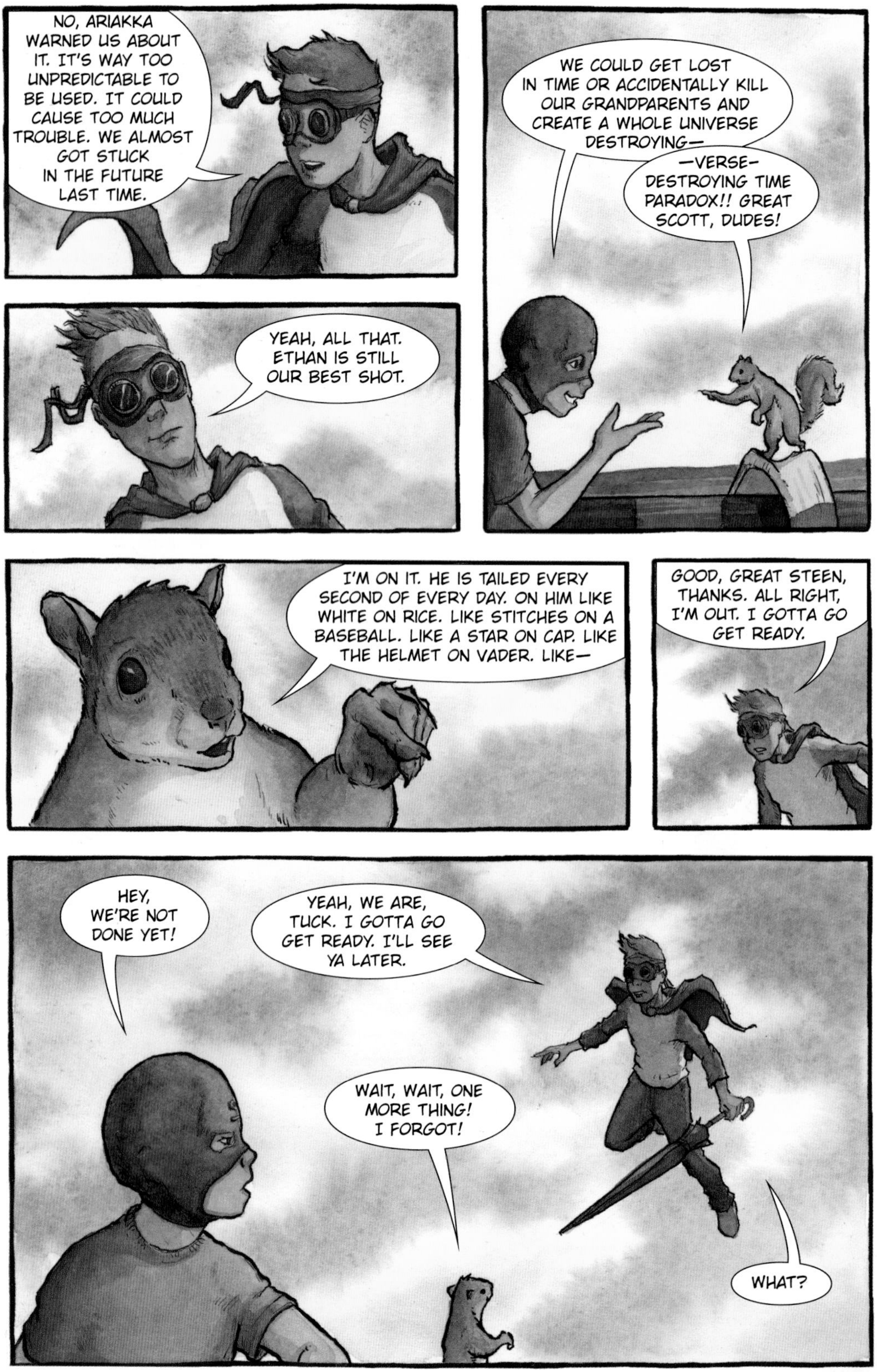
NO, ARIAKKA WARNED US ABOUT IT. IT'S WAY TOO UNPREDICTABLE TO BE USED. IT COULD CAUSE TOO MUCH TROUBLE. WE ALMOST GOT STUCK IN THE FUTURE LAST TIME.
WE COULD GET LOST IN TIME OR ACCIDENTALLY KILL OUR GRANDPARENTS AND CREATE A WHOLE UNIVERSE DESTROYING—
—VERSE-DESTROYING TIME PARADOX!! GREAT SCOTT, DUDES!
YEAH, ALL THAT. ETHAN IS STILL OUR BEST SHOT.
I'M ON IT. HE IS TAILED EVERY SECOND OF EVERY DAY. ON HIM LIKE WHITE ON RICE. LIKE STITCHES ON A BASEBALL. LIKE A STAR ON CAP. LIKE THE HELMET ON VADER. LIKE—
GOOD, GREAT STEEN, THANKS. ALL RIGHT, I'M OUT. I GOTTA GO GET READY.
HEY, WE'RE NOT DONE YET!
YEAH, WE ARE, TUCK. I GOTTA GO GET READY. I'LL SEE YA LATER.
WAIT, WAIT, ONE MORE THING! I FORGOT!
WHAT?

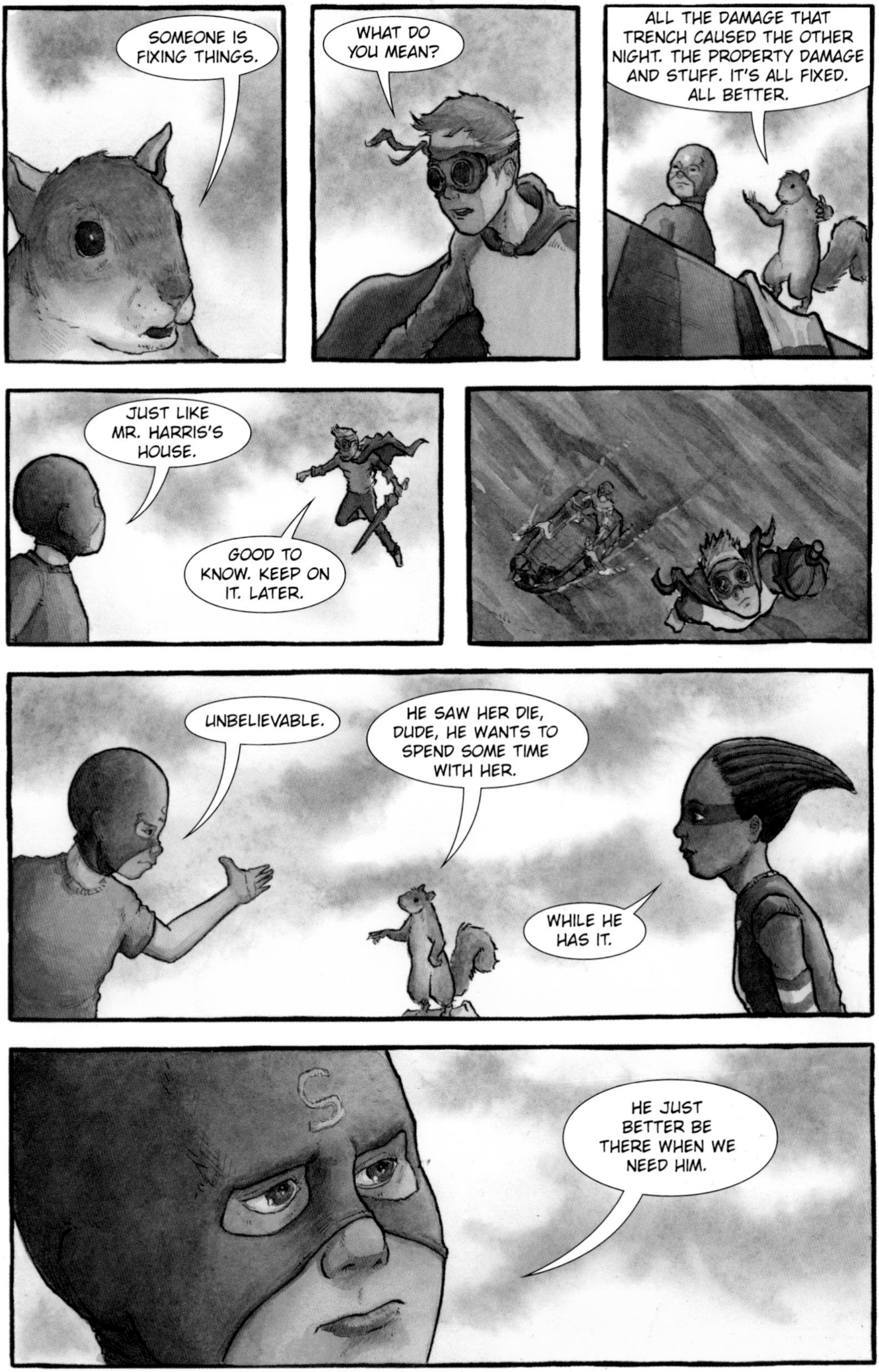
SOMEONE IS FIXING THINGS.
WHAT DO YOU MEAN?
ALL THE DAMAGE THAT TRENCH CAUSED THE OTHER NIGHT. THE PROPERTY DAMAGE AND STUFF. IT'S ALL FIXED. ALL BETTER.
JUST LIKE MR. HARRIS'S HOUSE.
GOOD TO KNOW. KEEP ON IT. LATER.
UNBELIEVABLE.
HE SAW HER DIE, DUDE, HE WANTS TO SPEND SOME TIME WITH HER.
WHILE HE HAS IT.
HE JUST BETTER BE THERE WHEN WE NEED HIM.

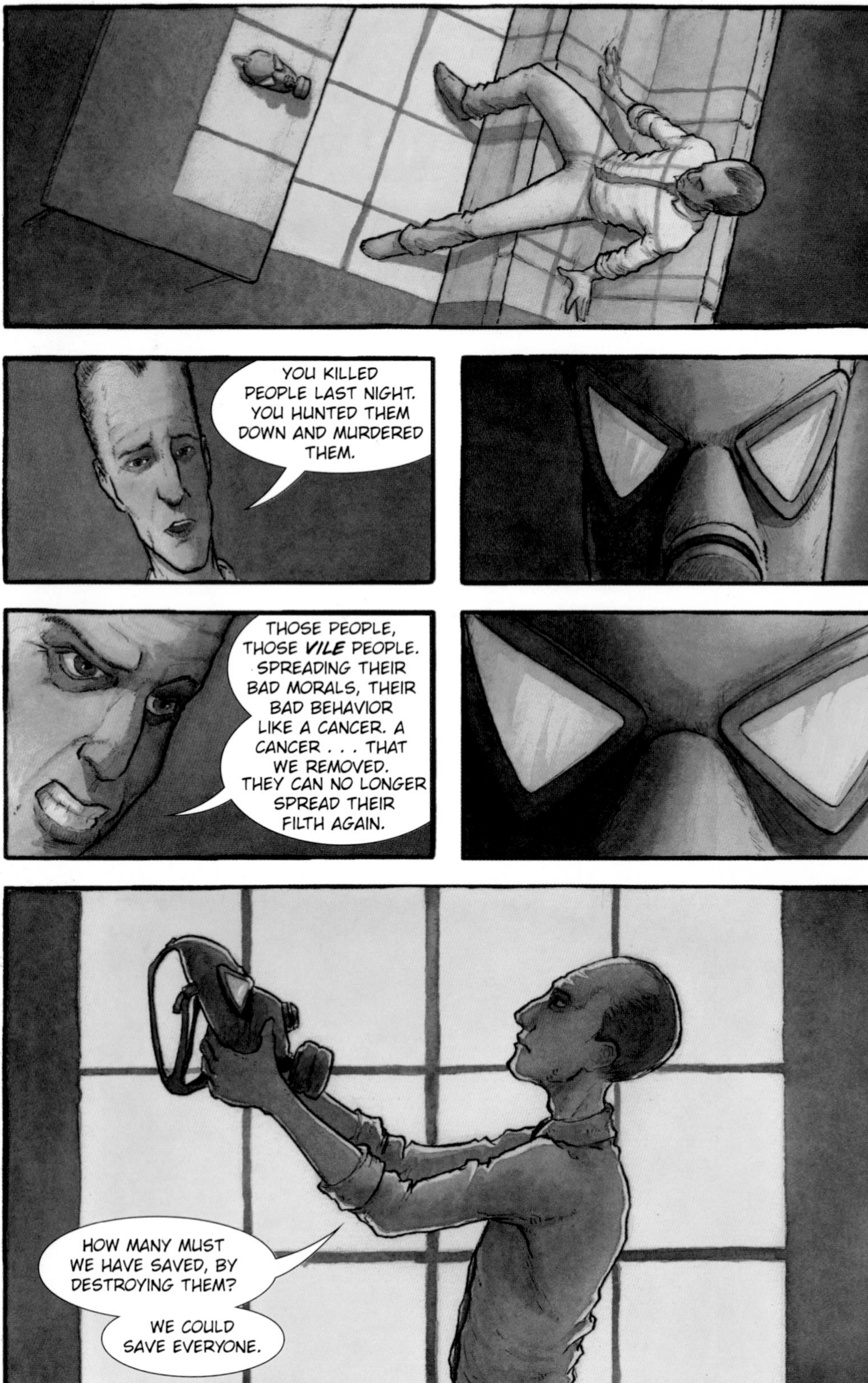
YOU KILLED PEOPLE LAST NIGHT. YOU HUNTED THEM DOWN AND MURDERED THEM.
THOSE PEOPLE, THOSE *VILE* PEOPLE. SPREADING THEIR BAD MORALS, THEIR BAD BEHAVIOR LIKE A CANCER. A CANCER . . . THAT WE REMOVED. THEY CAN NO LONGER SPREAD THEIR FILTH AGAIN.
HOW MANY MUST WE HAVE SAVED, BY DESTROYING THEM?
WE COULD SAVE EVERYONE.

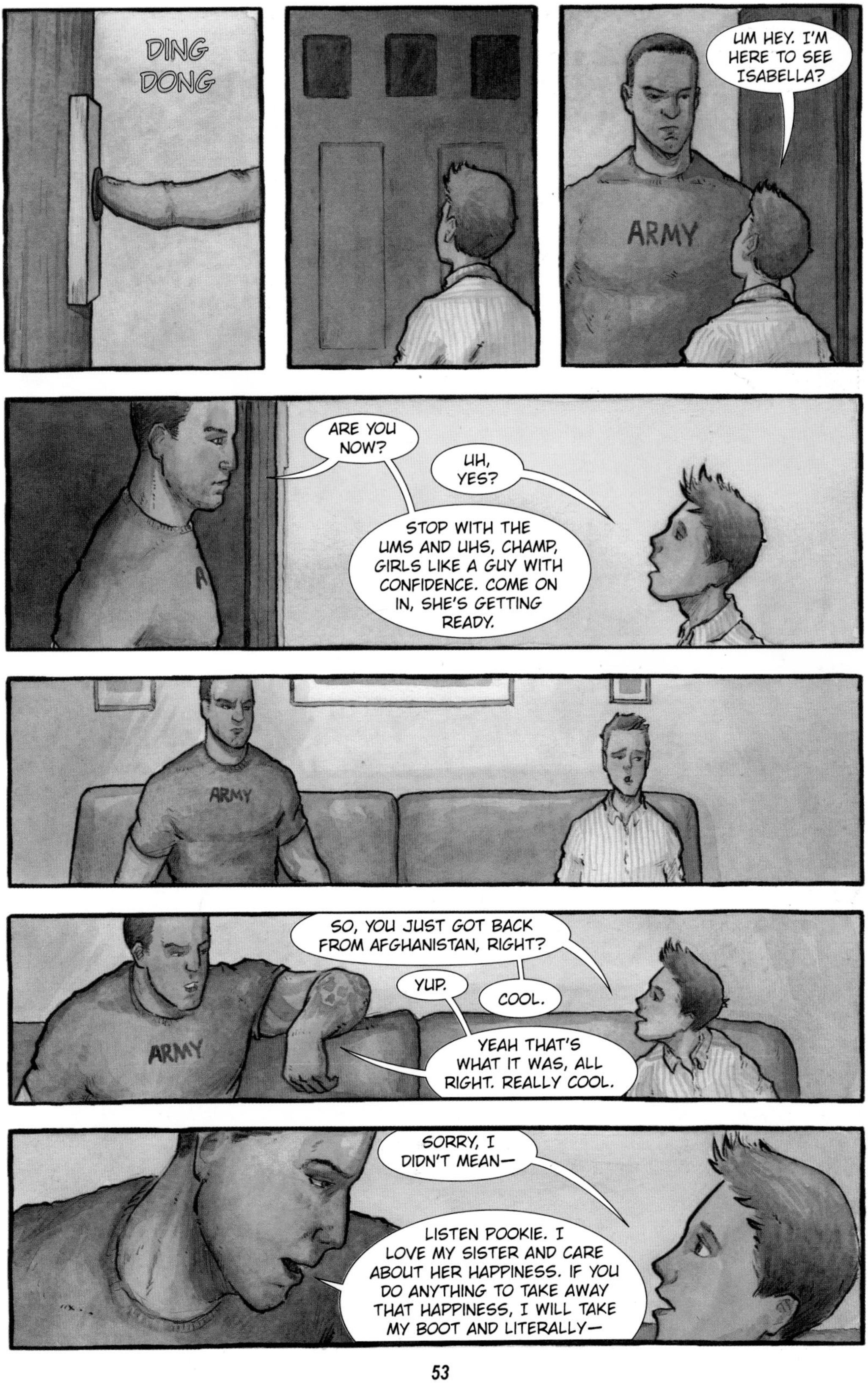
DING
DONG
UM HEY. I'M HERE TO SEE ISABELLA?
ARMY
ARE YOU NOW?
UH, YES?
STOP WITH THE UMS AND UHS, CHAMP, GIRLS LIKE A GUY WITH CONFIDENCE. COME ON IN, SHE'S GETTING READY.
ARMY
SO, YOU JUST GOT BACK FROM AFGHANISTAN, RIGHT?
YUP.
COOL.
YEAH THAT'S WHAT IT WAS, ALL RIGHT. REALLY COOL.
ARMY
SORRY, I DIDN'T MEAN—
LISTEN POOKIE. I LOVE MY SISTER AND CARE ABOUT HER HAPPINESS. IF YOU DO ANYTHING TO TAKE AWAY THAT HAPPINESS, I WILL TAKE MY BOOT AND LITERALLY—

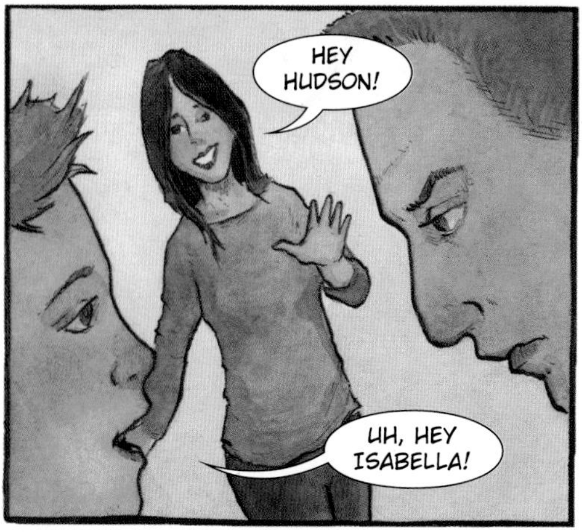
HEY HUDSON!
UH, HEY ISABELLA!

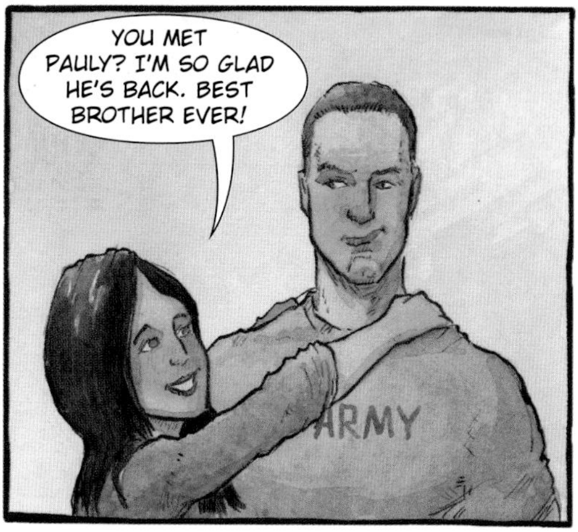
YOU MET PAULY? I'M SO GLAD HE'S BACK. BEST BROTHER EVER!
ARMY

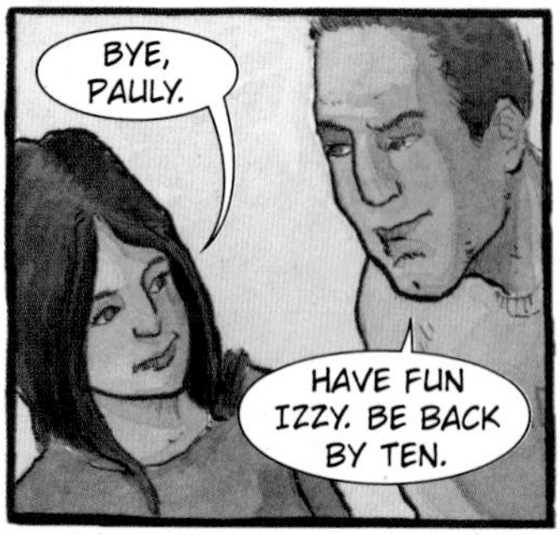
BYE, PAULY.
HAVE FUN IZZY. BE BACK BY TEN.

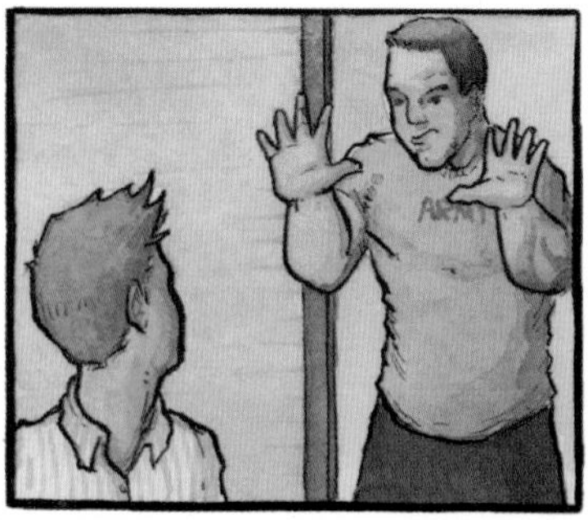

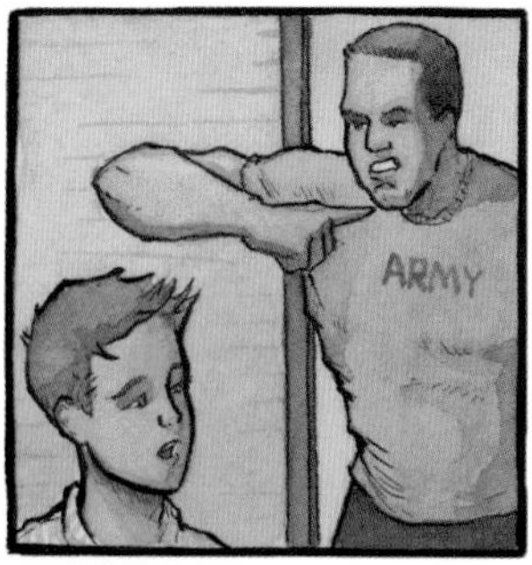
ARMY

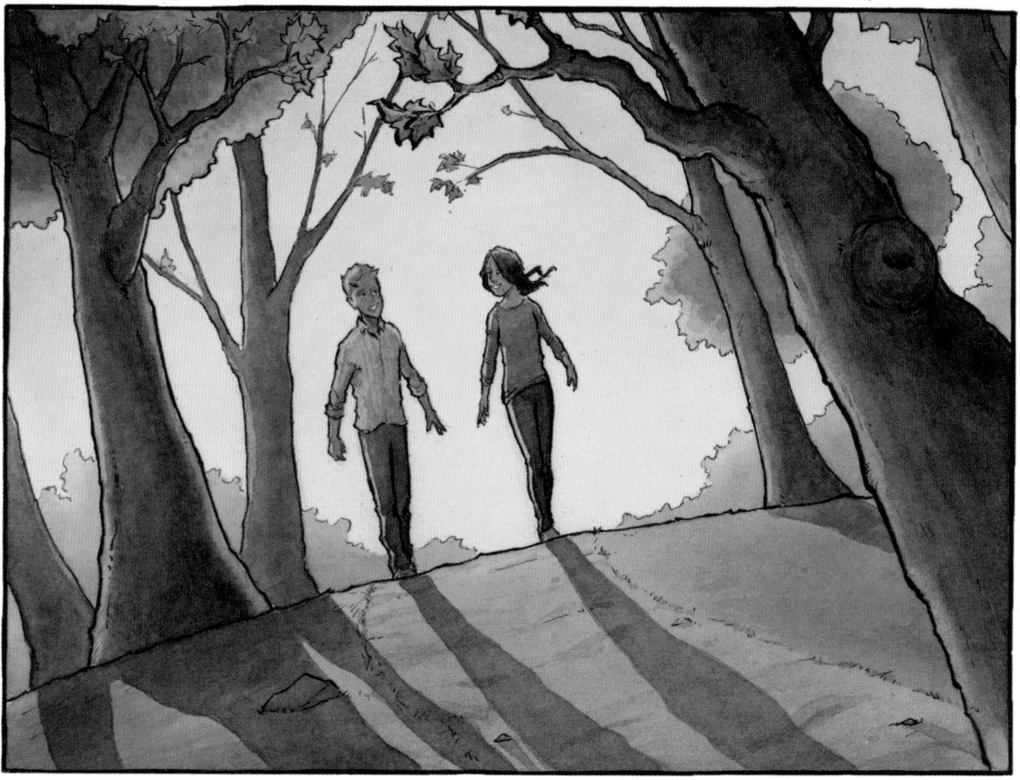

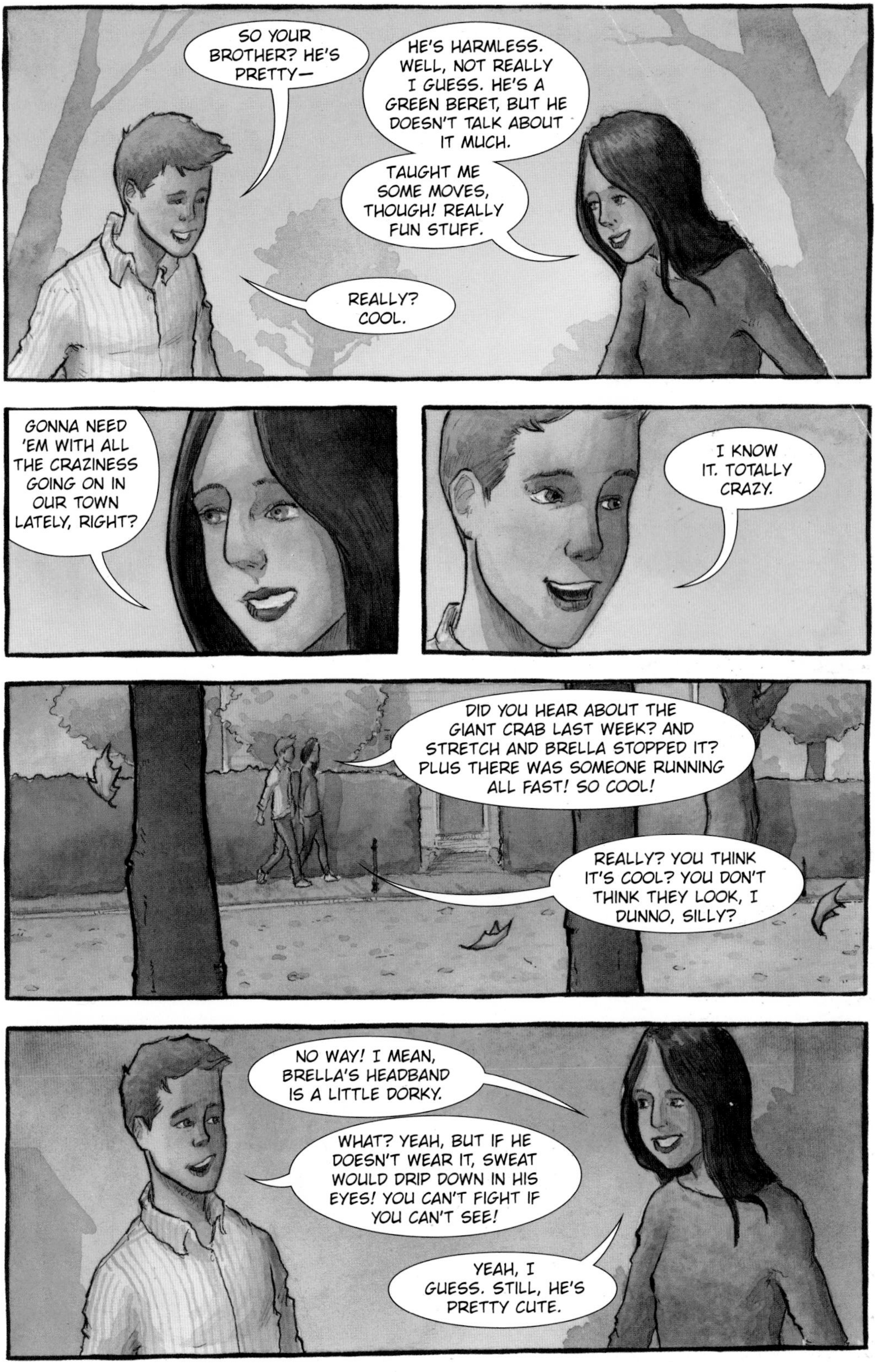
SO YOUR BROTHER? HE'S PRETTY—
HE'S HARMLESS. WELL, NOT REALLY I GUESS. HE'S A GREEN BERET, BUT HE DOESN'T TALK ABOUT IT MUCH.
TAUGHT ME SOME MOVES, THOUGH! REALLY FUN STUFF.
REALLY? COOL.
GONNA NEED 'EM WITH ALL THE CRAZINESS GOING ON IN OUR TOWN LATELY, RIGHT?
I KNOW IT. TOTALLY CRAZY.
DID YOU HEAR ABOUT THE GIANT CRAB LAST WEEK? AND STRETCH AND BRELLA STOPPED IT? PLUS THERE WAS SOMEONE RUNNING ALL FAST! SO COOL!
REALLY? YOU THINK IT'S COOL? YOU DON'T THINK THEY LOOK, I DUNNO, SILLY?
NO WAY! I MEAN, BRELLA'S HEADBAND IS A LITTLE DORKY.
WHAT? YEAH, BUT IF HE DOESN'T WEAR IT, SWEAT WOULD DRIP DOWN IN HIS EYES! YOU CAN'T FIGHT IF YOU CAN'T SEE!
YEAH, I GUESS. STILL, HE'S PRETTY CUTE.

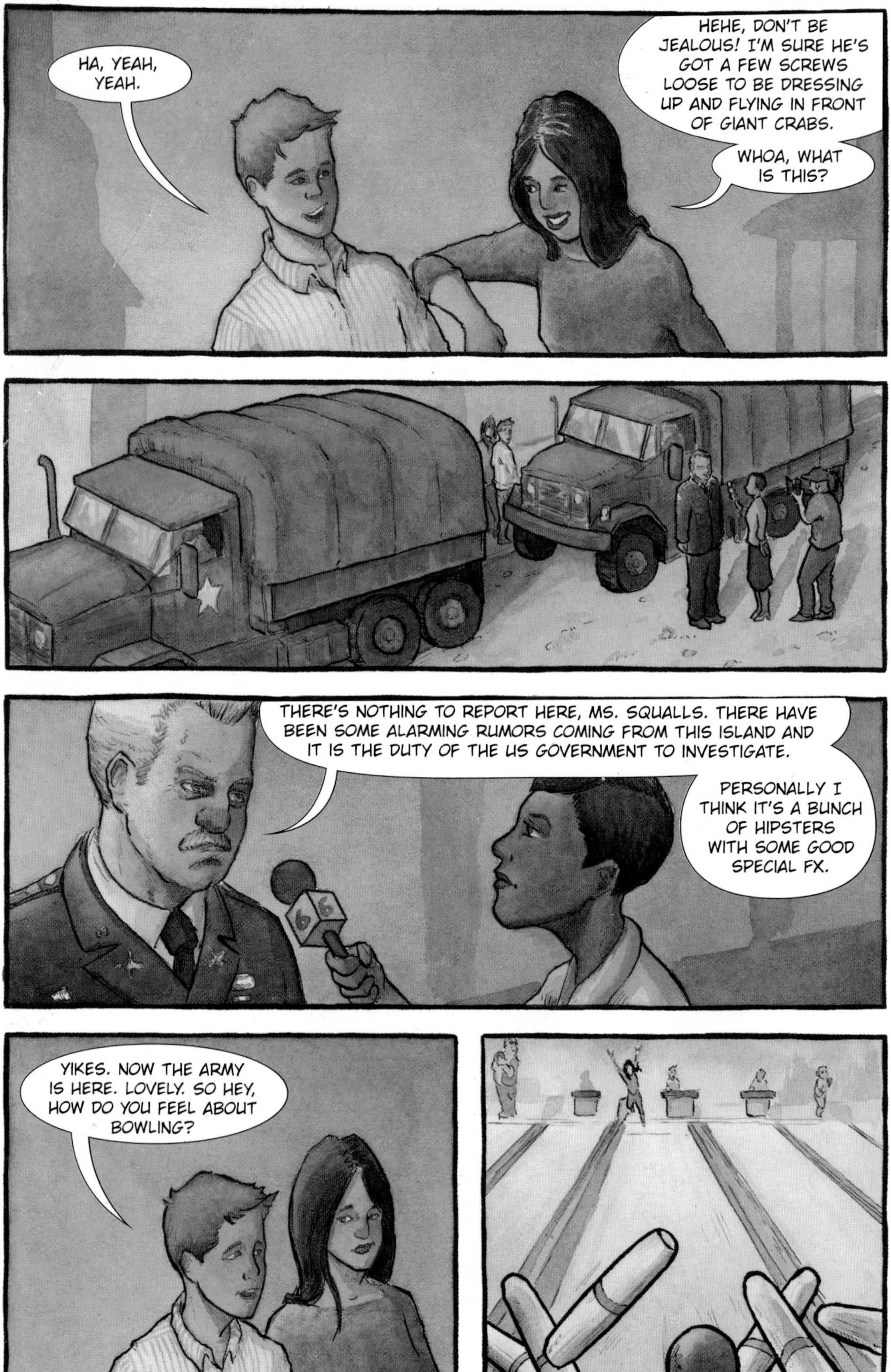
HA, YEAH, YEAH.
HEHE, DON'T BE JEALOUS! I'M SURE HE'S GOT A FEW SCREWS LOOSE TO BE DRESSING UP AND FLYING IN FRONT OF GIANT CRABS.
WHOA, WHAT IS THIS?
THERE'S NOTHING TO REPORT HERE, MS. SQUALLS. THERE HAVE BEEN SOME ALARMING RUMORS COMING FROM THIS ISLAND AND IT IS THE DUTY OF THE US GOVERNMENT TO INVESTIGATE.
PERSONALLY I THINK IT'S A BUNCH OF HIPSTERS WITH SOME GOOD SPECIAL FX.
YIKES. NOW THE ARMY IS HERE. LOVELY. SO HEY, HOW DO YOU FEEL ABOUT BOWLING?

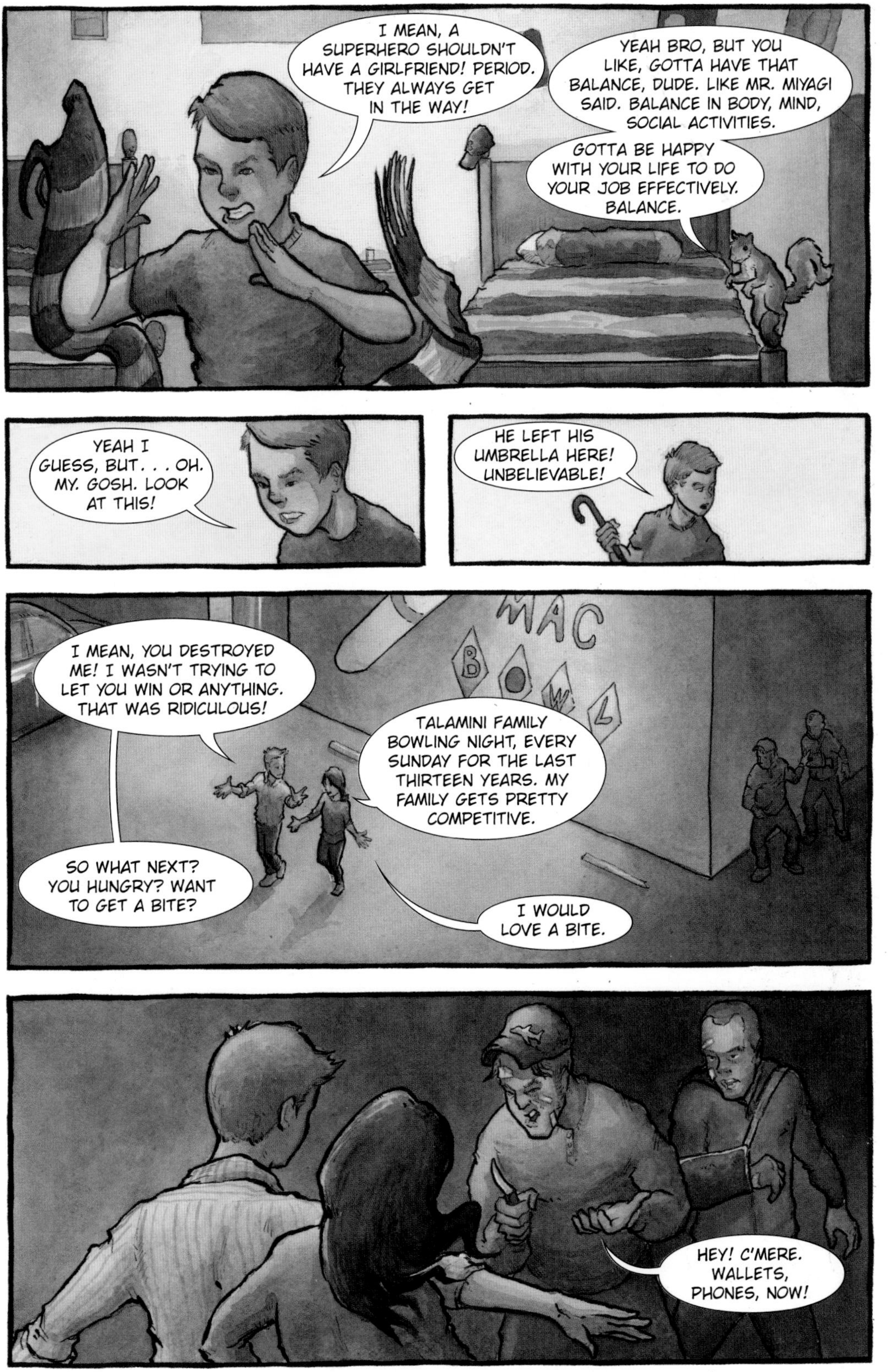
I MEAN, A SUPERHERO SHOULDN'T HAVE A GIRLFRIEND! PERIOD. THEY ALWAYS GET IN THE WAY!
YEAH BRO, BUT YOU LIKE, GOTTA HAVE THAT BALANCE, DUDE. LIKE MR. MIYAGI SAID. BALANCE IN BODY, MIND, SOCIAL ACTIVITIES.
GOTTA BE HAPPY WITH YOUR LIFE TO DO YOUR JOB EFFECTIVELY. BALANCE.
YEAH I GUESS, BUT. . . OH. MY. GOSH. LOOK AT THIS!
HE LEFT HIS UMBRELLA HERE! UNBELIEVABLE!
MAC
B O W L
I MEAN, YOU DESTROYED ME! I WASN'T TRYING TO LET YOU WIN OR ANYTHING. THAT WAS RIDICULOUS!
TALAMINI FAMILY BOWLING NIGHT, EVERY SUNDAY FOR THE LAST THIRTEEN YEARS. MY FAMILY GETS PRETTY COMPETITIVE.
SO WHAT NEXT? YOU HUNGRY? WANT TO GET A BITE?
I WOULD LOVE A BITE.
HEY! C'MERE. WALLETS, PHONES, NOW!

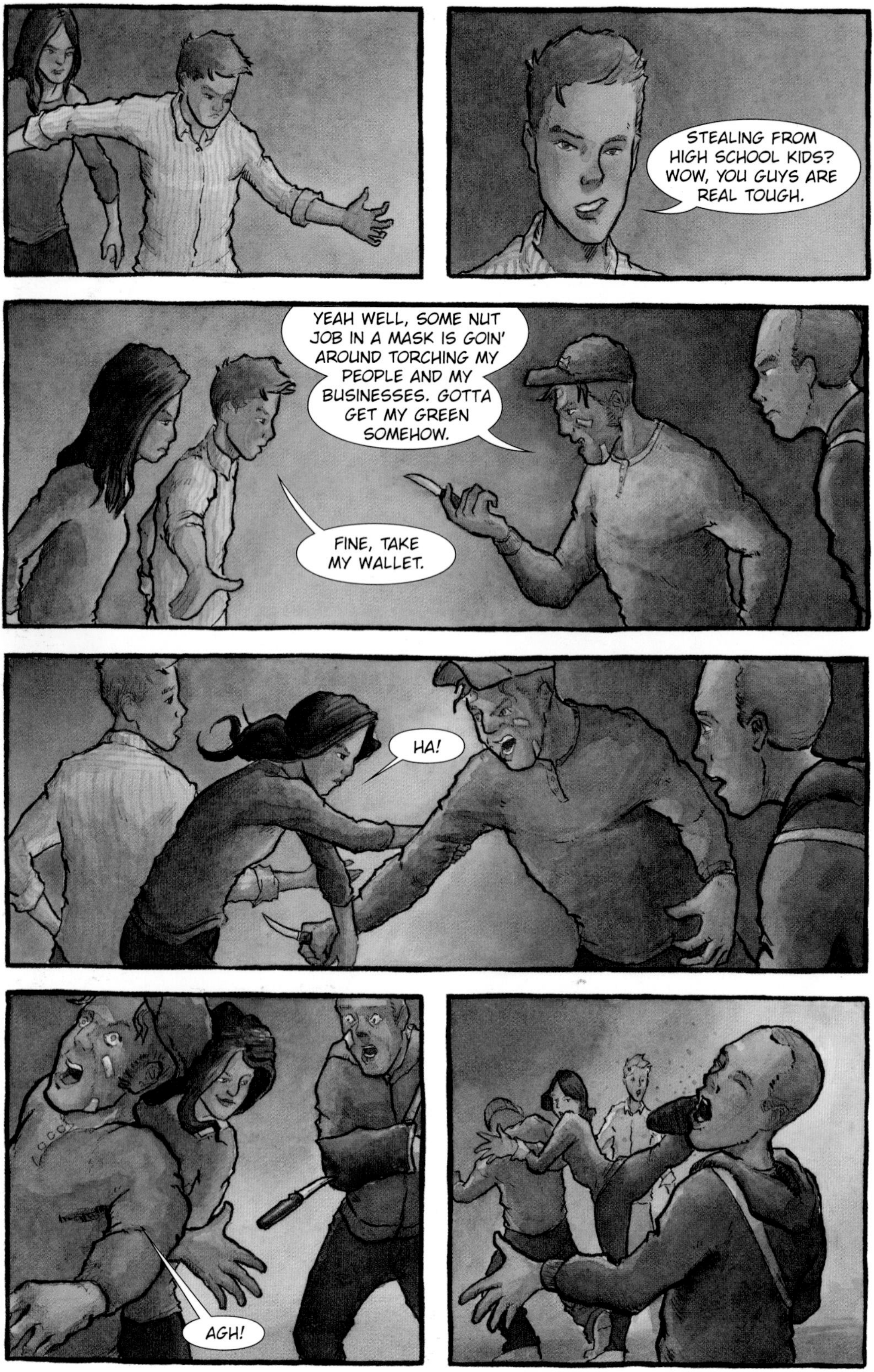
STEALING FROM HIGH SCHOOL KIDS? WOW, YOU GUYS ARE REAL TOUGH.
YEAH WELL, SOME NUT JOB IN A MASK IS GOIN' AROUND TORCHING MY PEOPLE AND MY BUSINESSES. GOTTA GET MY GREEN SOMEHOW.
FINE, TAKE MY WALLET.
HA!
AGH!

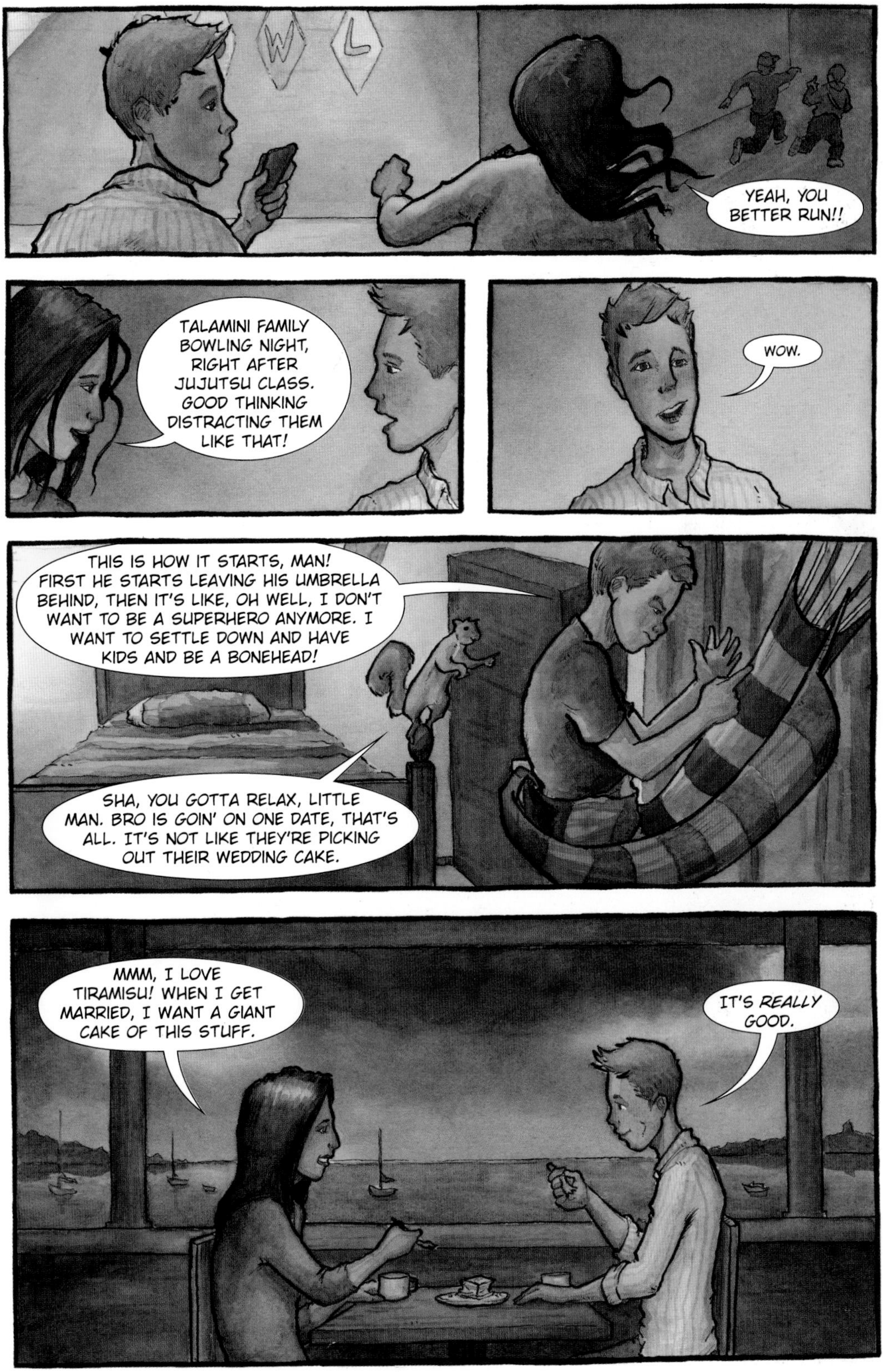
YEAH, YOU BETTER RUN!!
TALAMINI FAMILY BOWLING NIGHT, RIGHT AFTER JUJUTSU CLASS. GOOD THINKING DISTRACTING THEM LIKE THAT!
WOW.
THIS IS HOW IT STARTS, MAN! FIRST HE STARTS LEAVING HIS UMBRELLA BEHIND, THEN IT'S LIKE, OH WELL, I DON'T WANT TO BE A SUPERHERO ANYMORE. I WANT TO SETTLE DOWN AND HAVE KIDS AND BE A BONEHEAD!
SHA, YOU GOTTA RELAX, LITTLE MAN. BRO IS GOIN' ON ONE DATE, THAT'S ALL. IT'S NOT LIKE THEY'RE PICKING OUT THEIR WEDDING CAKE.
MMM, I LOVE TIRAMISU! WHEN I GET MARRIED, I WANT A GIANT CAKE OF THIS STUFF.
IT'S *REALLY* GOOD.

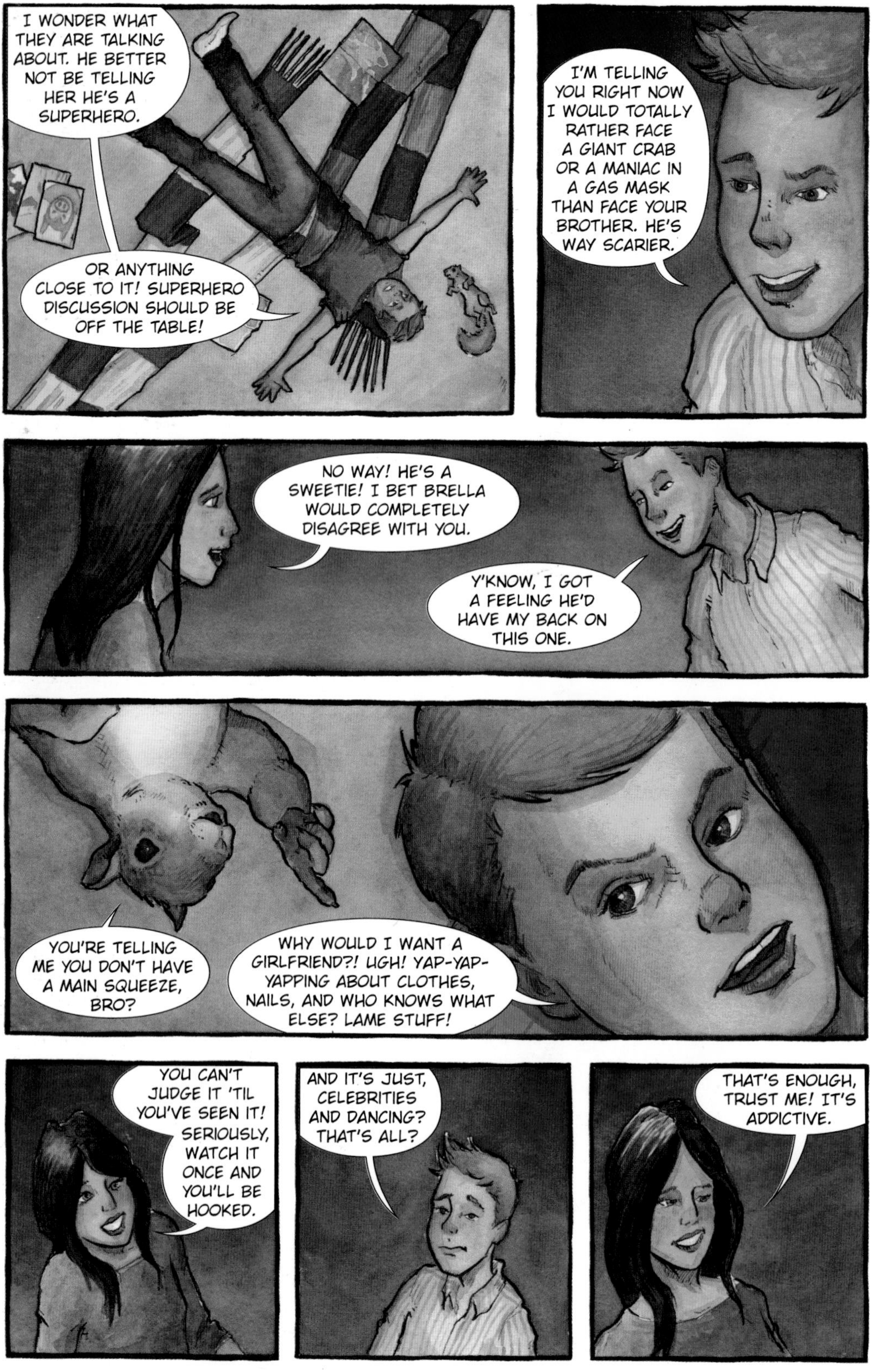
I WONDER WHAT THEY ARE TALKING ABOUT. HE BETTER NOT BE TELLING HER HE'S A SUPERHERO.
OR ANYTHING CLOSE TO IT! SUPERHERO DISCUSSION SHOULD BE OFF THE TABLE!
I'M TELLING YOU RIGHT NOW I WOULD TOTALLY RATHER FACE A GIANT CRAB OR A MANIAC IN A GAS MASK THAN FACE YOUR BROTHER. HE'S WAY SCARIER.
NO WAY! HE'S A SWEETIE! I BET BRELLA WOULD COMPLETELY DISAGREE WITH YOU.
Y'KNOW, I GOT A FEELING HE'D HAVE MY BACK ON THIS ONE.
YOU'RE TELLING ME YOU DON'T HAVE A MAIN SQUEEZE, BRO?
WHY WOULD I WANT A GIRLFRIEND?! UGH! YAP-YAP-YAPPING ABOUT CLOTHES, NAILS, AND WHO KNOWS WHAT ELSE? LAME STUFF!
YOU CAN'T JUDGE IT 'TIL YOU'VE SEEN IT! SERIOUSLY, WATCH IT ONCE AND YOU'LL BE HOOKED.
AND IT'S JUST, CELEBRITIES AND DANCING? THAT'S ALL?
THAT'S ENOUGH, TRUST ME! IT'S ADDICTIVE.

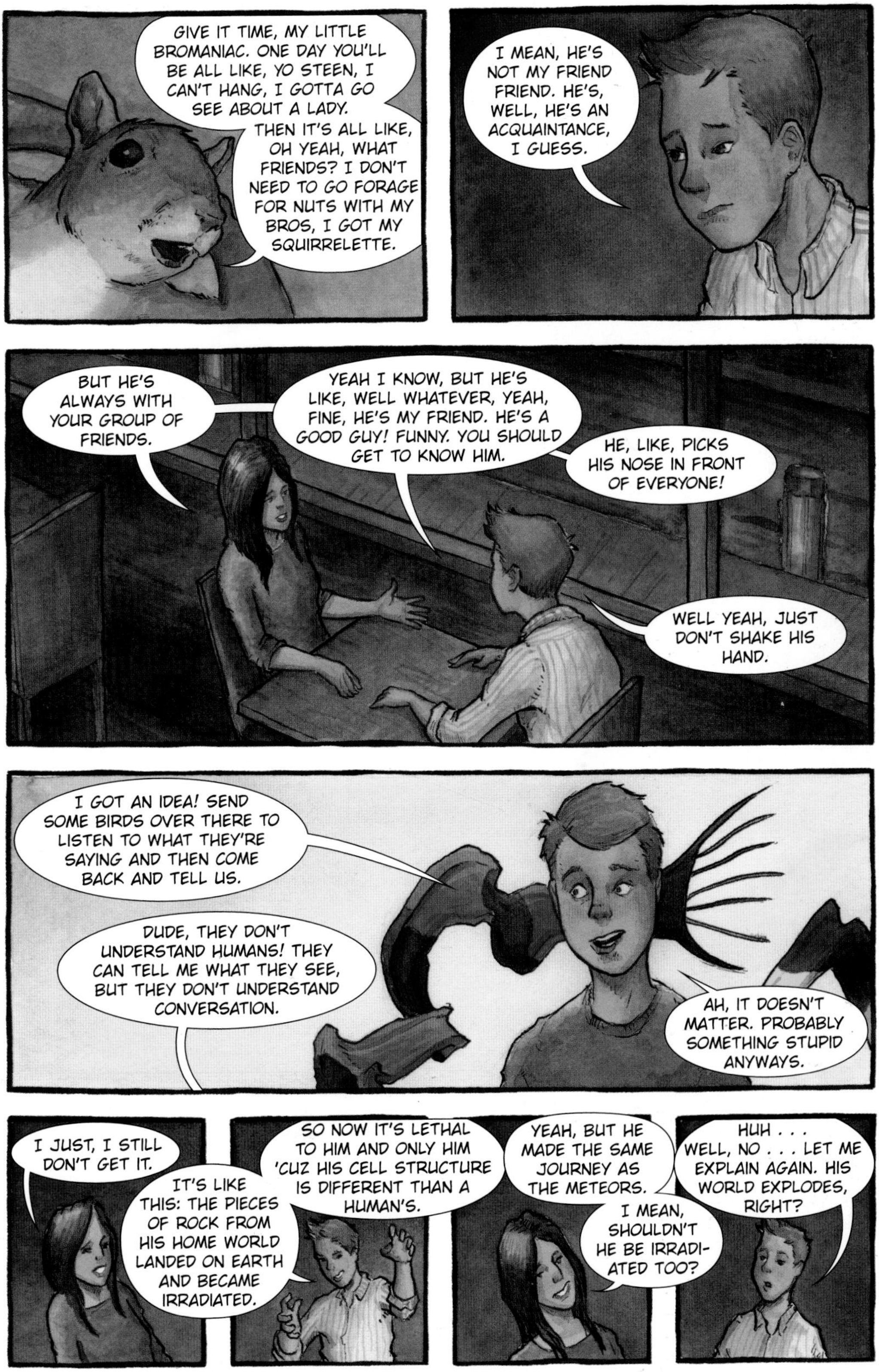
GIVE IT TIME, MY LITTLE BROMANIAC. ONE DAY YOU'LL BE ALL LIKE, YO STEEN, I CAN'T HANG, I GOTTA GO SEE ABOUT A LADY.
THEN IT'S ALL LIKE, OH YEAH, WHAT FRIENDS? I DON'T NEED TO GO FORAGE FOR NUTS WITH MY BROS, I GOT MY SQUIRRELETTE.
I MEAN, HE'S NOT MY FRIEND FRIEND. HE'S, WELL, HE'S AN ACQUAINTANCE, I GUESS.
BUT HE'S ALWAYS WITH YOUR GROUP OF FRIENDS.
YEAH I KNOW, BUT HE'S LIKE, WELL WHATEVER, YEAH, FINE, HE'S MY FRIEND. HE'S A GOOD GUY! FUNNY. YOU SHOULD GET TO KNOW HIM.
HE, LIKE, PICKS HIS NOSE IN FRONT OF EVERYONE!
WELL YEAH, JUST DON'T SHAKE HIS HAND.
I GOT AN IDEA! SEND SOME BIRDS OVER THERE TO LISTEN TO WHAT THEY'RE SAYING AND THEN COME BACK AND TELL US.
DUDE, THEY DON'T UNDERSTAND HUMANS! THEY CAN TELL ME WHAT THEY SEE, BUT THEY DON'T UNDERSTAND CONVERSATION.
AH, IT DOESN'T MATTER. PROBABLY SOMETHING STUPID ANYWAYS.
I JUST, I STILL DON'T GET IT.
IT'S LIKE THIS: THE PIECES OF ROCK FROM HIS HOME WORLD LANDED ON EARTH AND BECAME IRRADIATED.
SO NOW IT'S LETHAL TO HIM AND ONLY HIM 'CUZ HIS CELL STRUCTURE IS DIFFERENT THAN A HUMAN'S.
YEAH, BUT HE MADE THE SAME JOURNEY AS THE METEORS.
I MEAN, SHOULDN'T HE BE IRRADI-ATED TOO?
HUH . . . WELL, NO . . . LET ME EXPLAIN AGAIN. HIS WORLD EXPLODES, RIGHT?

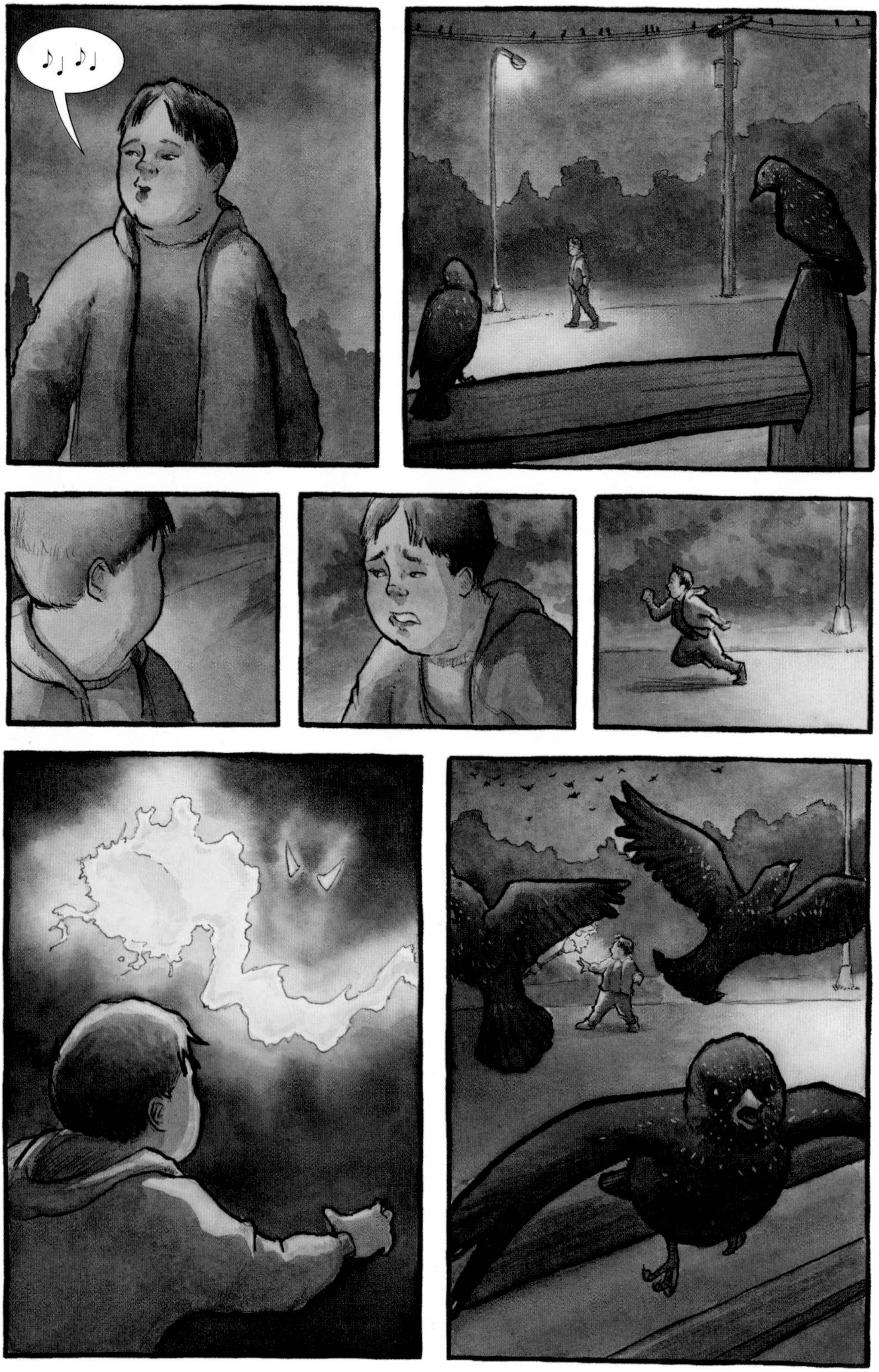

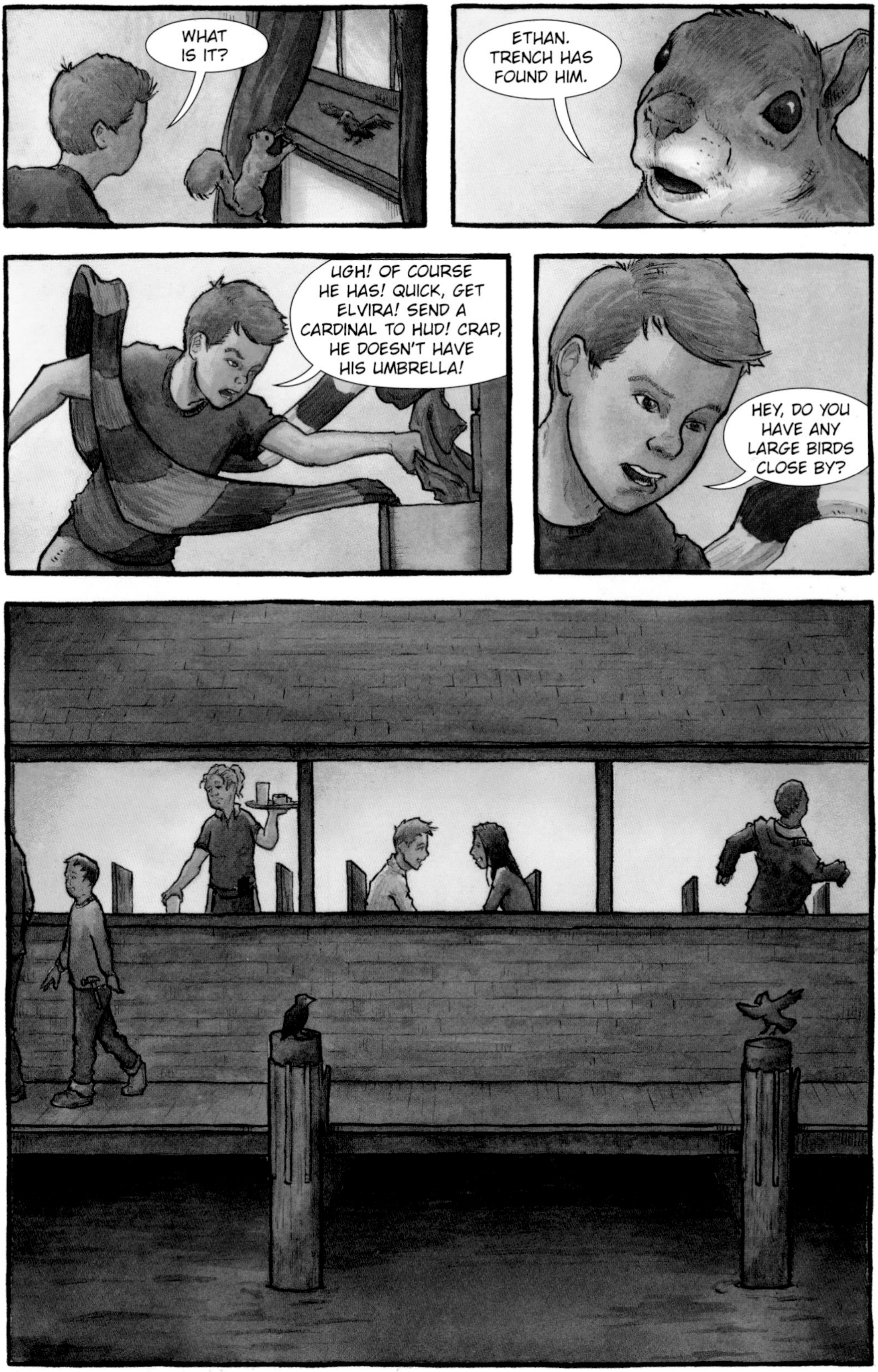
WHAT IS IT?
ETHAN. TRENCH HAS FOUND HIM.
UGH! OF COURSE HE HAS! QUICK, GET ELVIRA! SEND A CARDINAL TO HUD! CRAP, HE DOESN'T HAVE HIS UMBRELLA!
HEY, DO YOU HAVE ANY LARGE BIRDS CLOSE BY?

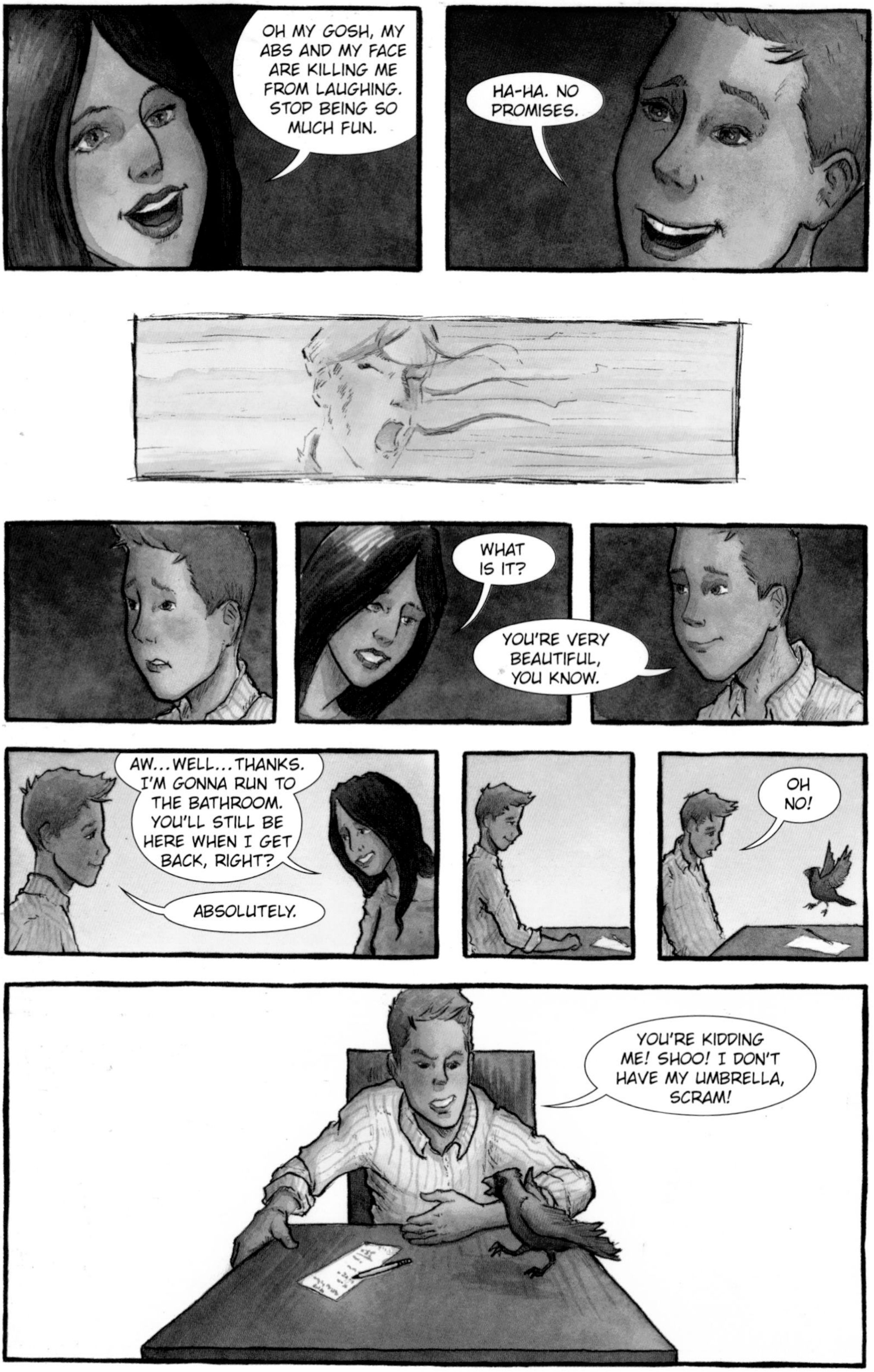
OH MY GOSH, MY ABS AND MY FACE ARE KILLING ME FROM LAUGHING. STOP BEING SO MUCH FUN.
HA-HA. NO PROMISES.
WHAT IS IT?
YOU'RE VERY BEAUTIFUL, YOU KNOW.
AW...WELL...THANKS. I'M GONNA RUN TO THE BATHROOM. YOU'LL STILL BE HERE WHEN I GET BACK, RIGHT?
ABSOLUTELY.
OH NO!
YOU'RE KIDDING ME! SHOO! I DON'T HAVE MY UMBRELLA, SCRAM!

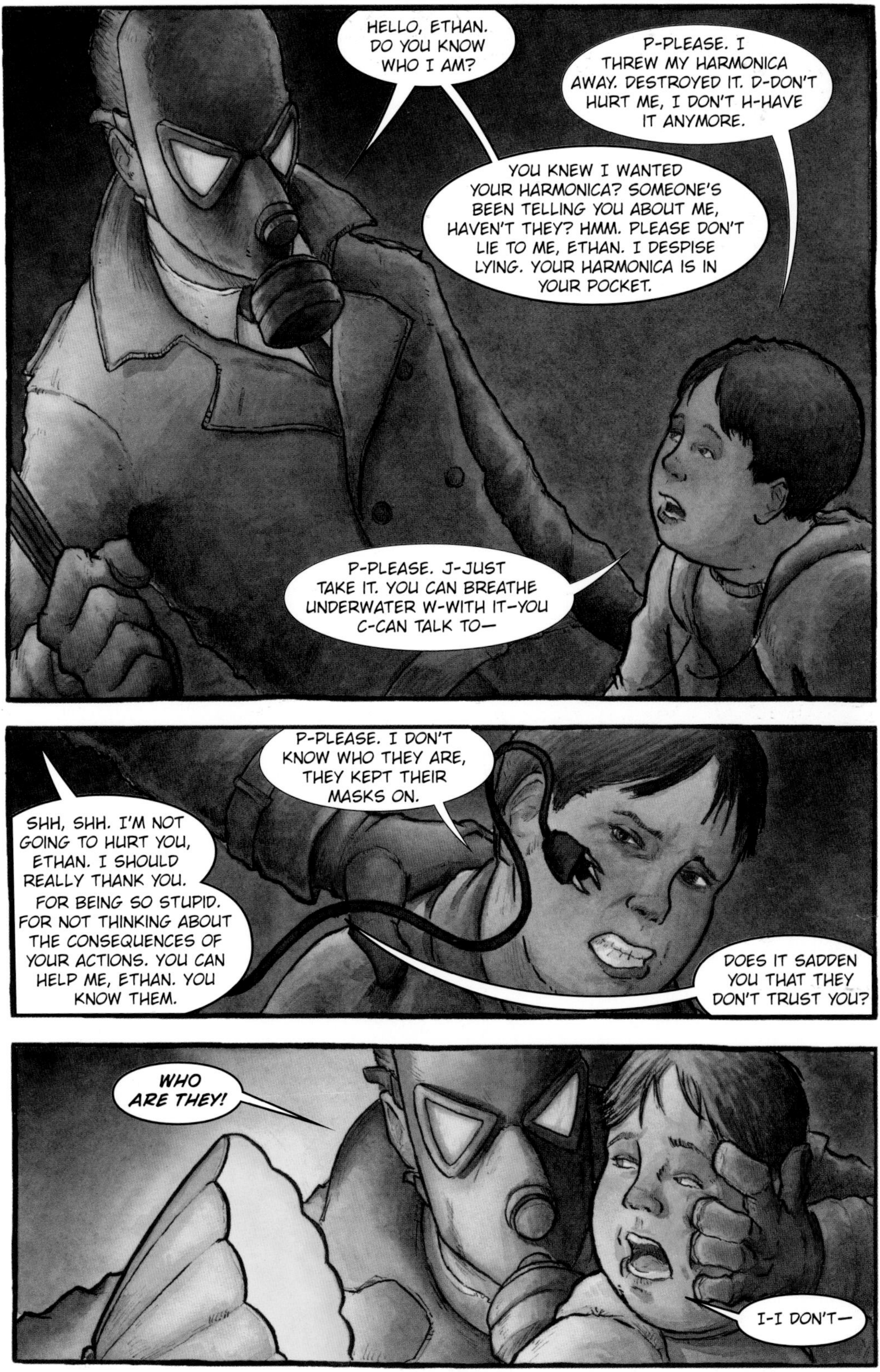
HELLO, ETHAN. DO YOU KNOW WHO I AM?
P-PLEASE. I THREW MY HARMONICA AWAY. DESTROYED IT. D-DON'T HURT ME, I DON'T H-HAVE IT ANYMORE.
YOU KNEW I WANTED YOUR HARMONICA? SOMEONE'S BEEN TELLING YOU ABOUT ME, HAVEN'T THEY? HMM. PLEASE DON'T LIE TO ME, ETHAN. I DESPISE LYING. YOUR HARMONICA IS IN YOUR POCKET.
P-PLEASE. J-JUST TAKE IT. YOU CAN BREATHE UNDERWATER W-WITH IT—YOU C-CAN TALK TO—
P-PLEASE. I DON'T KNOW WHO THEY ARE, THEY KEPT THEIR MASKS ON.
SHH, SHH. I'M NOT GOING TO HURT YOU, ETHAN. I SHOULD REALLY THANK YOU.
FOR BEING SO STUPID. FOR NOT THINKING ABOUT THE CONSEQUENCES OF YOUR ACTIONS. YOU CAN HELP ME, ETHAN. YOU KNOW THEM.
DOES IT SADDEN YOU THAT THEY DON'T TRUST YOU?
WHO ARE THEY!
I-I DON'T—

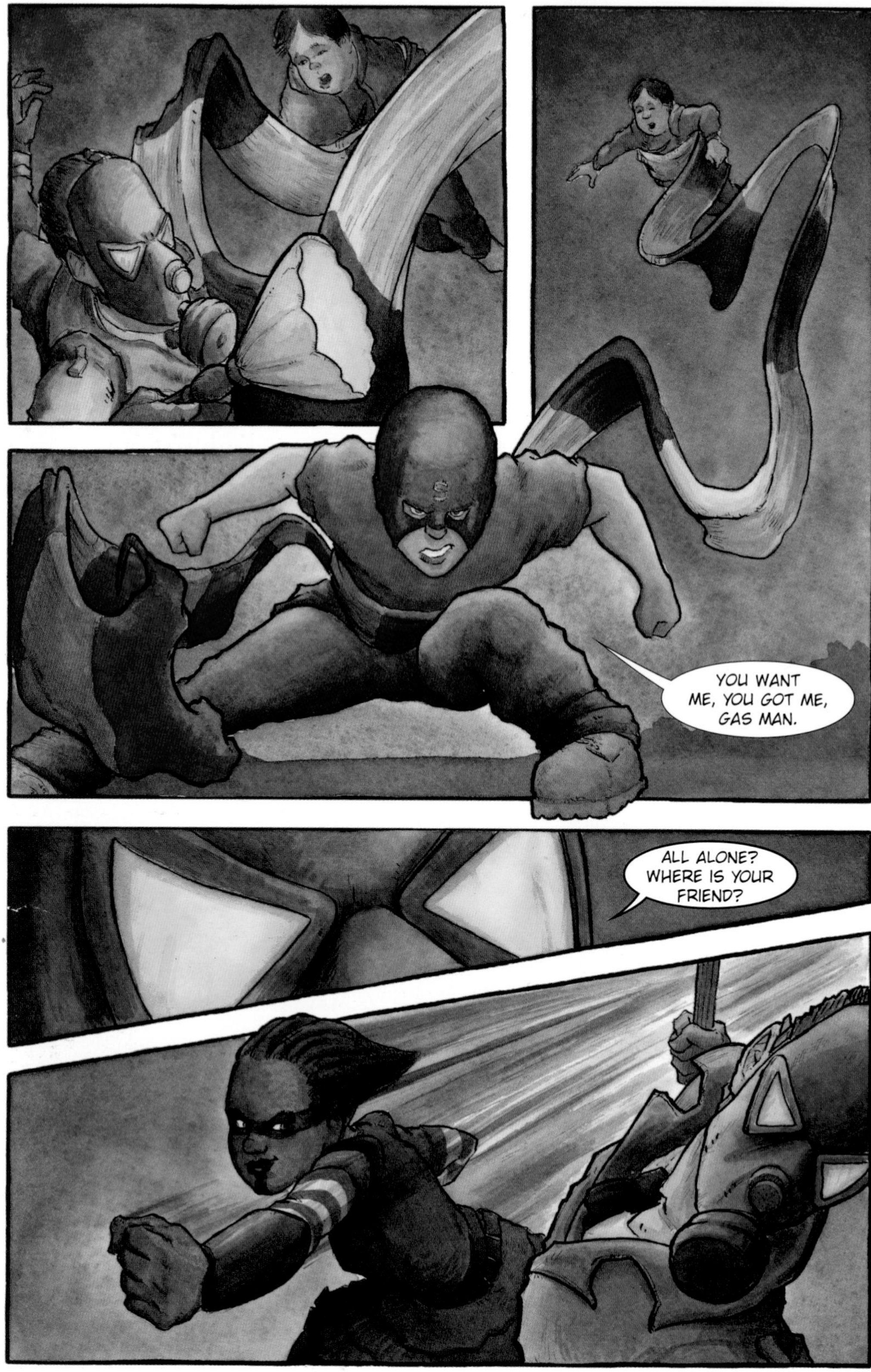
YOU WANT ME, YOU GOT ME, GAS MAN.
ALL ALONE? WHERE IS YOUR FRIEND?

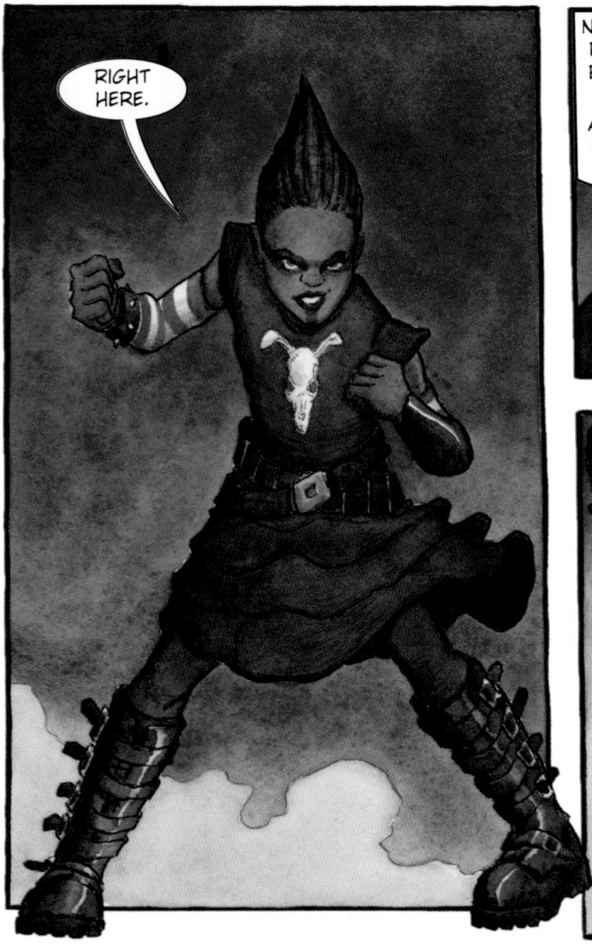
RIGHT HERE.

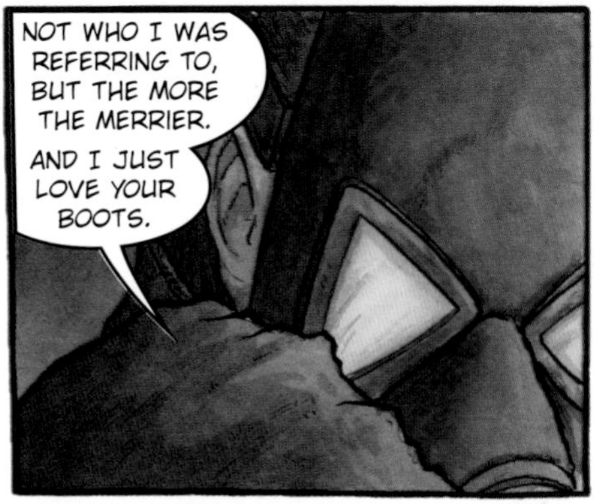
NOT WHO I WAS REFERRING TO, BUT THE MORE THE MERRIER.
AND I JUST LOVE YOUR BOOTS.

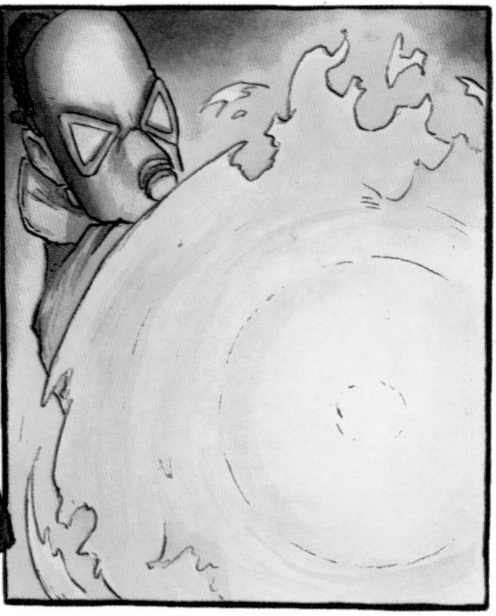

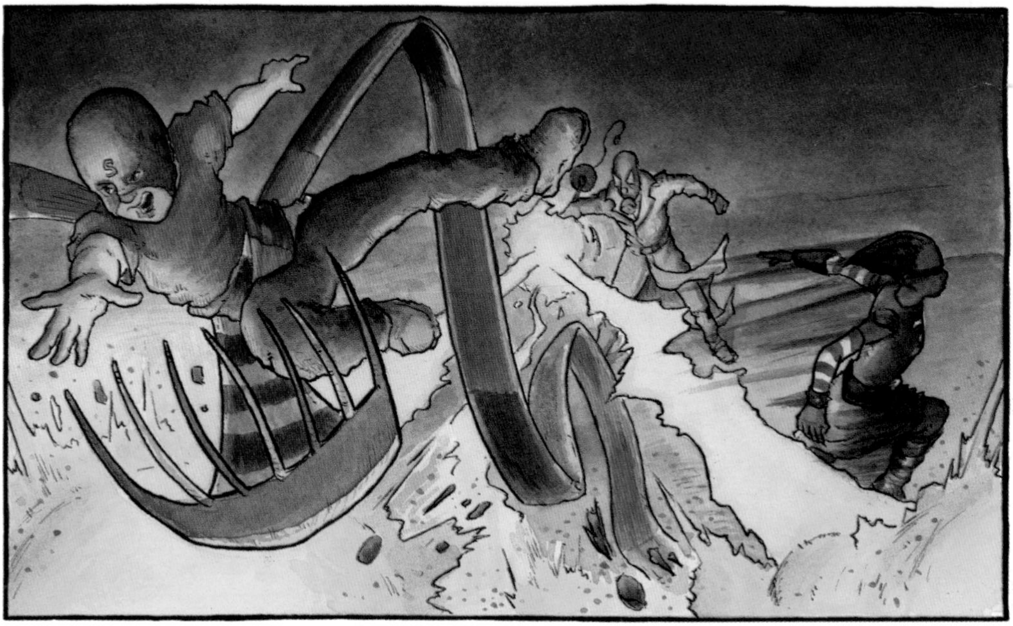

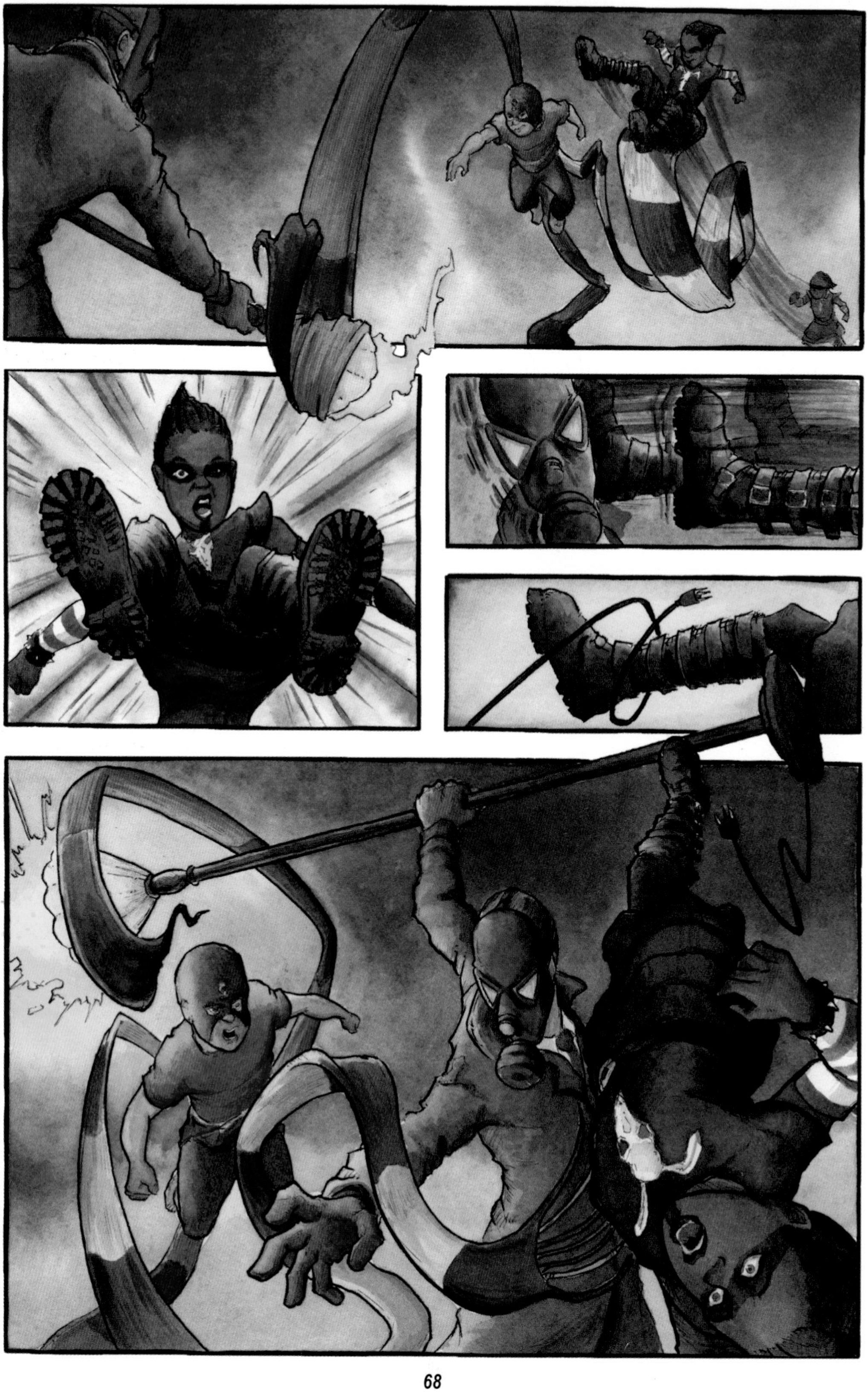

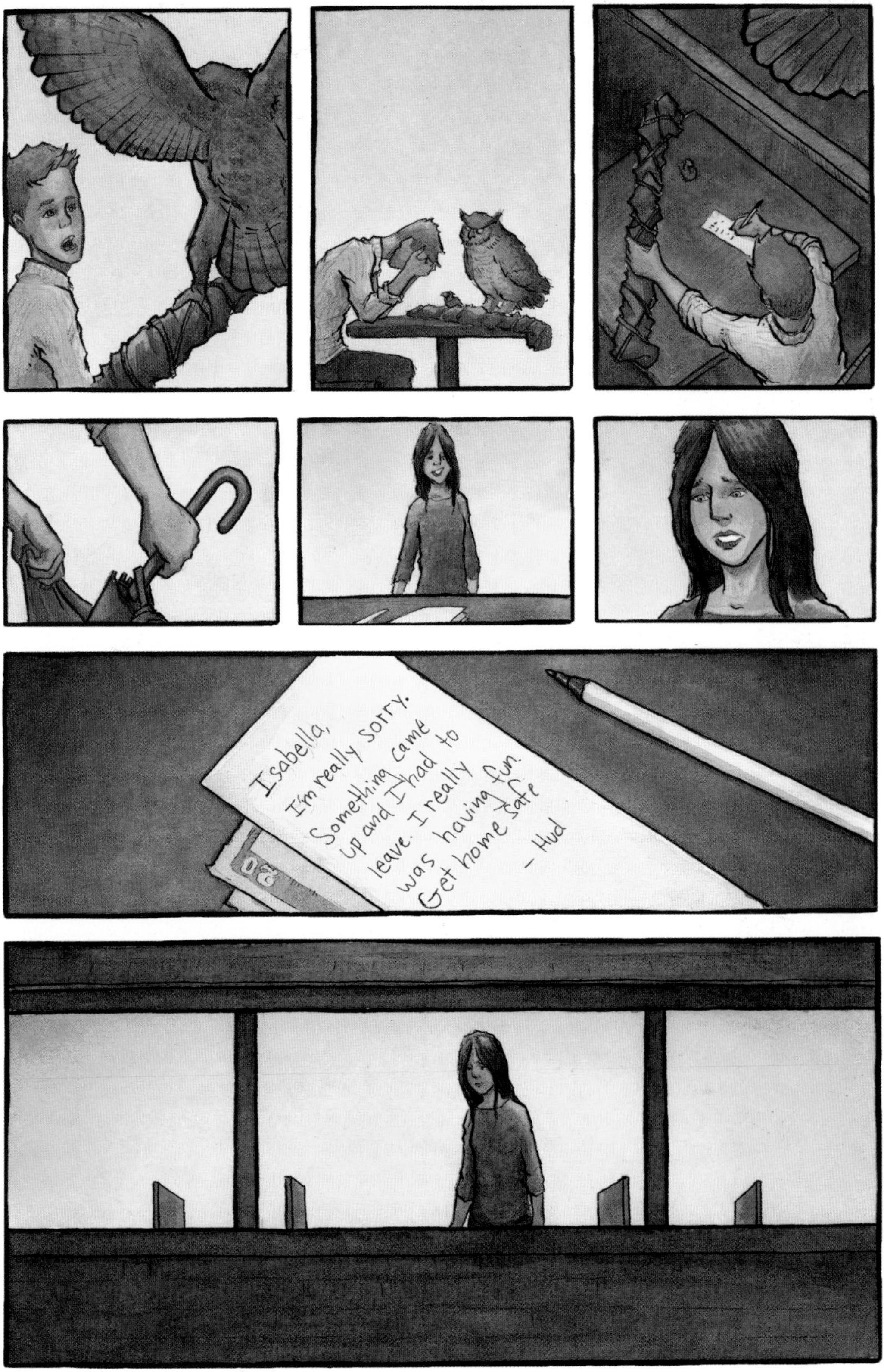
Isabella,
I'm really sorry.
Something came
up and I had to
leave. I really
was having fun.
Get home safe
- Hud

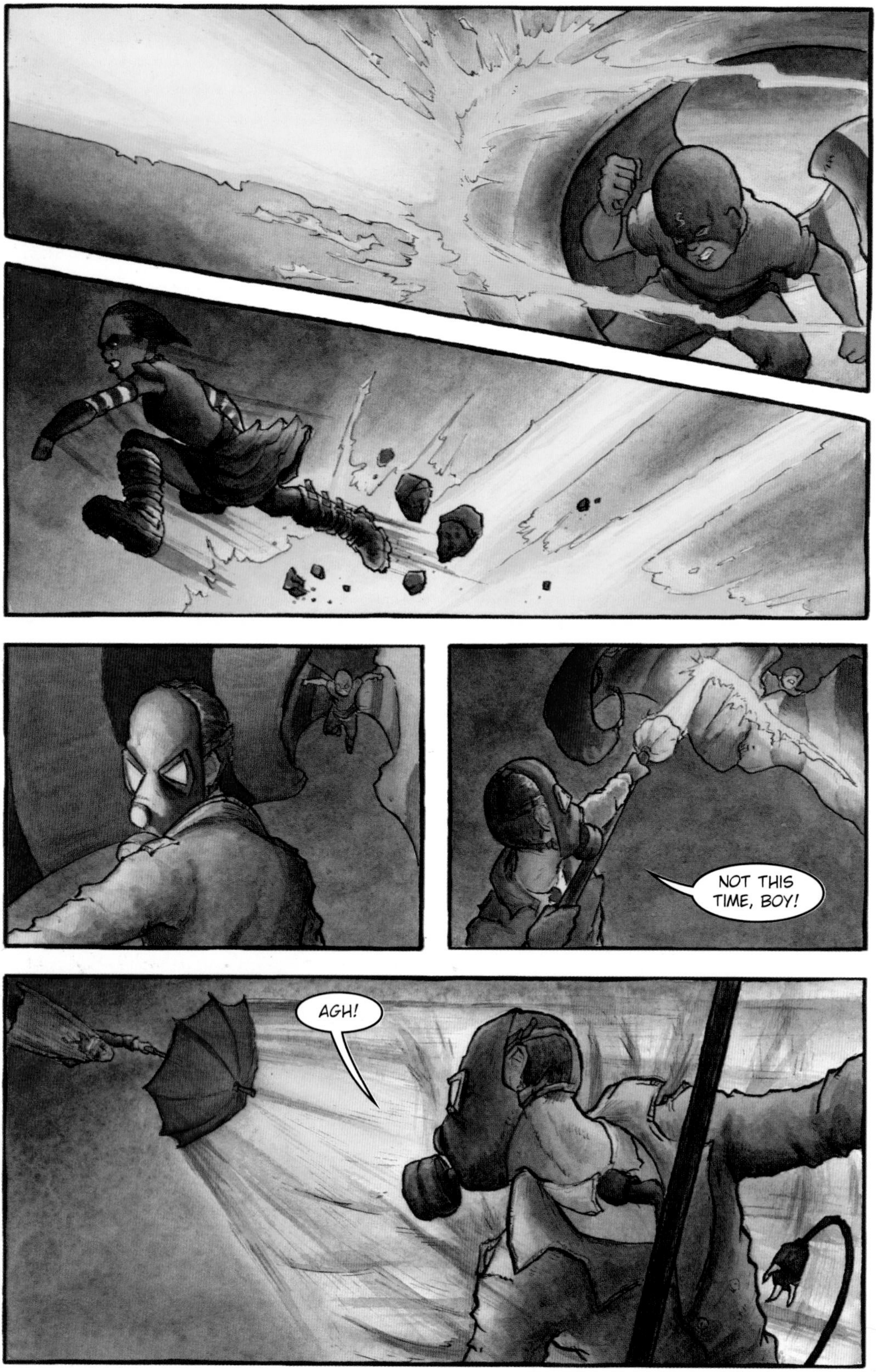
NOT THIS TIME, BOY!
AGH!

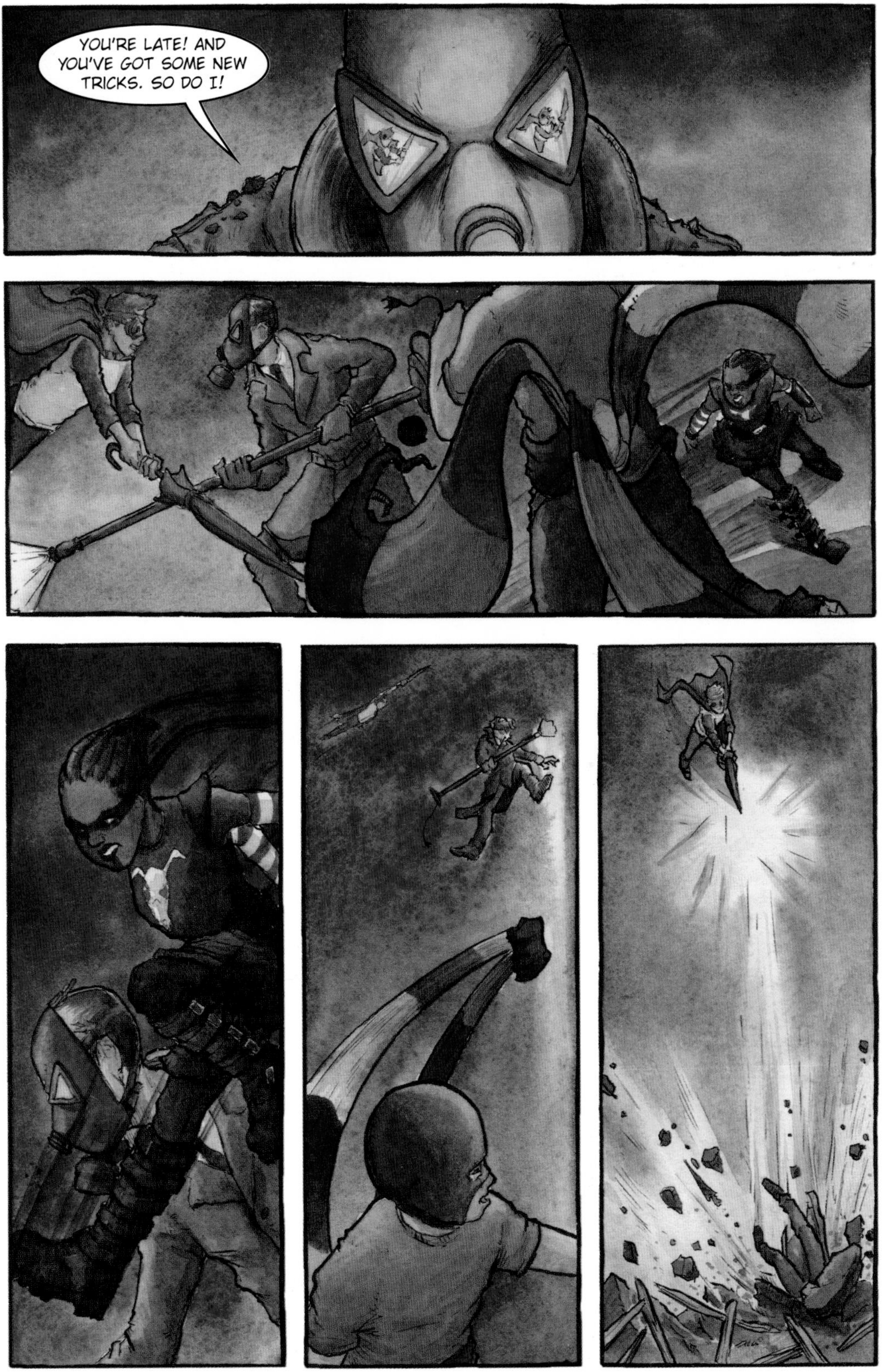
YOU'RE LATE! AND YOU'VE GOT SOME NEW TRICKS. SO DO I!

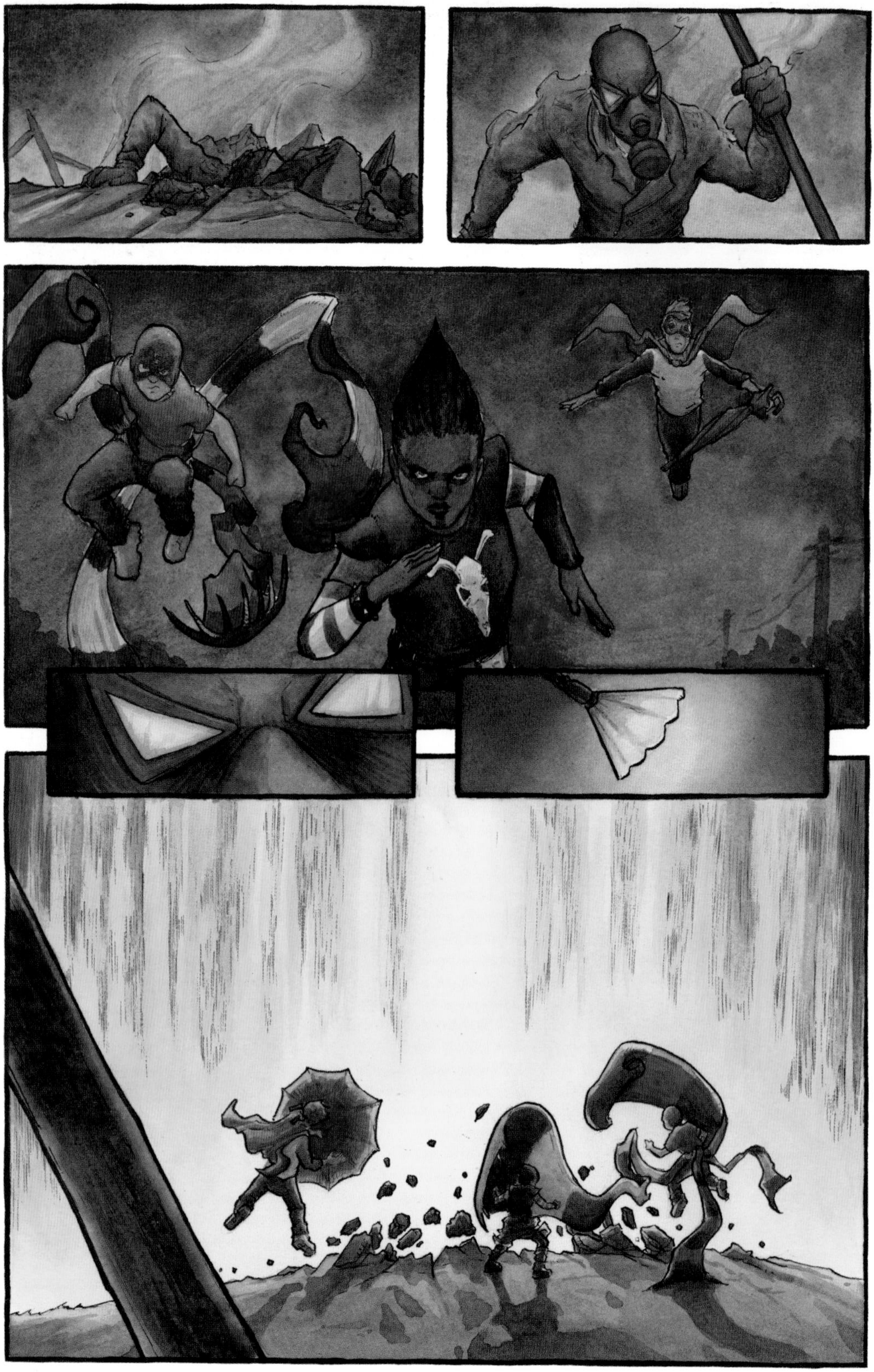

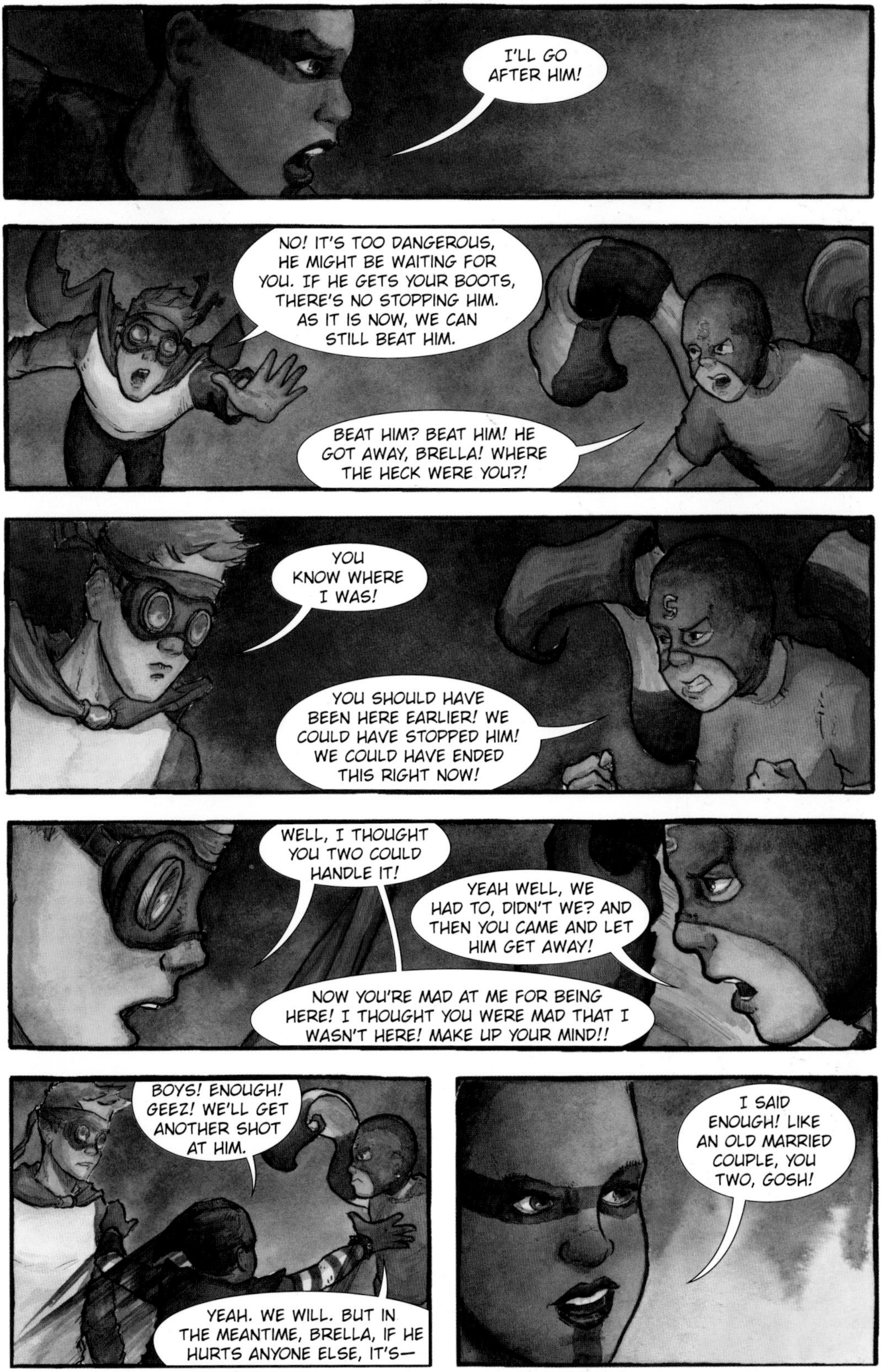
I'LL GO AFTER HIM!
NO! IT'S TOO DANGEROUS, HE MIGHT BE WAITING FOR YOU. IF HE GETS YOUR BOOTS, THERE'S NO STOPPING HIM. AS IT IS NOW, WE CAN STILL BEAT HIM.
BEAT HIM? BEAT HIM! HE GOT AWAY, BRELLA! WHERE THE HECK WERE YOU?!
YOU KNOW WHERE I WAS!
YOU SHOULD HAVE BEEN HERE EARLIER! WE COULD HAVE STOPPED HIM! WE COULD HAVE ENDED THIS RIGHT NOW!
WELL, I THOUGHT YOU TWO COULD HANDLE IT!
YEAH WELL, WE HAD TO, DIDN'T WE? AND THEN YOU CAME AND LET HIM GET AWAY!
NOW YOU'RE MAD AT ME FOR BEING HERE! I THOUGHT YOU WERE MAD THAT I WASN'T HERE! MAKE UP YOUR MIND!!
BOYS! ENOUGH! GEEZ! WE'LL GET ANOTHER SHOT AT HIM.
YEAH. WE WILL. BUT IN THE MEANTIME, BRELLA, IF HE HURTS ANYONE ELSE, IT'S—
I SAID ENOUGH! LIKE AN OLD MARRIED COUPLE, YOU TWO, GOSH!

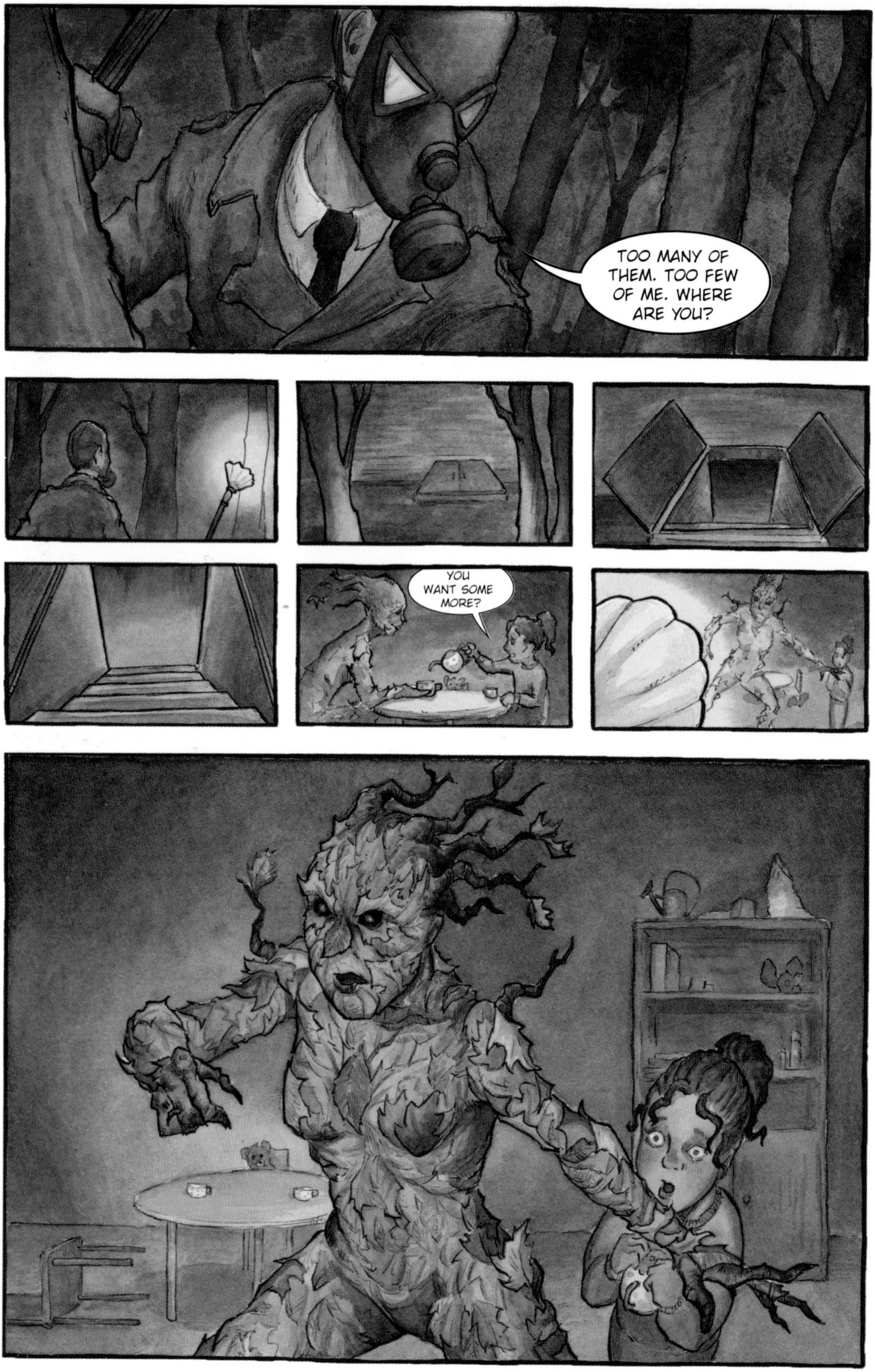
TOO MANY OF THEM. TOO FEW OF ME. WHERE ARE YOU?
YOU WANT SOME MORE?

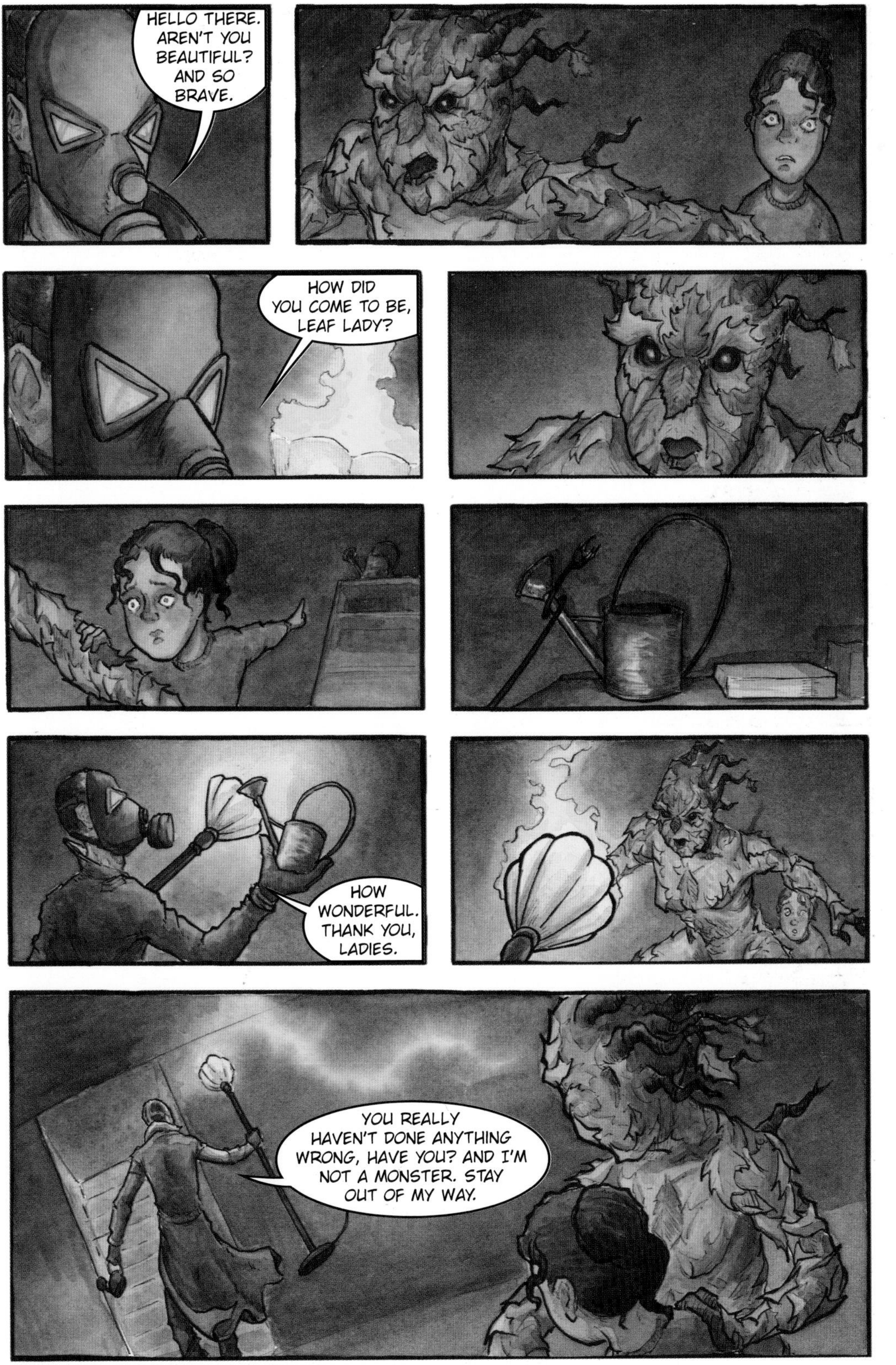
HELLO THERE. AREN'T YOU BEAUTIFUL? AND SO BRAVE.
HOW DID YOU COME TO BE, LEAF LADY?
HOW WONDERFUL. THANK YOU, LADIES.
YOU REALLY HAVEN'T DONE ANYTHING WRONG, HAVE YOU? AND I'M NOT A MONSTER. STAY OUT OF MY WAY.

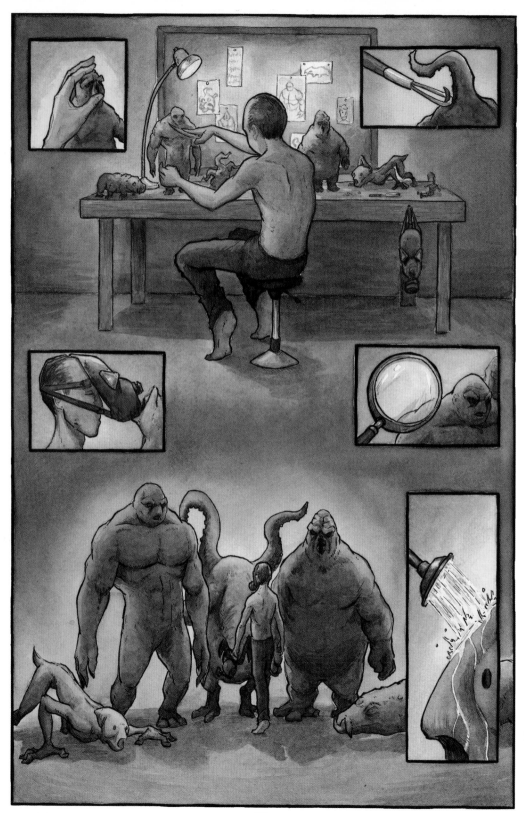

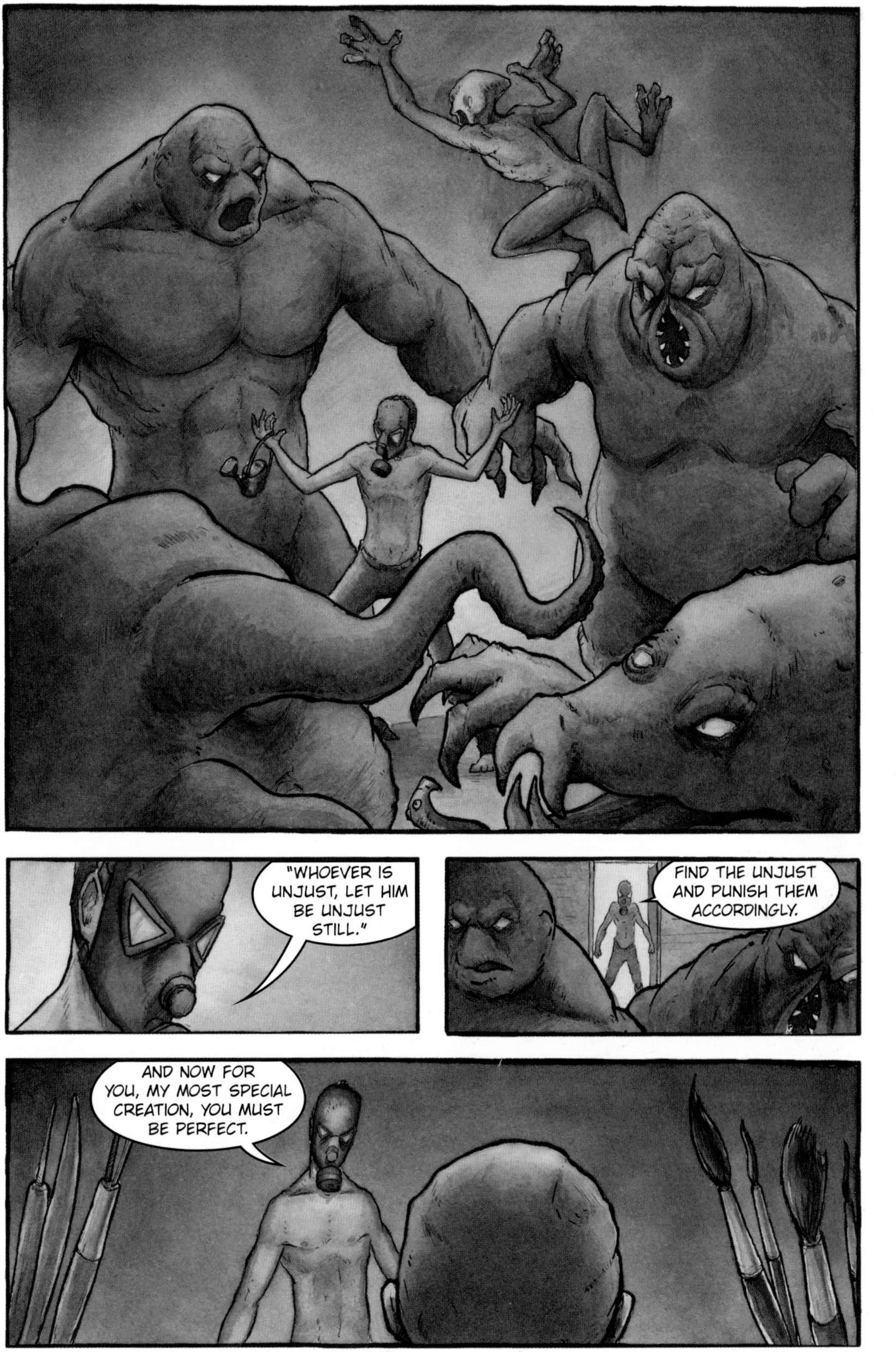
"WHOEVER IS UNJUST, LET HIM BE UNJUST STILL."
FIND THE UNJUST AND PUNISH THEM ACCORDINGLY.
AND NOW FOR YOU, MY MOST SPECIAL CREATION, YOU MUST BE PERFECT.

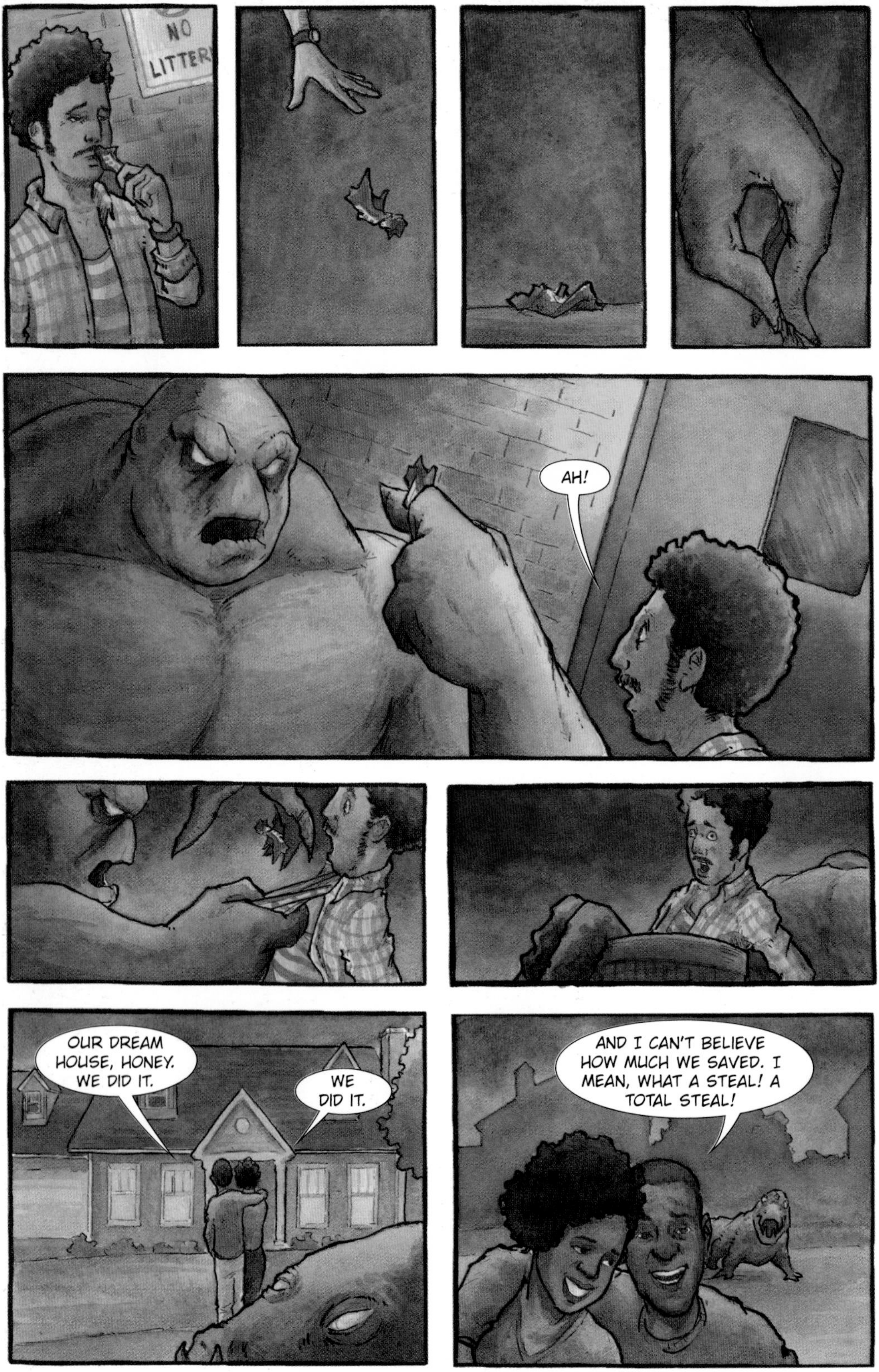
NO LITTER
AH!
OUR DREAM HOUSE, HONEY. WE DID IT.
WE DID IT.
AND I CAN'T BELIEVE HOW MUCH WE SAVED. I MEAN, WHAT A STEAL! A TOTAL STEAL!

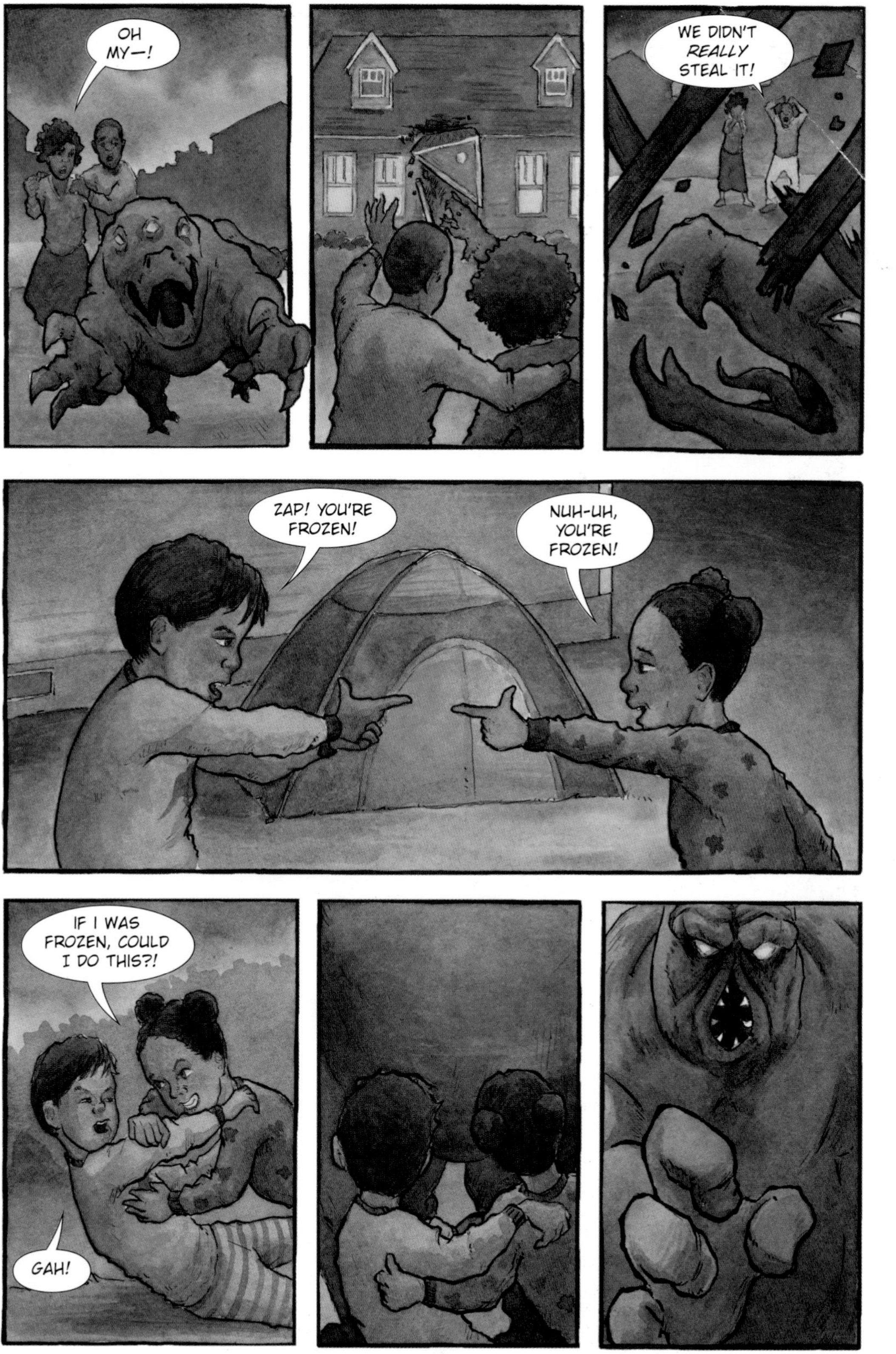
OH MY—!
WE DIDN'T REALLY STEAL IT!
ZAP! YOU'RE FROZEN!
NUH-UH, YOU'RE FROZEN!
IF I WAS FROZEN, COULD I DO THIS?!
GAH!

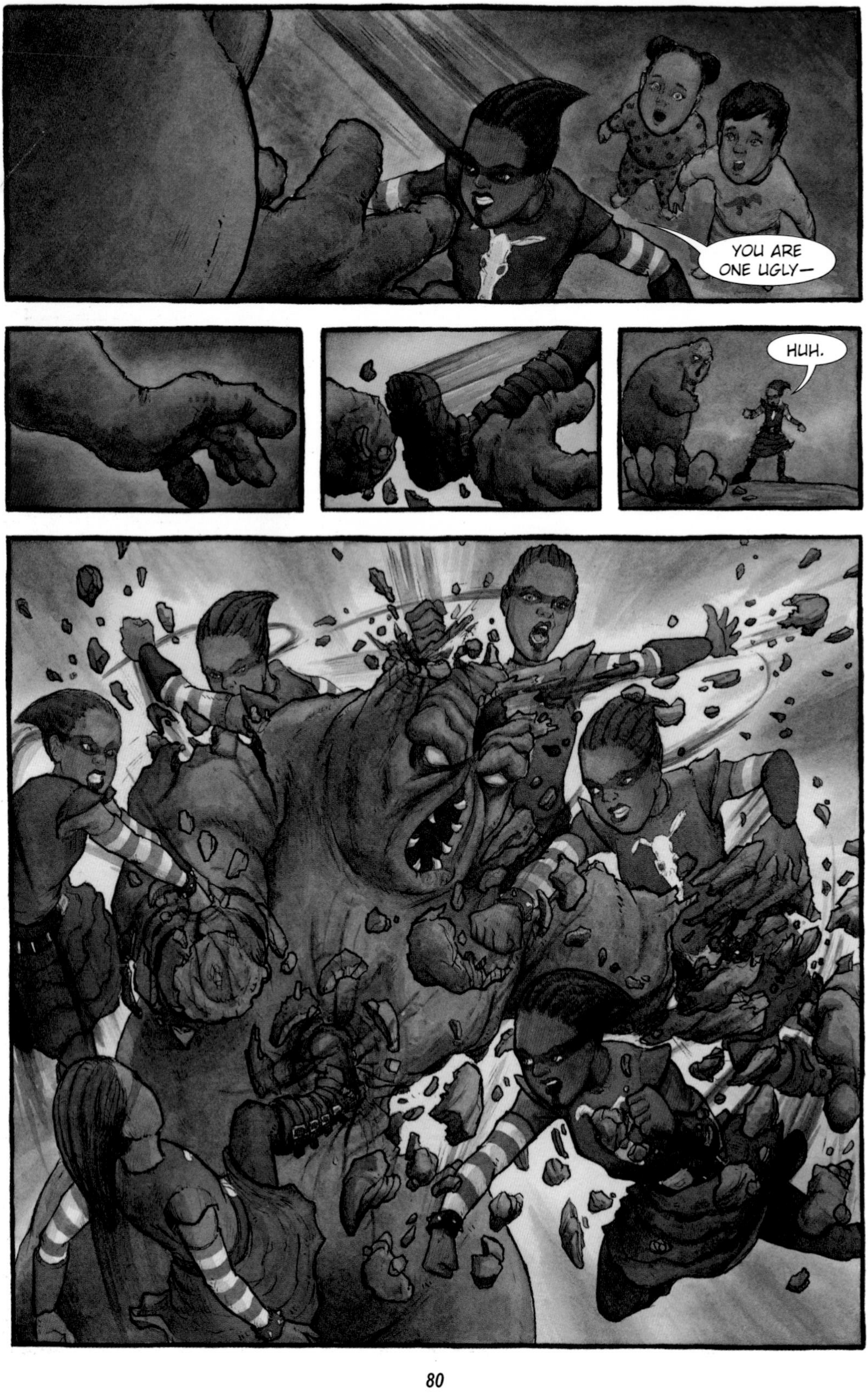
YOU ARE ONE UGLY—
HUH.

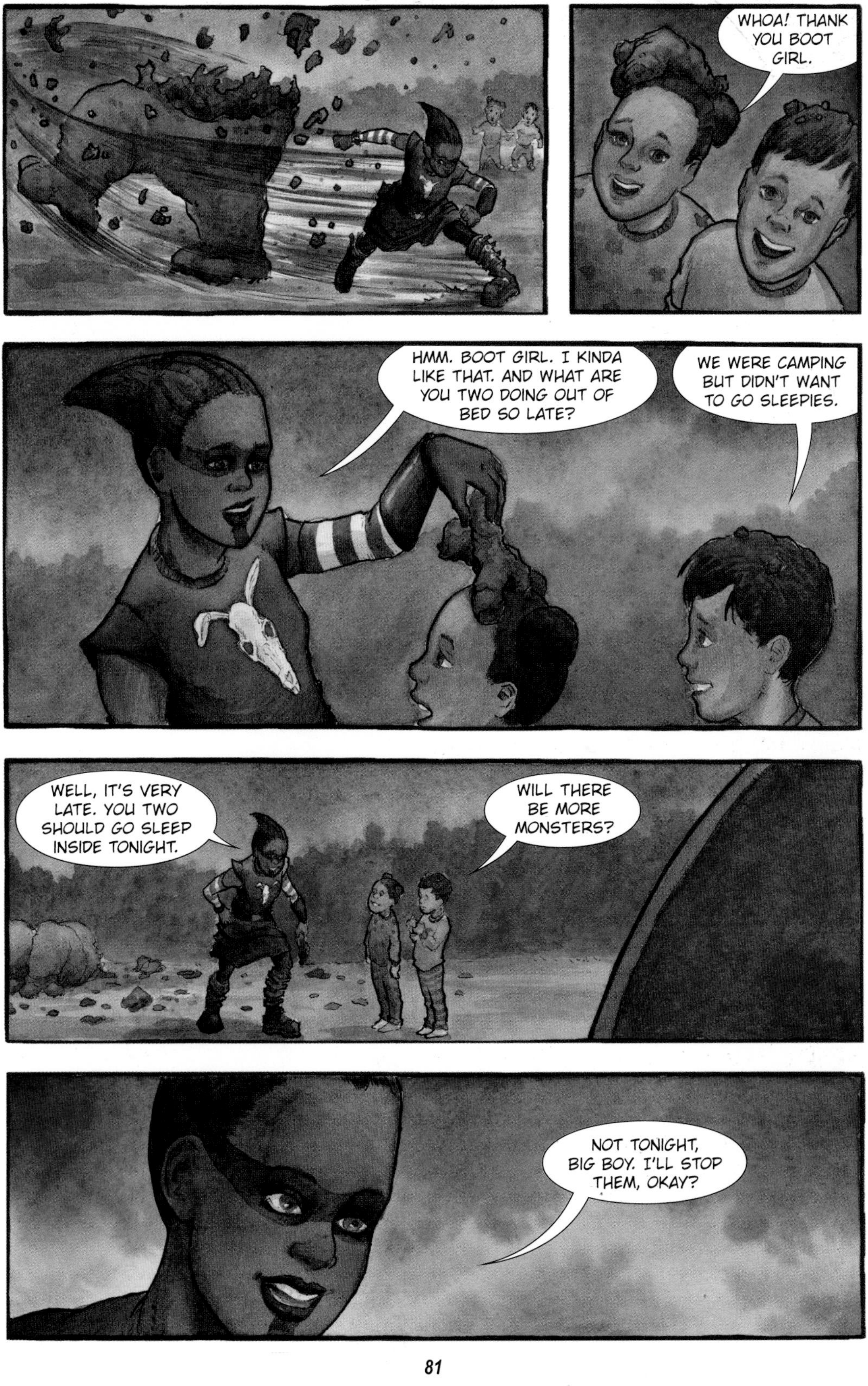
WHOA! THANK YOU BOOT GIRL.
HMM. BOOT GIRL. I KINDA LIKE THAT. AND WHAT ARE YOU TWO DOING OUT OF BED SO LATE?
WE WERE CAMPING BUT DIDN'T WANT TO GO SLEEPIES.
WELL, IT'S VERY LATE. YOU TWO SHOULD GO SLEEP INSIDE TONIGHT.
WILL THERE BE MORE MONSTERS?
NOT TONIGHT, BIG BOY. I'LL STOP THEM, OKAY?

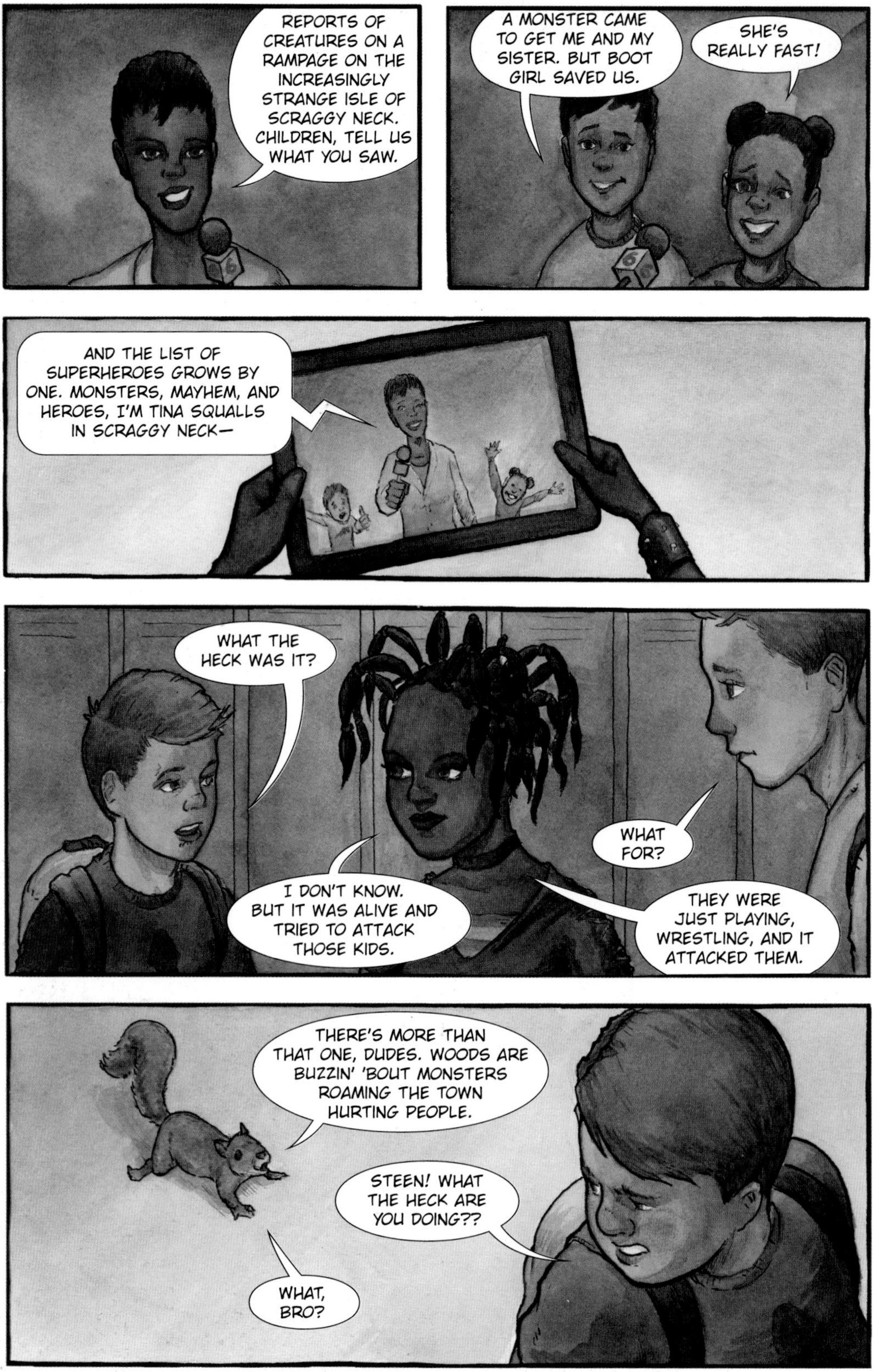
REPORTS OF CREATURES ON A RAMPAGE ON THE INCREASINGLY STRANGE ISLE OF SCRAGGY NECK. CHILDREN, TELL US WHAT YOU SAW.
A MONSTER CAME TO GET ME AND MY SISTER. BUT BOOT GIRL SAVED US.
SHE'S REALLY FAST!
AND THE LIST OF SUPERHEROES GROWS BY ONE. MONSTERS, MAYHEM, AND HEROES, I'M TINA SQUALLS IN SCRAGGY NECK—
WHAT THE HECK WAS IT?
I DON'T KNOW. BUT IT WAS ALIVE AND TRIED TO ATTACK THOSE KIDS.
WHAT FOR?
THEY WERE JUST PLAYING, WRESTLING, AND IT ATTACKED THEM.
THERE'S MORE THAN THAT ONE, DUDES. WOODS ARE BUZZIN' 'BOUT MONSTERS ROAMING THE TOWN HURTING PEOPLE.
STEEN! WHAT THE HECK ARE YOU DOING??
WHAT, BRO?

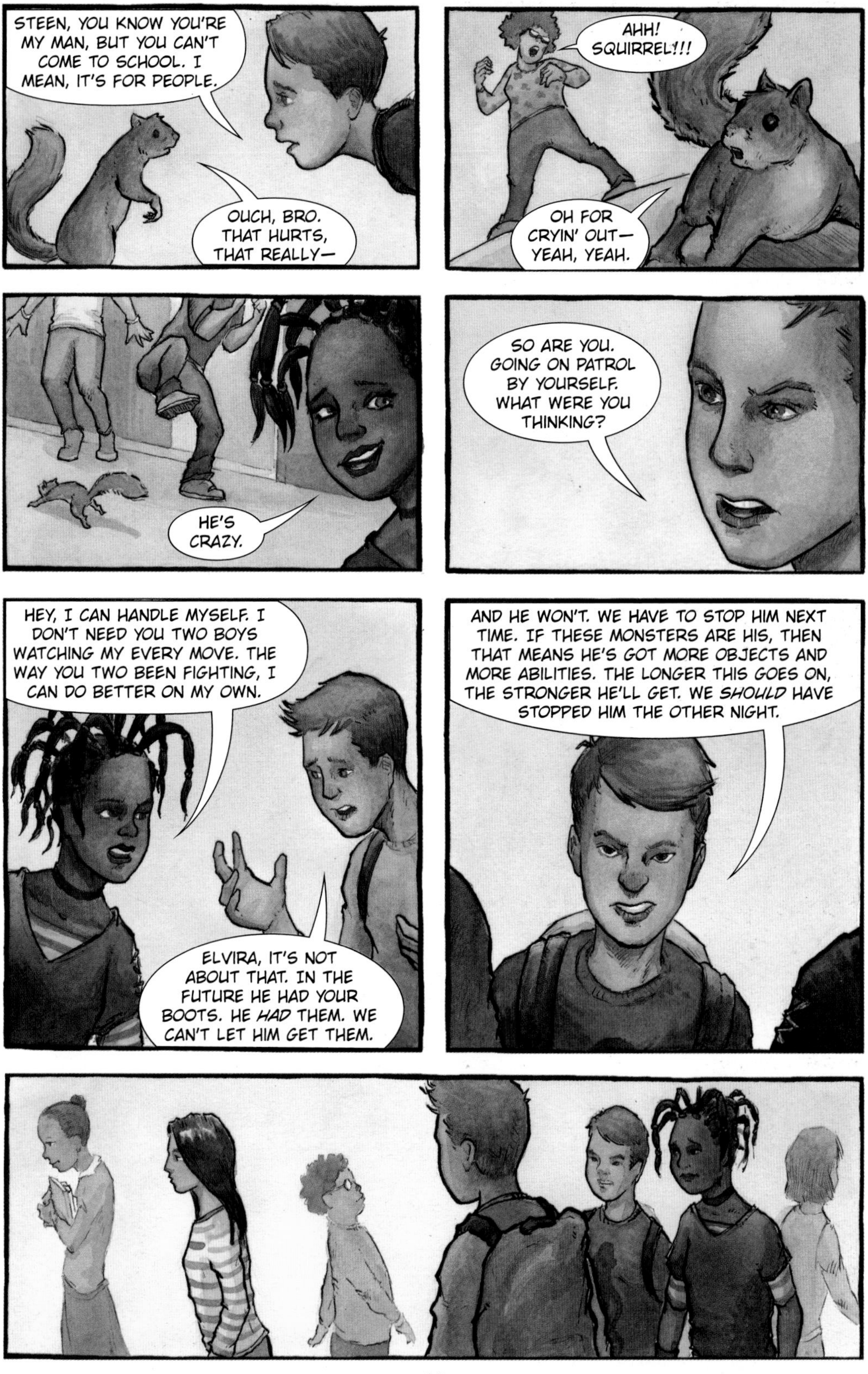
STEEN, YOU KNOW YOU'RE MY MAN, BUT YOU CAN'T COME TO SCHOOL. I MEAN, IT'S FOR PEOPLE.
OUCH, BRO. THAT HURTS, THAT REALLY—
AHH! SQUIRREL!!!
OH FOR CRYIN' OUT— YEAH, YEAH.
HE'S CRAZY.
SO ARE YOU. GOING ON PATROL BY YOURSELF. WHAT WERE YOU THINKING?
HEY, I CAN HANDLE MYSELF. I DON'T NEED YOU TWO BOYS WATCHING MY EVERY MOVE. THE WAY YOU TWO BEEN FIGHTING, I CAN DO BETTER ON MY OWN.
ELVIRA, IT'S NOT ABOUT THAT. IN THE FUTURE HE HAD YOUR BOOTS. HE *HAD* THEM. WE CAN'T LET HIM GET THEM.
AND HE WON'T. WE HAVE TO STOP HIM NEXT TIME. IF THESE MONSTERS ARE HIS, THEN THAT MEANS HE'S GOT MORE OBJECTS AND MORE ABILITIES. THE LONGER THIS GOES ON, THE STRONGER HE'LL GET. WE *SHOULD* HAVE STOPPED HIM THE OTHER NIGHT.

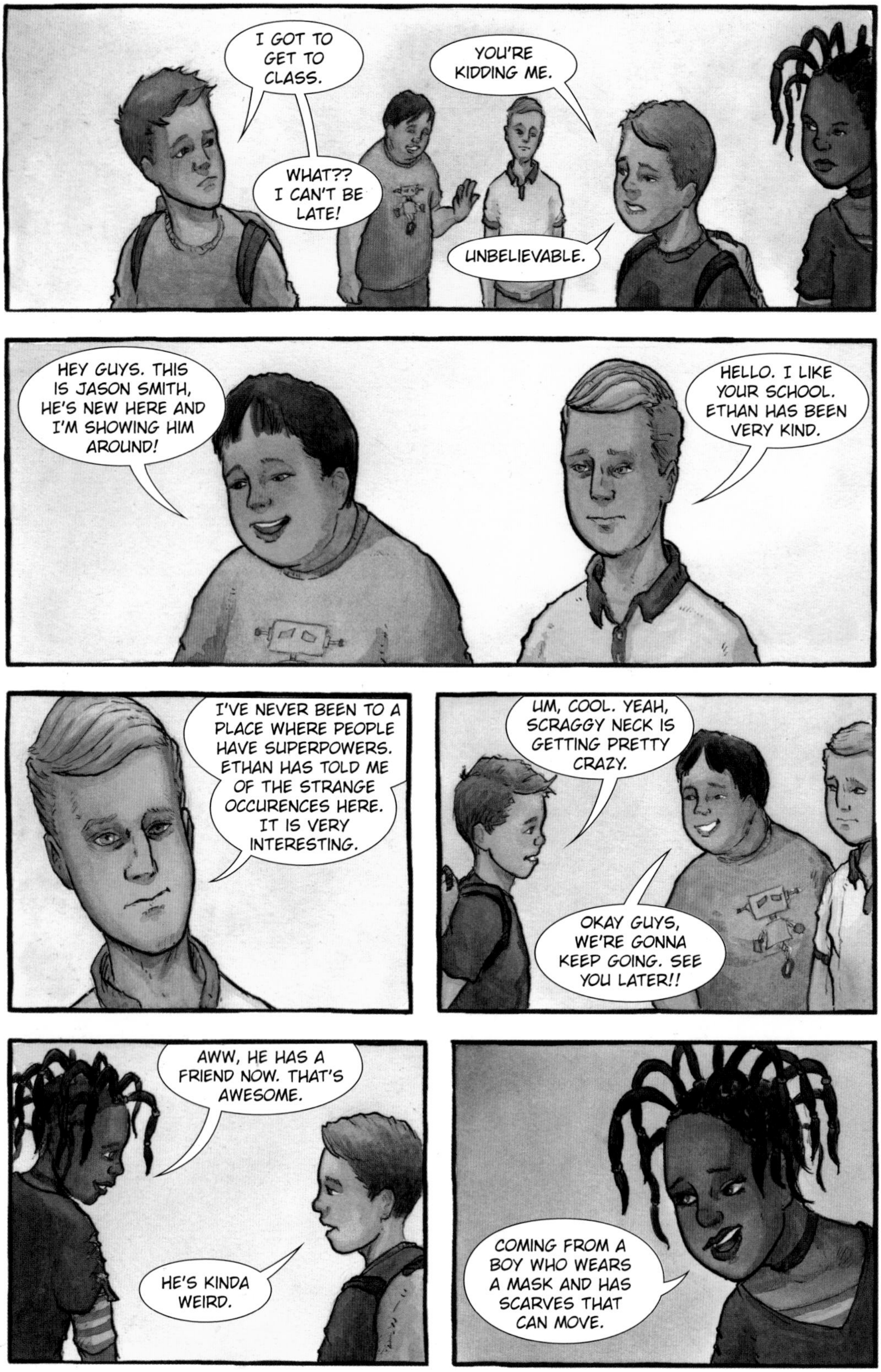
I GOT TO GET TO CLASS.
WHAT?? I CAN'T BE LATE!
YOU'RE KIDDING ME.
UNBELIEVABLE.
HEY GUYS. THIS IS JASON SMITH, HE'S NEW HERE AND I'M SHOWING HIM AROUND!
HELLO. I LIKE YOUR SCHOOL. ETHAN HAS BEEN VERY KIND.
I'VE NEVER BEEN TO A PLACE WHERE PEOPLE HAVE SUPERPOWERS. ETHAN HAS TOLD ME OF THE STRANGE OCCURENCES HERE. IT IS VERY INTERESTING.
UM, COOL. YEAH, SCRAGGY NECK IS GETTING PRETTY CRAZY.
OKAY GUYS, WE'RE GONNA KEEP GOING. SEE YOU LATER!!
AWW, HE HAS A FRIEND NOW. THAT'S AWESOME.
HE'S KINDA WEIRD.
COMING FROM A BOY WHO WEARS A MASK AND HAS SCARVES THAT CAN MOVE.

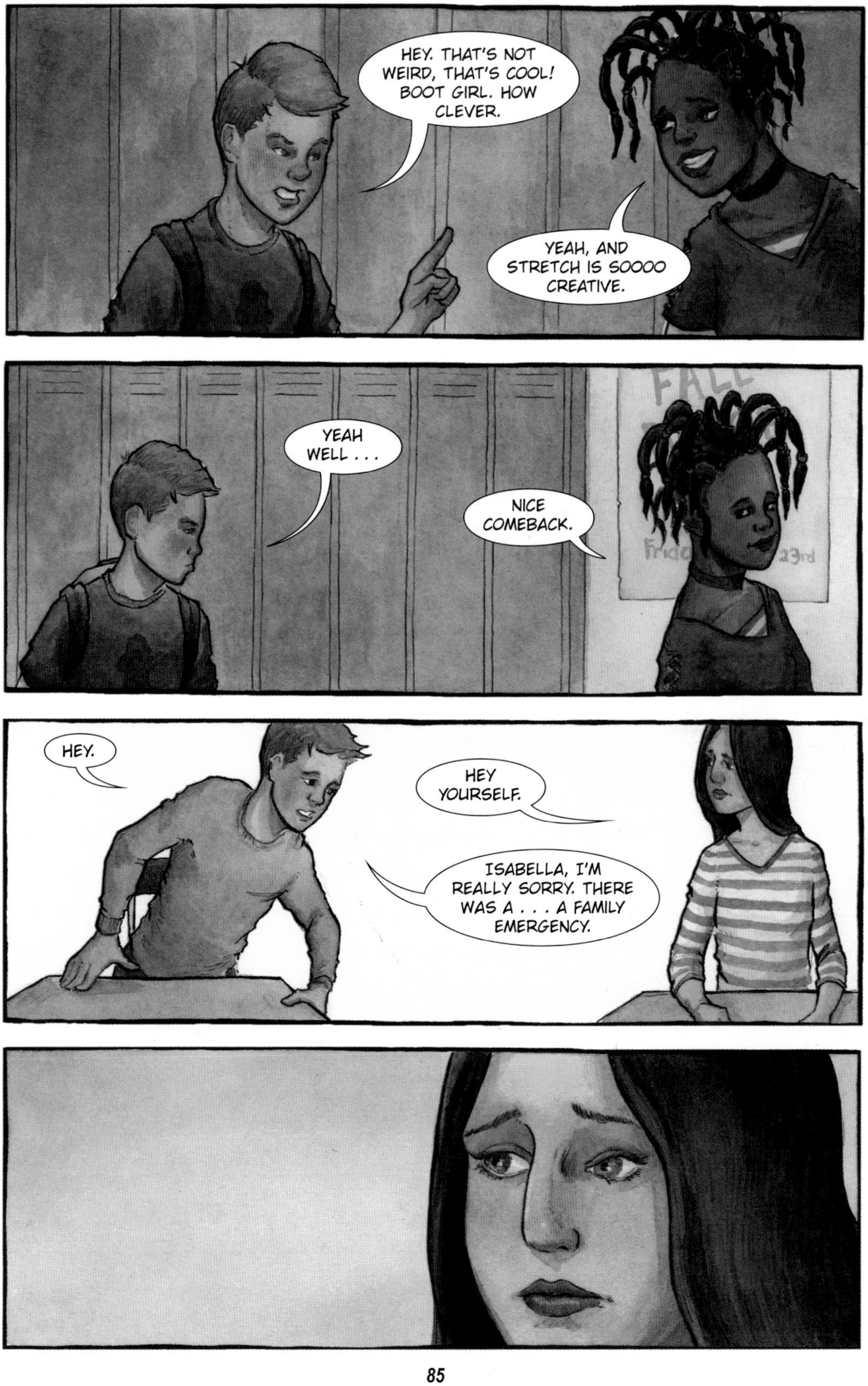
HEY. THAT'S NOT WEIRD, THAT'S COOL! BOOT GIRL. HOW CLEVER.
YEAH, AND STRETCH IS SOOOO CREATIVE.
YEAH WELL . . .
NICE COMEBACK.
23rd
HEY.
HEY YOURSELF.
ISABELLA, I'M REALLY SORRY. THERE WAS A . . . A FAMILY EMERGENCY.

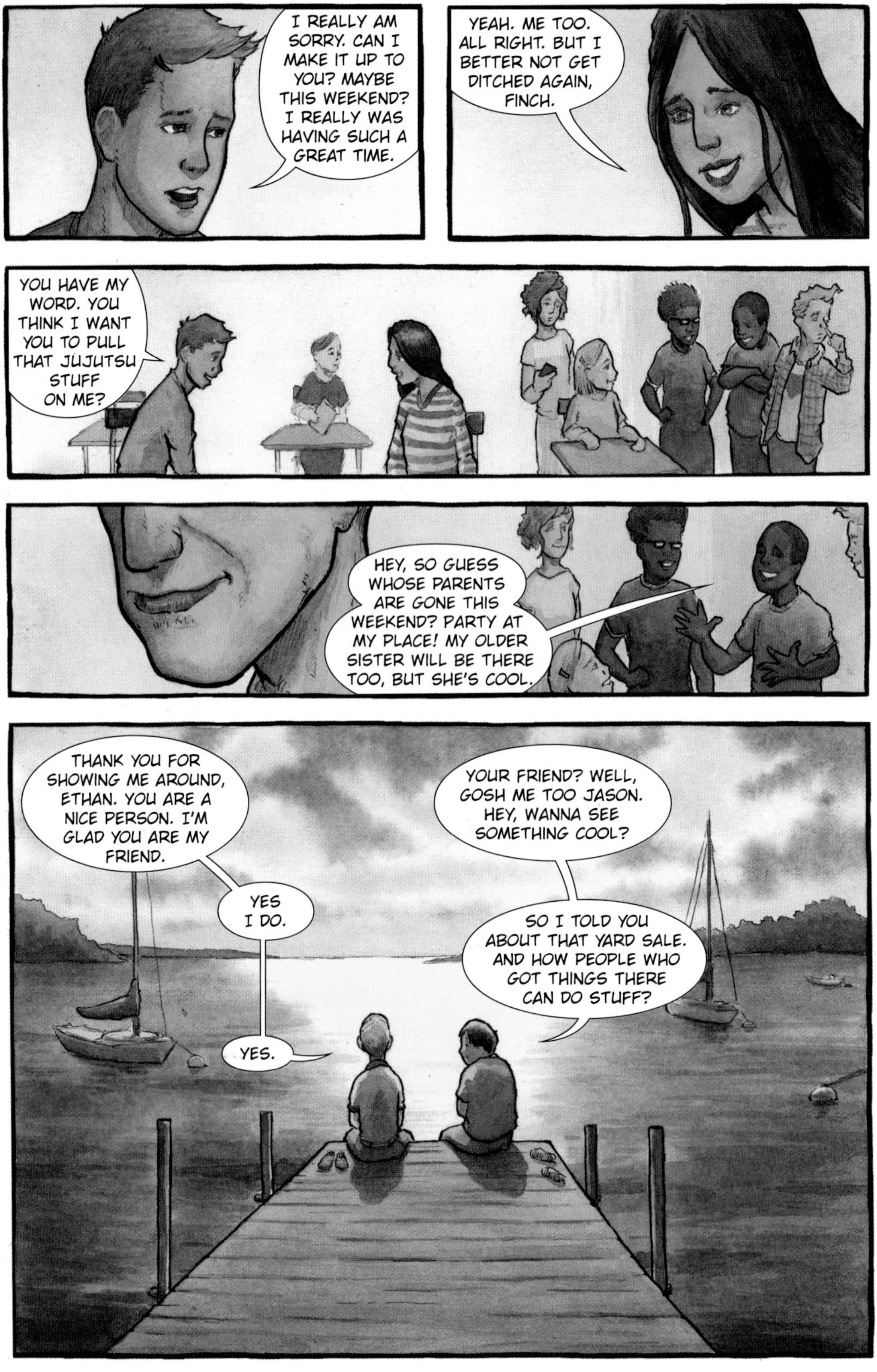
I REALLY AM SORRY. CAN I MAKE IT UP TO YOU? MAYBE THIS WEEKEND? I REALLY WAS HAVING SUCH A GREAT TIME.
YEAH. ME TOO. ALL RIGHT. BUT I BETTER NOT GET DITCHED AGAIN, FINCH.
YOU HAVE MY WORD. YOU THINK I WANT YOU TO PULL THAT JUJUTSU STUFF ON ME?
HEY, SO GUESS WHOSE PARENTS ARE GONE THIS WEEKEND? PARTY AT MY PLACE! MY OLDER SISTER WILL BE THERE TOO, BUT SHE'S COOL.
THANK YOU FOR SHOWING ME AROUND, ETHAN. YOU ARE A NICE PERSON. I'M GLAD YOU ARE MY FRIEND.
YOUR FRIEND? WELL, GOSH ME TOO JASON. HEY, WANNA SEE SOMETHING COOL?
YES I DO.
SO I TOLD YOU ABOUT THAT YARD SALE. AND HOW PEOPLE WHO GOT THINGS THERE CAN DO STUFF?
YES.

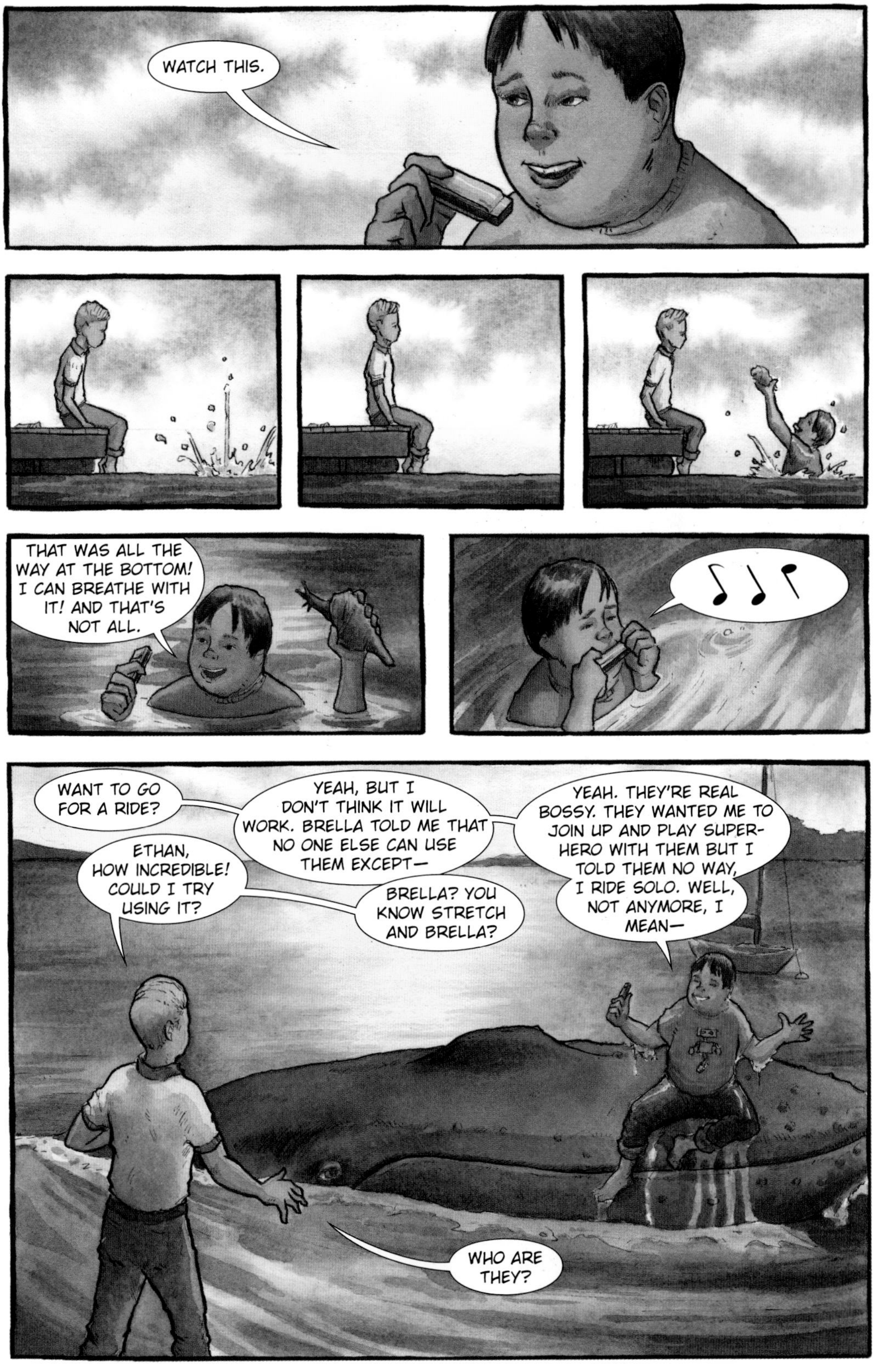
WATCH THIS.
THAT WAS ALL THE WAY AT THE BOTTOM! I CAN BREATHE WITH IT! AND THAT'S NOT ALL.
WANT TO GO FOR A RIDE?
ETHAN, HOW INCREDIBLE! COULD I TRY USING IT?
YEAH, BUT I DON'T THINK IT WILL WORK. BRELLA TOLD ME THAT NO ONE ELSE CAN USE THEM EXCEPT—
BRELLA? YOU KNOW STRETCH AND BRELLA?
YEAH. THEY'RE REAL BOSSY. THEY WANTED ME TO JOIN UP AND PLAY SUPER-HERO WITH THEM BUT I TOLD THEM NO WAY, I RIDE SOLO. WELL, NOT ANYMORE, I MEAN—
WHO ARE THEY?

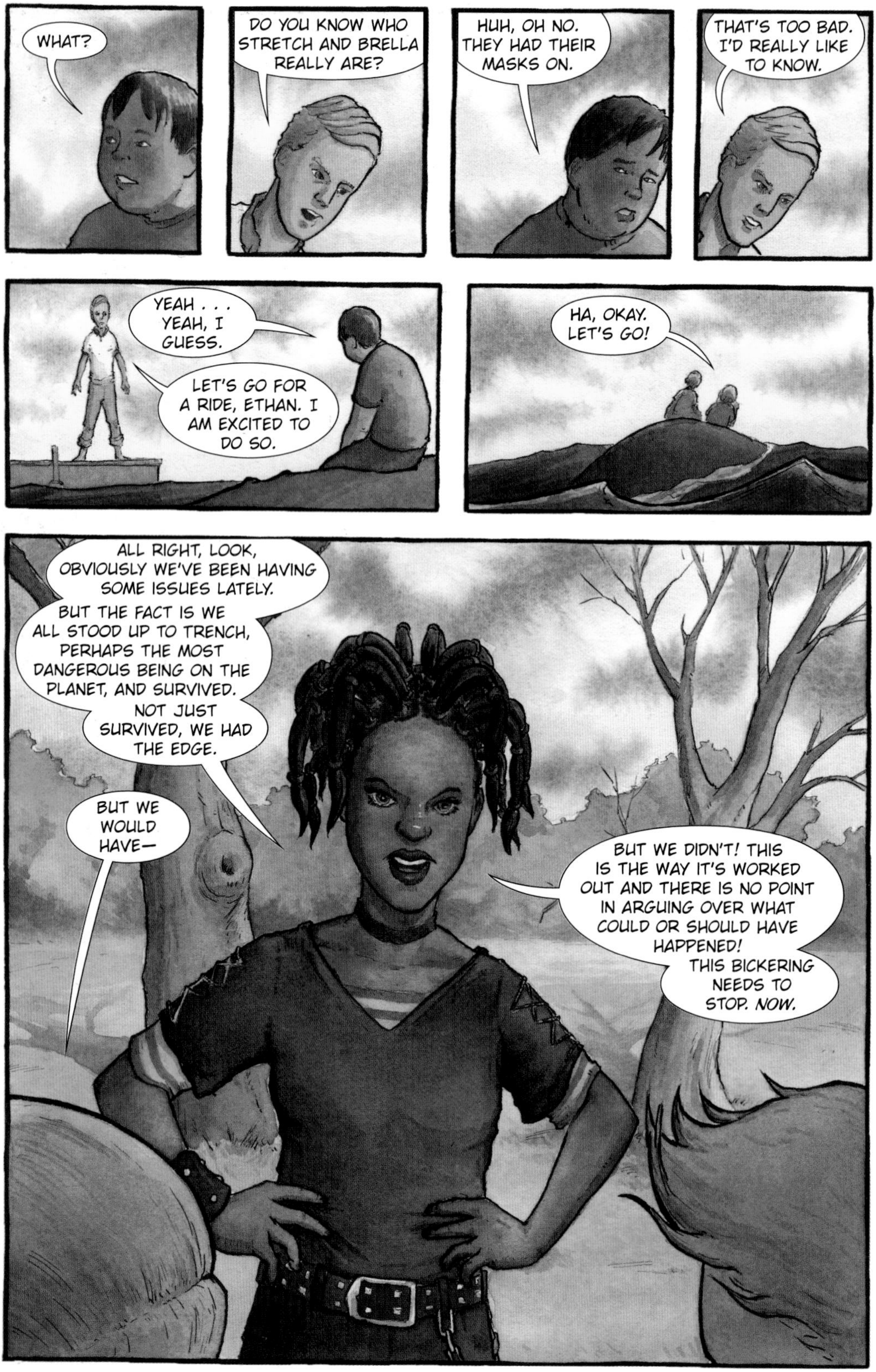
WHAT?
DO YOU KNOW WHO STRETCH AND BRELLA REALLY ARE?
HUH, OH NO. THEY HAD THEIR MASKS ON.
THAT'S TOO BAD. I'D REALLY LIKE TO KNOW.
YEAH . . . YEAH, I GUESS.
LET'S GO FOR A RIDE, ETHAN. I AM EXCITED TO DO SO.
HA, OKAY. LET'S GO!
ALL RIGHT, LOOK, OBVIOUSLY WE'VE BEEN HAVING SOME ISSUES LATELY.
BUT THE FACT IS WE ALL STOOD UP TO TRENCH, PERHAPS THE MOST DANGEROUS BEING ON THE PLANET, AND SURVIVED.
NOT JUST SURVIVED, WE HAD THE EDGE.
BUT WE WOULD HAVE—
BUT WE DIDN'T! THIS IS THE WAY IT'S WORKED OUT AND THERE IS NO POINT IN ARGUING OVER WHAT COULD OR SHOULD HAVE HAPPENED!
THIS BICKERING NEEDS TO STOP. NOW.

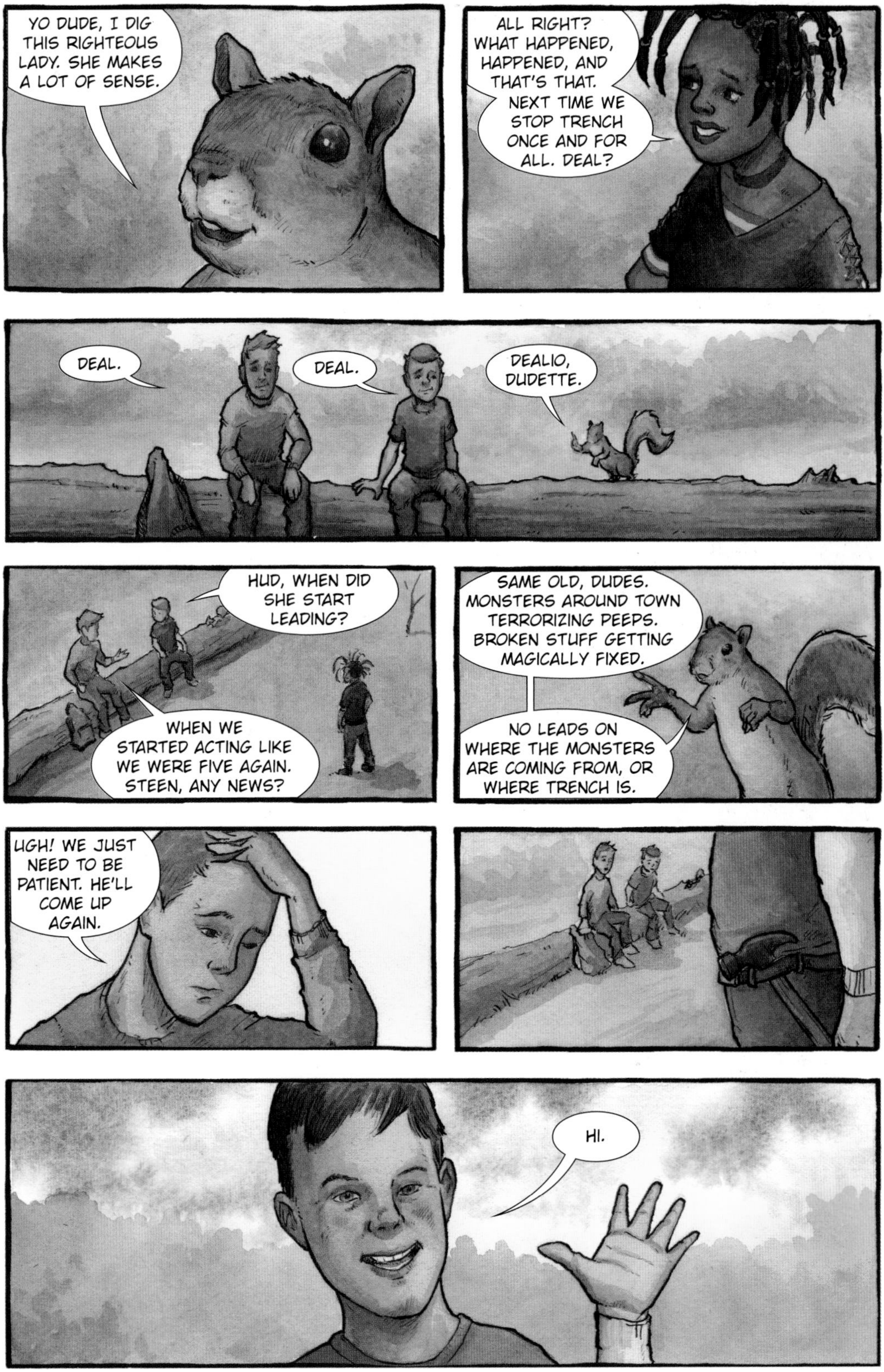
YO DUDE, I DIG THIS RIGHTEOUS LADY. SHE MAKES A LOT OF SENSE.
ALL RIGHT? WHAT HAPPENED, HAPPENED, AND THAT'S THAT.
NEXT TIME WE STOP TRENCH ONCE AND FOR ALL. DEAL?
DEAL.
DEAL.
DEALIO, DUDETTE.
HUD, WHEN DID SHE START LEADING?
WHEN WE STARTED ACTING LIKE WE WERE FIVE AGAIN. STEEN, ANY NEWS?
SAME OLD, DUDES. MONSTERS AROUND TOWN TERRORIZING PEEPS. BROKEN STUFF GETTING MAGICALLY FIXED.
NO LEADS ON WHERE THE MONSTERS ARE COMING FROM, OR WHERE TRENCH IS.
UGH! WE JUST NEED TO BE PATIENT. HE'LL COME UP AGAIN.
HI.

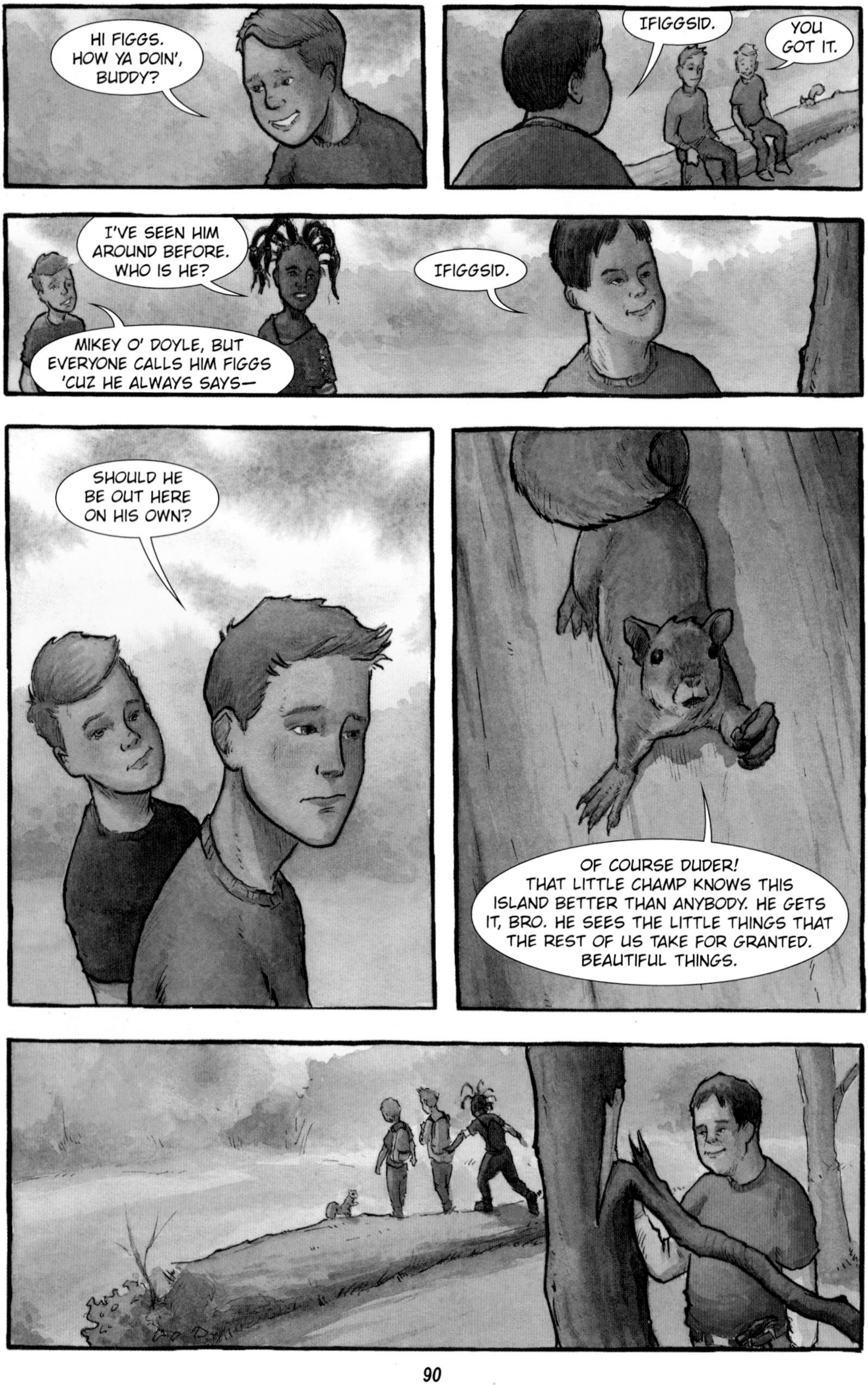
HI FIGGS. HOW YA DOIN', BUDDY?
IFIGGSID.
YOU GOT IT.
I'VE SEEN HIM AROUND BEFORE. WHO IS HE?
MIKEY O' DOYLE, BUT EVERYONE CALLS HIM FIGGS 'CUZ HE ALWAYS SAYS—
IFIGGSID.
SHOULD HE BE OUT HERE ON HIS OWN?
OF COURSE DUDER! THAT LITTLE CHAMP KNOWS THIS ISLAND BETTER THAN ANYBODY. HE GETS IT, BRO. HE SEES THE LITTLE THINGS THAT THE REST OF US TAKE FOR GRANTED. BEAUTIFUL THINGS.

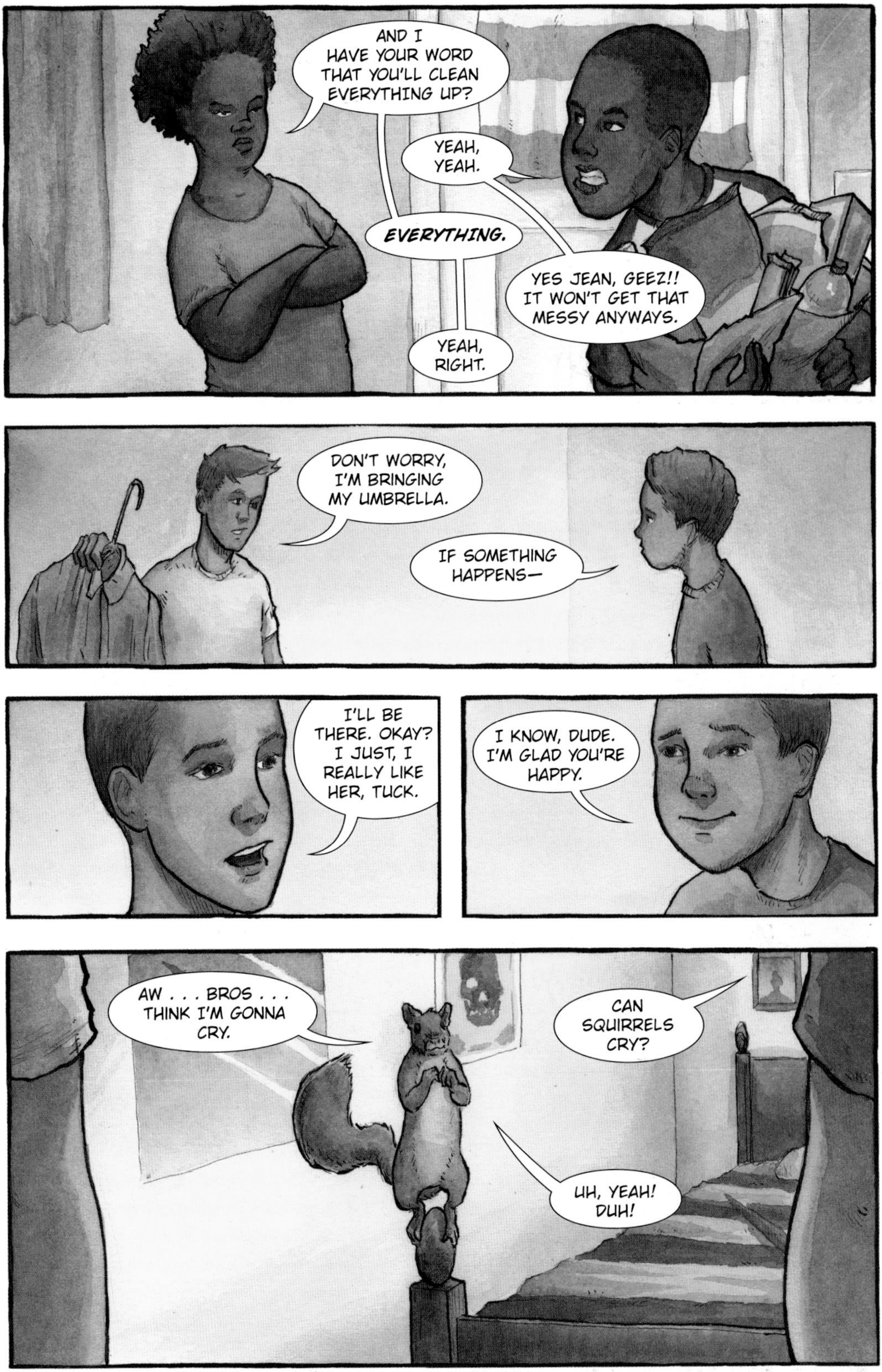
AND I HAVE YOUR WORD THAT YOU'LL CLEAN EVERYTHING UP?
YEAH, YEAH.
EVERYTHING.
YES JEAN, GEEZ!! IT WON'T GET THAT MESSY ANYWAYS.
YEAH, RIGHT.
DON'T WORRY, I'M BRINGING MY UMBRELLA.
IF SOMETHING HAPPENS—
I'LL BE THERE. OKAY? I JUST, I REALLY LIKE HER, TUCK.
I KNOW, DUDE. I'M GLAD YOU'RE HAPPY.
AW . . . BROS . . . THINK I'M GONNA CRY.
CAN SQUIRRELS CRY?
UH, YEAH! DUH!

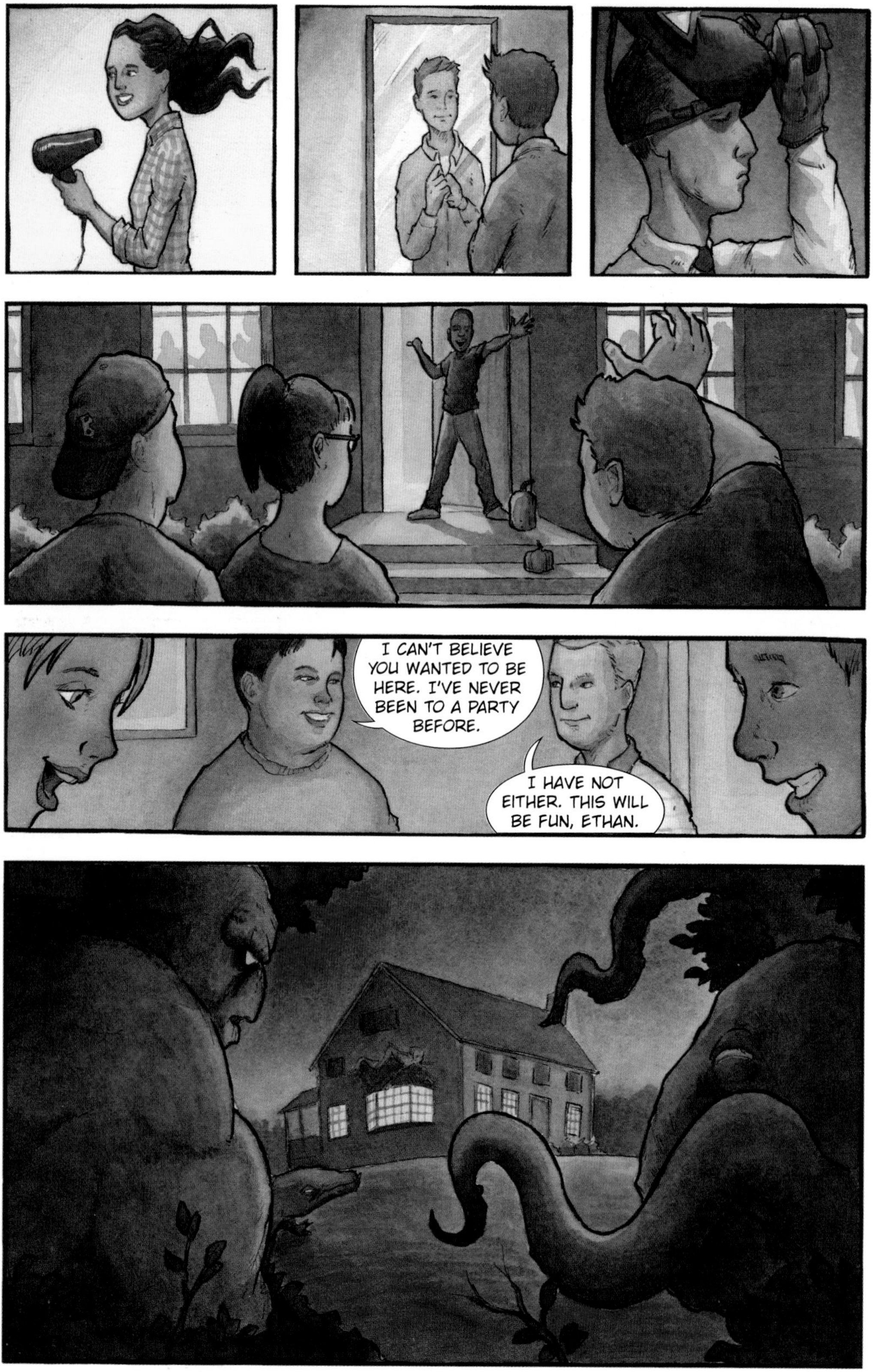
I CAN'T BELIEVE YOU WANTED TO BE HERE. I'VE NEVER BEEN TO A PARTY BEFORE.
I HAVE NOT EITHER. THIS WILL BE FUN, ETHAN.

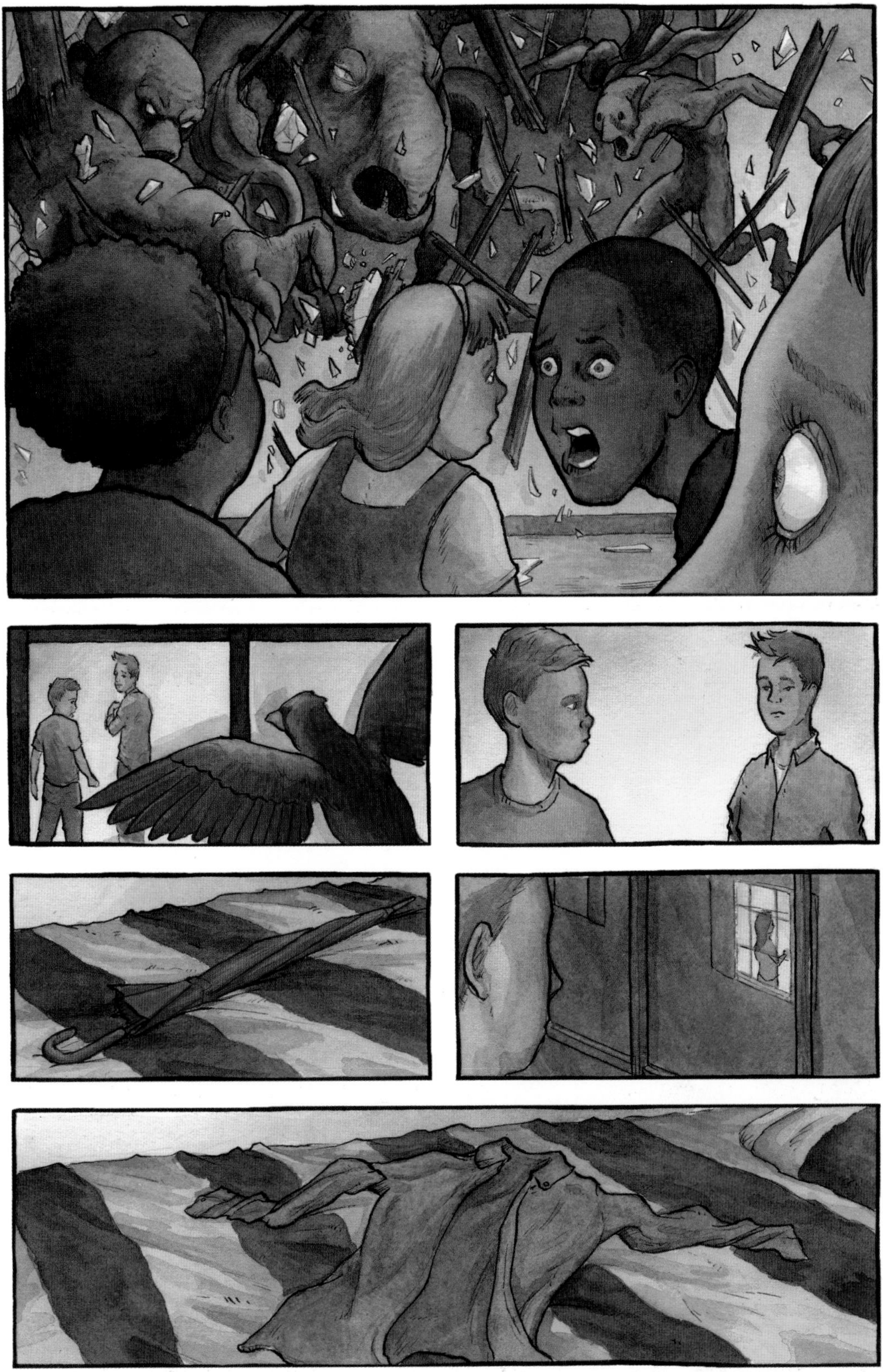

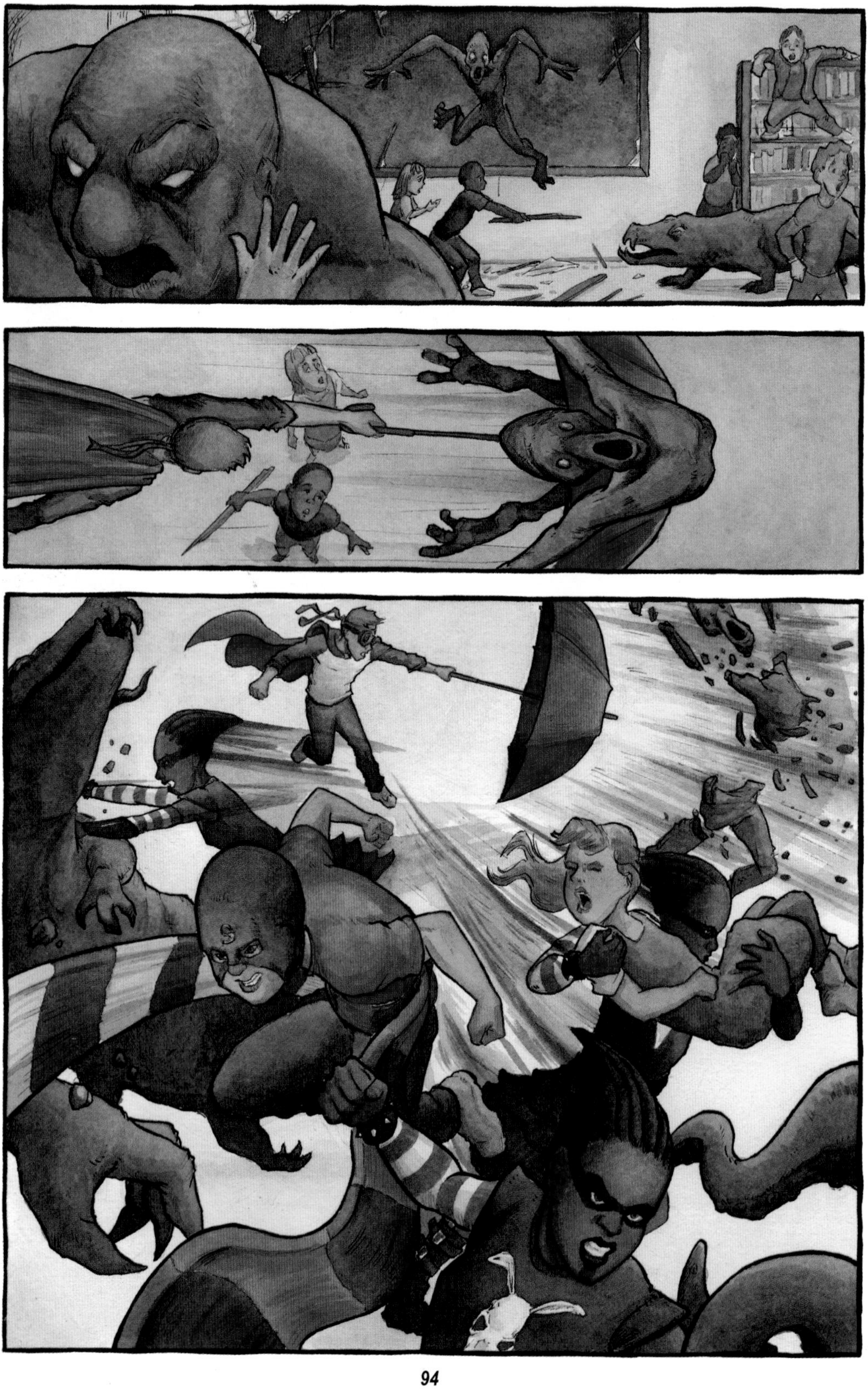

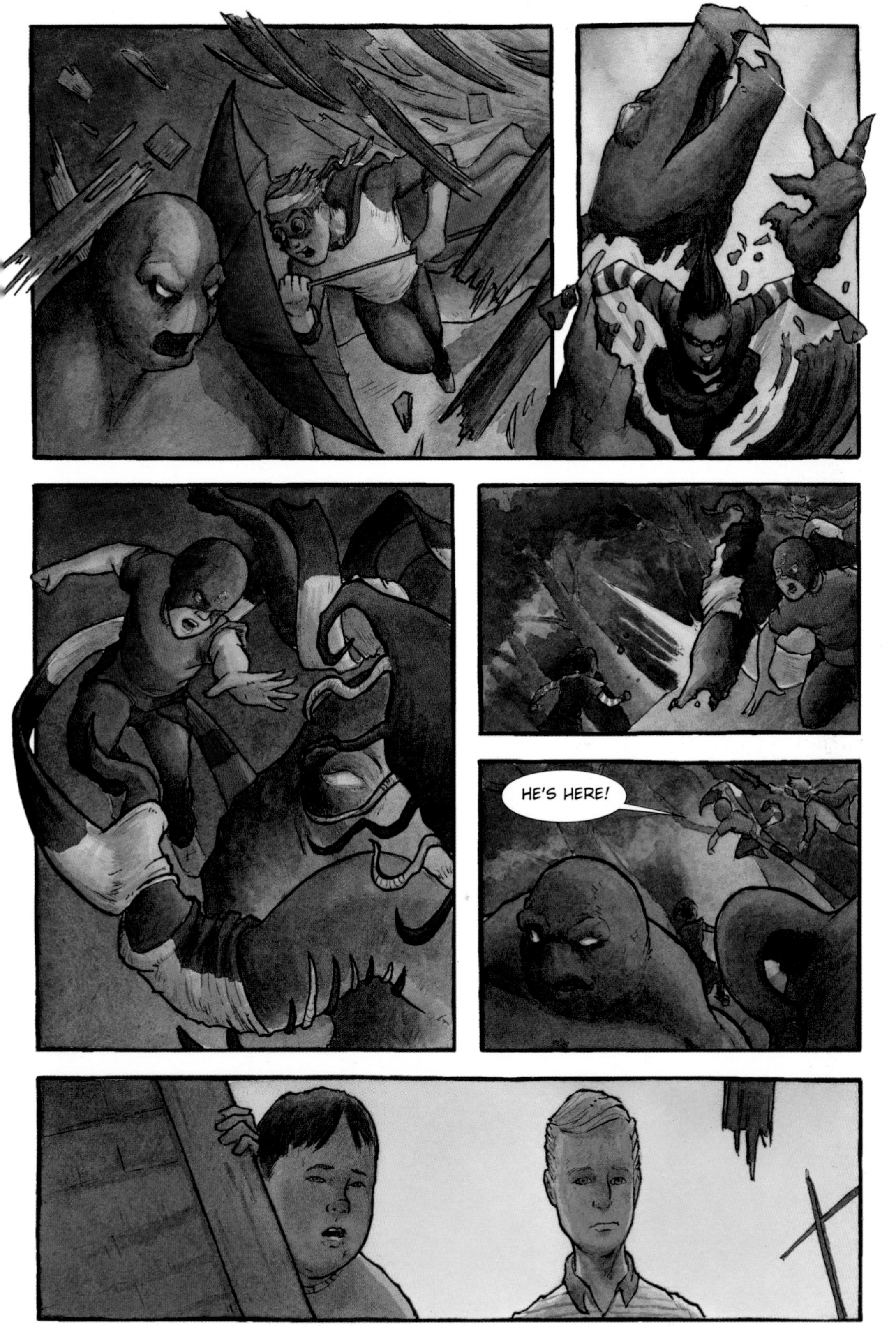
HE'S HERE!

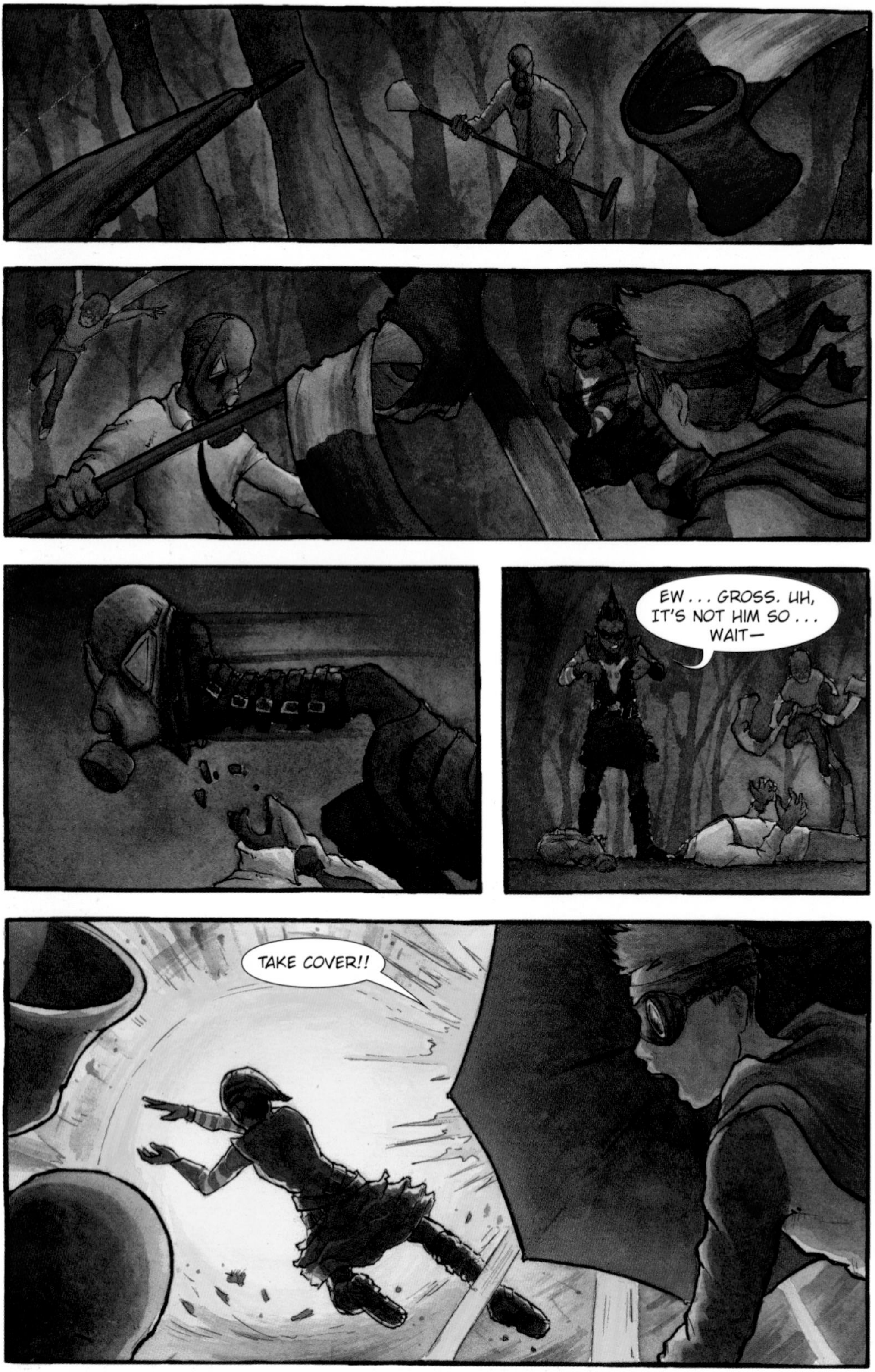
EW . . . GROSS. UH, IT'S NOT HIM SO . . . WAIT—
TAKE COVER!!

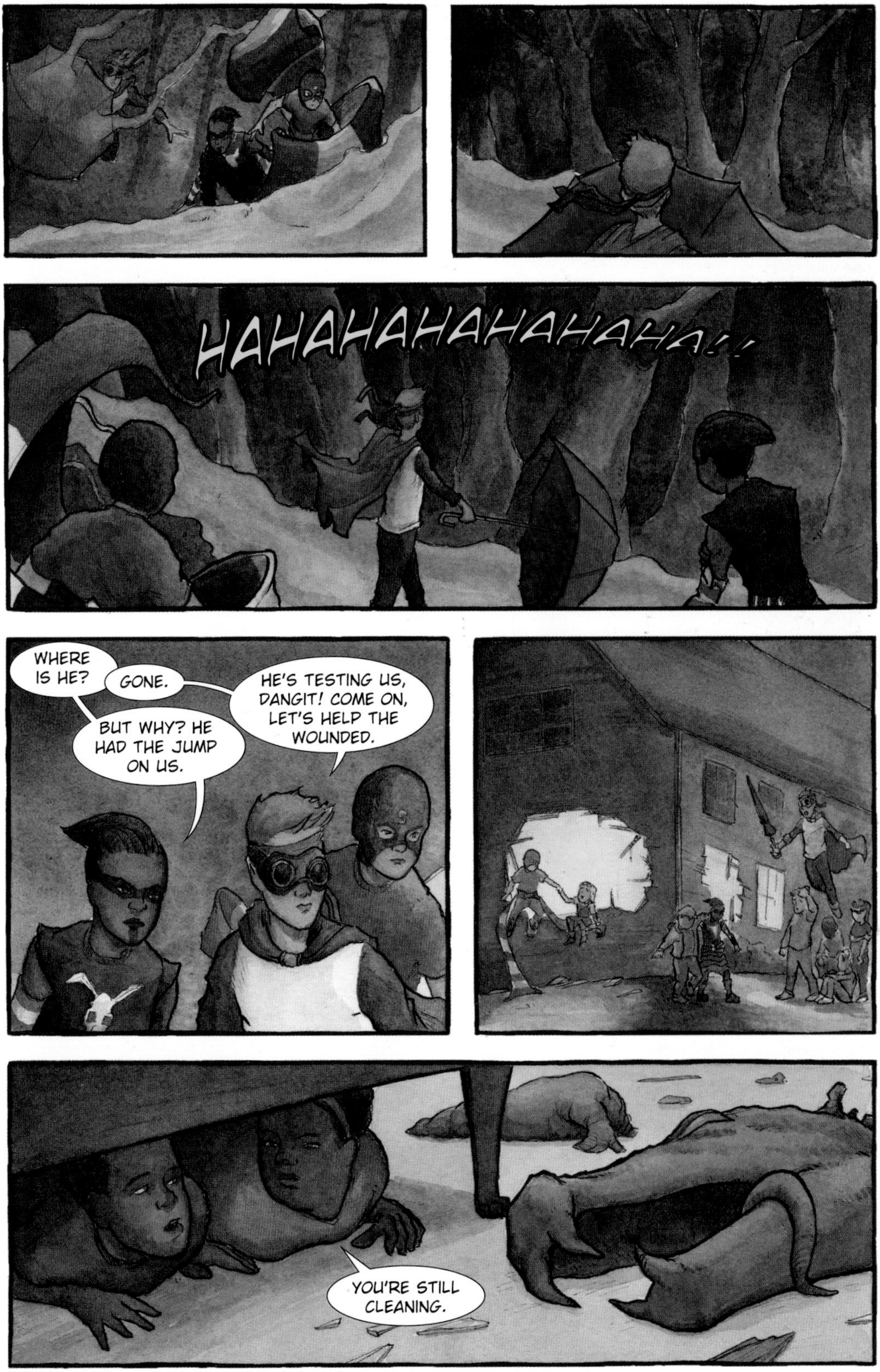
HAHAHAHAHAHAHAHA!!
WHERE IS HE?
GONE.
BUT WHY? HE HAD THE JUMP ON US.
HE'S TESTING US, DANGIT! COME ON, LET'S HELP THE WOUNDED.
YOU'RE STILL CLEANING.

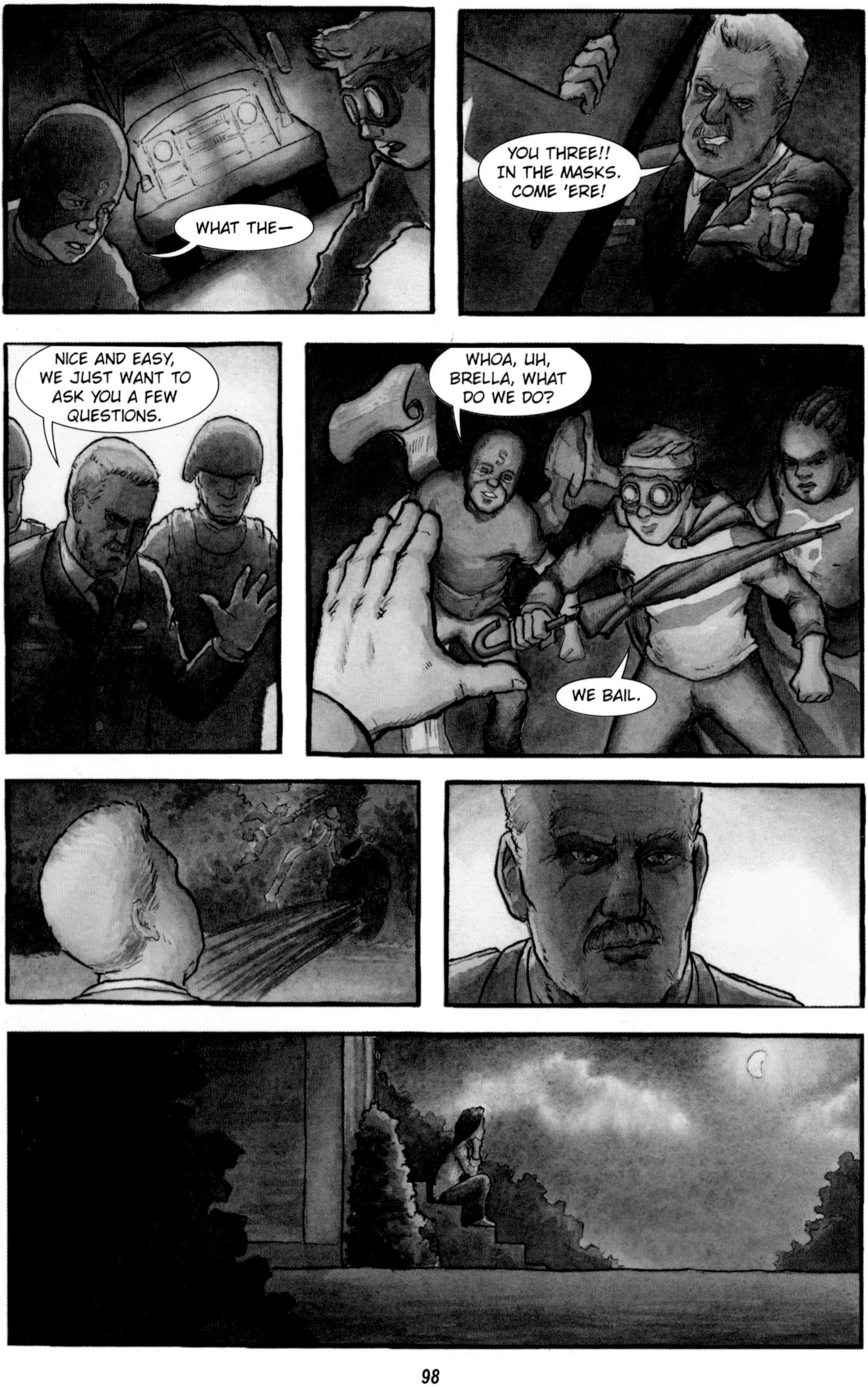
WHAT THE—
YOU THREE!! IN THE MASKS. COME 'ERE!
NICE AND EASY, WE JUST WANT TO ASK YOU A FEW QUESTIONS.
WHOA, UH, BRELLA, WHAT DO WE DO?
WE BAIL.

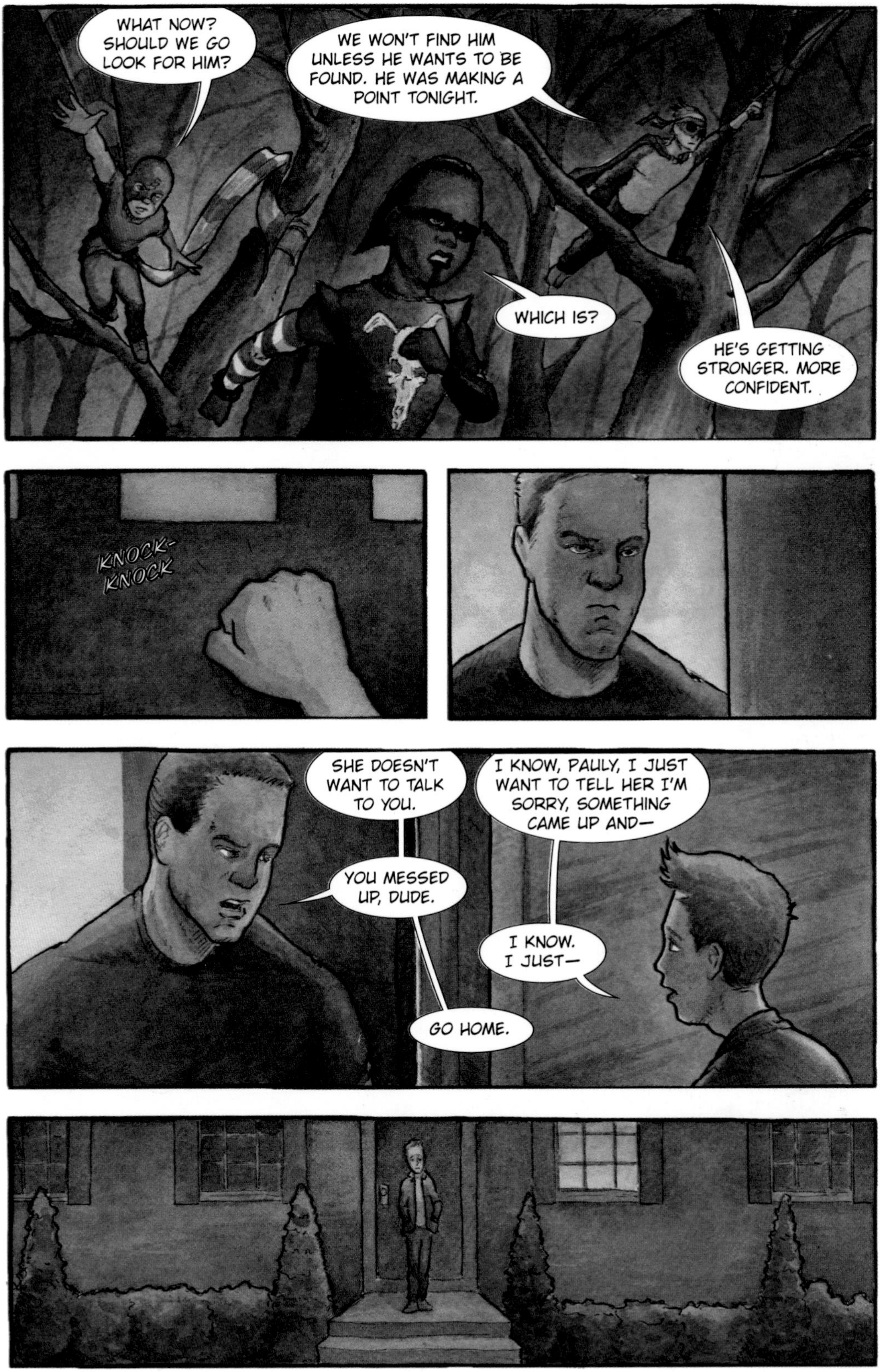
WHAT NOW? SHOULD WE GO LOOK FOR HIM?
WE WON'T FIND HIM UNLESS HE WANTS TO BE FOUND. HE WAS MAKING A POINT TONIGHT.
WHICH IS?
HE'S GETTING STRONGER. MORE CONFIDENT.
KNOCK-KNOCK
SHE DOESN'T WANT TO TALK TO YOU.
YOU MESSED UP, DUDE.
GO HOME.
I KNOW, PAULY, I JUST WANT TO TELL HER I'M SORRY, SOMETHING CAME UP AND—
I KNOW. I JUST—

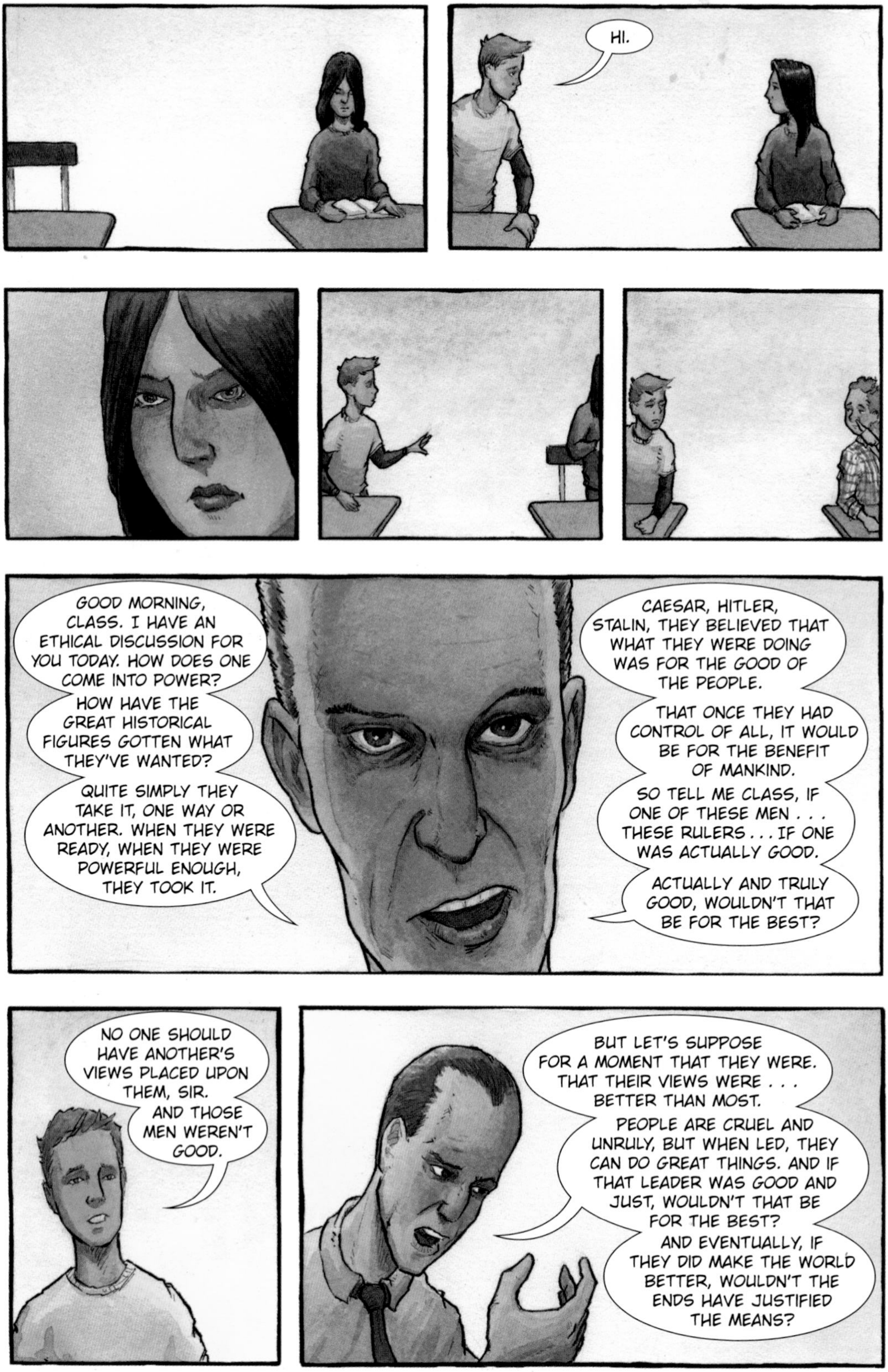
HI.
GOOD MORNING, CLASS. I HAVE AN ETHICAL DISCUSSION FOR YOU TODAY. HOW DOES ONE COME INTO POWER?
HOW HAVE THE GREAT HISTORICAL FIGURES GOTTEN WHAT THEY'VE WANTED?
QUITE SIMPLY THEY TAKE IT, ONE WAY OR ANOTHER. WHEN THEY WERE READY, WHEN THEY WERE POWERFUL ENOUGH, THEY TOOK IT.
CAESAR, HITLER, STALIN, THEY BELIEVED THAT WHAT THEY WERE DOING WAS FOR THE GOOD OF THE PEOPLE.
THAT ONCE THEY HAD CONTROL OF ALL, IT WOULD BE FOR THE BENEFIT OF MANKIND.
SO TELL ME CLASS, IF ONE OF THESE MEN . . . THESE RULERS . . . IF ONE WAS ACTUALLY GOOD.
ACTUALLY AND TRULY GOOD, WOULDN'T THAT BE FOR THE BEST?
NO ONE SHOULD HAVE ANOTHER'S VIEWS PLACED UPON THEM, SIR.
AND THOSE MEN WEREN'T GOOD.
BUT LET'S SUPPOSE FOR A MOMENT THAT THEY WERE. THAT THEIR VIEWS WERE . . . BETTER THAN MOST.
PEOPLE ARE CRUEL AND UNRULY, BUT WHEN LED, THEY CAN DO GREAT THINGS. AND IF THAT LEADER WAS GOOD AND JUST, WOULDN'T THAT BE FOR THE BEST?
AND EVENTUALLY, IF THEY DID MAKE THE WORLD BETTER, WOULDN'T THE ENDS HAVE JUSTIFIED THE MEANS?

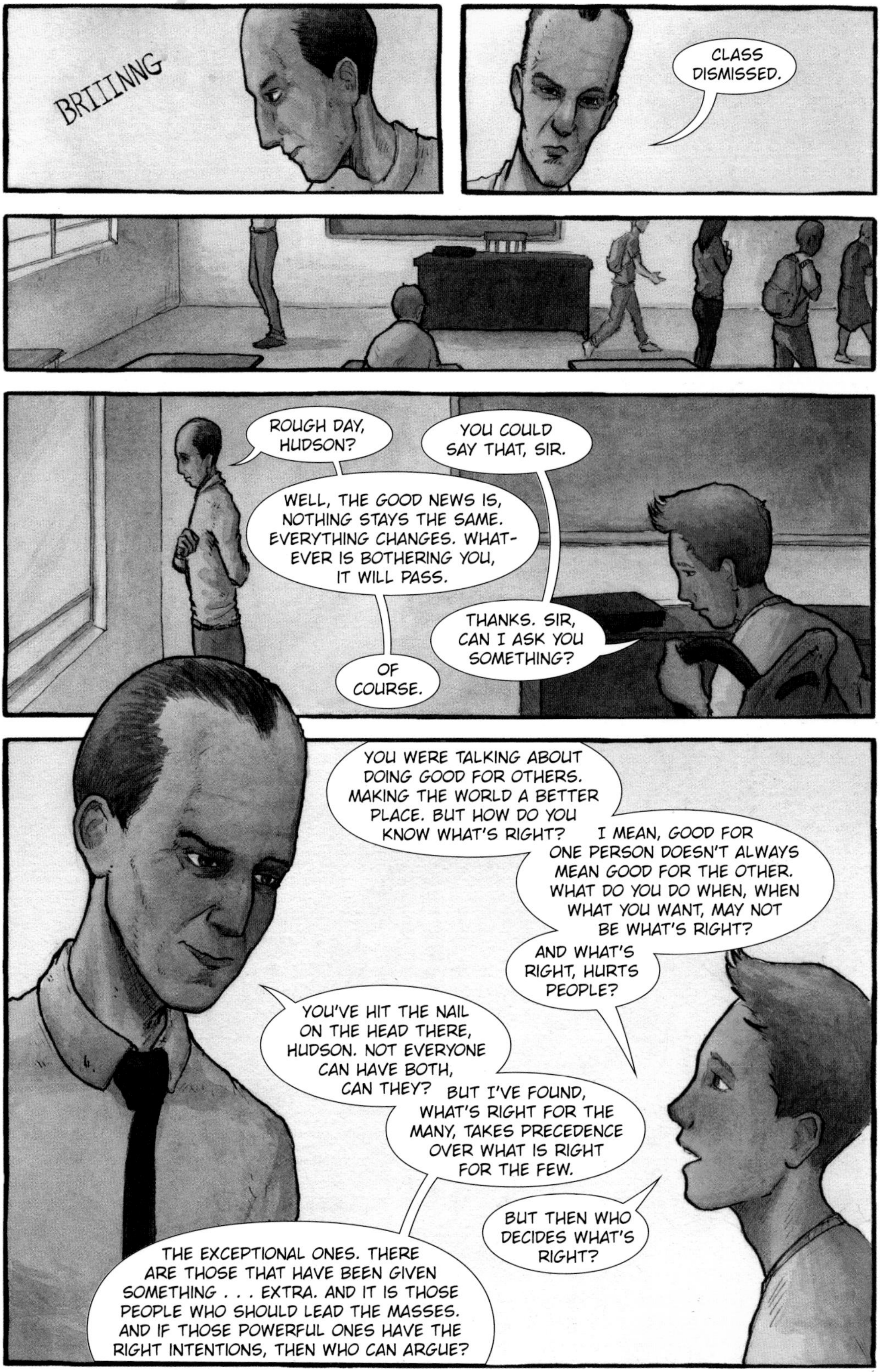
BRIIINNG
CLASS DISMISSED.
ROUGH DAY, HUDSON?
YOU COULD SAY THAT, SIR.
WELL, THE GOOD NEWS IS, NOTHING STAYS THE SAME. EVERYTHING CHANGES. WHATEVER IS BOTHERING YOU, IT WILL PASS.
THANKS. SIR, CAN I ASK YOU SOMETHING?
OF COURSE.
YOU WERE TALKING ABOUT DOING GOOD FOR OTHERS. MAKING THE WORLD A BETTER PLACE. BUT HOW DO YOU KNOW WHAT'S RIGHT?
I MEAN, GOOD FOR ONE PERSON DOESN'T ALWAYS MEAN GOOD FOR THE OTHER. WHAT DO YOU DO WHEN, WHEN WHAT YOU WANT, MAY NOT BE WHAT'S RIGHT?
AND WHAT'S RIGHT, HURTS PEOPLE?
YOU'VE HIT THE NAIL ON THE HEAD THERE, HUDSON. NOT EVERYONE CAN HAVE BOTH, CAN THEY?
BUT I'VE FOUND, WHAT'S RIGHT FOR THE MANY, TAKES PRECEDENCE OVER WHAT IS RIGHT FOR THE FEW.
BUT THEN WHO DECIDES WHAT'S RIGHT?
THE EXCEPTIONAL ONES. THERE ARE THOSE THAT HAVE BEEN GIVEN SOMETHING . . . EXTRA. AND IT IS THOSE PEOPLE WHO SHOULD LEAD THE MASSES. AND IF THOSE POWERFUL ONES HAVE THE RIGHT INTENTIONS, THEN WHO CAN ARGUE?

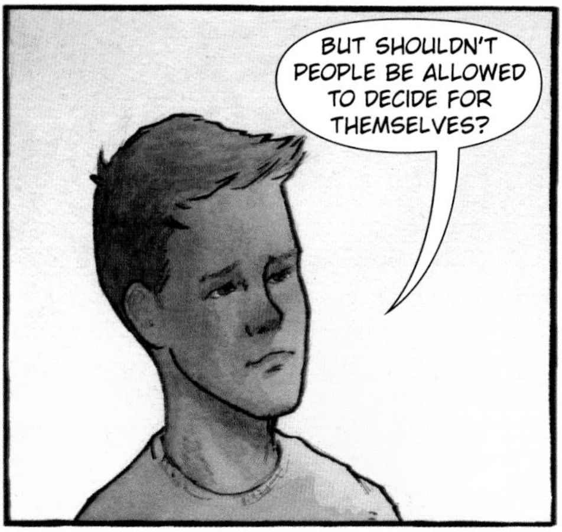
BUT SHOULDN'T PEOPLE BE ALLOWED TO DECIDE FOR THEMSELVES?

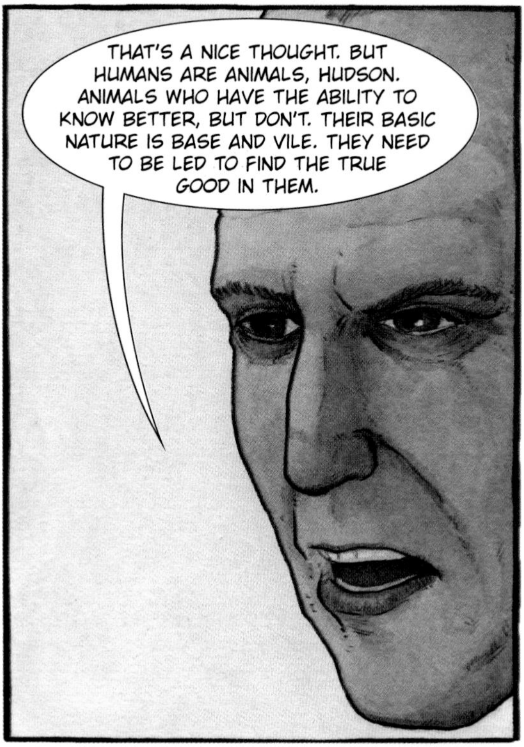
THAT'S A NICE THOUGHT. BUT HUMANS ARE ANIMALS, HUDSON. ANIMALS WHO HAVE THE ABILITY TO KNOW BETTER, BUT DON'T. THEIR BASIC NATURE IS BASE AND VILE. THEY NEED TO BE LED TO FIND THE TRUE GOOD IN THEM.

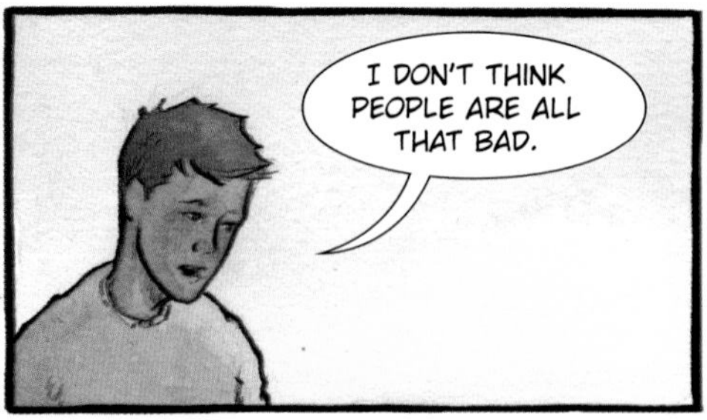
I DON'T THINK PEOPLE ARE ALL THAT BAD.

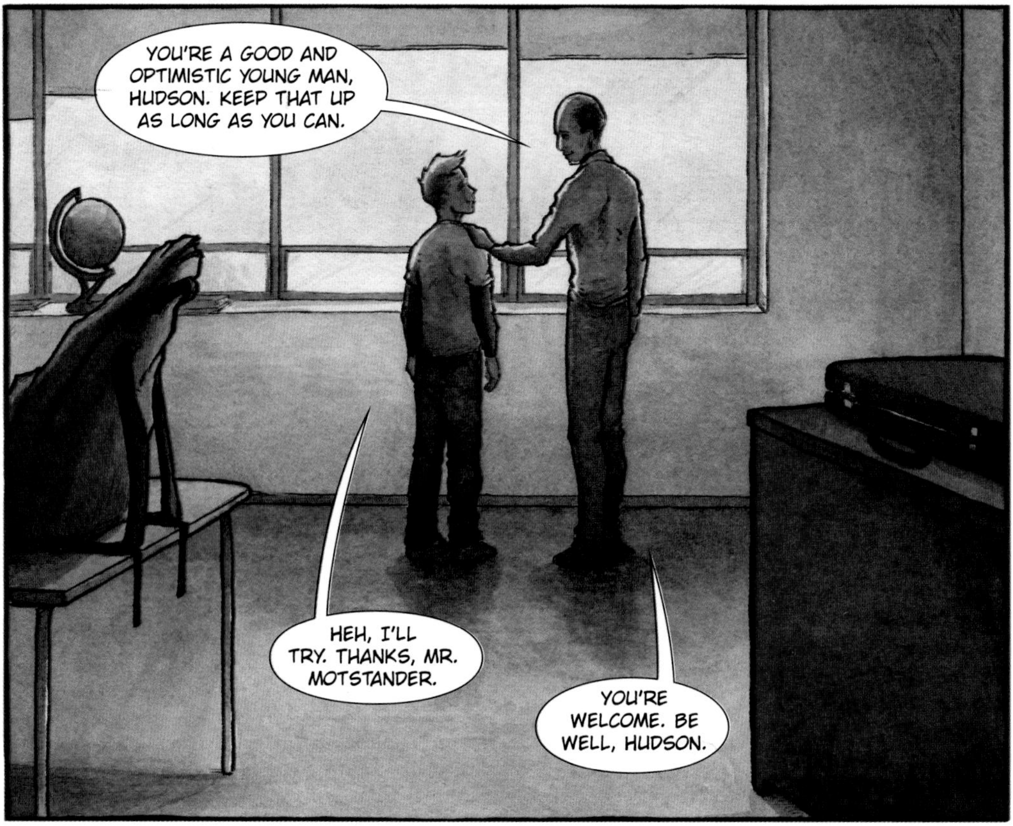
YOU'RE A GOOD AND OPTIMISTIC YOUNG MAN, HUDSON. KEEP THAT UP AS LONG AS YOU CAN.
HEH, I'LL TRY. THANKS, MR. MOTSTANDER.
YOU'RE WELCOME. BE WELL, HUDSON.

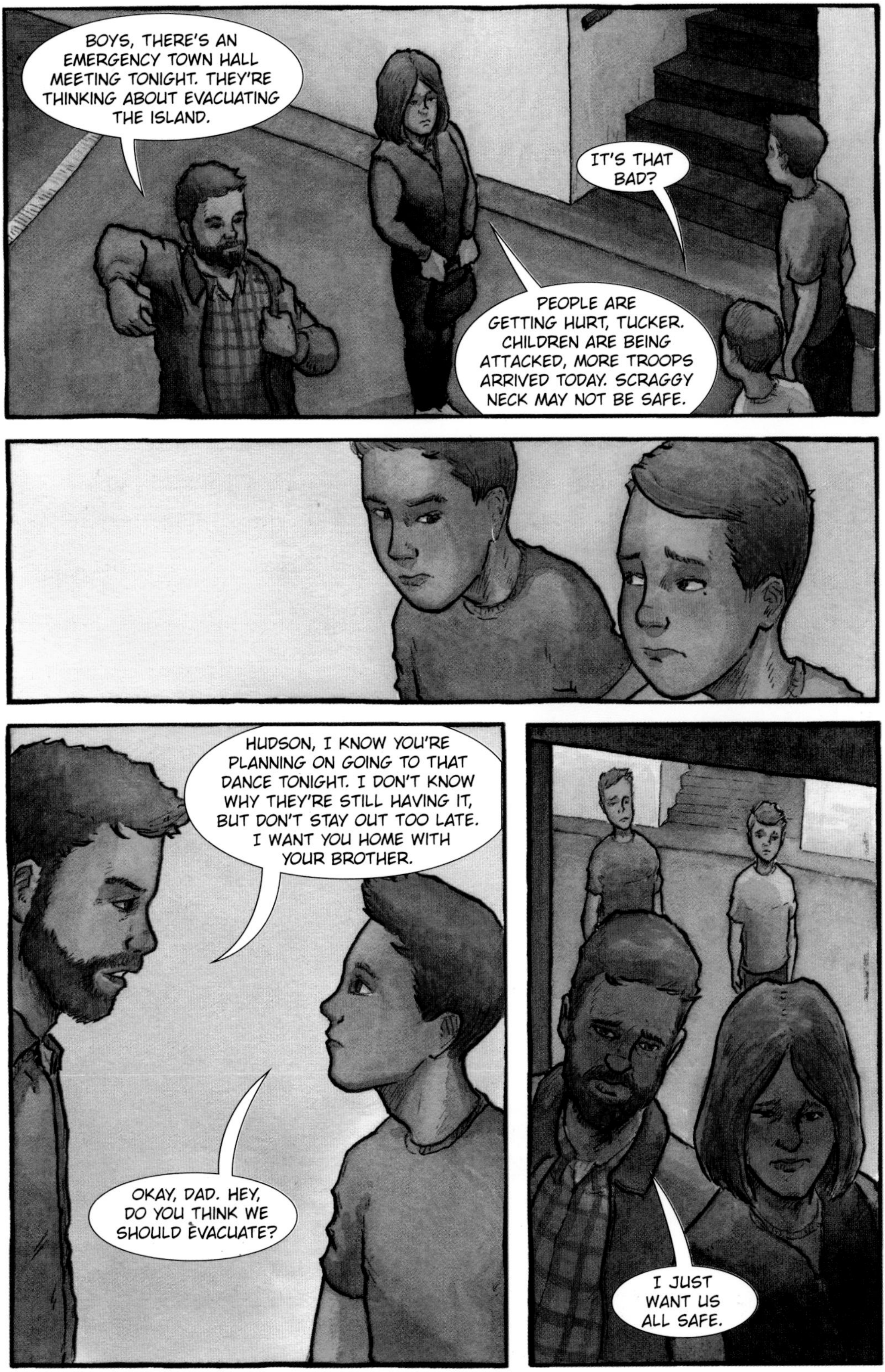
BOYS, THERE'S AN EMERGENCY TOWN HALL MEETING TONIGHT. THEY'RE THINKING ABOUT EVACUATING THE ISLAND.
IT'S THAT BAD?
PEOPLE ARE GETTING HURT, TUCKER. CHILDREN ARE BEING ATTACKED, MORE TROOPS ARRIVED TODAY. SCRAGGY NECK MAY NOT BE SAFE.
HUDSON, I KNOW YOU'RE PLANNING ON GOING TO THAT DANCE TONIGHT. I DON'T KNOW WHY THEY'RE STILL HAVING IT, BUT DON'T STAY OUT TOO LATE. I WANT YOU HOME WITH YOUR BROTHER.
OKAY, DAD. HEY, DO YOU THINK WE SHOULD EVACUATE?
I JUST WANT US ALL SAFE.

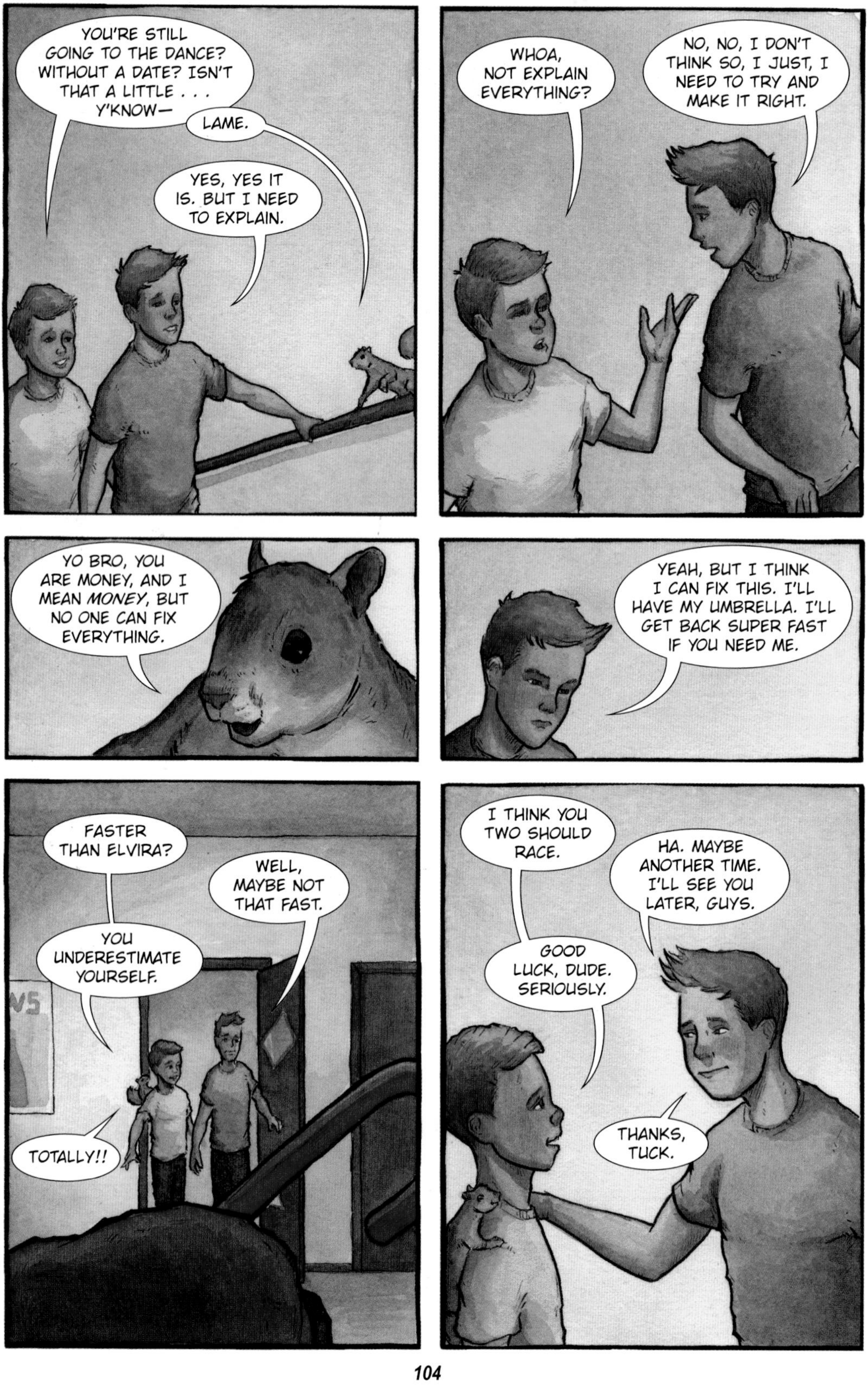
YOU'RE STILL GOING TO THE DANCE? WITHOUT A DATE? ISN'T THAT A LITTLE . . . Y'KNOW—
LAME.
YES, YES IT IS. BUT I NEED TO EXPLAIN.
WHOA, NOT EXPLAIN EVERYTHING?
NO, NO, I DON'T THINK SO, I JUST, I NEED TO TRY AND MAKE IT RIGHT.
YO BRO, YOU ARE MONEY, AND I MEAN *MONEY*, BUT NO ONE CAN FIX EVERYTHING.
YEAH, BUT I THINK I CAN FIX THIS. I'LL HAVE MY UMBRELLA. I'LL GET BACK SUPER FAST IF YOU NEED ME.
FASTER THAN ELVIRA?
WELL, MAYBE NOT THAT FAST.
YOU UNDERESTIMATE YOURSELF.
TOTALLY!!
I THINK YOU TWO SHOULD RACE.
HA. MAYBE ANOTHER TIME. I'LL SEE YOU LATER, GUYS.
GOOD LUCK, DUDE. SERIOUSLY.
THANKS, TUCK.

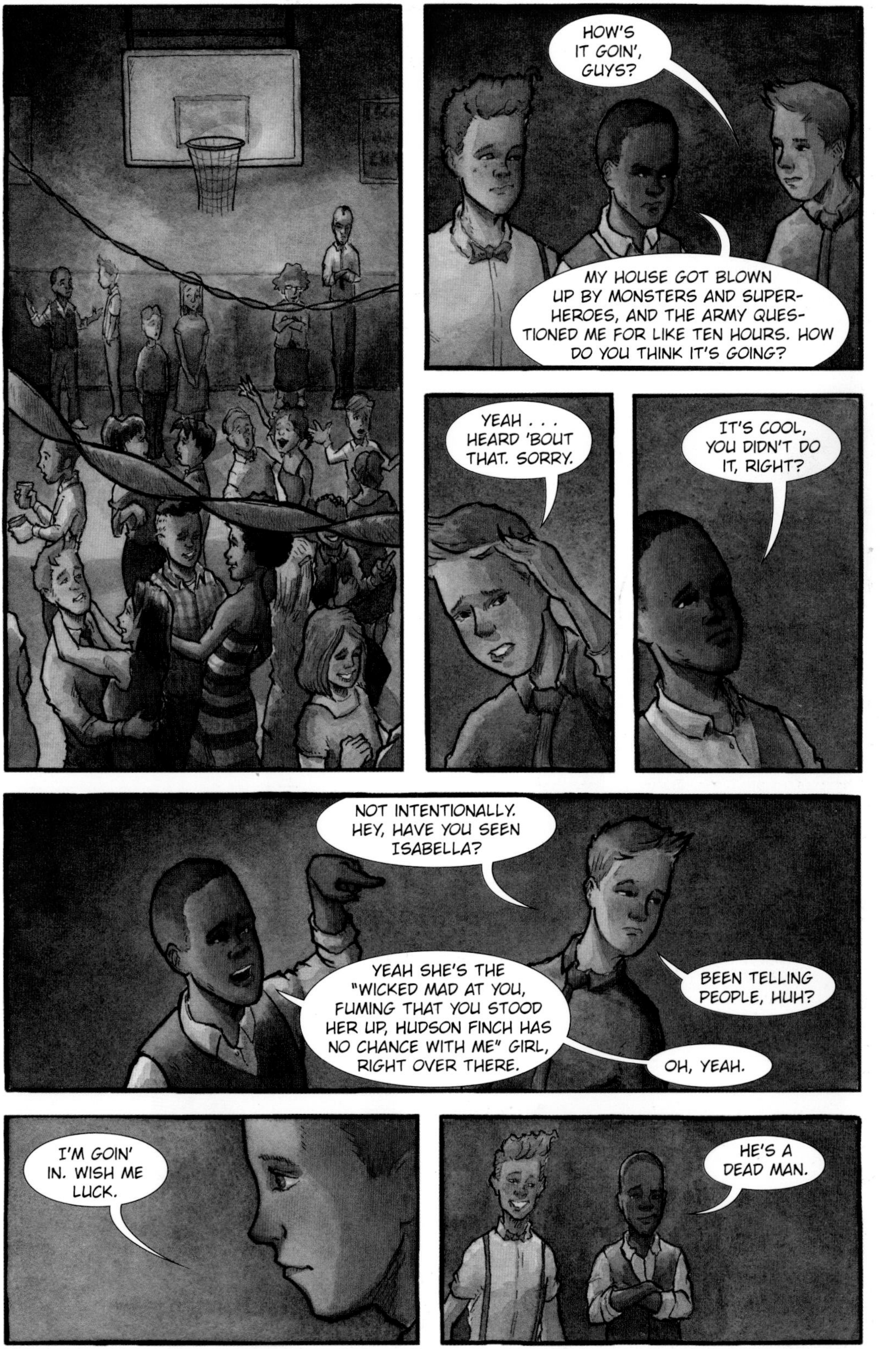
HOW'S IT GOIN', GUYS?
MY HOUSE GOT BLOWN UP BY MONSTERS AND SUPER-HEROES, AND THE ARMY QUES-TIONED ME FOR LIKE TEN HOURS. HOW DO YOU THINK IT'S GOING?
YEAH . . . HEARD 'BOUT THAT. SORRY.
IT'S COOL, YOU DIDN'T DO IT, RIGHT?
NOT INTENTIONALLY. HEY, HAVE YOU SEEN ISABELLA?
YEAH SHE'S THE "WICKED MAD AT YOU, FUMING THAT YOU STOOD HER UP, HUDSON FINCH HAS NO CHANCE WITH ME" GIRL, RIGHT OVER THERE.
BEEN TELLING PEOPLE, HUH?
OH, YEAH.
I'M GOIN' IN. WISH ME LUCK.
HE'S A DEAD MAN.

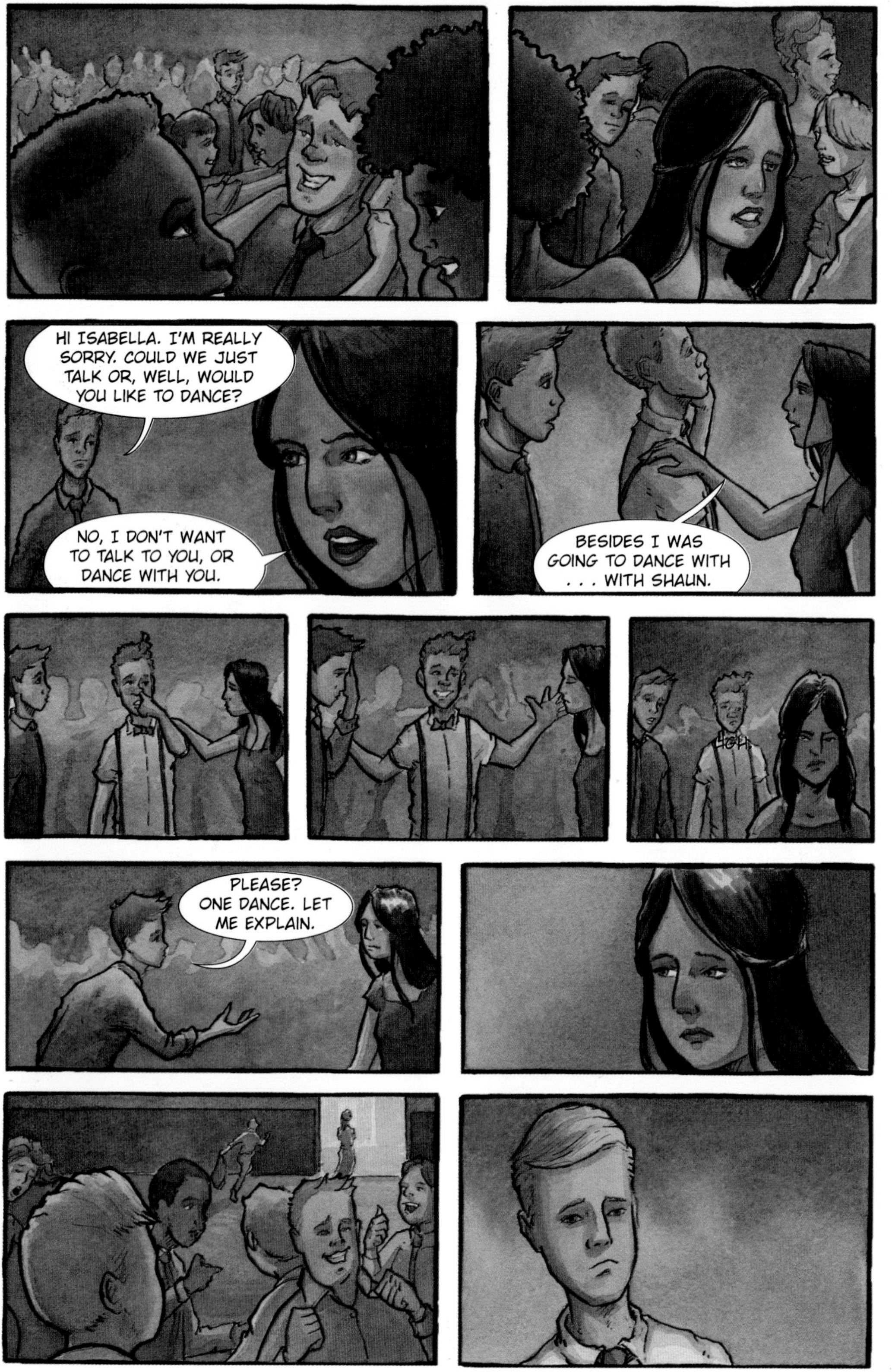
HI ISABELLA. I'M REALLY SORRY. COULD WE JUST TALK OR, WELL, WOULD YOU LIKE TO DANCE?
NO, I DON'T WANT TO TALK TO YOU, OR DANCE WITH YOU.
BESIDES I WAS GOING TO DANCE WITH . . . WITH SHAUN.
PLEASE? ONE DANCE. LET ME EXPLAIN.

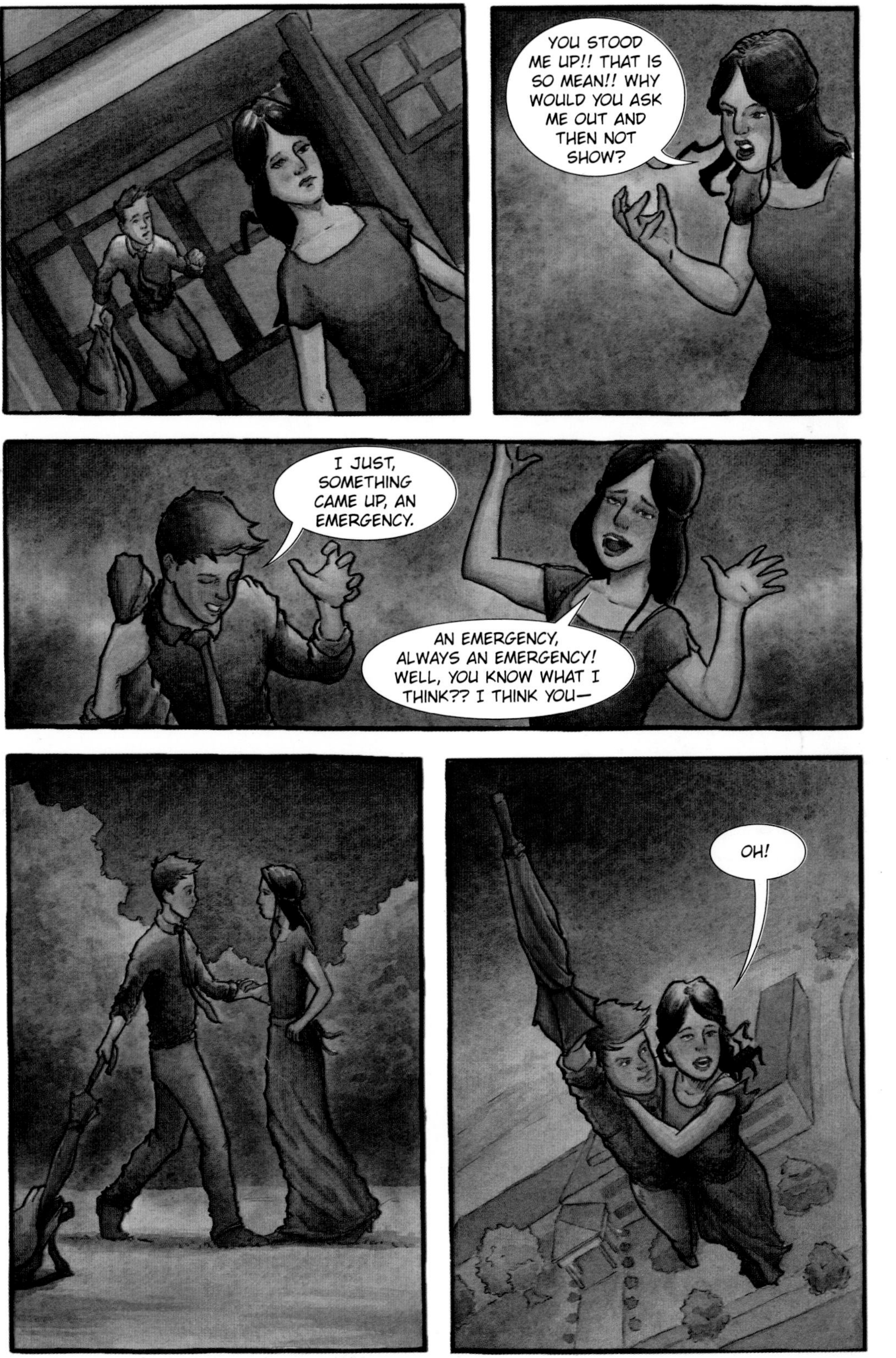
YOU STOOD ME UP!! THAT IS SO MEAN!! WHY WOULD YOU ASK ME OUT AND THEN NOT SHOW?
I JUST, SOMETHING CAME UP, AN EMERGENCY.
AN EMERGENCY, ALWAYS AN EMERGENCY! WELL, YOU KNOW WHAT I THINK?? I THINK YOU—
OH!

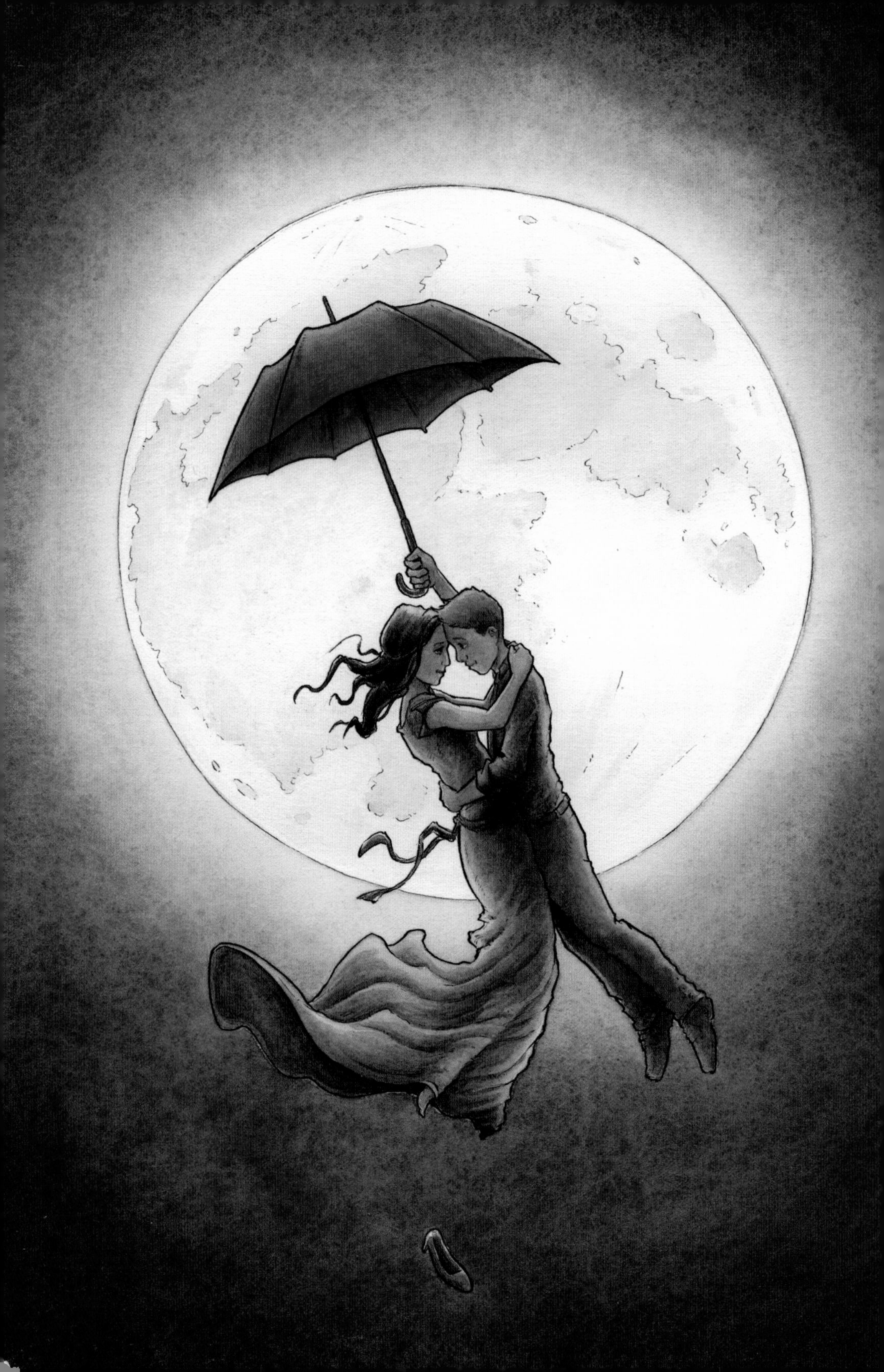

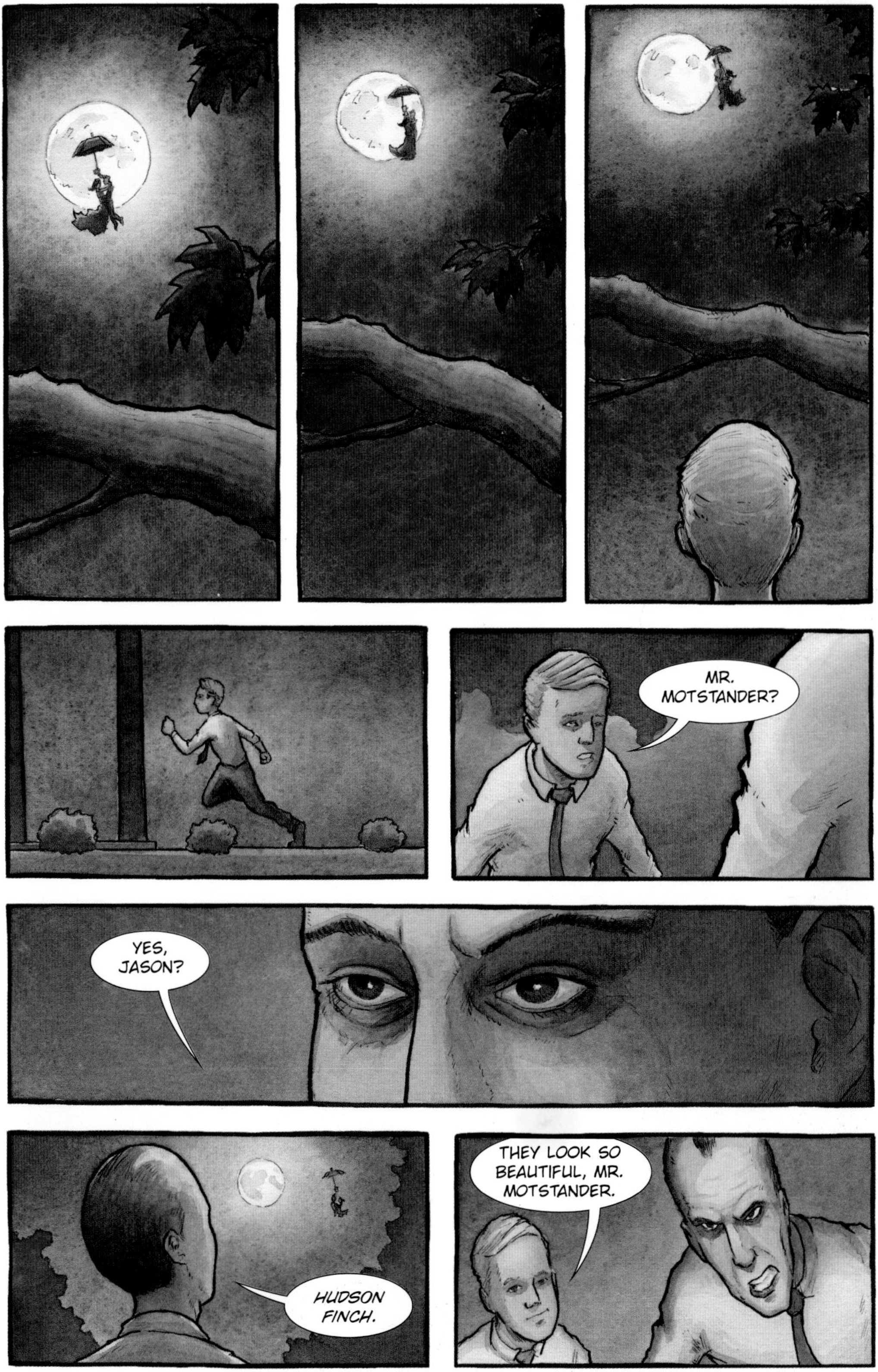
MR. MOTSTANDER?
YES, JASON?
HUDSON FINCH.
THEY LOOK SO BEAUTIFUL, MR. MOTSTANDER.

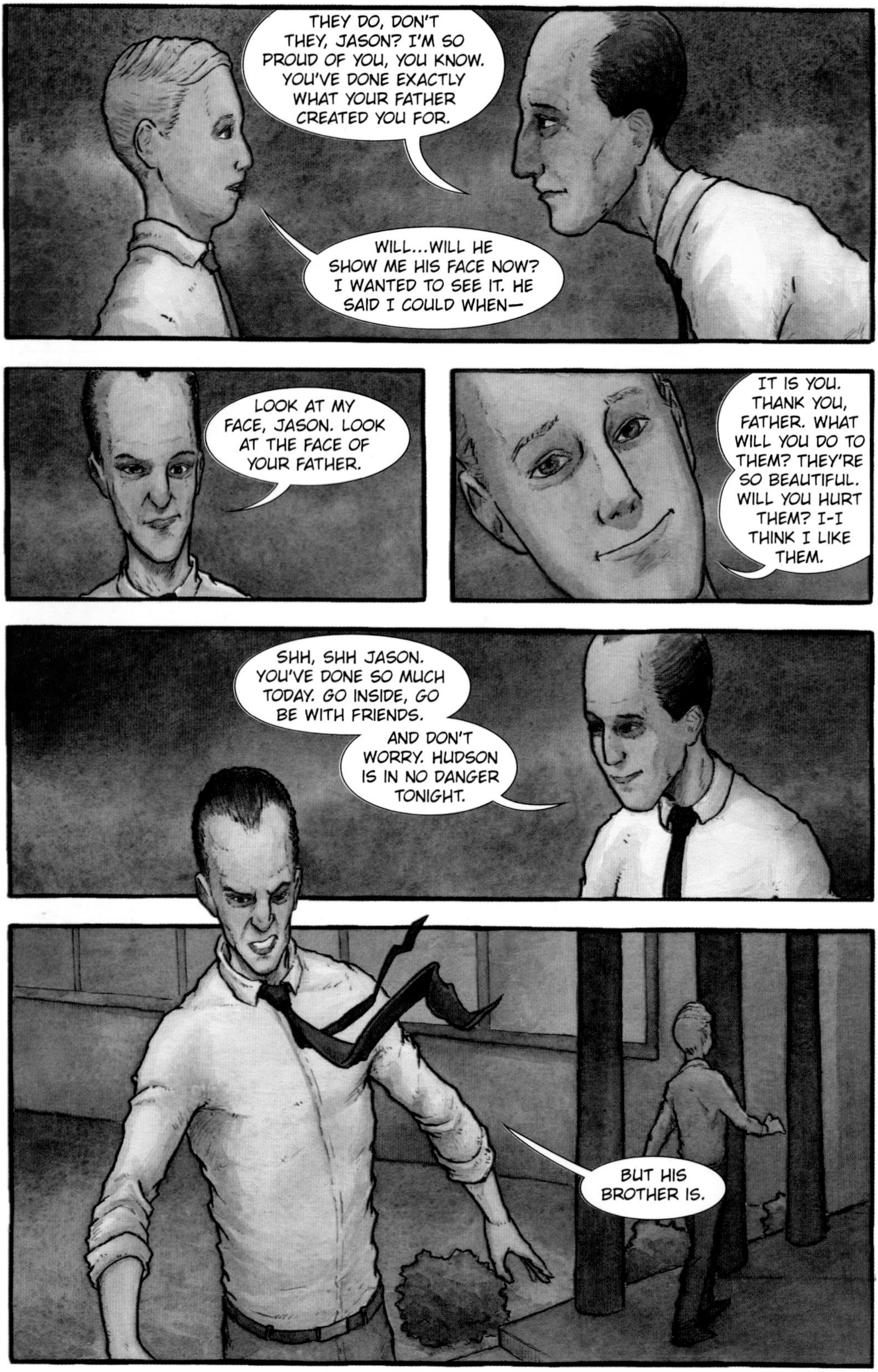
THEY DO, DON'T THEY, JASON? I'M SO PROUD OF YOU, YOU KNOW. YOU'VE DONE EXACTLY WHAT YOUR FATHER CREATED YOU FOR.
WILL...WILL HE SHOW ME HIS FACE NOW? I WANTED TO SEE IT. HE SAID I COULD WHEN—
LOOK AT MY FACE, JASON. LOOK AT THE FACE OF YOUR FATHER.
IT IS YOU. THANK YOU, FATHER. WHAT WILL YOU DO TO THEM? THEY'RE SO BEAUTIFUL. WILL YOU HURT THEM? I-I THINK I LIKE THEM.
SHH, SHH JASON. YOU'VE DONE SO MUCH TODAY. GO INSIDE, GO BE WITH FRIENDS.
AND DON'T WORRY. HUDSON IS IN NO DANGER TONIGHT.
BUT HIS BROTHER IS.

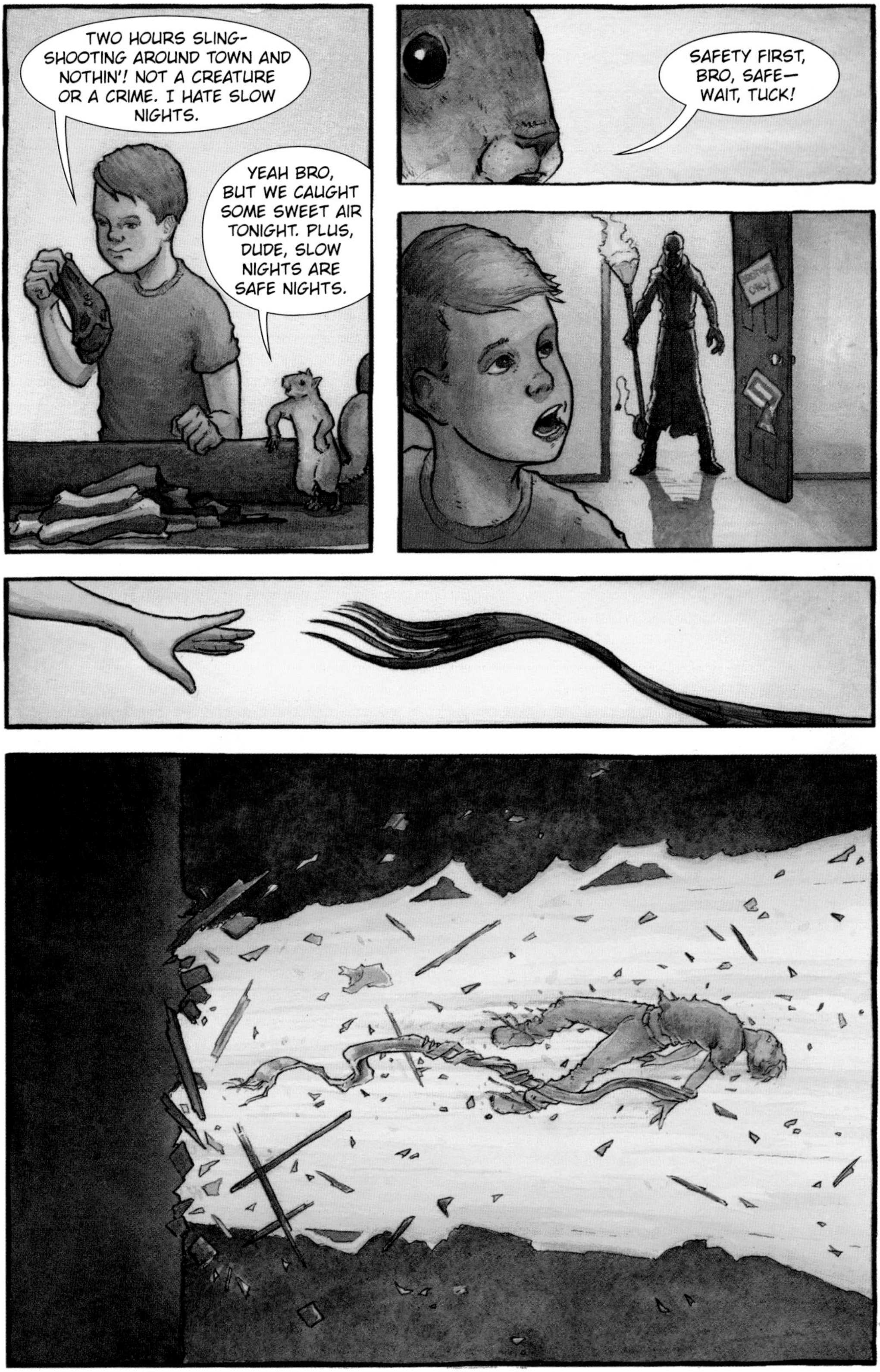
TWO HOURS SLING-SHOOTING AROUND TOWN AND NOTHIN'! NOT A CREATURE OR A CRIME. I HATE SLOW NIGHTS.
YEAH BRO, BUT WE CAUGHT SOME SWEET AIR TONIGHT. PLUS, DUDE, SLOW NIGHTS ARE SAFE NIGHTS.
SAFETY FIRST, BRO, SAFE—WAIT, TUCK!

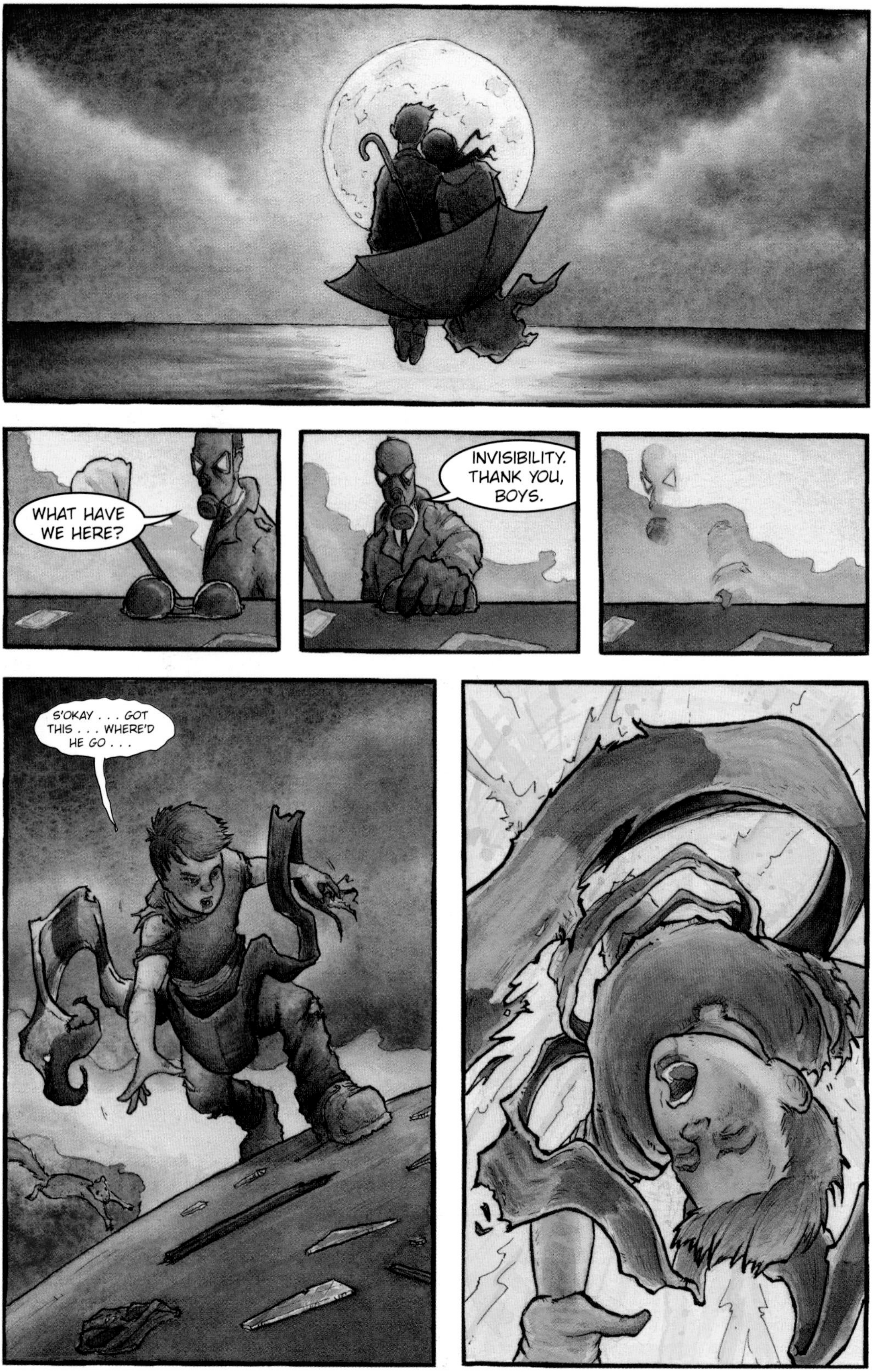
WHAT HAVE WE HERE?
INVISIBILITY. THANK YOU, BOYS.
S'OKAY . . . GOT THIS . . . WHERE'D HE GO . . .

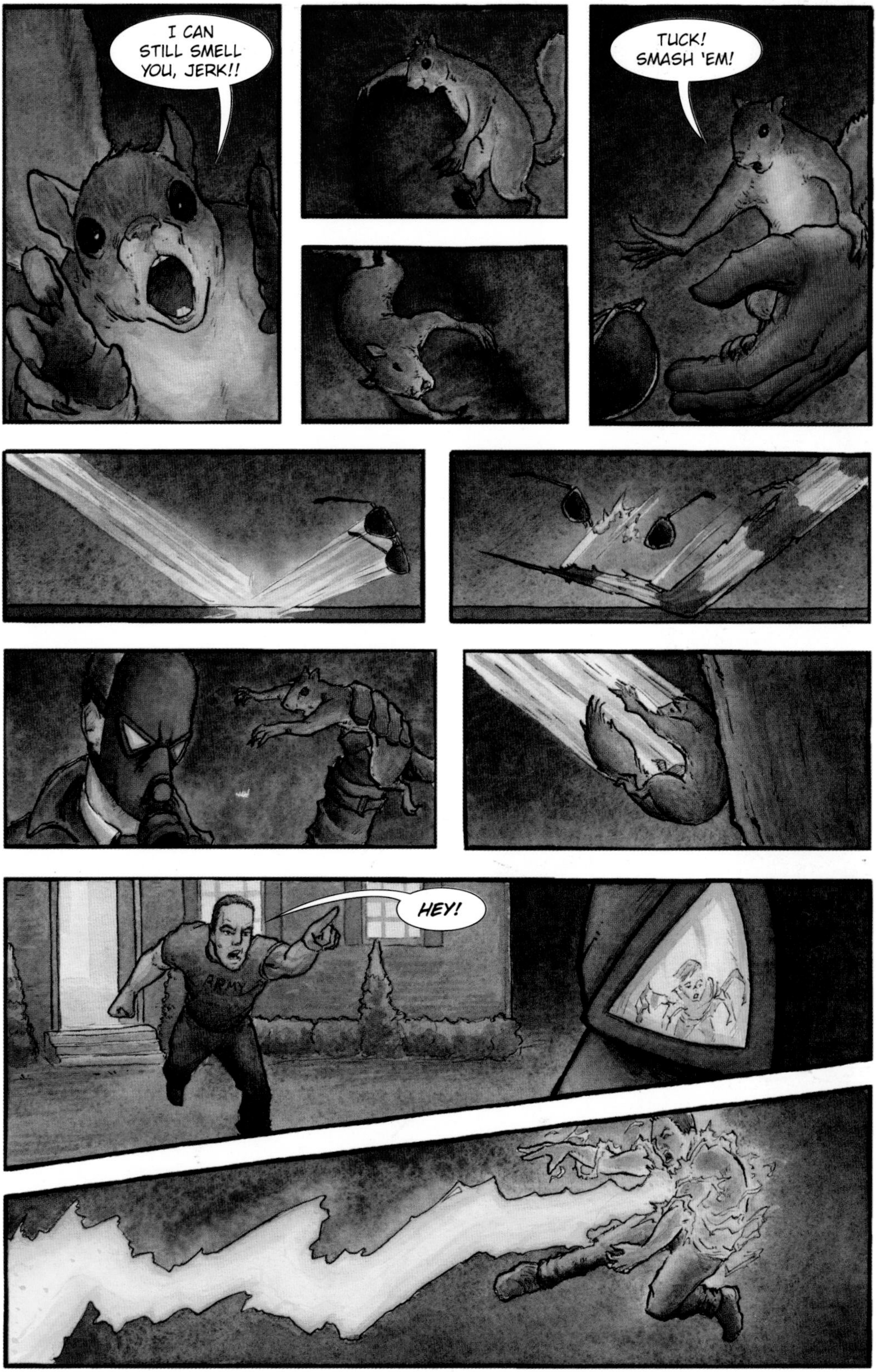
I CAN STILL SMELL YOU, JERK!!
TUCK! SMASH 'EM!
HEY!

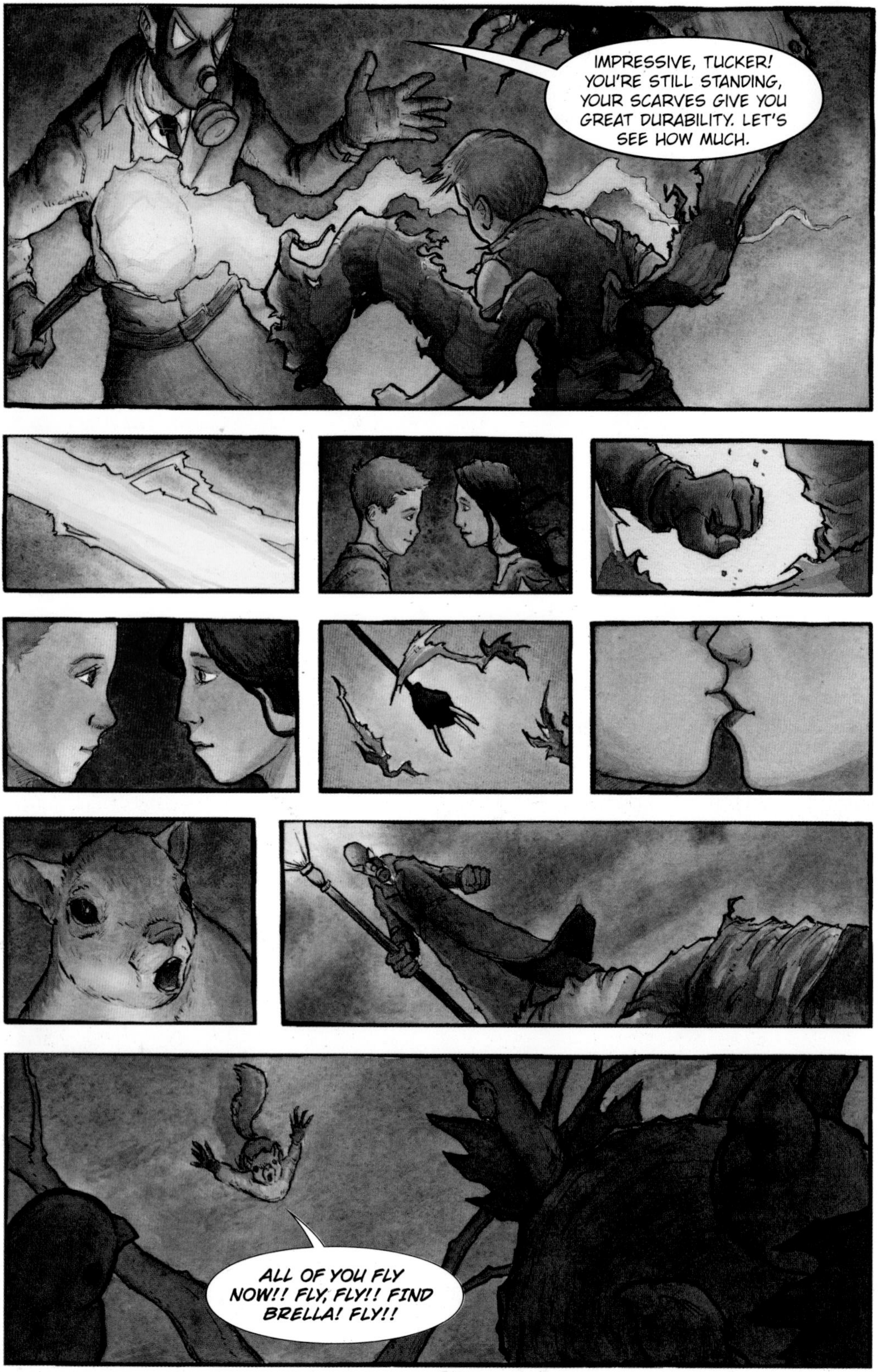
IMPRESSIVE, TUCKER! YOU'RE STILL STANDING, YOUR SCARVES GIVE YOU GREAT DURABILITY. LET'S SEE HOW MUCH.
ALL OF YOU FLY NOW!! FLY, FLY!! FIND BRELLA! FLY!!

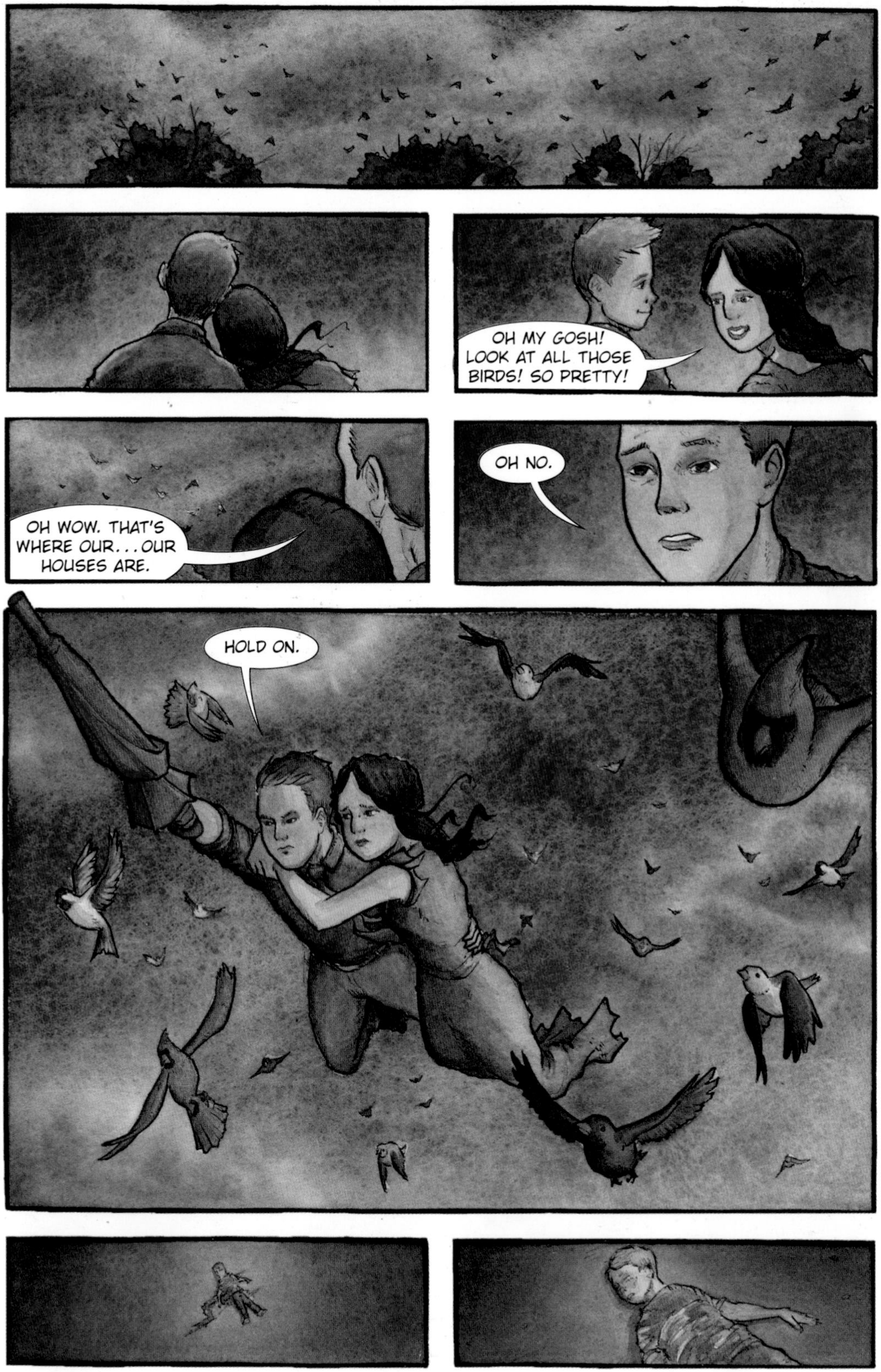
OH MY GOSH! LOOK AT ALL THOSE BIRDS! SO PRETTY!
OH WOW. THAT'S WHERE OUR. . . OUR HOUSES ARE.
OH NO.
HOLD ON.

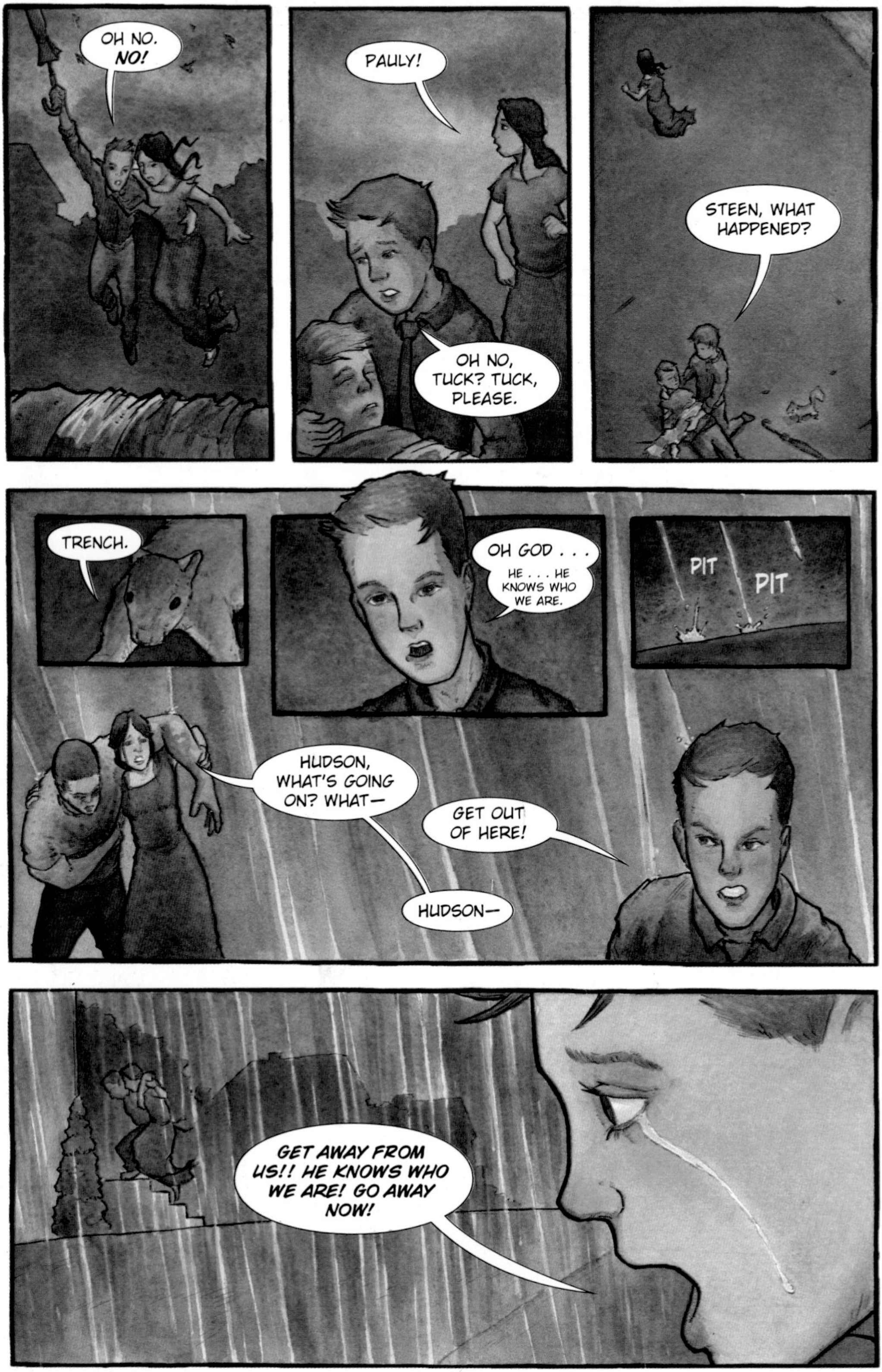
OH NO. NO!
PAULY!
OH NO, TUCK? TUCK, PLEASE.
STEEN, WHAT HAPPENED?
TRENCH.
OH GOD . . .
HE . . . HE KNOWS WHO WE ARE.
PIT
PIT
HUDSON, WHAT'S GOING ON? WHAT—
HUDSON—
GET OUT OF HERE!
GET AWAY FROM US!! HE KNOWS WHO WE ARE! GO AWAY NOW!

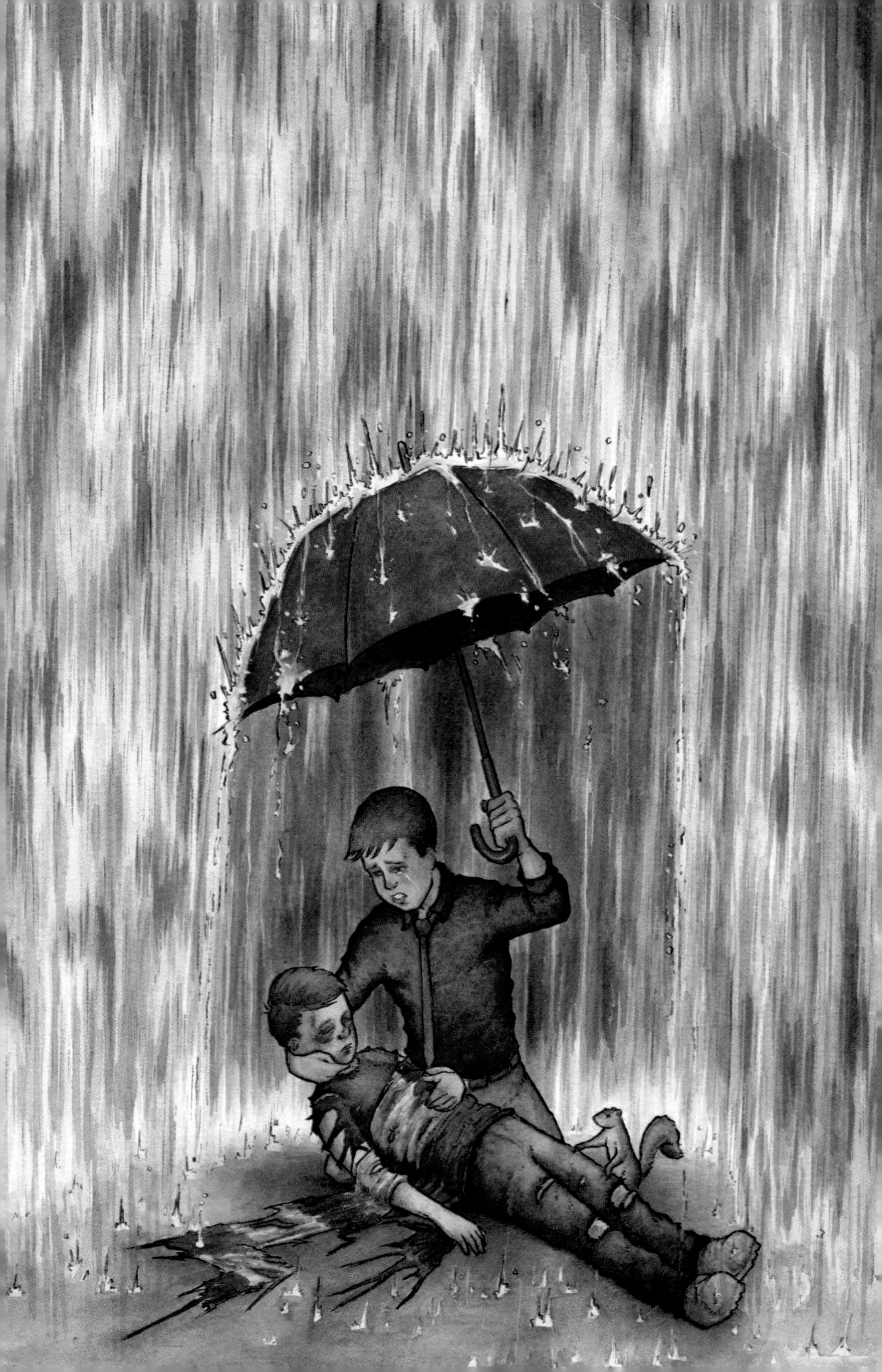

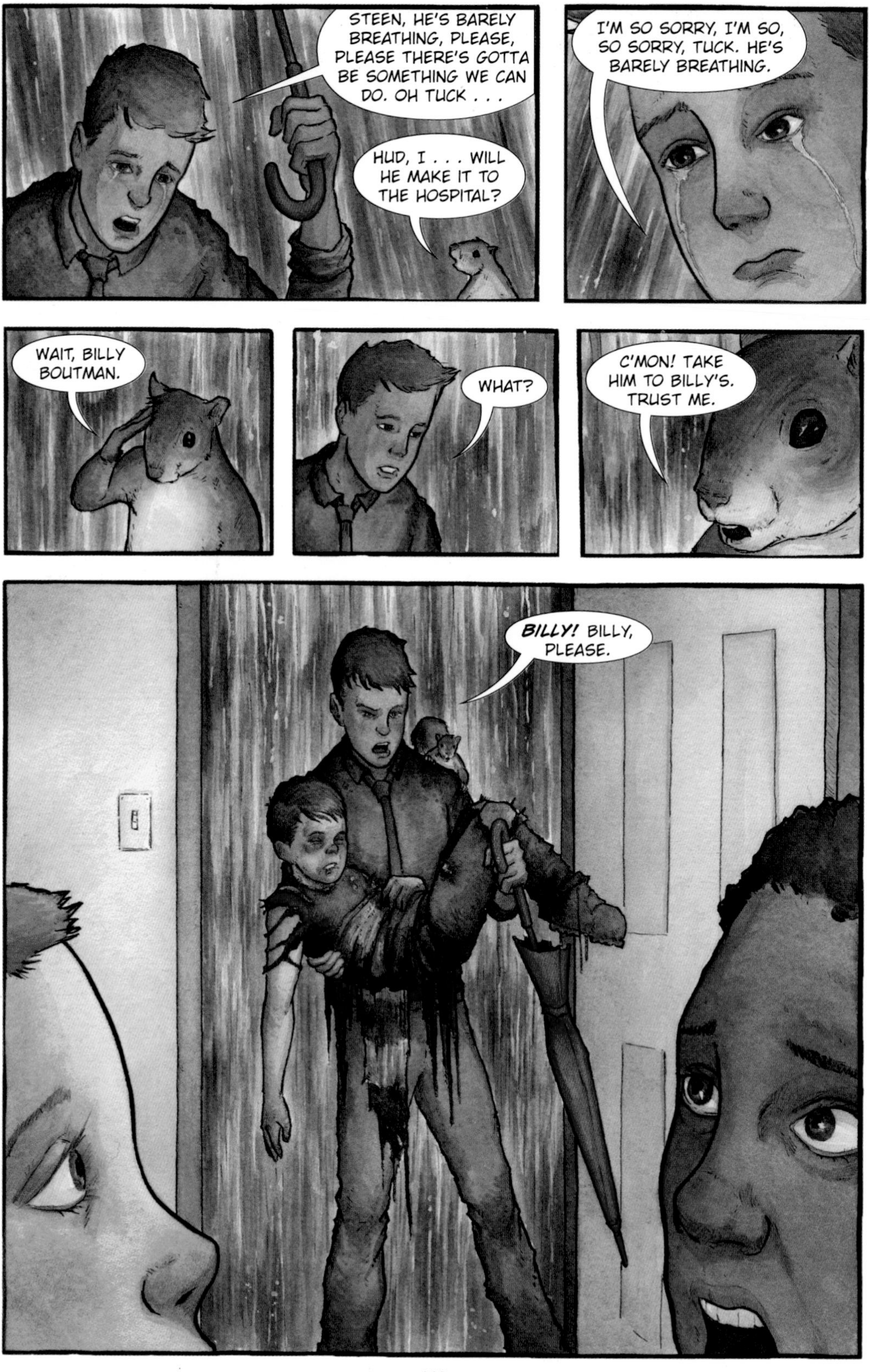
STEEN, HE'S BARELY BREATHING, PLEASE, PLEASE THERE'S GOTTA BE SOMETHING WE CAN DO. OH TUCK . . .
HUD, I . . . WILL HE MAKE IT TO THE HOSPITAL?
I'M SO SORRY, I'M SO, SO SORRY, TUCK. HE'S BARELY BREATHING.
WAIT, BILLY BOUTMAN.
WHAT?
C'MON! TAKE HIM TO BILLY'S. TRUST ME.
BILLY! BILLY, PLEASE.

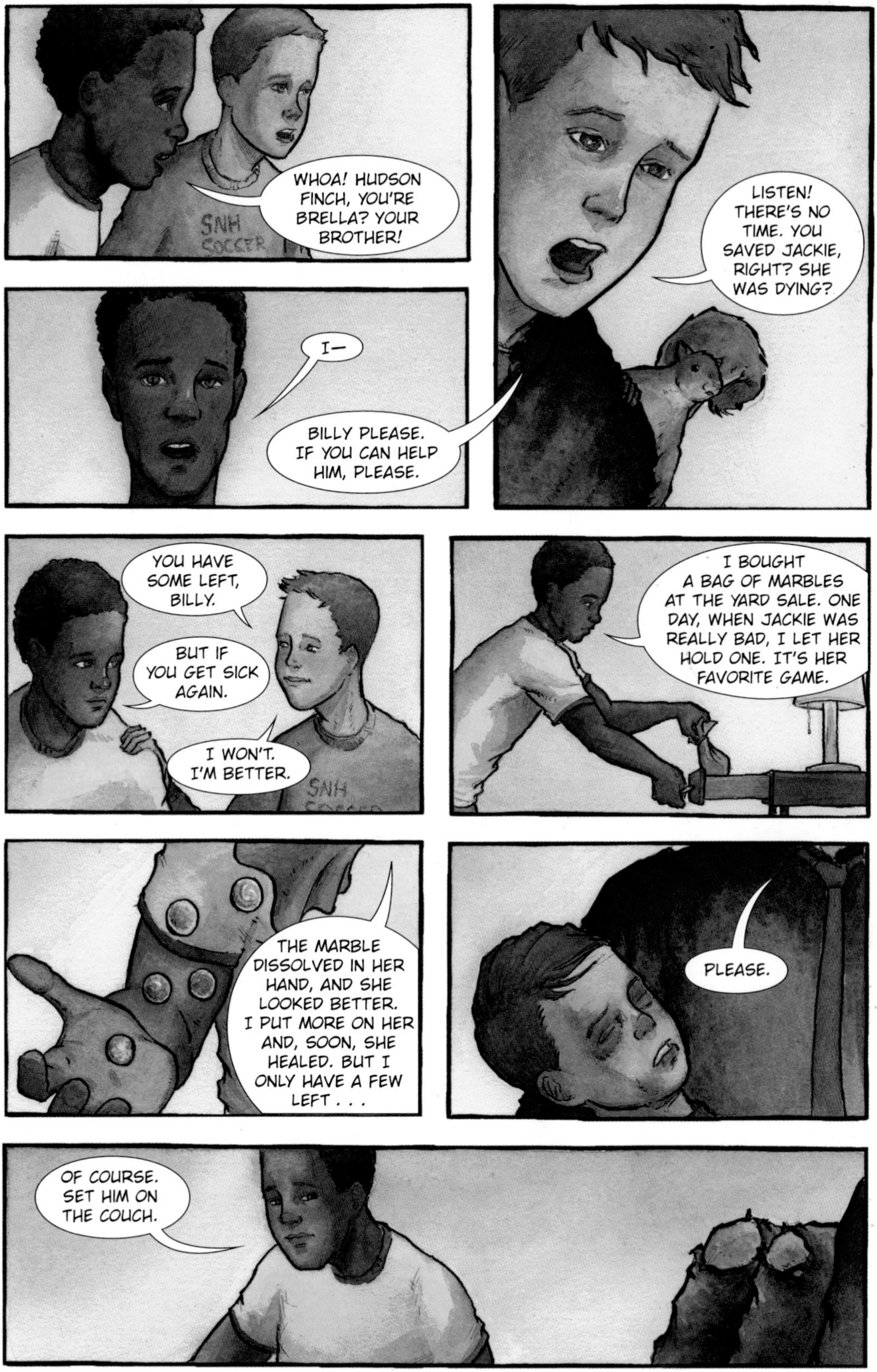

WHOA! HUDSON FINCH, YOU'RE BRELLA? YOUR BROTHER!
SNH SOCCER
LISTEN! THERE'S NO TIME. YOU SAVED JACKIE, RIGHT? SHE WAS DYING?
I—
BILLY PLEASE. IF YOU CAN HELP HIM, PLEASE.
YOU HAVE SOME LEFT, BILLY.
BUT IF YOU GET SICK AGAIN.
I WON'T. I'M BETTER.
SNH
I BOUGHT A BAG OF MARBLES AT THE YARD SALE. ONE DAY, WHEN JACKIE WAS REALLY BAD, I LET HER HOLD ONE. IT'S HER FAVORITE GAME.
THE MARBLE DISSOLVED IN HER HAND, AND SHE LOOKED BETTER. I PUT MORE ON HER AND, SOON, SHE HEALED. BUT I ONLY HAVE A FEW LEFT . . .
PLEASE.
OF COURSE. SET HIM ON THE COUCH.

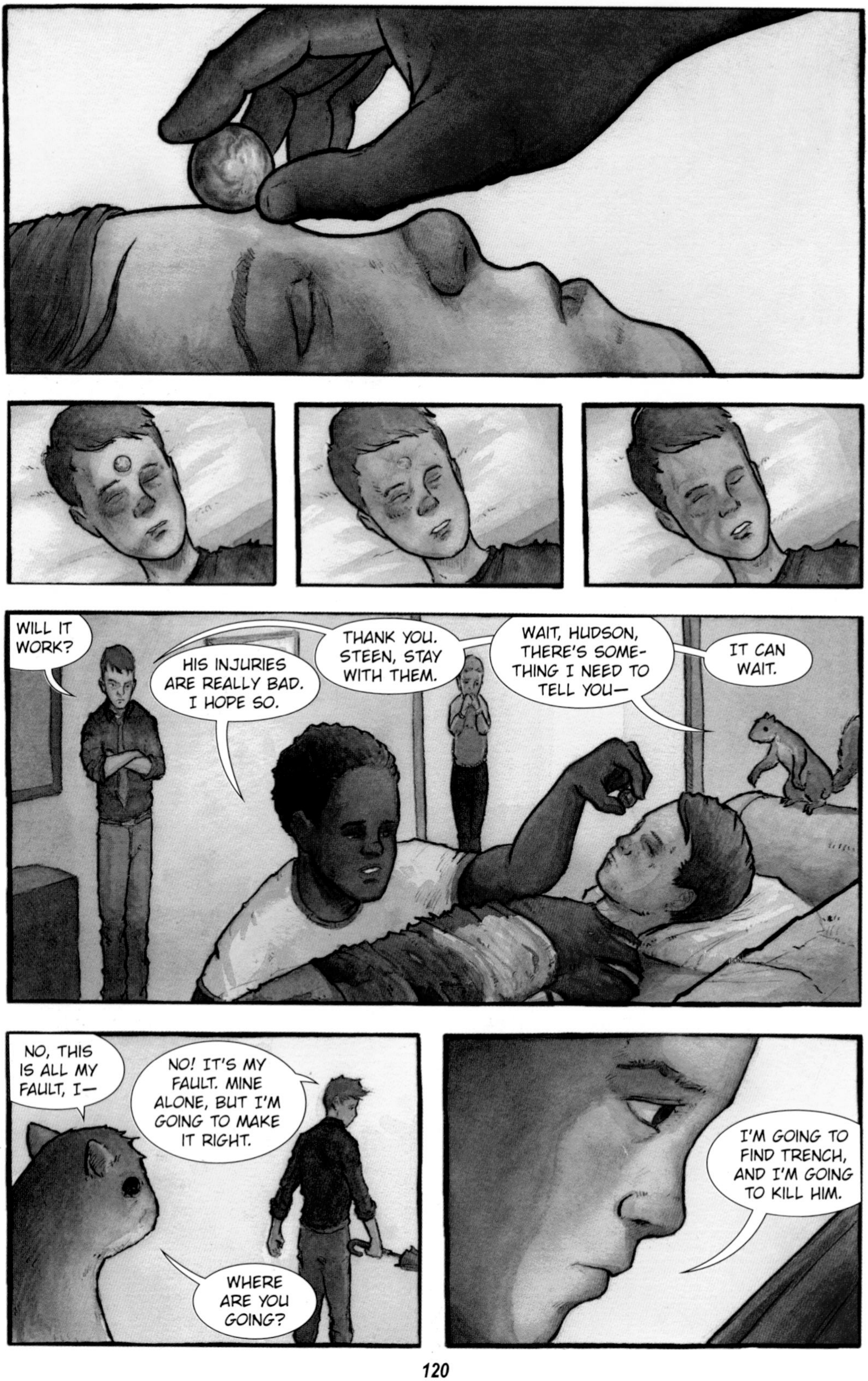
WILL IT WORK?
HIS INJURIES ARE REALLY BAD. I HOPE SO.
THANK YOU. STEEN, STAY WITH THEM.
WAIT, HUDSON, THERE'S SOME-THING I NEED TO TELL YOU—
IT CAN WAIT.
NO, THIS IS ALL MY FAULT, I—
NO! IT'S MY FAULT. MINE ALONE, BUT I'M GOING TO MAKE IT RIGHT.
WHERE ARE YOU GOING?
I'M GOING TO FIND TRENCH, AND I'M GOING TO KILL HIM.

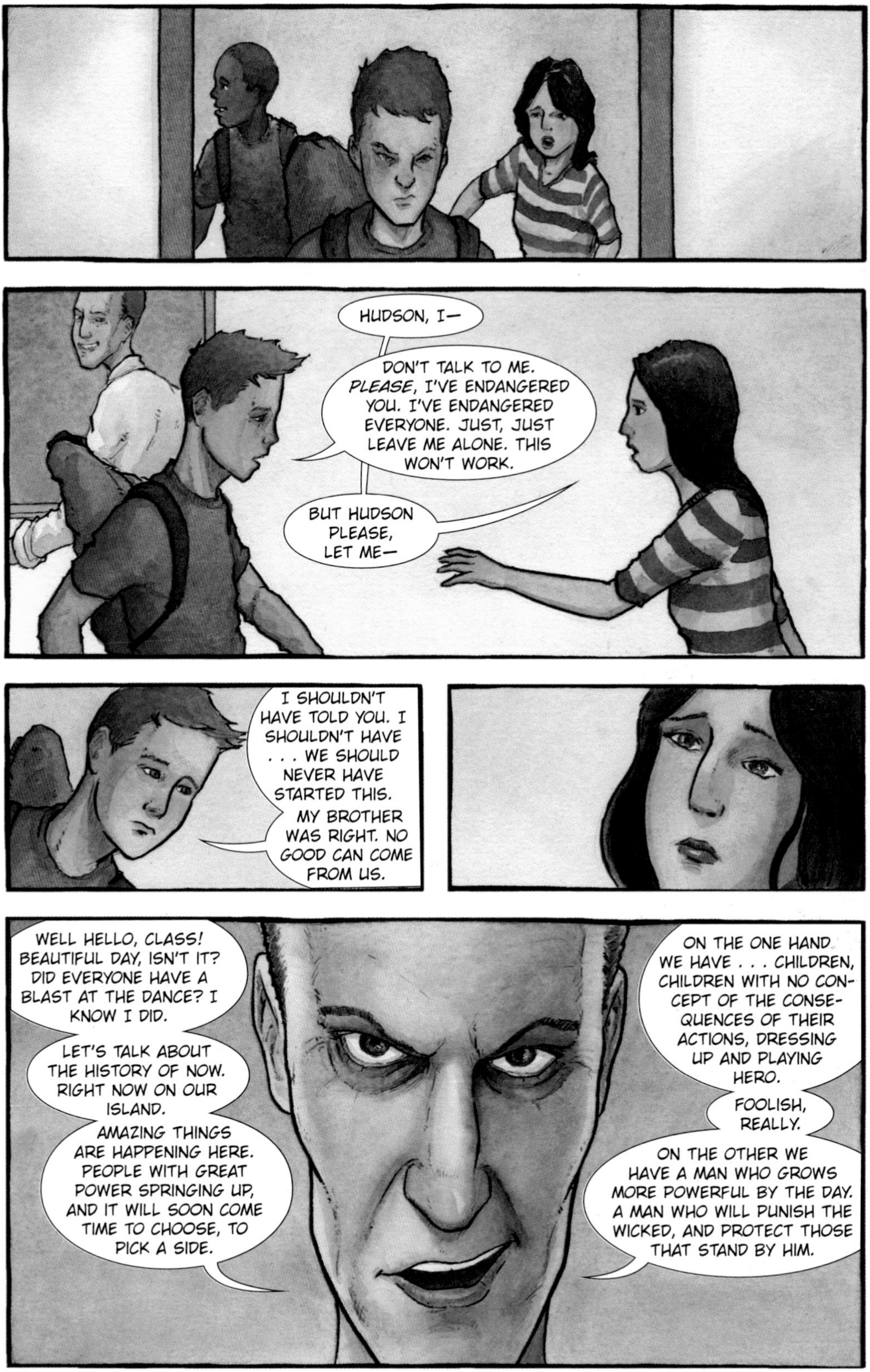
HUDSON, I—
DON'T TALK TO ME. *PLEASE*, I'VE ENDANGERED YOU. I'VE ENDANGERED EVERYONE. JUST, JUST LEAVE ME ALONE. THIS WON'T WORK.
BUT HUDSON PLEASE, LET ME—
I SHOULDN'T HAVE TOLD YOU. I SHOULDN'T HAVE . . . WE SHOULD NEVER HAVE STARTED THIS.
MY BROTHER WAS RIGHT. NO GOOD CAN COME FROM US.
WELL HELLO, CLASS! BEAUTIFUL DAY, ISN'T IT? DID EVERYONE HAVE A BLAST AT THE DANCE? I KNOW I DID.
LET'S TALK ABOUT THE HISTORY OF NOW. RIGHT NOW ON OUR ISLAND.
AMAZING THINGS ARE HAPPENING HERE. PEOPLE WITH GREAT POWER SPRINGING UP, AND IT WILL SOON COME TIME TO CHOOSE, TO PICK A SIDE.
ON THE ONE HAND WE HAVE . . . CHILDREN, CHILDREN WITH NO CONCEPT OF THE CONSEQUENCES OF THEIR ACTIONS, DRESSING UP AND PLAYING HERO.
FOOLISH, REALLY.
ON THE OTHER WE HAVE A MAN WHO GROWS MORE POWERFUL BY THE DAY. A MAN WHO WILL PUNISH THE WICKED, AND PROTECT THOSE THAT STAND BY HIM.

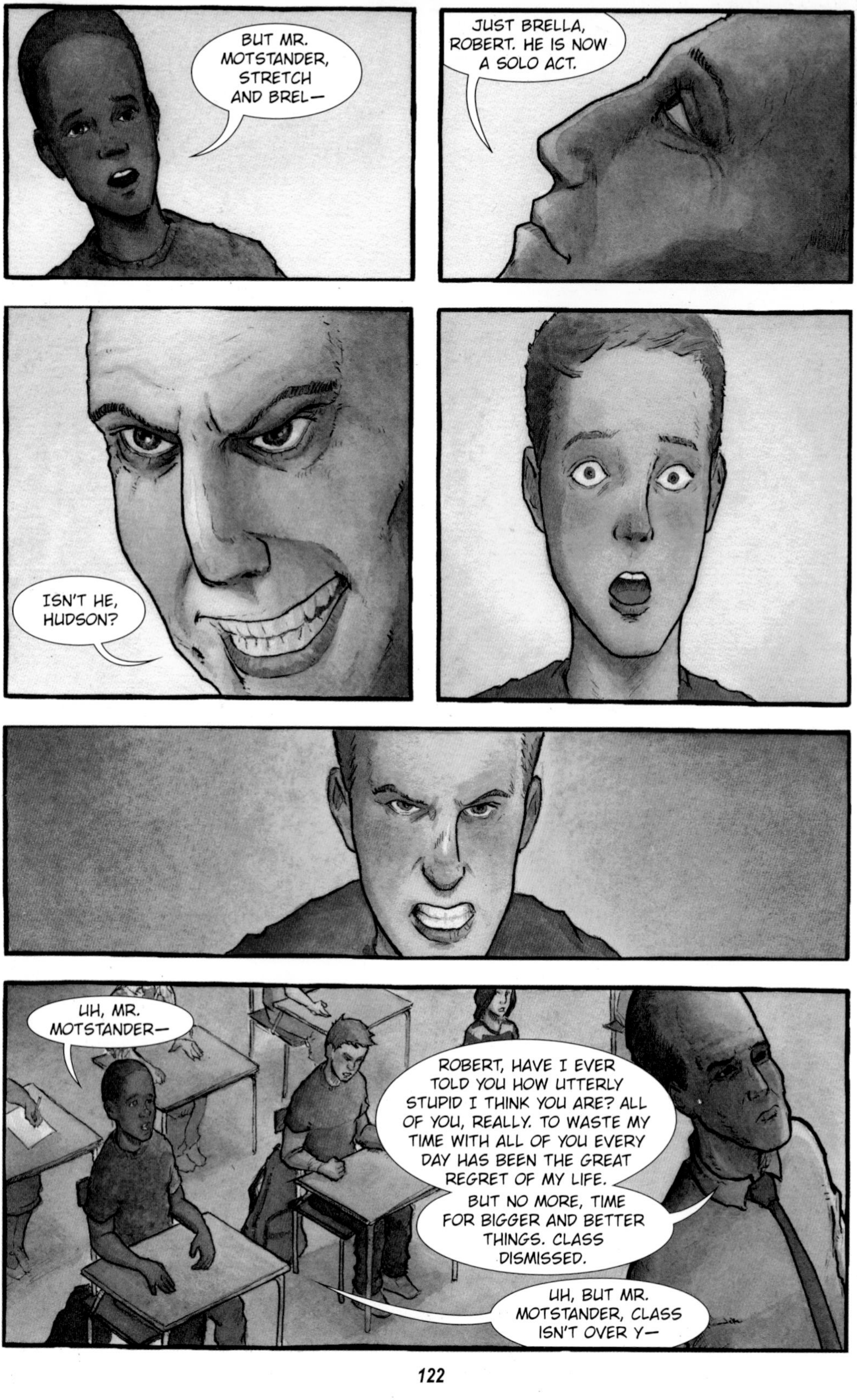
BUT MR. MOTSTANDER, STRETCH AND BREL—
JUST BRELLA, ROBERT. HE IS NOW A SOLO ACT.
ISN'T HE, HUDSON?
UH, MR. MOTSTANDER—
ROBERT, HAVE I EVER TOLD YOU HOW UTTERLY STUPID I THINK YOU ARE? ALL OF YOU, REALLY. TO WASTE MY TIME WITH ALL OF YOU EVERY DAY HAS BEEN THE GREAT REGRET OF MY LIFE.
BUT NO MORE, TIME FOR BIGGER AND BETTER THINGS. CLASS DISMISSED.
UH, BUT MR. MOTSTANDER, CLASS ISN'T OVER Y—

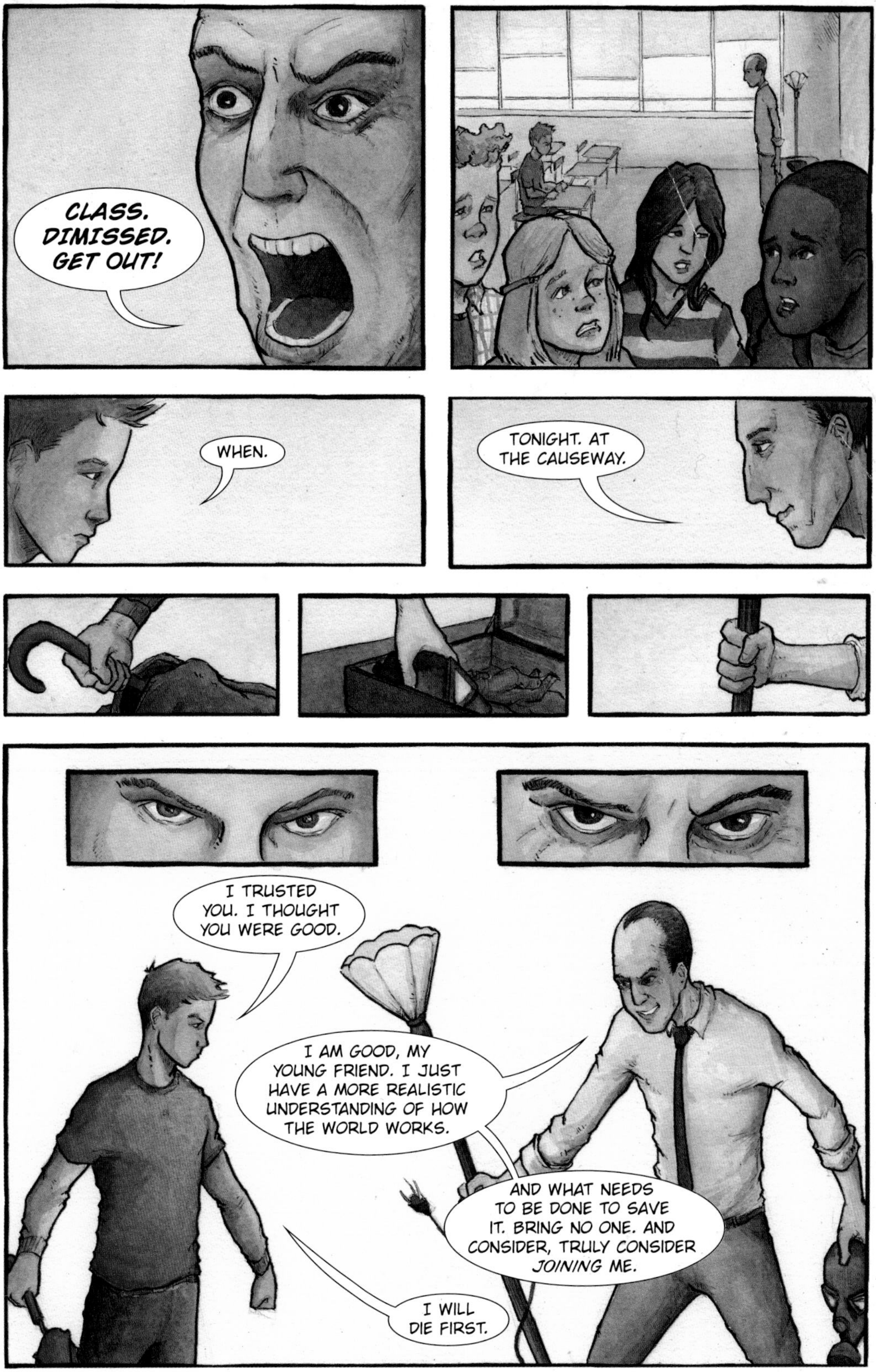

CLASS. DIMISSED. GET OUT!
WHEN.
TONIGHT. AT THE CAUSEWAY.
I TRUSTED YOU. I THOUGHT YOU WERE GOOD.
I AM GOOD, MY YOUNG FRIEND. I JUST HAVE A MORE REALISTIC UNDERSTANDING OF HOW THE WORLD WORKS.
AND WHAT NEEDS TO BE DONE TO SAVE IT. BRING NO ONE. AND CONSIDER, TRULY CONSIDER *JOINING* ME.
I WILL DIE FIRST.

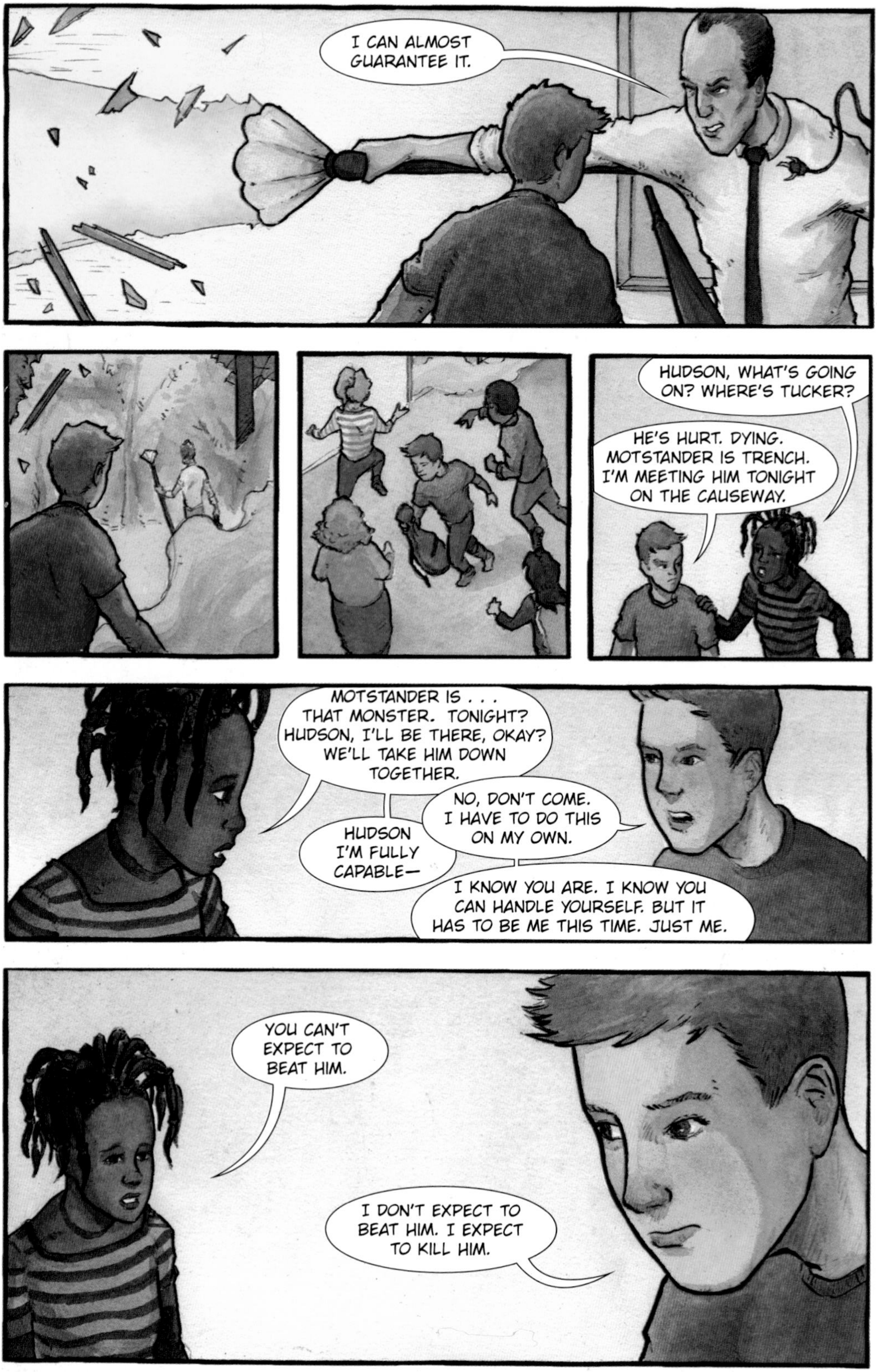

I CAN ALMOST GUARANTEE IT.
HUDSON, WHAT'S GOING ON? WHERE'S TUCKER?
HE'S HURT. DYING. MOTSTANDER IS TRENCH. I'M MEETING HIM TONIGHT ON THE CAUSEWAY.
MOTSTANDER IS . . . THAT MONSTER. TONIGHT? HUDSON, I'LL BE THERE, OKAY? WE'LL TAKE HIM DOWN TOGETHER.
NO, DON'T COME. I HAVE TO DO THIS ON MY OWN.
HUDSON I'M FULLY CAPABLE—
I KNOW YOU ARE. I KNOW YOU CAN HANDLE YOURSELF. BUT IT HAS TO BE ME THIS TIME. JUST ME.
YOU CAN'T EXPECT TO BEAT HIM.
I DON'T EXPECT TO BEAT HIM. I EXPECT TO KILL HIM.

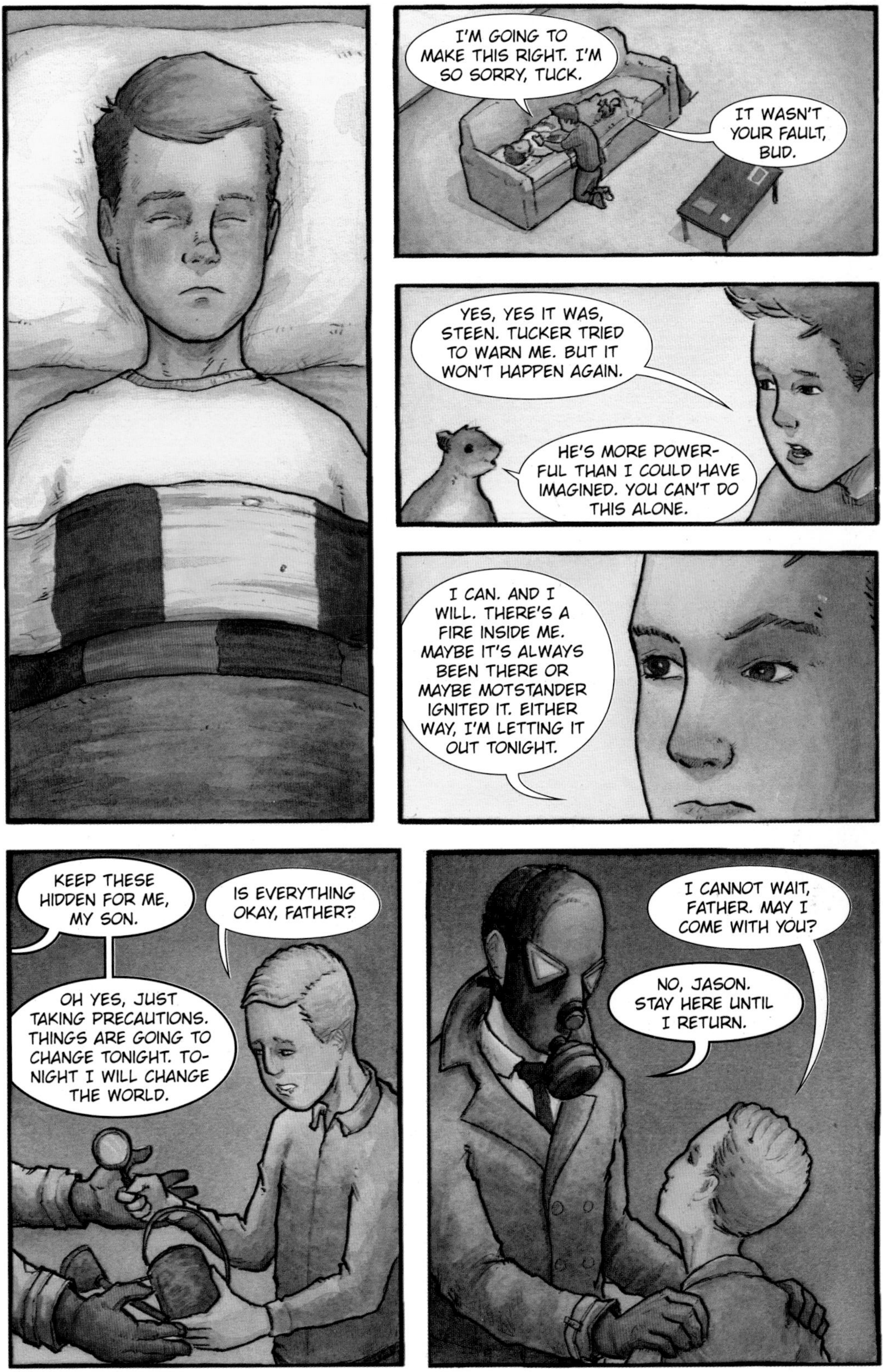
I'M GOING TO MAKE THIS RIGHT. I'M SO SORRY, TUCK.
IT WASN'T YOUR FAULT, BUD.
YES, YES IT WAS, STEEN. TUCKER TRIED TO WARN ME. BUT IT WON'T HAPPEN AGAIN.
HE'S MORE POWER-FUL THAN I COULD HAVE IMAGINED. YOU CAN'T DO THIS ALONE.
I CAN. AND I WILL. THERE'S A FIRE INSIDE ME. MAYBE IT'S ALWAYS BEEN THERE OR MAYBE MOTSTANDER IGNITED IT. EITHER WAY, I'M LETTING IT OUT TONIGHT.
KEEP THESE HIDDEN FOR ME, MY SON.
IS EVERYTHING OKAY, FATHER?
OH YES, JUST TAKING PRECAUTIONS. THINGS ARE GOING TO CHANGE TONIGHT. TO-NIGHT I WILL CHANGE THE WORLD.
I CANNOT WAIT, FATHER. MAY I COME WITH YOU?
NO, JASON. STAY HERE UNTIL I RETURN.

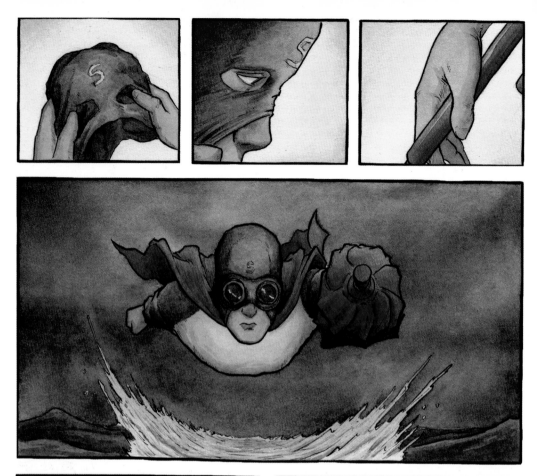

BEFORE WE BEGIN, I WANT YOU TO—

YOU HURT MY BROTHER!!!

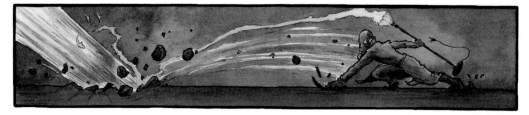

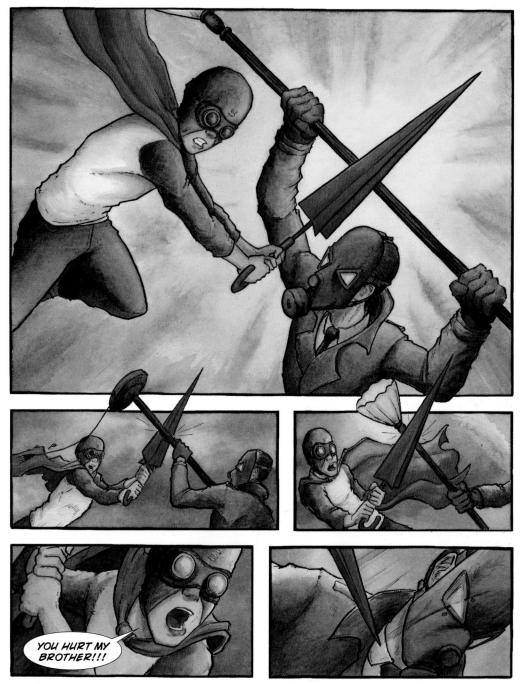

LOOK AT WHAT YOU'VE BECOME! YOU SEE WHAT I'VE BROUGHT OUT IN YOU? YOU NEEDED THIS!

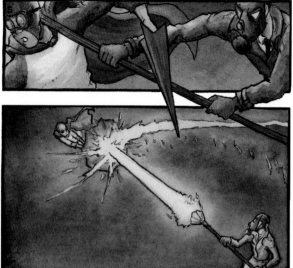

BRELLA AND TRENCH, DROP YOUR WEAPONS AND WALK TOWARD THE TRUCK SLOWLY. WE HAVE ENOUGH FIREPOWER TO—

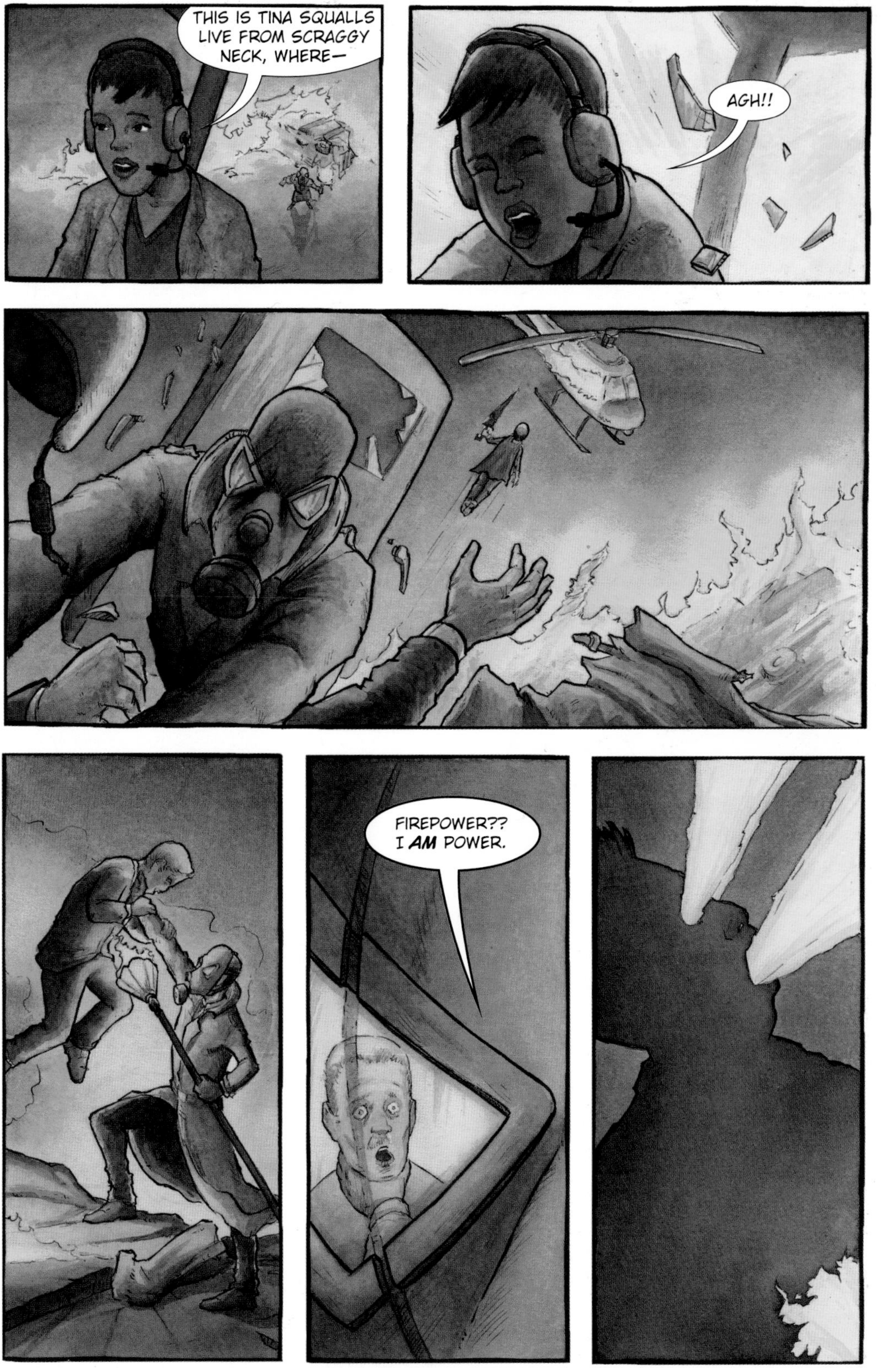
THIS IS TINA SQUALLS LIVE FROM SCRAGGY NECK, WHERE—
AGH!!
FIREPOWER?? I **AM** POWER.

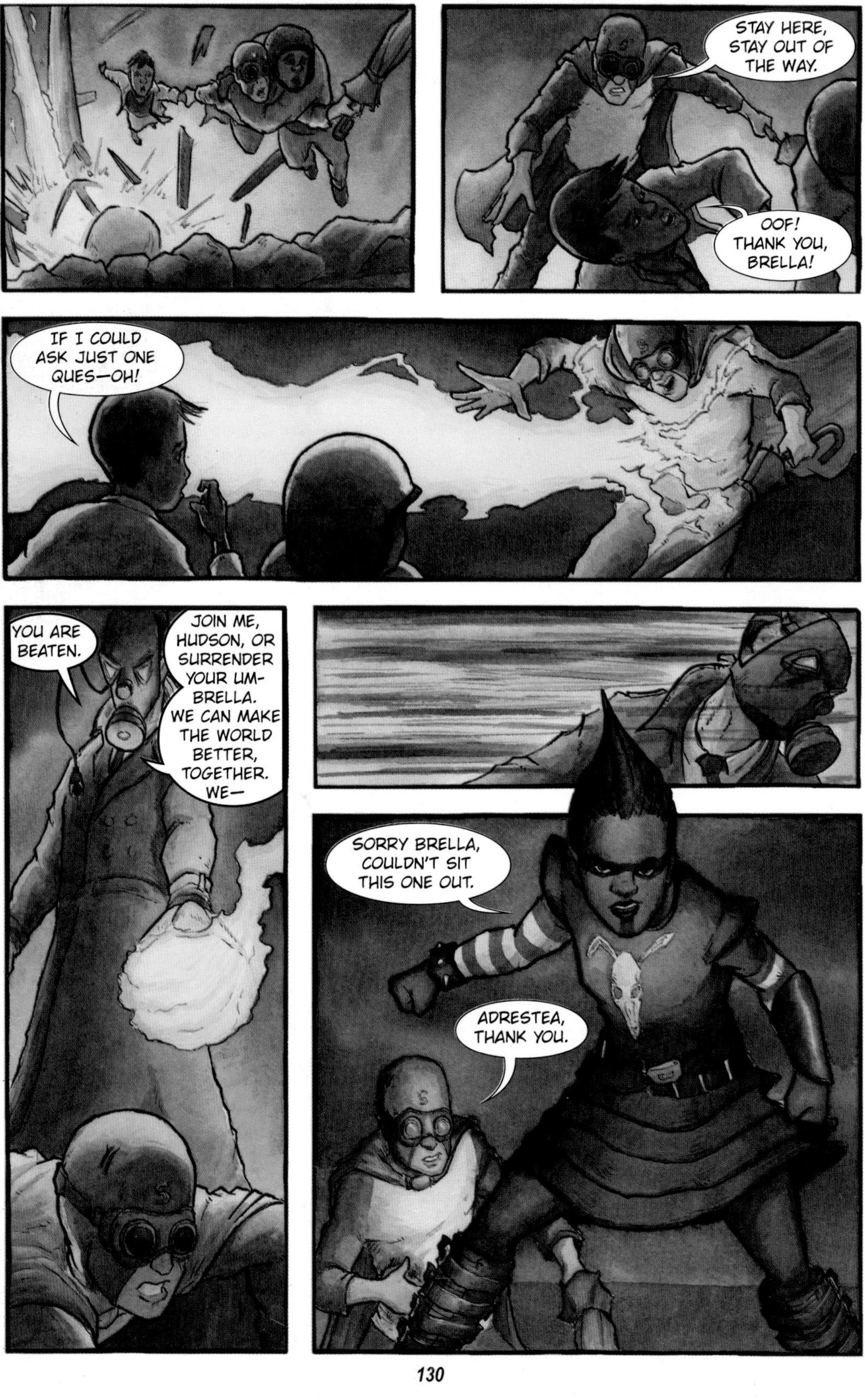
STAY HERE, STAY OUT OF THE WAY.
OOF! THANK YOU, BRELLA!
IF I COULD ASK JUST ONE QUES—OH!
YOU ARE BEATEN.
JOIN ME, HUDSON, OR SURRENDER YOUR UM-BRELLA. WE CAN MAKE THE WORLD BETTER, TOGETHER. WE—
SORRY BRELLA, COULDN'T SIT THIS ONE OUT.
ADRESTEA, THANK YOU.

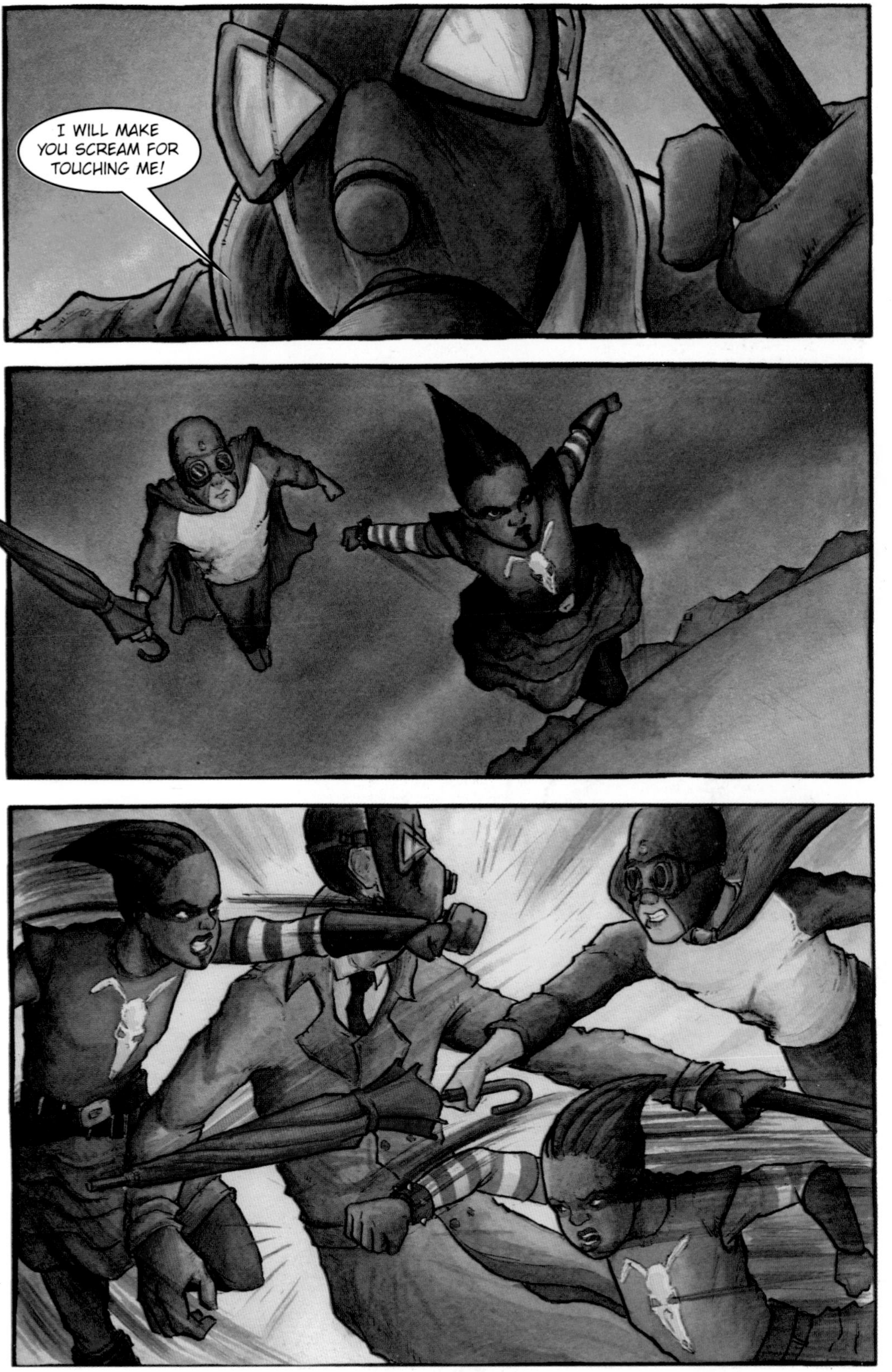
I WILL MAKE YOU SCREAM FOR TOUCHING ME!

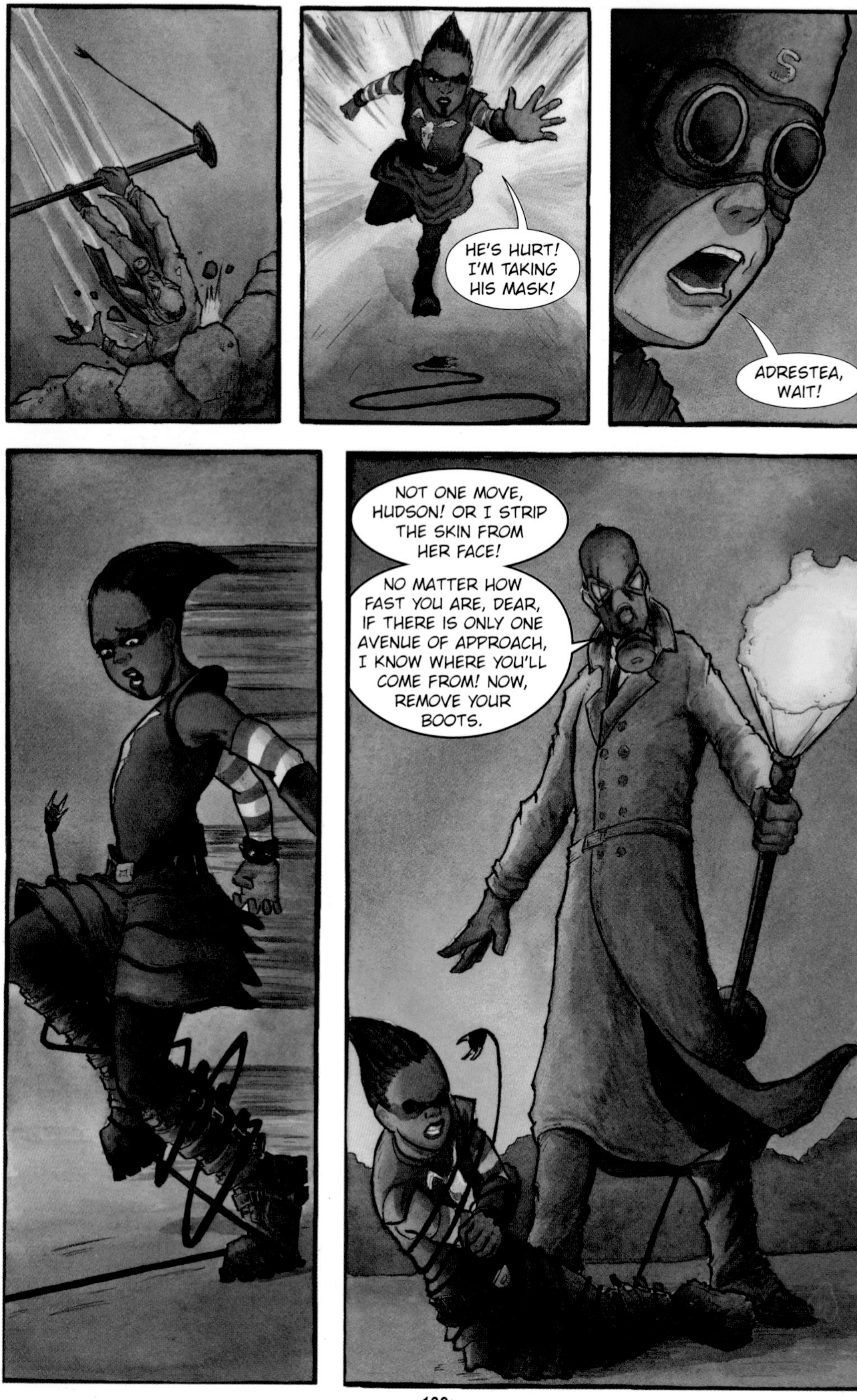
HE'S HURT! I'M TAKING HIS MASK!
ADRESTEA, WAIT!
NOT ONE MOVE, HUDSON! OR I STRIP THE SKIN FROM HER FACE!
NO MATTER HOW FAST YOU ARE, DEAR, IF THERE IS ONLY ONE AVENUE OF APPROACH, I KNOW WHERE YOU'LL COME FROM! NOW, REMOVE YOUR BOOTS.

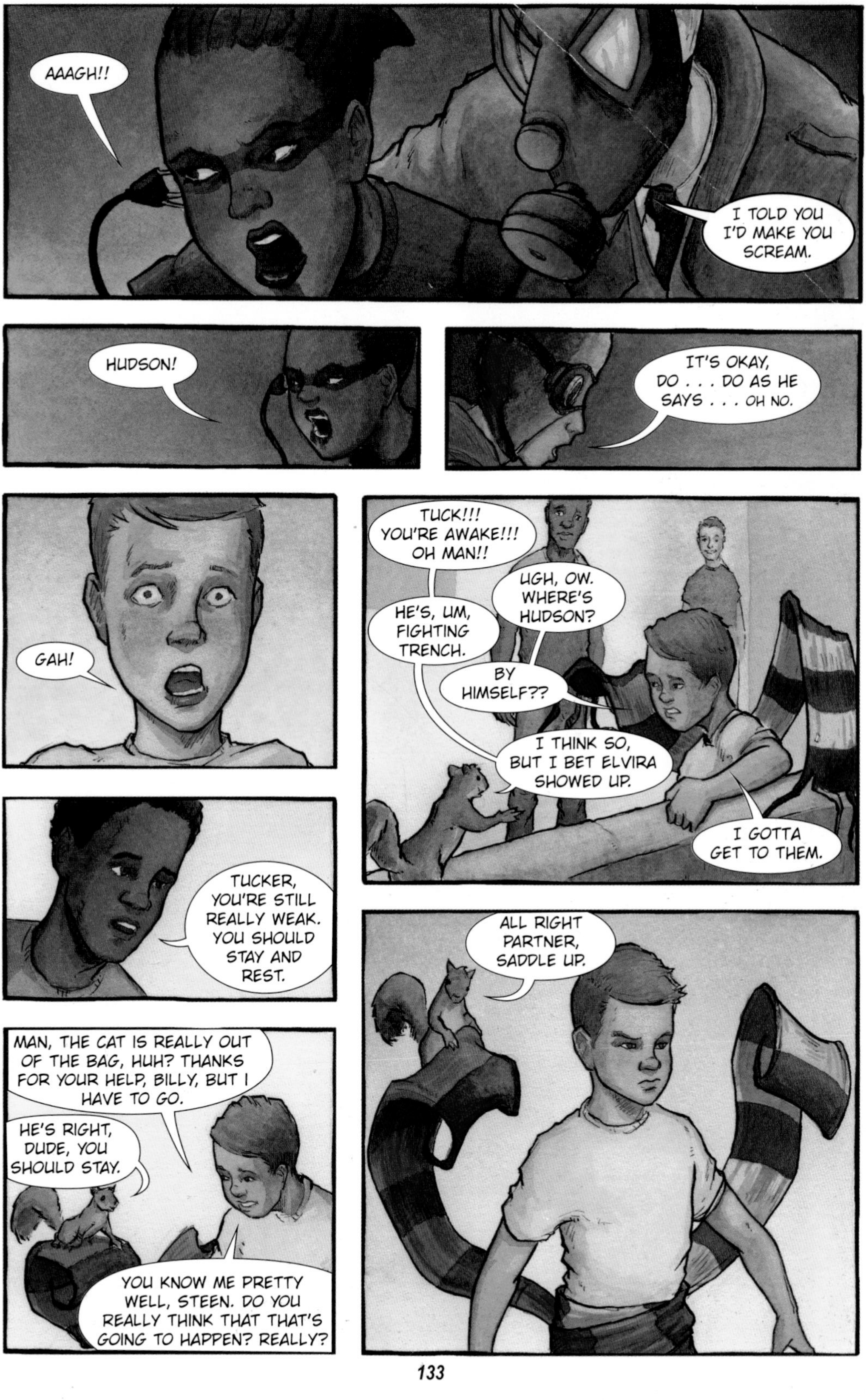
AAAGH!!
I TOLD YOU I'D MAKE YOU SCREAM.
HUDSON!
IT'S OKAY, DO . . . DO AS HE SAYS . . . OH NO.
GAH!
TUCK!!! YOU'RE AWAKE!!! OH MAN!!
UGH, OW. WHERE'S HUDSON?
HE'S, UM, FIGHTING TRENCH.
BY HIMSELF??
I THINK SO, BUT I BET ELVIRA SHOWED UP.
I GOTTA GET TO THEM.
TUCKER, YOU'RE STILL REALLY WEAK. YOU SHOULD STAY AND REST.
ALL RIGHT PARTNER, SADDLE UP.
MAN, THE CAT IS REALLY OUT OF THE BAG, HUH? THANKS FOR YOUR HELP, BILLY, BUT I HAVE TO GO.
HE'S RIGHT, DUDE, YOU SHOULD STAY.
YOU KNOW ME PRETTY WELL, STEEN. DO YOU REALLY THINK THAT THAT'S GOING TO HAPPEN? REALLY?

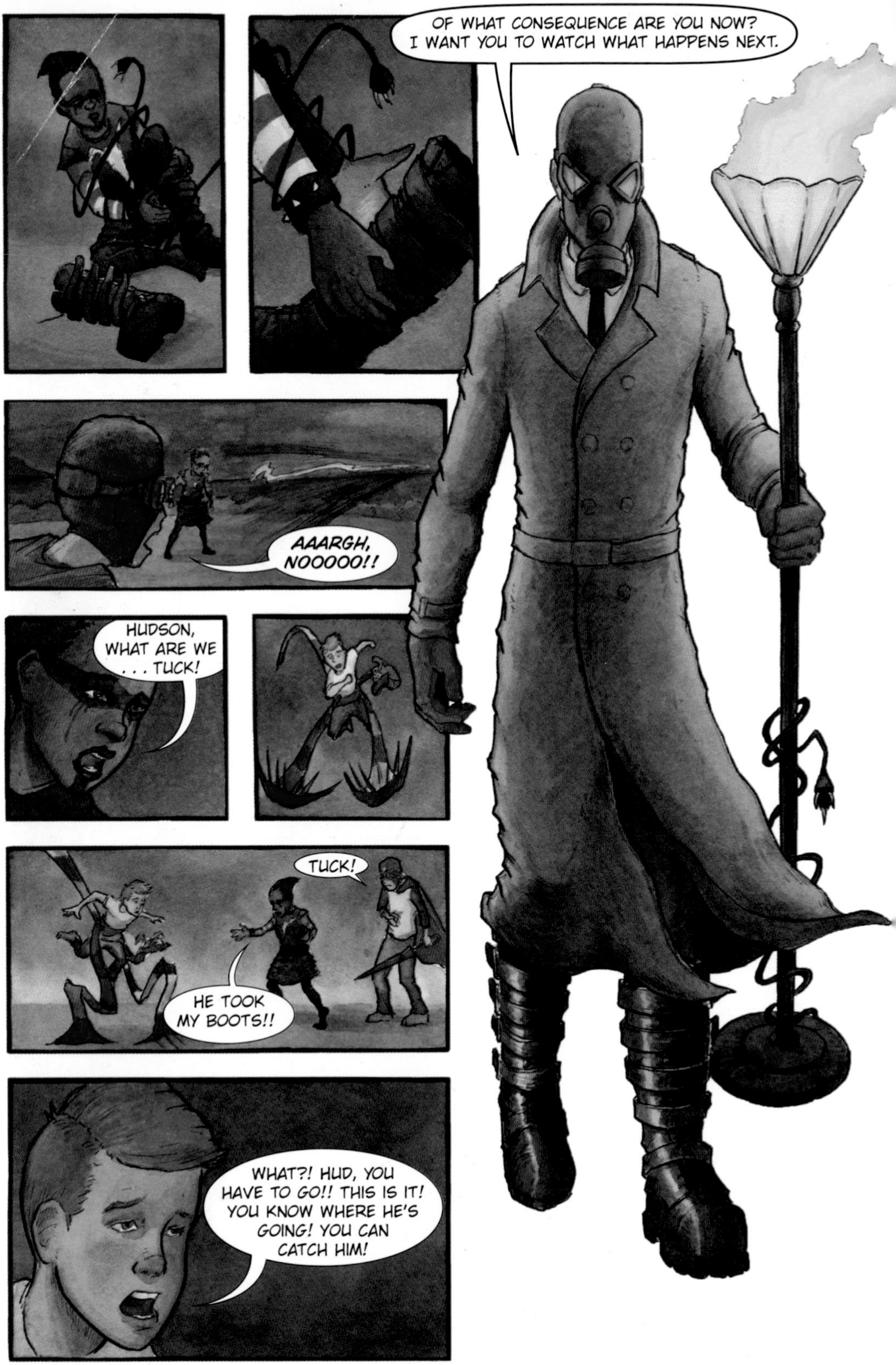
OF WHAT CONSEQUENCE ARE YOU NOW? I WANT YOU TO WATCH WHAT HAPPENS NEXT.
AAARGH, NOOOOO!!
HUDSON, WHAT ARE WE . . . TUCK!
TUCK!
HE TOOK MY BOOTS!!
WHAT?! HUD, YOU HAVE TO GO!! THIS IS IT! YOU KNOW WHERE HE'S GOING! YOU CAN CATCH HIM!

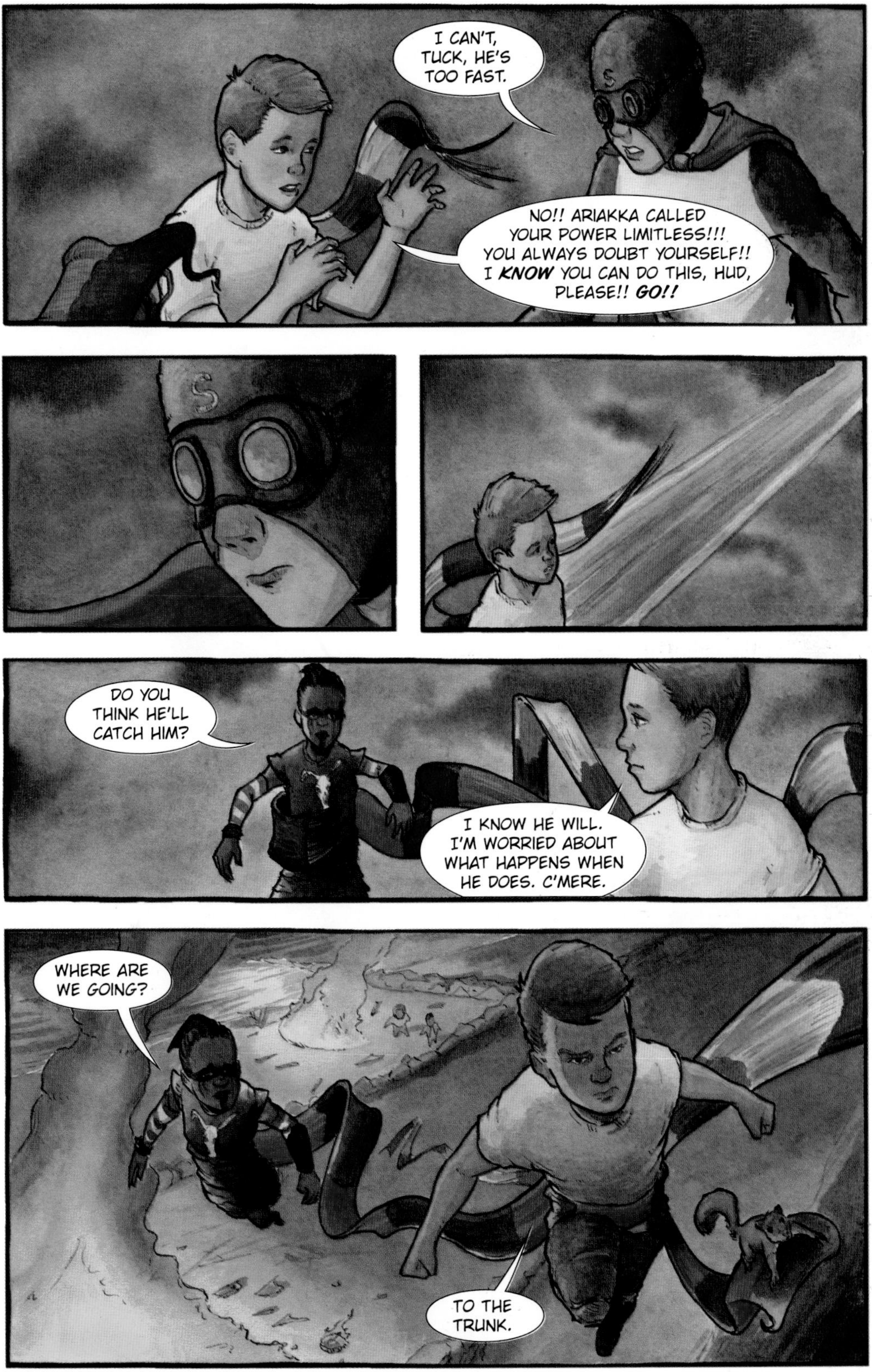
I CAN'T, TUCK, HE'S TOO FAST.
NO!! ARIAKKA CALLED YOUR POWER LIMITLESS!!! YOU ALWAYS DOUBT YOURSELF!! I **KNOW** YOU CAN DO THIS, HUD, PLEASE!! **GO!!**
DO YOU THINK HE'LL CATCH HIM?
I KNOW HE WILL. I'M WORRIED ABOUT WHAT HAPPENS WHEN HE DOES. C'MERE.
WHERE ARE WE GOING?
TO THE TRUNK.

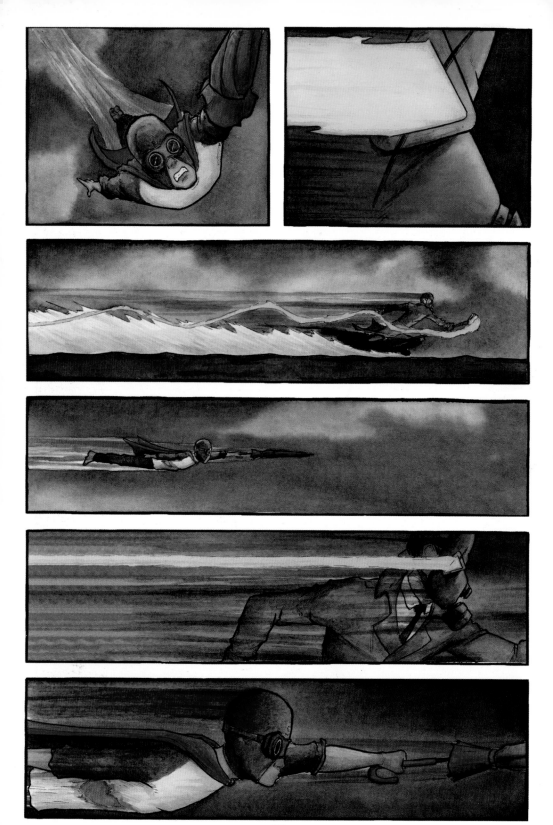

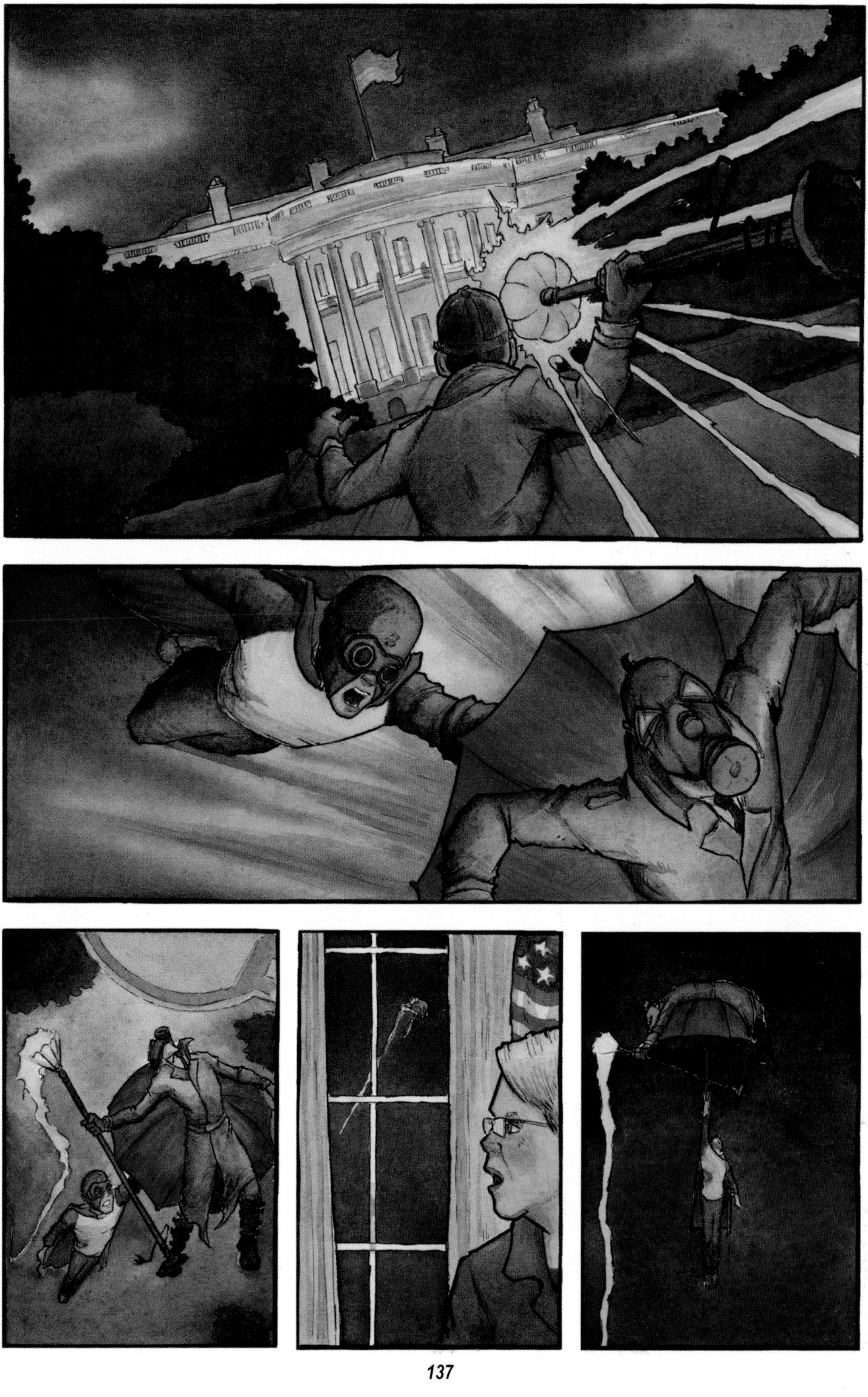

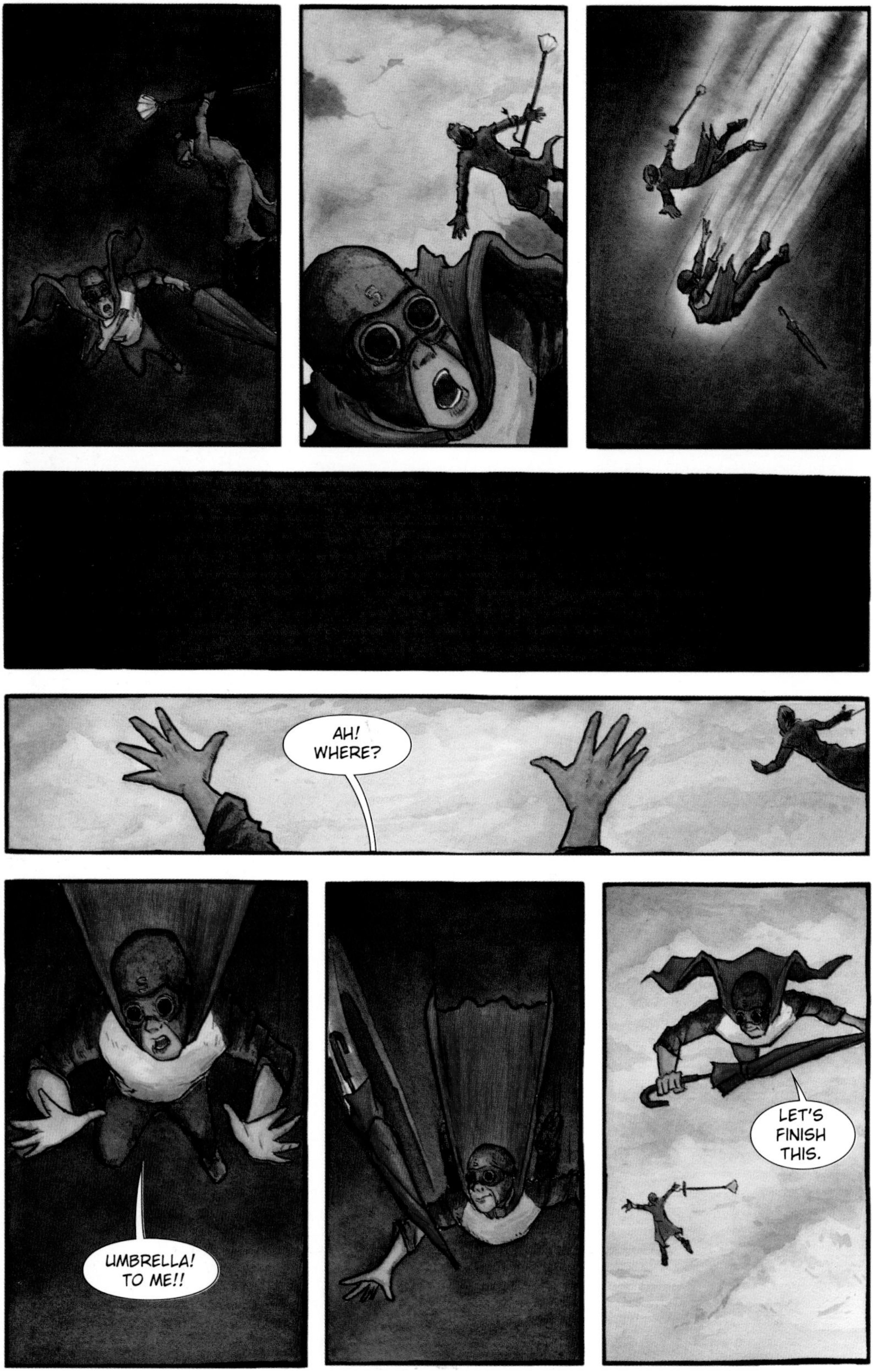
AH! WHERE?
UMBRELLA! TO ME!!
LET'S FINISH THIS.

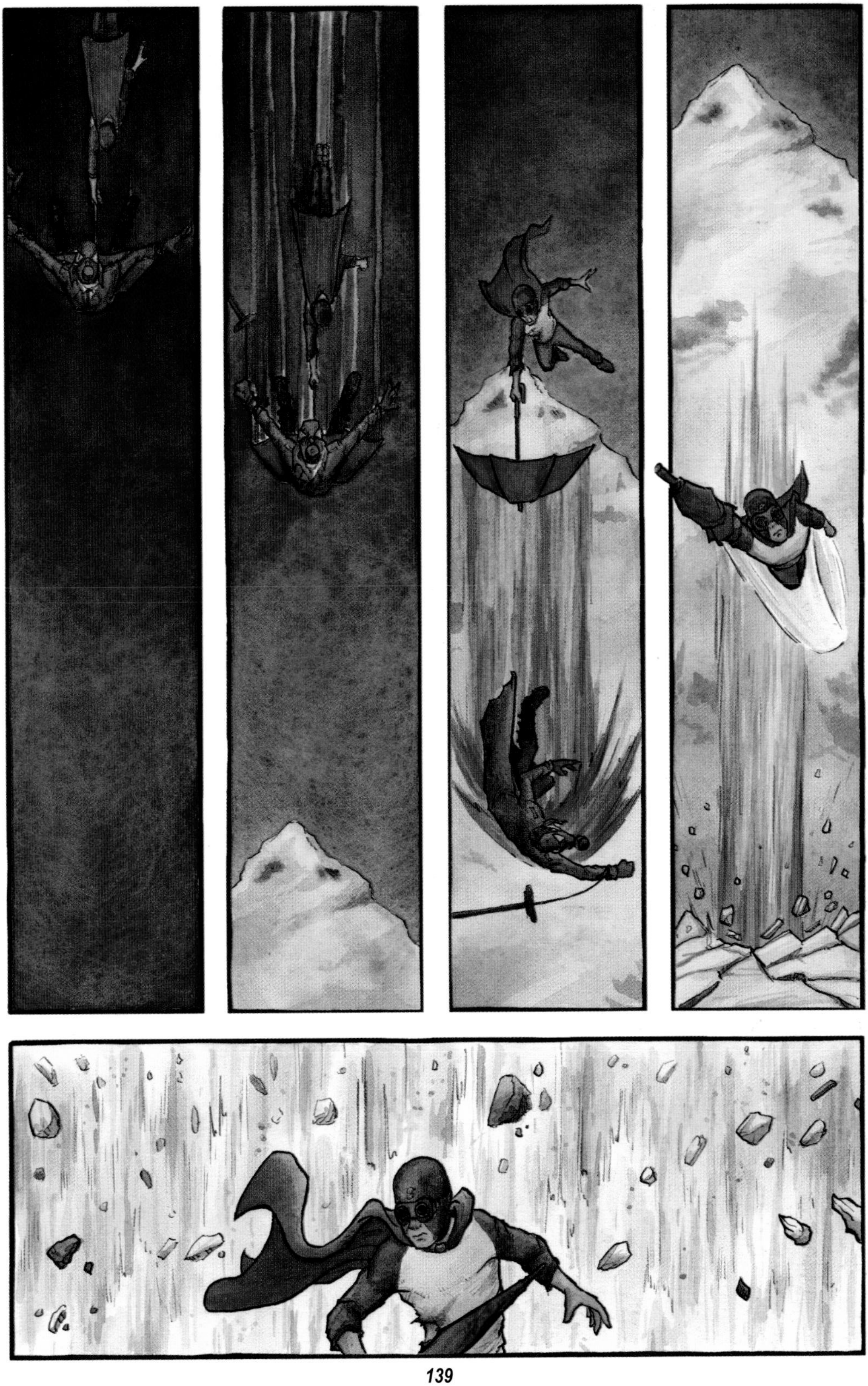

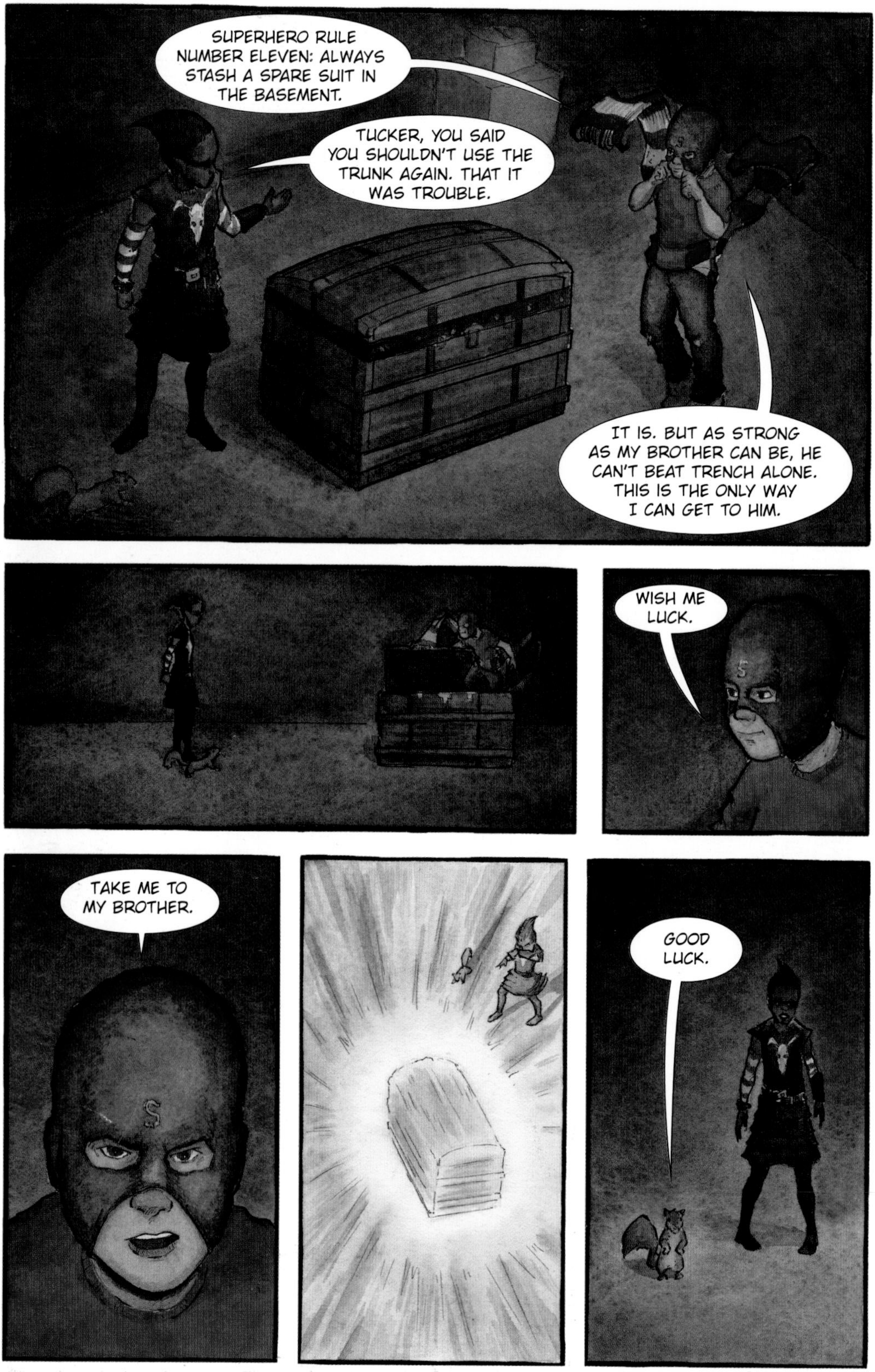
SUPERHERO RULE NUMBER ELEVEN: ALWAYS STASH A SPARE SUIT IN THE BASEMENT.
TUCKER, YOU SAID YOU SHOULDN'T USE THE TRUNK AGAIN. THAT IT WAS TROUBLE.
IT IS. BUT AS STRONG AS MY BROTHER CAN BE, HE CAN'T BEAT TRENCH ALONE. THIS IS THE ONLY WAY I CAN GET TO HIM.
WISH ME LUCK.
TAKE ME TO MY BROTHER.
GOOD LUCK.

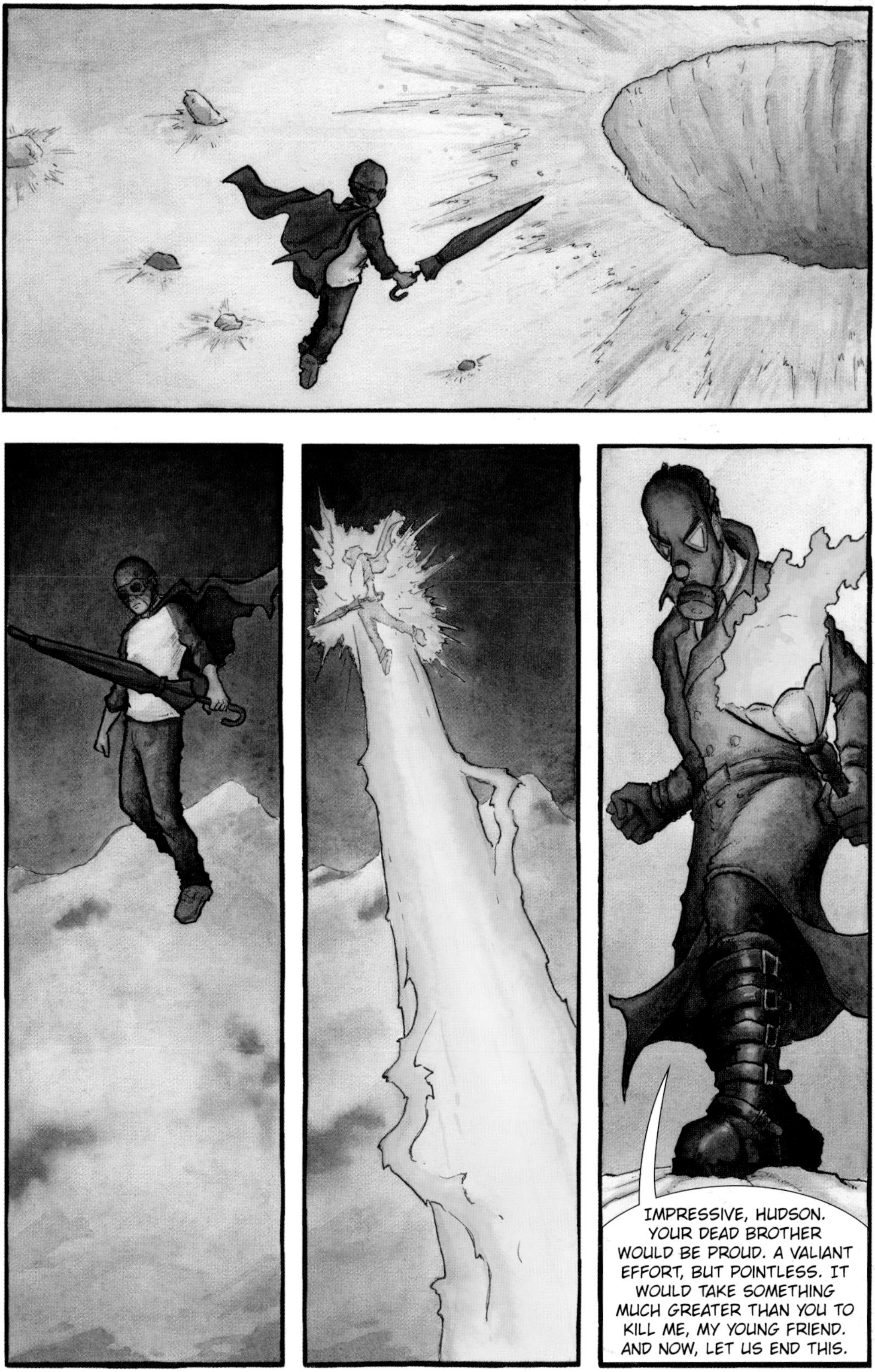
IMPRESSIVE, HUDSON. YOUR DEAD BROTHER WOULD BE PROUD. A VALIANT EFFORT, BUT POINTLESS. IT WOULD TAKE SOMETHING MUCH GREATER THAN YOU TO KILL ME, MY YOUNG FRIEND. AND NOW, LET US END THIS.

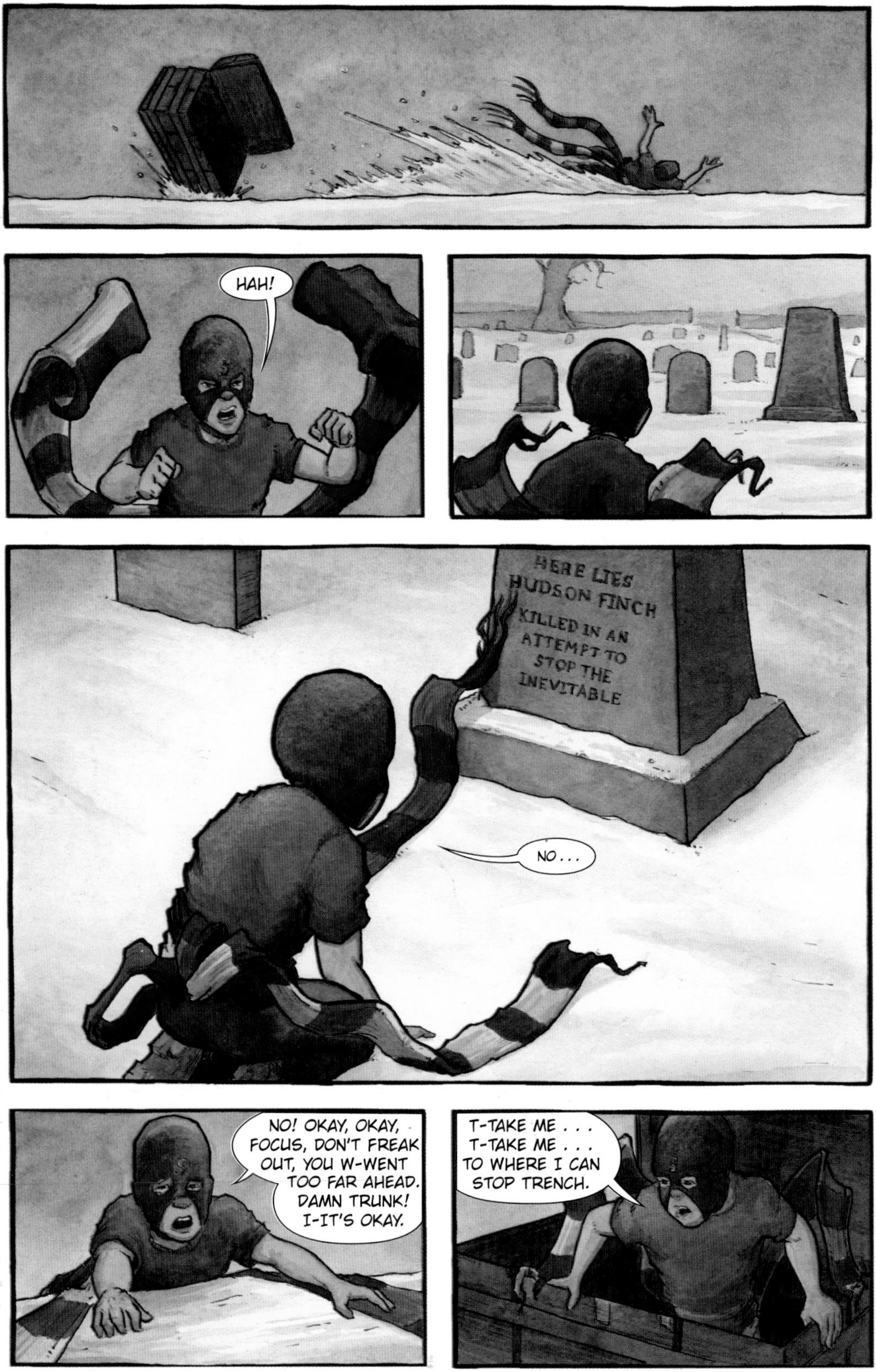
HAH!
HERE LIES HUDSON FINCH
KILLED IN AN ATTEMPT TO STOP THE INEVITABLE
NO . . .
NO! OKAY, OKAY, FOCUS, DON'T FREAK OUT, YOU W-WENT TOO FAR AHEAD. DAMN TRUNK! I-IT'S OKAY.
T-TAKE ME . . . T-TAKE ME . . . TO WHERE I CAN STOP TRENCH.

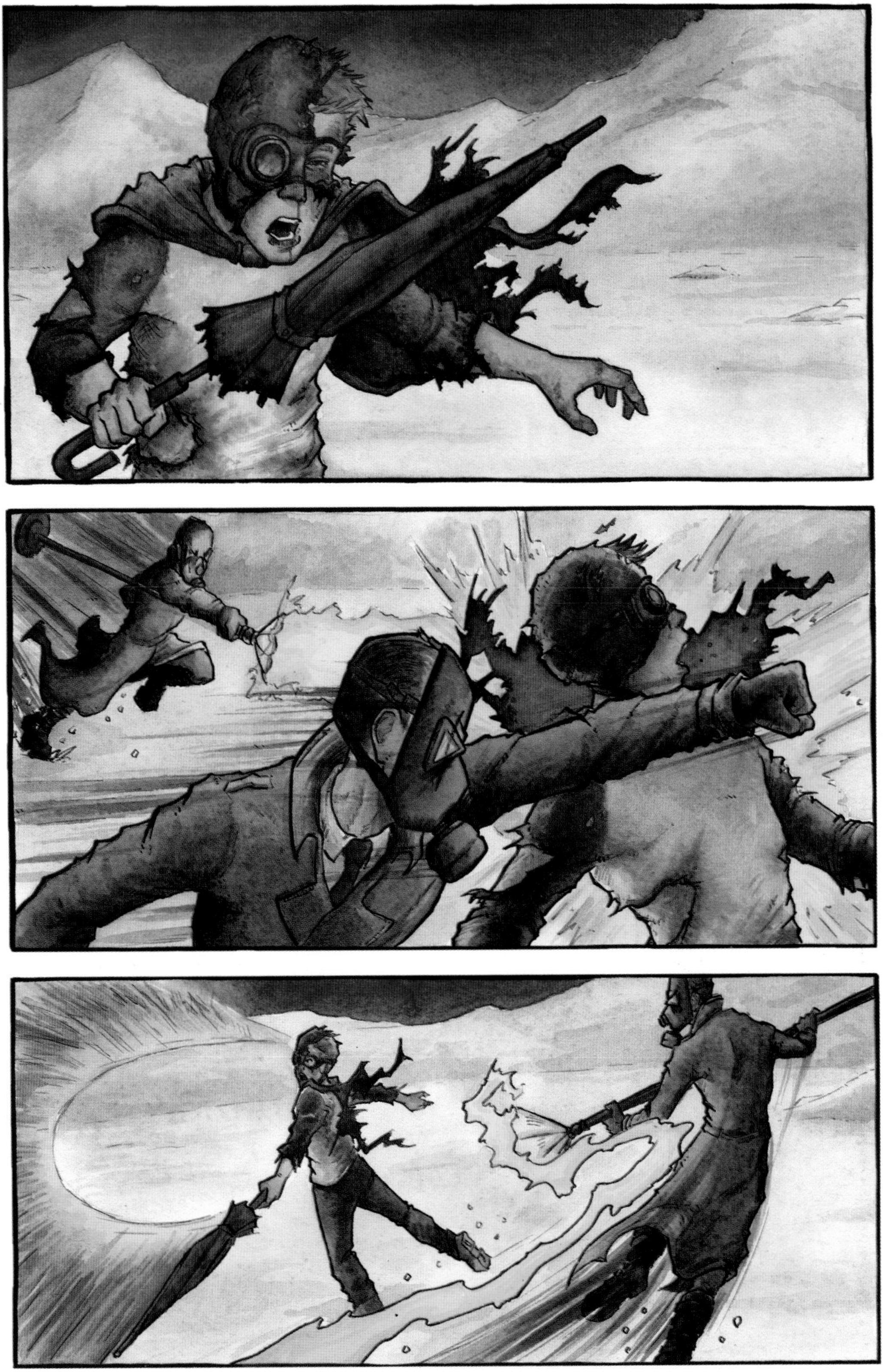

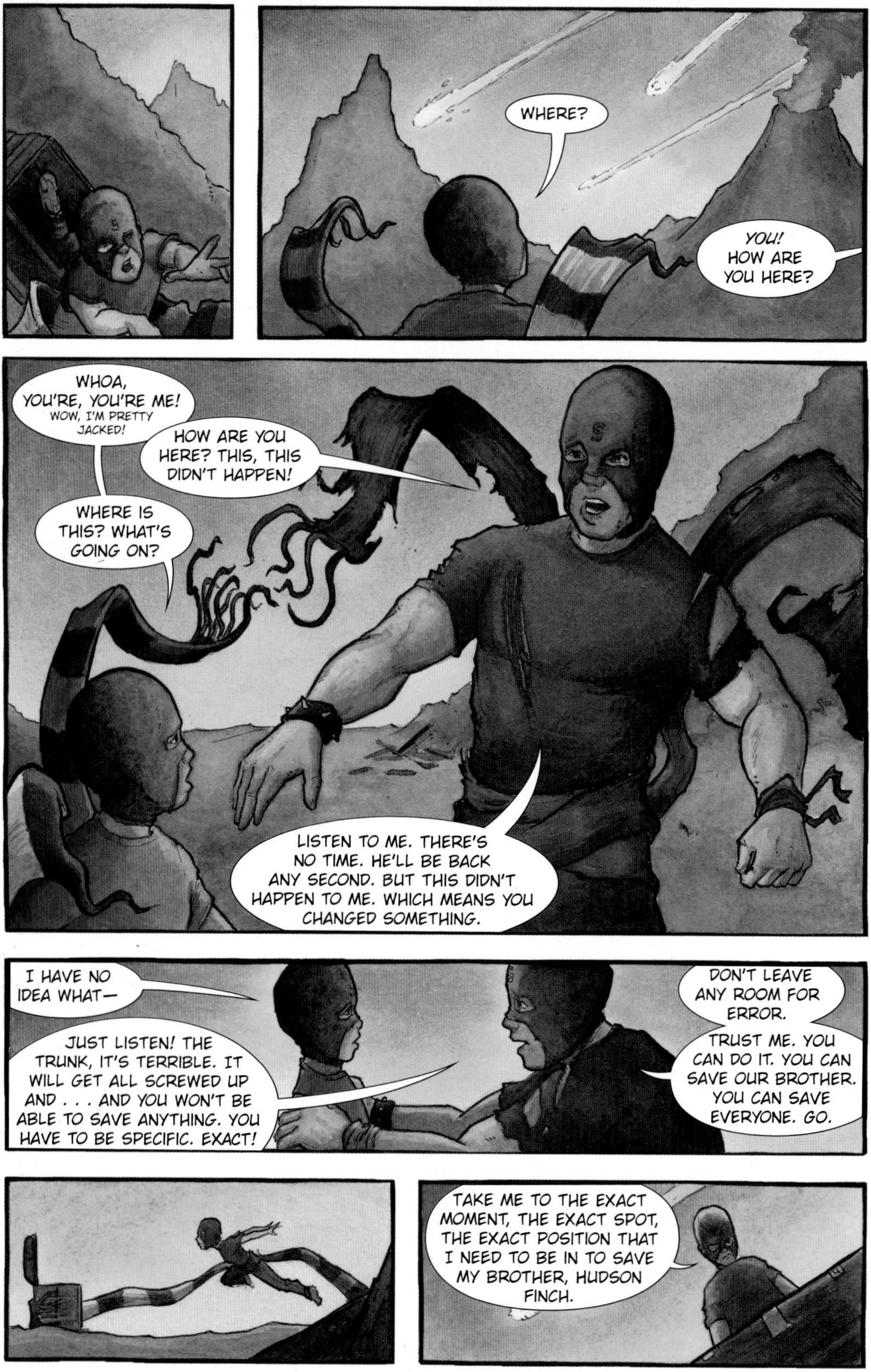
WHERE?
YOU! HOW ARE YOU HERE?
WHOA, YOU'RE, YOU'RE ME! WOW, I'M PRETTY JACKED!
HOW ARE YOU HERE? THIS, THIS DIDN'T HAPPEN!
WHERE IS THIS? WHAT'S GOING ON?
LISTEN TO ME. THERE'S NO TIME. HE'LL BE BACK ANY SECOND. BUT THIS DIDN'T HAPPEN TO ME. WHICH MEANS YOU CHANGED SOMETHING.
I HAVE NO IDEA WHAT—
JUST LISTEN! THE TRUNK, IT'S TERRIBLE. IT WILL GET ALL SCREWED UP AND . . . AND YOU WON'T BE ABLE TO SAVE ANYTHING. YOU HAVE TO BE SPECIFIC. EXACT!
DON'T LEAVE ANY ROOM FOR ERROR.
TRUST ME. YOU CAN DO IT. YOU CAN SAVE OUR BROTHER. YOU CAN SAVE EVERYONE. GO.
TAKE ME TO THE EXACT MOMENT, THE EXACT SPOT, THE EXACT POSITION THAT I NEED TO BE IN TO SAVE MY BROTHER, HUDSON FINCH.

IT WAS INEVITABLE, HUDSON.

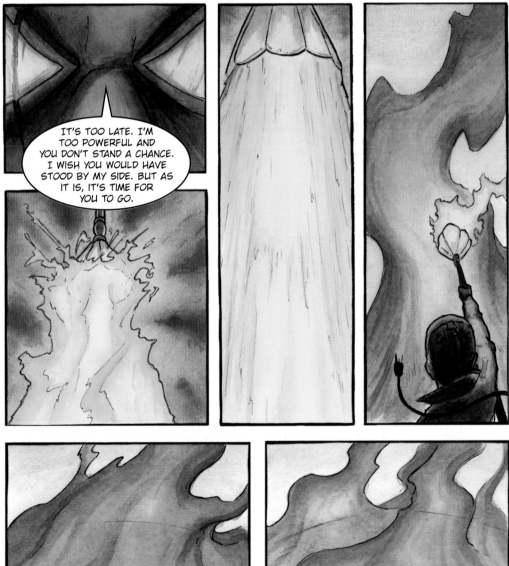

IT'S TOO LATE. I'M TOO POWERFUL AND YOU DON'T STAND A CHANCE. I WISH YOU WOULD HAVE STOOD BY MY SIDE. BUT AS IT IS, IT'S TIME FOR YOU TO GO.

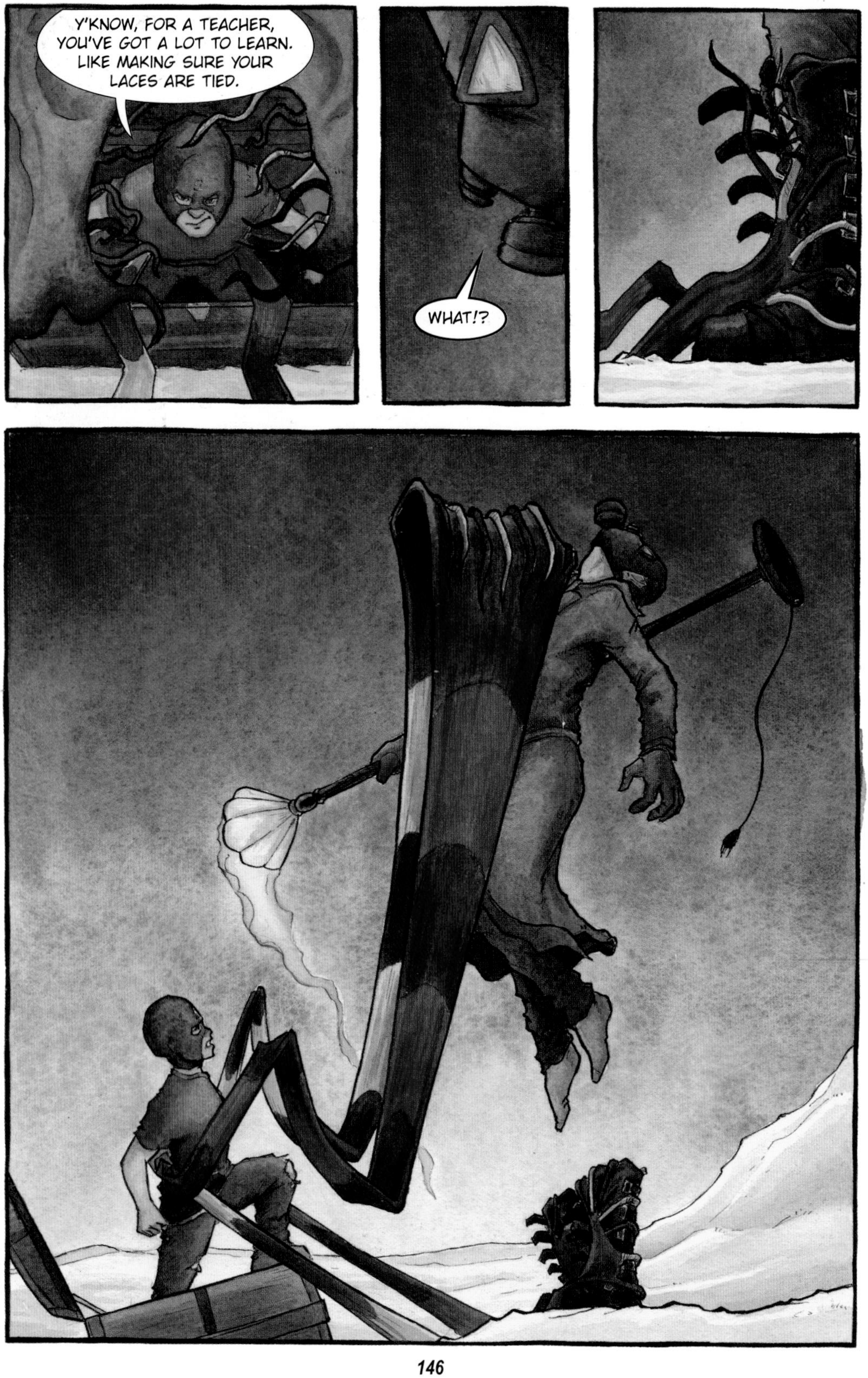
Y'KNOW, FOR A TEACHER, YOU'VE GOT A LOT TO LEARN. LIKE MAKING SURE YOUR LACES ARE TIED.
WHAT!?

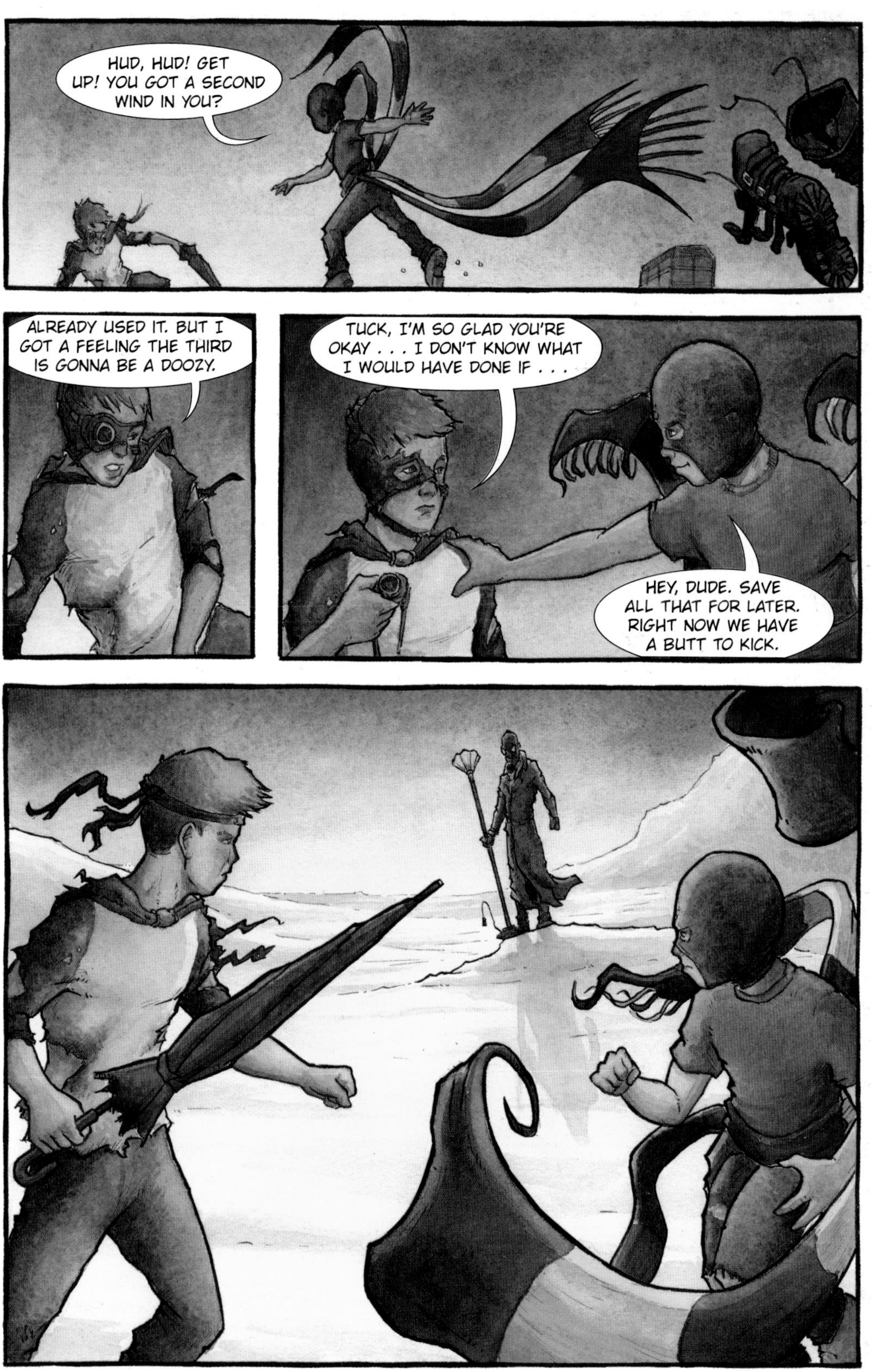
HUD, HUD! GET UP! YOU GOT A SECOND WIND IN YOU?
ALREADY USED IT. BUT I GOT A FEELING THE THIRD IS GONNA BE A DOOZY.
TUCK, I'M SO GLAD YOU'RE OKAY . . . I DON'T KNOW WHAT I WOULD HAVE DONE IF . . .
HEY, DUDE. SAVE ALL THAT FOR LATER. RIGHT NOW WE HAVE A BUTT TO KICK.

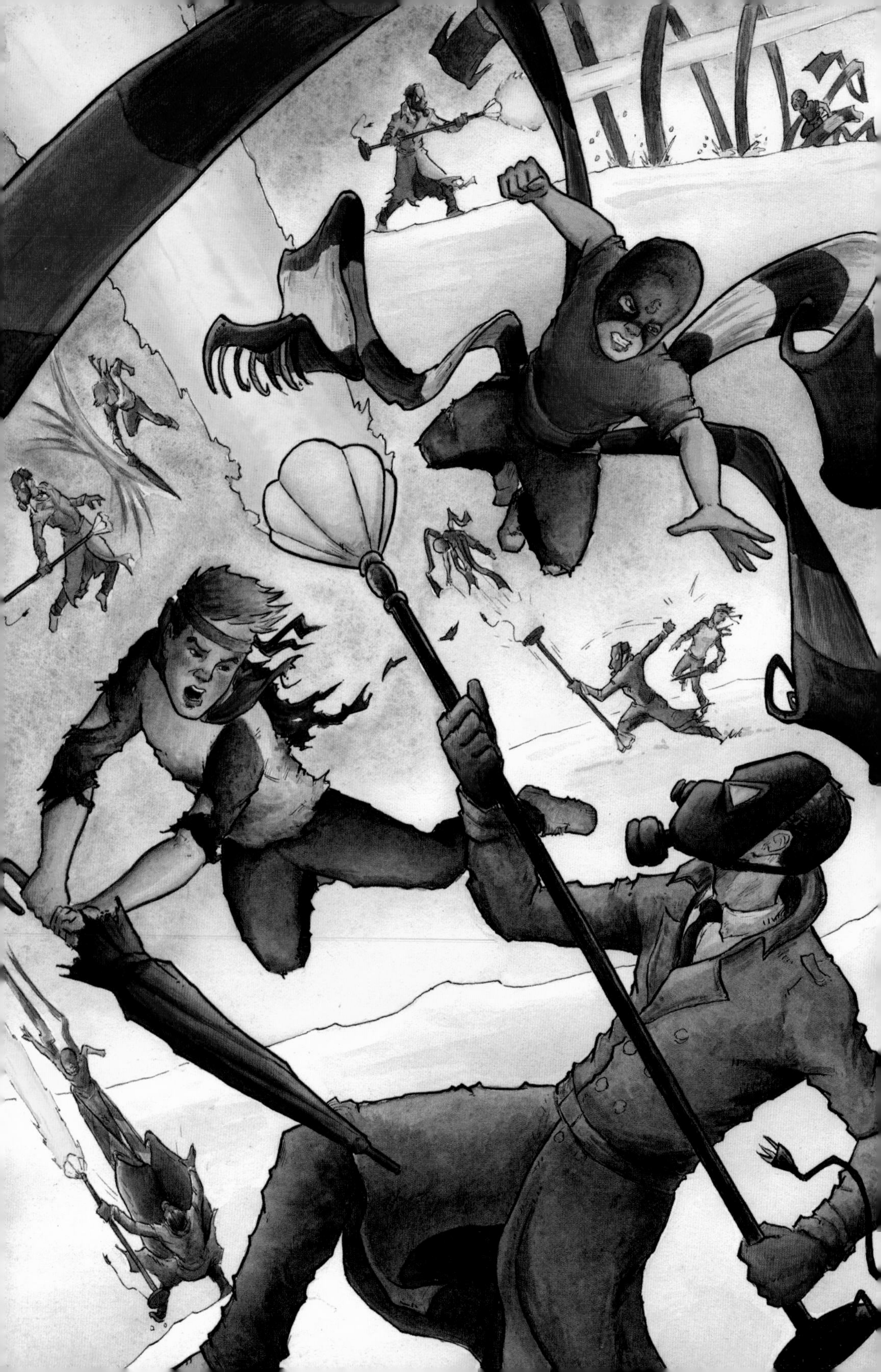

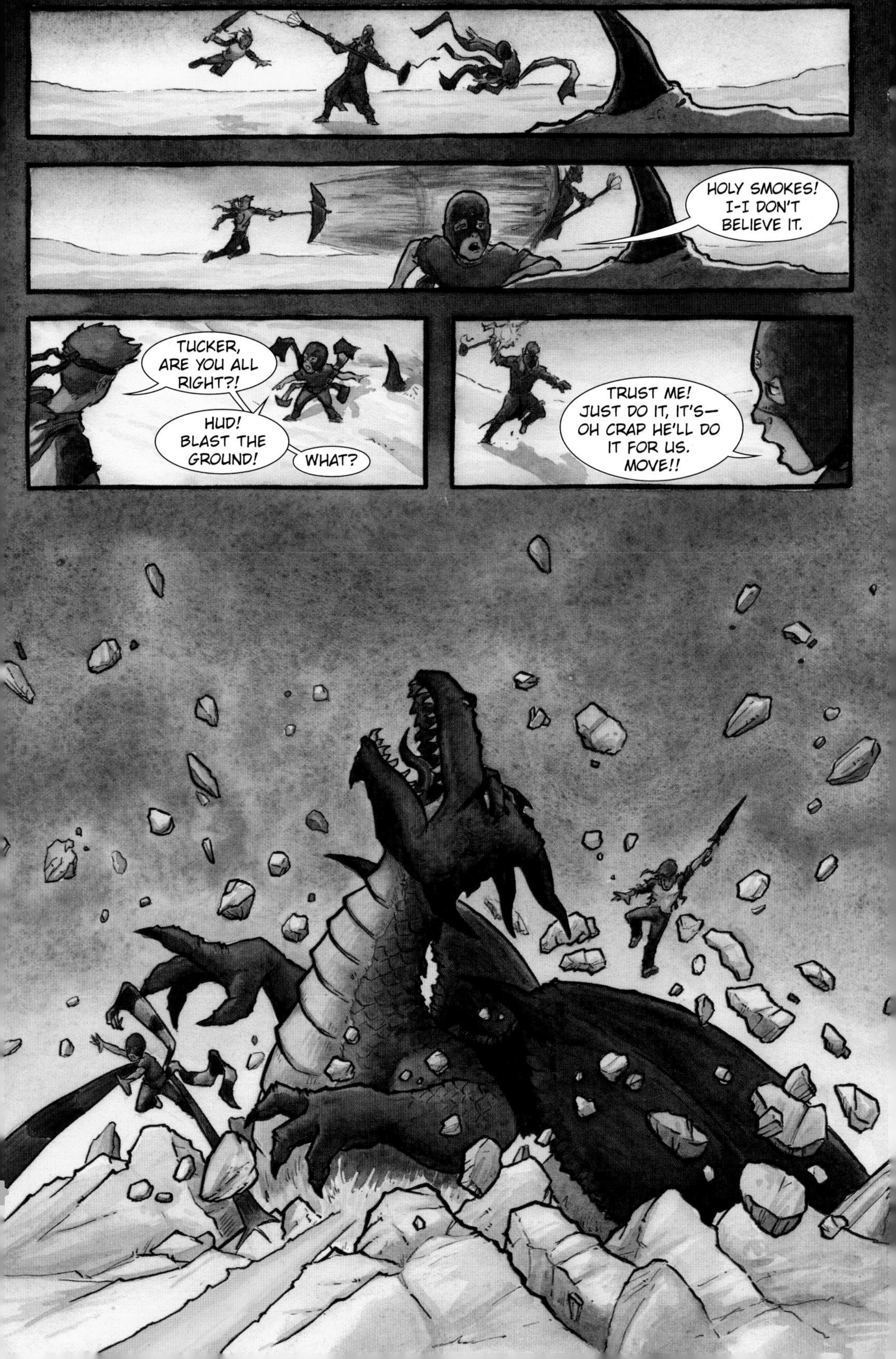
HOLY SMOKES! I-I DON'T BELIEVE IT.
TUCKER, ARE YOU ALL RIGHT?!
HUD! BLAST THE GROUND!
WHAT?
TRUST ME! JUST DO IT, IT'S—OH CRAP HE'LL DO IT FOR US. MOVE!!

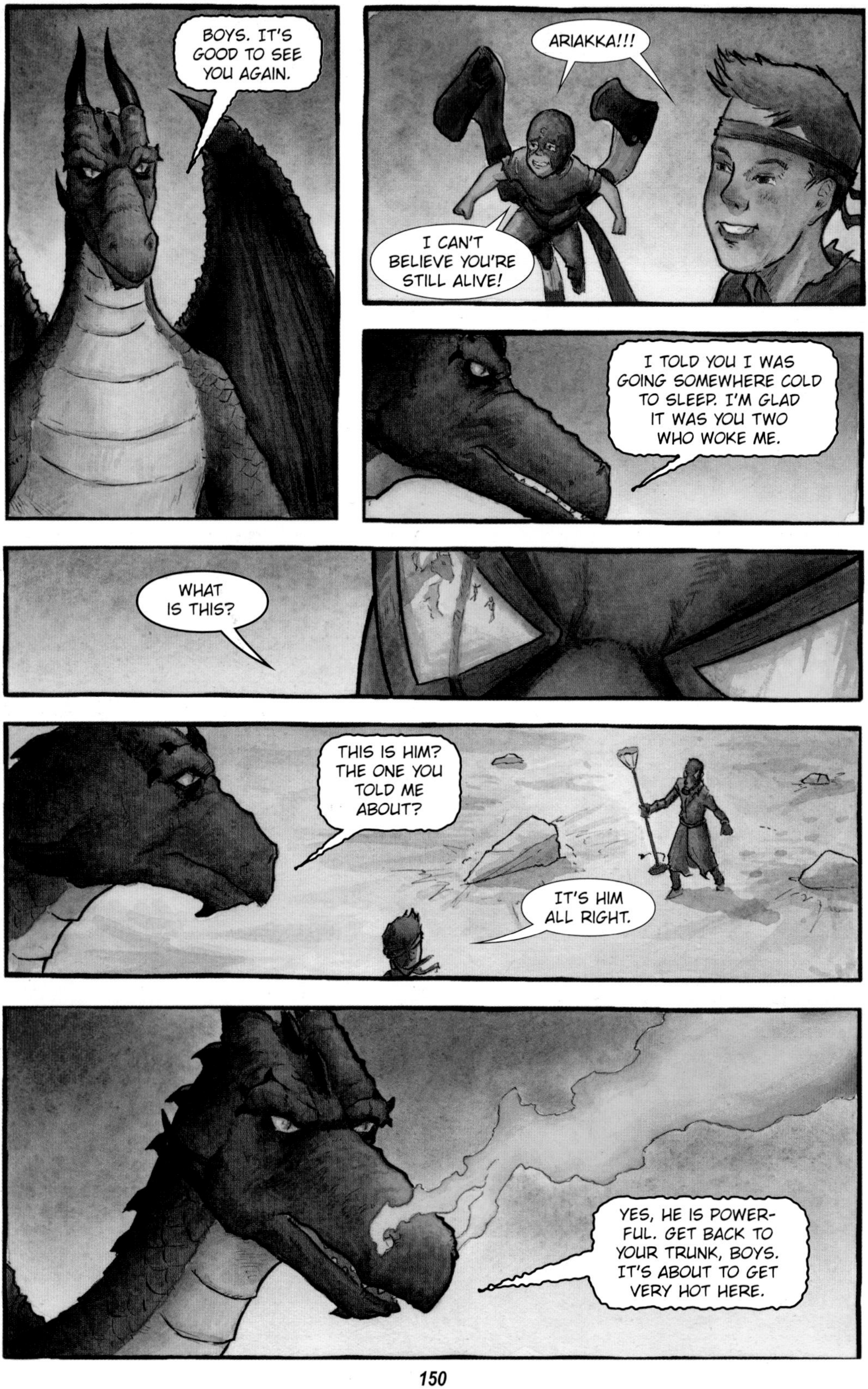
BOYS. IT'S GOOD TO SEE YOU AGAIN.
ARIAKKA!!!
I CAN'T BELIEVE YOU'RE STILL ALIVE!
I TOLD YOU I WAS GOING SOMEWHERE COLD TO SLEEP. I'M GLAD IT WAS YOU TWO WHO WOKE ME.
WHAT IS THIS?
THIS IS HIM? THE ONE YOU TOLD ME ABOUT?
IT'S HIM ALL RIGHT.
YES, HE IS POWER-FUL. GET BACK TO YOUR TRUNK, BOYS. IT'S ABOUT TO GET VERY HOT HERE.

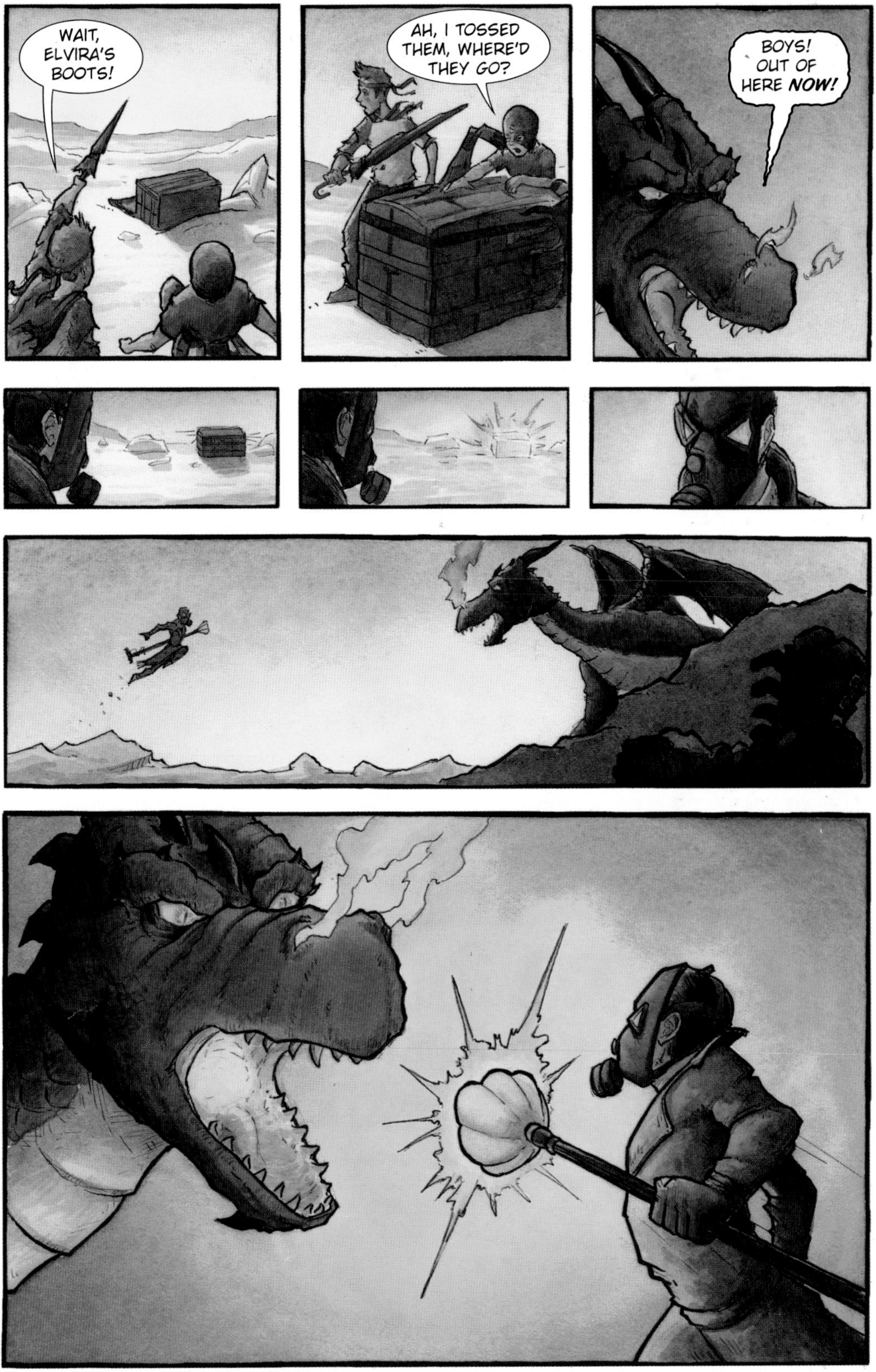
WAIT, ELVIRA'S BOOTS!
AH, I TOSSED THEM, WHERE'D THEY GO?
BOYS! OUT OF HERE **NOW!**

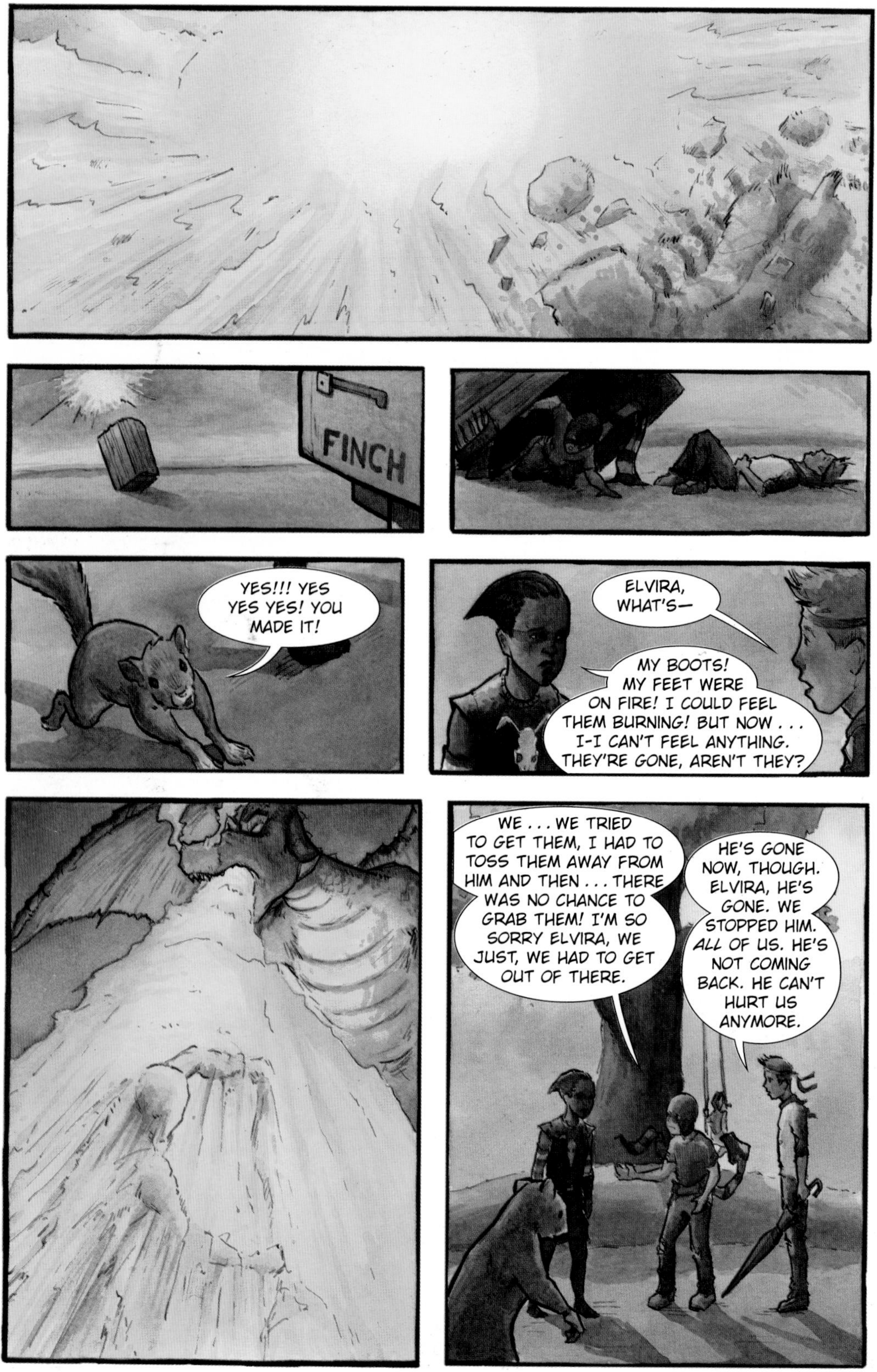
FINCH
YES!!! YES YES YES! YOU MADE IT!
ELVIRA, WHAT'S—
MY BOOTS! MY FEET WERE ON FIRE! I COULD FEEL THEM BURNING! BUT NOW . . . I-I CAN'T FEEL ANYTHING. THEY'RE GONE, AREN'T THEY?
WE . . . WE TRIED TO GET THEM, I HAD TO TOSS THEM AWAY FROM HIM AND THEN . . . THERE WAS NO CHANCE TO GRAB THEM! I'M SO SORRY ELVIRA, WE JUST, WE HAD TO GET OUT OF THERE.
HE'S GONE NOW, THOUGH. ELVIRA, HE'S GONE. WE STOPPED HIM. ALL OF US. HE'S NOT COMING BACK. HE CAN'T HURT US ANYMORE.

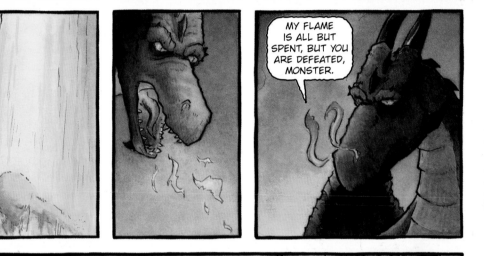

MY FLAME IS ALL BUT SPENT, BUT YOU ARE DEFEATED, MONSTER.

HI.

HI.

HOW'S YOUR BROTHER?

HE'S OKAY. A FEW BURNS, BUT HE'S TOUGH.

RUNS IN THE FAMILY.

HEH. HOW'S YOURS?

OKAY. HE'S TOUGH TOO.

RUNS IN THE FAMILY. SO, HE'S GONE? YOU BEAT THE BAD GUY?

YES. HE'S TOAST.

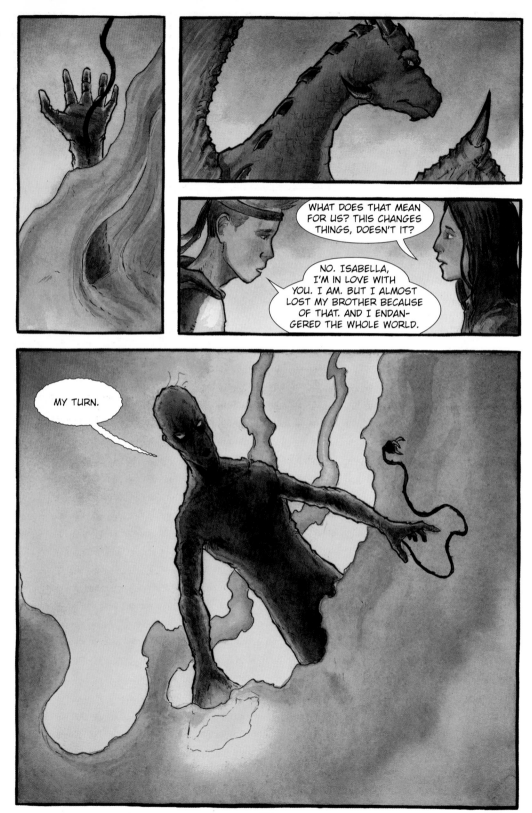

WHAT DOES THAT MEAN FOR US? THIS CHANGES THINGS, DOESN'T IT?

NO. ISABELLA, I'M IN LOVE WITH YOU. I AM. BUT I ALMOST LOST MY BROTHER BECAUSE OF THAT. AND I ENDANGERED THE WHOLE WORLD.

MY TURN.

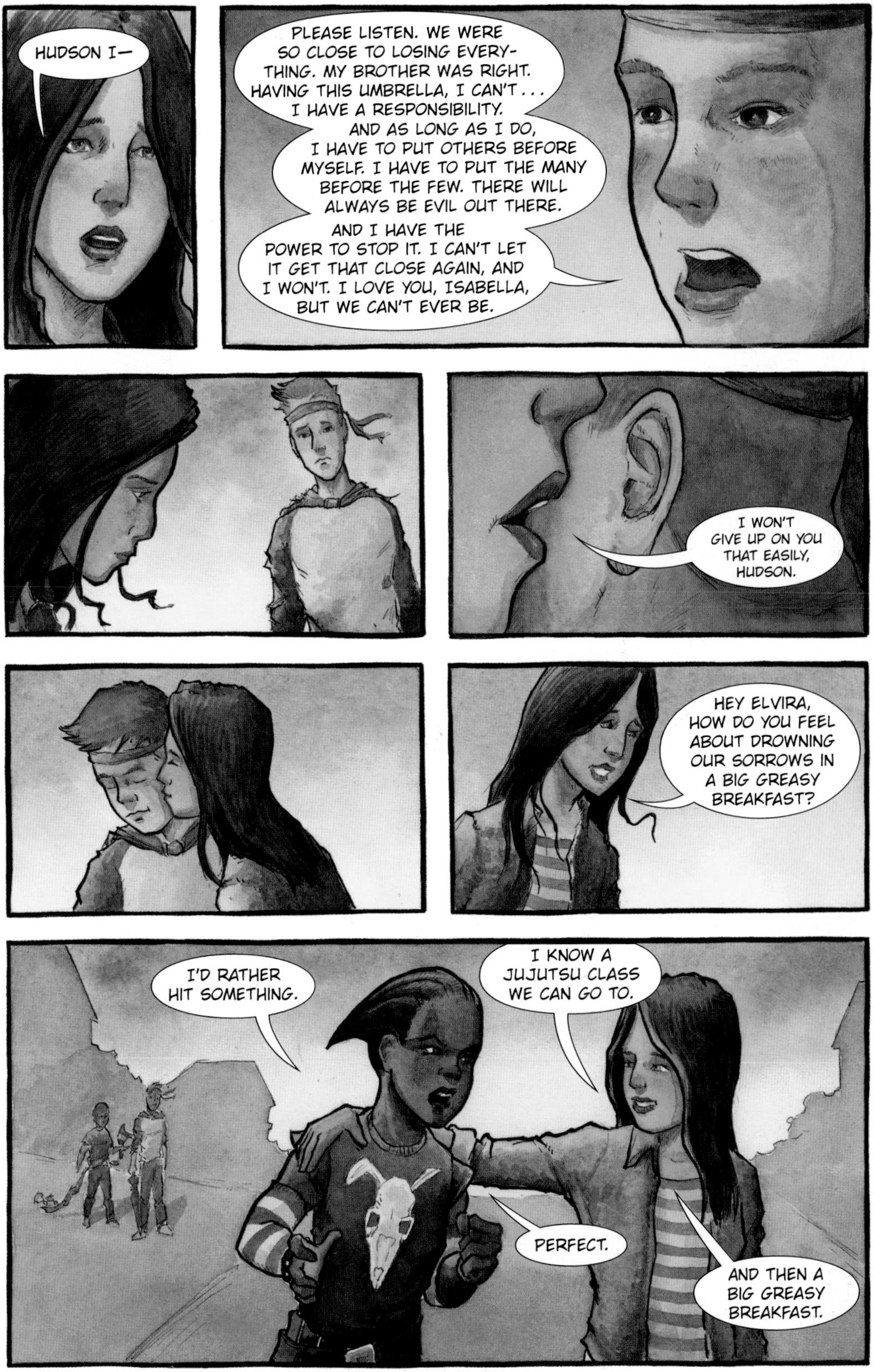
HUDSON I—
PLEASE LISTEN. WE WERE SO CLOSE TO LOSING EVERY-THING. MY BROTHER WAS RIGHT. HAVING THIS UMBRELLA, I CAN'T . . . I HAVE A RESPONSIBILITY.
AND AS LONG AS I DO, I HAVE TO PUT OTHERS BEFORE MYSELF. I HAVE TO PUT THE MANY BEFORE THE FEW. THERE WILL ALWAYS BE EVIL OUT THERE.
AND I HAVE THE POWER TO STOP IT. I CAN'T LET IT GET THAT CLOSE AGAIN, AND I WON'T. I LOVE YOU, ISABELLA, BUT WE CAN'T EVER BE.
I WON'T GIVE UP ON YOU THAT EASILY, HUDSON.
HEY ELVIRA, HOW DO YOU FEEL ABOUT DROWNING OUR SORROWS IN A BIG GREASY BREAKFAST?
I'D RATHER HIT SOMETHING.
I KNOW A JUJUTSU CLASS WE CAN GO TO.
PERFECT.
AND THEN A BIG GREASY BREAKFAST.

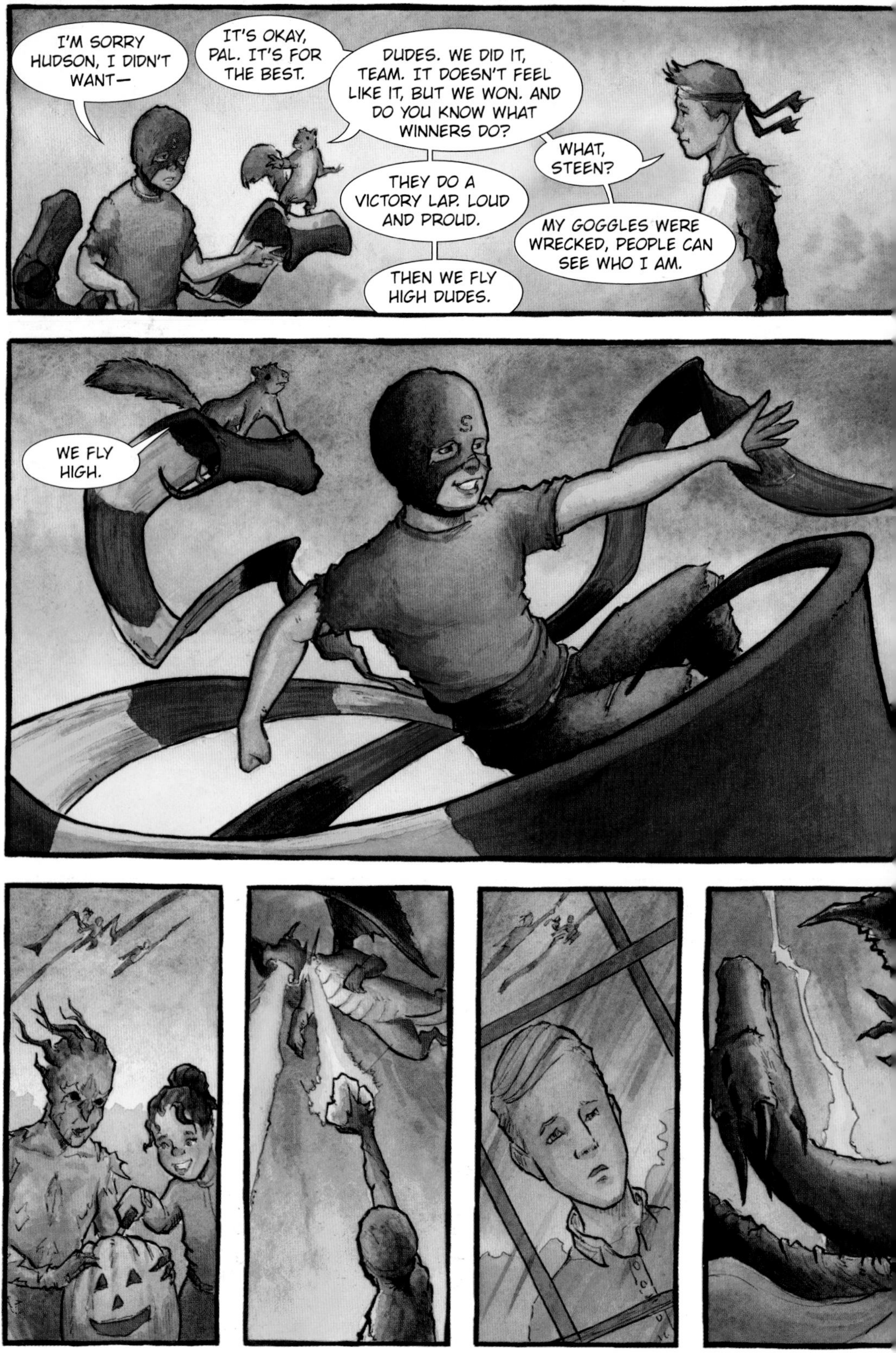
I'M SORRY HUDSON, I DIDN'T WANT—
IT'S OKAY, PAL. IT'S FOR THE BEST.
DUDES. WE DID IT, TEAM. IT DOESN'T FEEL LIKE IT, BUT WE WON. AND DO YOU KNOW WHAT WINNERS DO?
WHAT, STEEN?
THEY DO A VICTORY LAP. LOUD AND PROUD.
MY GOGGLES WERE WRECKED, PEOPLE CAN SEE WHO I AM.
THEN WE FLY HIGH DUDES.
WE FLY HIGH.

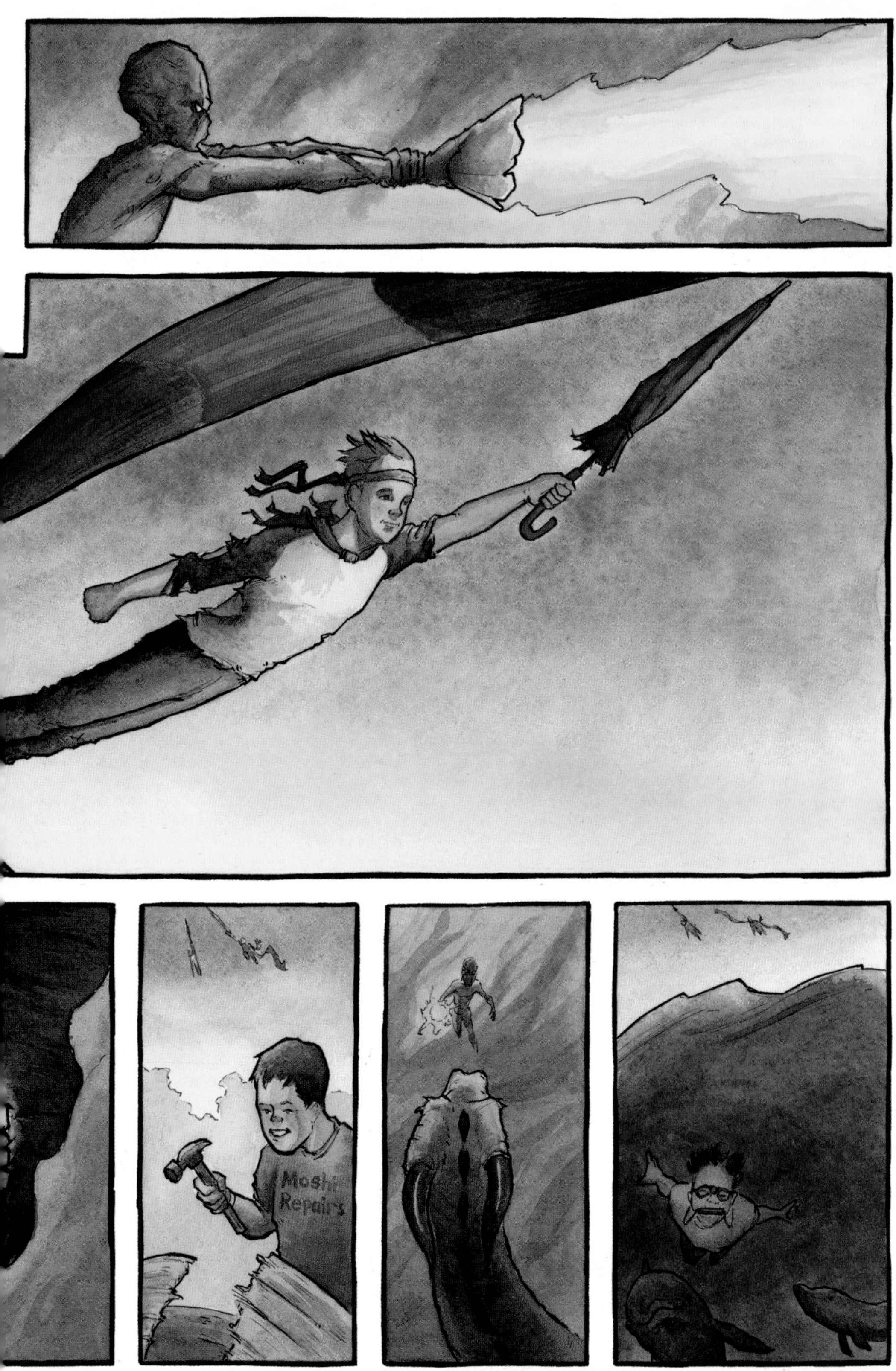
Moshi Repairs

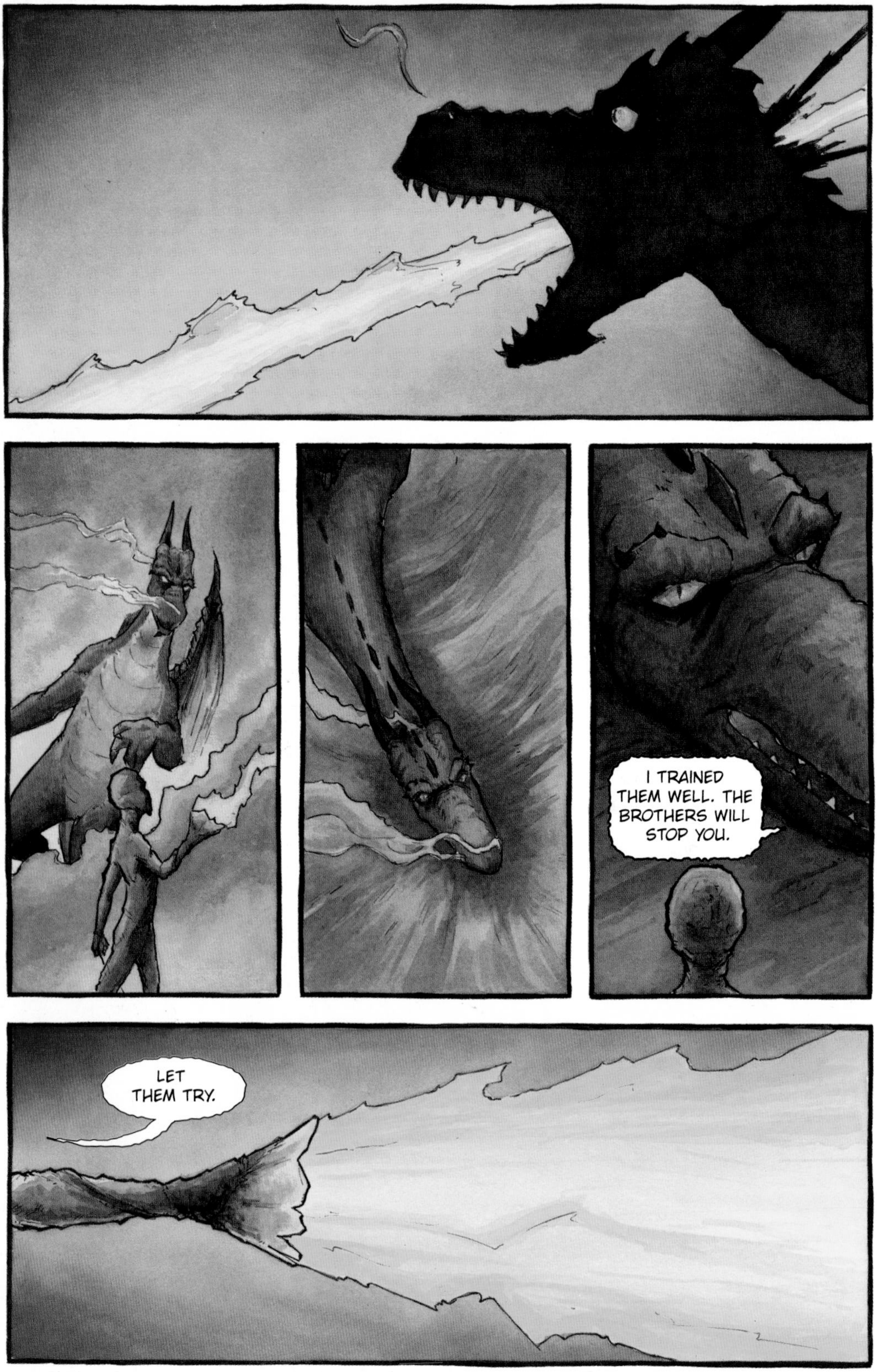
I TRAINED THEM WELL. THE BROTHERS WILL STOP YOU.
LET THEM TRY.